Once To Die

A Novel of Catholic Christian Suspense

T.S. EPPERSON

Multivalent Press

For information, email: information@MultivalentPress.com.

Cover design by W.D. Epperson

ISBN: 979-8-9866064-0-8

First Edition 2022

Contents

Note From the Author

Hello, Friend.

Once To Die is the first book in a series of novels, which I hope you will find entertaining and thought-provoking.

Someone told me long ago that a writer should write a story she or he would enjoy reading. In my case, that is a story where complex characters walk in haste or run to achieve a goal as lives hang in the balance. As circumstances intervene, they encounter setbacks, and blindsiding twists and turns that prevent them from completing their all-important task. And the clock is always ticking.

I find a story most exciting when the stakes are even higher than life and death, delving into the deeper question of what will happen in eternity. *The Other Side of Dead* is a series that explores those deep questions.

To put it simply, I enjoy stories that mimic the real world in which we live. Not many of us humans are truly good through and through. Most of us strive but fail to be as good as we would like to be. Even the holiest and most devout people struggle with some core weakness, or temptation, like St. Paul's "thorn in the flesh."

The other side of that coin is that few people are truly evil to the core. Even the most heinous villains in human history were trying to achieve what they believed to be some "greater good" as they carried out their despicable deeds.

I like a quote attributed to Professor Peter Kreeft, which says "There are only two kinds of people: sinners, who think they're saints; and saints, who know they're sinners."

Once To Die is an adventure of one young man's heroic journey from self-reliance and spiritual indifference, to profound humility and spiritual awakening. My hope is that you may find in the story an honest look at the temptations, the hardships, the difficulties with which the narrow road to heaven is paved, and come away with a fresh resolve to get up and try yet again.

When you've read the book, I'd love to hear from you. You can connect with me at:

T.S.Epperson@multivalentpress.com

facebook.com/T.S.Epperson

MultivalentPress.com/T.S.Epperson

God bless you on your journey,
T.S. Epperson

Prologue

The squeal of an old-time radio tuner screeched out of the darkness. An orchestra faded in, then out, through some static, to some idiots making stupid jokes. Then to more static, to a male talk show host's voice.

"Sandy, if I've said it once on this show, I've said it a thousand times. The homeless problem in this city is out of control. I know the bleeding hearts want us to think of these people as victims, but the truth is, most of them are homeless by choice."

"Stan… that may be true, but in the story we're following tonight, a young man did fall victim to brutal violence."

"I know that, and I don't wish anyone harm. But I'm going to go out on a limb here, and predict that when the smoke clears, the evidence will prove that the violence was perpetrated by another homeless person, or by gang members. Two parts of the same problem. What does the evidence say so far?"

"Stan, all we've been able to determine, is that he was bludgeoned by a blunt object. A baseball bat was found abandoned at the scene, and it appears to be the murder weapon. DNA samples are being processed to confirm."

"So, early findings are consistent with my prediction," Stan said. "Have they identified the victim?"

"Yes, but they're not releasing the name because they are searching for the next of kin."

"Do we know anything at all about the victim?"

"Not much, other than he lived in a makeshift shelter beside a dumpster. Police say he engaged in petty crime, scavenging, and stealing. He stole food from restaurants and supplies from construction sites."

"So, it is just as I was saying. He was unremarkable in life, and in death, he disappears into a landscape of statistics that are becoming increasingly disturbing. This is the end of another wasted life like so many blighting our inner city."

"Still, it is sad to see this happen to such a young person."

"It is, sad, Sandy. And these tragic stories are becoming all too familiar. It is hard to fathom why any young person would choose to squander their life in that way."

"I agree, Stan. Officials who work with the homeless say they tried repeatedly to give him a fresh start, but he was too stubborn to accept help."

"Sandy, you've proven my point. His could have been a story of overcoming odds. Instead, his life ends as a tragic example of wasted human potential."

"I guess the core lesson in this is that we should not waste the opportunities we are given."

"Exactly. And in brighter news, next we'll interview the fireman who rescued a baby owl today, and we have this week's winning kitten story."

Silence.

Perry wanted to vomit. He wanted to cry. He screamed, but it was like the sound didn't go anywhere. It stayed close around him. He screamed again. He began to sob and curse. "Why would you let me hear that?"

No response came. Only darkness and silence.

Dark draped upon dark, growing darker still. He felt a pressure closing against him. The floor collapsed, and he was falling, rolling, tumbling over, and over. hands flailing, finding nothing, It was the worst feeling ever. A stab of panic. *This is it. I'm finally falling into the bad place.*

A rumbling male voice, deep and sinister like that of a great beast growling through a mouthful of spit, said,

"I told you God would let you down, Perry."

September 4

Things were always going to go only one way for Perry. Mama was smiling at him and singing a nursery rhyme when a little leather-faced demon jumped up on her shoulder and started ripping at her hair. She screamed and fought back. A second one, scowling yellow eyes, jumped on her other shoulder, and a third one, ugly face all crinkled up in a jagged-tooth grin, jumped on her back, clamped a bony arm across her neck, and started scratching at her chest with dark little claws.

"Daddy!" Perry shouted. "Help Mama! Daddy, please help her!"

But Daddy was in a chair snoring with his hand resting on the bed. Mama was screaming and crying, so Perry grabbed a plastic dinosaur and started biting the demons as hard as he could with it. The plastic teeth bending, wouldn't cut into the leathery demon skin, even with Perry making his most ferocious growling noises.

"Daddy get up and fight!" he shouted. "Why don't you get up and fight?"

One of the demons turned, hissed and leapt toward Perry, and he jerked so hard he woke up, blinking at the morning sun flooding in through the plastic canopy. It was the same lousy dream he'd dreamed at least nine hundred times. His heart pounded inside his chest, like it was trying to get out. *Calm down, man.* He filled his lungs with air, let out the breath slowly. A few times breathing like that, he started to feel a little better, but his heart was still racing. Mama had to have been the nicest and the prettiest woman in the whole world, but that didn't make any difference. She was still just as dead.

The dumpster stank like sin on Sunday. All his life, Perry had been looking for a way to get away from that stinking dumpster, but no matter how hard he worked, what he tried, things never got better. That stink was always there, sticking to him, following him everywhere he went, and everybody could smell it a mile away. All these mornings were getting to be the same. Wake up scared half to death, fight to push back the hopeless, then work himself up to get out and start going after it again. What if one day he couldn't work himself up? It bothered him, but he never told anybody. What if one day he couldn't fight anymore? He'd Just spend the rest of his days laying here next to the dumpster in this filth. Perry sighed. *Nothin' good's gonna happen 'less I get up and make it happen.*

The cool of the ground had his muscles and bones stiff. Everything hurt. But the pebble under his left shoulder blade was the worst. There was always one thing that hurt more than everything else. Right now, it was the pebble. The softness of the cardboard boxes covered the bumps of the asphalt but didn't give protection from pebbles or glass. It would be nice to sweep that pebble out of there. But he couldn't without untying the plastic canopy and taking everything apart. Perry rolled onto his right side, away from the pebble. A big rat peered at him from under the dumpster. He smiled at it, and the rat smiled back. They twitched their noses at each other. Perry laughed. He pulled the scratchy green blanket up over his head. *A real wool Army blanket* something that Dad's buddy at the surplus store gave them. *Rough against yer face but warm. Stuff like that don't come along every day. Way better than newspapers. Hmm. What could I do about pebbles? There oughta be somethin'.* A smart guy like him could figure it out if he tried. He lay quiet, letting his mind work. The soft stuff he'd been gettin' was too soft. Pebbles and glass could push right through. He needed somethin' hard to keep out the hard stuff. The soft stuff could go on top of that. *Yeh. That's it. Them junk houses in Roxbury. Down there I could prob'ly get a piece of tin or somethin'. Or go over where they were building that high-rise downtown, get inside the construction fence and borrow somethin'. One of those.*

His belly growled like a mangy dog. Should get up and go find some food, but man, the warm blanket made it tough. He lifted a corner of it, let a little cool air in. The nights were gonna start getting nippy. No surprise, Boston in September. It was still nice most days, but he needed to gather more clothes, maybe some more blankets before winter set in for real. He dropped the blanket back over his face. It smelled wet out there. *Is this trash day? No, today's Wednesday. Trash day is Monday, worst day of the week. Have to get up, take the whole shelter apart so they can lift the dumpster.* That one time he was late getting the shelter untied, they left without dumping it. Old man Ming, owner of the restaurant, chewed him out and pitched all his cardboard and plastic into the dumpster. That put him back to square one, with nothin'. He rolled back over. Onto the pebble.

"Aww, *booger* noodles." He sat up. Cold plastic hit him in the face and morning air flooded in. Perry sighed again. *Another day in paradise. But it don't do no good to sit here and feel sorry. Nobody gonna come along and give us a hand up.* If they were ever gonna get ahead in life, it was on him and nobody else.

Glancing over, the place where Dad oughta be was empty. He snorted disgust and crawled out onto the wet asphalt. *Where in hell is the old man?* He wiped his wet hands against his down vest and stuffed 'em into the fluffy pockets. He turned and found Dad curled up, butt and legs on the wet asphalt, arms hugging himself, shoulder snuggled against the cold green steel of the dumpster. Prob'ly freezing, too drunk to know. Scruffy whiskers pressed down on his chest; green cap pulled low over his face. Matted gray hair stringy against the collar of his filthy Army jacket. His clothes matched perfect. With the stinking dumpster. Him snoring down there, useless like that was ... there probably wasn't even a word for how aggrivatin' it was. An army of one. Rot. His chest was rising and falling, so at least he wasn't dead. Perry placed a ragged boot against his shoulder and shoved him over against the brick wall.

"Wake up, Dad."

The old man grunted, his head fell back, showing the wrinkled face, mouth open to the sky, the whole front row of gums. Perry spit on the asphalt in disgust. *Home sweet home. Jeez.* He felt guilty for thinking bad about their spot. They was lucky to have it. There wasn't too many places in Boston like this alley. Most places, people just put the dumpster right out on the street. But old man Ming's restaurant had a back door that opened onto a narrow alley. It was quiet back here, and private. The alley had a wide end big enough for a garbage truck, and a little narrow end barely wide enough to walk through. The high brick walls was like the walls of a castle. If they hadn't had this spot, they'd have been sleepin' in doorways all these years, or right out on the street. Perry fixed his mind not to talk bad about their spot or about old man Ming, no more.

The first day he met Mr. Ming, Perry was a sniffling little boy, only six, looking up at this strange man with a flat-topped hat and long black ponytail. He was about to freeze, snuggled against Dad, beside the dumpster. Mr. Ming come out with big garbage bags. First, he was real angry, seein' Dad, who was drunk as usual. But then he seen Perry, paused for a minute, and his eyes went kinda soft. He pitched the bags in the dumpster and went back inside without saying a word. Couple minutes later, Mrs. Ming came out, nice little Chinese lady, brought them two boxes of hot food and two fancy red tablecloths. She wrapped Perry in one and gave the other to Dad. That was it. They'd been livin' here for the fifteen years since. He shouldn't never think nothin' bad about the Mings.

Far down at the wide end of the alley, a street sweeper swoosh-swoosh-swooshed its way by. *Clean gutters for the drunks to lay in.* He stretched his arms a little to get the blood moving. He turned his shoulders side to side, enjoying the way it stretched his back muscles. He did a couple slow-motion punches in front of him, raised his fists high up, did a little two-step victory dance.

"The welterweight champion uuuuh thuuuuuh werrrrrrld!" His announcer's voice echoed off the high walls, like Madison Square Garden. "Whaaaah, the crowd goes wild!" He did another victory shuffle, fists held high, moving backward in a little circle this time, shook his fists down, slapped his arms with his hands. *Waking up now. Stiffness lettin' go. Prob'ly gonna be a pretty good day. Maybe something awesome will happen. Maybe find some cool stuff.* He was proud of the new idea for the shelter. *Gonna take action on that. Jump on the T and ride the rails down into Roxbury. First, gotta find some food.*

••••••••••

The skinny end of the alley was a short passageway between two buildings, barely wide enough for Perry's shoulders. He stopped in the shadows at the end of the passage and peeped out left and right. Dad taught him to always look both ways before stepping out onto a sidewalk. *No cops. Good.* He almost jumped out of his skin when someone behind him said "Perry." He spun around and jumped out of his skin again. *Bobby.* He couldn't believe it. He wanted to take off sprinting, but he couldn't move at all. He opened his mouth, but nothing came out.

"Perry, help me."

"Bobby?"

There with him in the little skinny part of the alley, Bobby reaching his hand out toward him, desperate. A blue-green light was shining on Bobby, like he was in a dark room somewhere.

"Bobby, is that you?" It was. It was his best friend in the world, no way he could be wrong about it. Bobby standing there, a scared look on his face, reaching out to him. Perry gathered his courage and reached out to take his hand. A jolt of electricity, frozen. An icy sensation shot through his hand and arm, into his heart. His hand passed right through Bobby's hand like it wasn't there. Like it was a freezing electrified mist.

"Help me, Perry," he said again.

"Bobby, how can I help you, bruh? What do you need me to do?"

"Help me." Bobby was real sad and started to fade, like the end of a movie.

"Bobby! Don't go, man. We'll figure it out. How can I help Bobby? Bobby!"

He was staring at an empty alley, looking at the wide opening way over on the other end. He shuddered from head to toe. Sick to his stomach. He had to get out of there. Perry stepped quick out of the alley, turned left, east toward the tall Chinatown Gate. He checked behind him, everything normal, morning sunlight painting the buildings and sidewalks a warm orange color. He shuddered again. He passed under the gate. He never could see why they called it that. There wasn't no gate, just two huge pillars, and above that, somethin' like the top of a big fancy Chinese house. But that's what they called it. A gate. He checked behind him again, to make sure Bobby wasn't following him. He turned left outside the gate, north through the planters and benches until he reached the far end of the Chinatown Park.

Standing on the curb at Essex, he had a creepy feeling tingling his spine and kept looking around to make sure there wasn't any ghosts sneaking up behind him. A couple cars zoomed by. He quick-stepped across three lanes of Essex, cross-walked right across Lincoln, turned left on the far side. Heading up Lincoln, east again. Past the big parking garage, he could see the tall buildings and the shopping plaza where Lincoln met Summer Street. At the corner of Summer, he paused at the three-way where Lincoln flowed into Summer, and Bedford flowed out. He peeped left past the island between the three streets, then right. A couple doors down, across from the big high rise banking center, his friend, the old newsman was rolling his magazine rack out onto the sidewalk. No traffic on Summer Street yet, still early. Business types still a couple hours out. He took a few more big breaths, pushed them out slow, trying to settle down. He brushed himself off, shook one more long tingle off his spine, put on a big wise-guy grin, and headed toward Gillespie Periodicals.

••••••••••••

The street kid, his face pale inside the hood in the cold morning light, turned the corner onto Summer. His black stringy hair was sticking out of the sweatshirt beside his cheeks. Giovanni had been watching for him. As he did every morning, the young man hailed him,

"Hey, good morning, Mr. Geppetto!"

Giovanni swept the sidewalk, frowning. "Good morning, Master Perry."

"Hey, what's the news, newsman? Anything good shakin'?"

"See for yourself."

"Nah, I don't got time to read that trash. Mostly all lies anyway."

"How you know when you never read?"

"I got ears, don't I? I'm payin' attention everywhere. Don't gotta read, 'cause everyone else reads and blabs about it all day—at the bus stop, on the Metro, on the sidewalks."

"Hmpf."

"World's all messed up, Mr. G. Powerful people screwing the little guy. Nobody gettin' ahead but the ones already ahead. And them richer and richer."

"You got it all figured out, huh, Perry?"

"Yeh. You know I do. You been seein' me all these years. I can do about anything I wanna do."

Giovanni turned to him but didn't say anything.

"Want a cup a coffee, Geppetto?"

"No, but help yourself."

"Thanks, Geppetto."

Perry was upbeat, as usual. By his mood, you'd never guess he slept by a dumpster last night.

"Hey, Geppetto?"

"Yes Perry?"

"You ever seen a ghost?"

Giovanni gave him a serious look. "That's personal. None of your business."

"But Geppetto, I really wanna know. I'm not playin." Giovanni paused. The boy was being sincere.

"By the time you get to my age, Perry, there are many ghosts. Too many."

That disturbed the young man. "Why do you ask me that, Perry?"

"I don't know, Geppetto. Just wonderin'."

"Perry, why you call me Geppetto, when you know my name is Giovanni? You do that to disrespect me?"

"Naw, it ain't like that. I just think it fits you. Like you *seem* like Geppetto, so I *call* you Geppetto."

"Yeah? Well, maybe I call you *Pinocchio*."

"Like you my old man or somethin'? Naw. I already got one old man to take care of. Don't need another one. By the way, you seen him? Gone two nights, he finally come home. He's back at our spot sleepin' it off."

"No, I have not seen him yet." Giovanni smiled. "Hey, your old man should be Geppetto."

"Yeah? Why's that?"

"Cause all he ever wanted was a real boy, and instead he get a braying little jackass."

"Ha! Good one, Geppetto. That's funny. Hey, thanks for the donut!"

"I did not say you could have a donut, you little hoodlum."

"Now you mention it, I think I *will* take that paper you offered."

"Help Wanted section in the back."

"Yeah? Maybe there's an executive position for me in one of these high-rises, you think?"

"Anything better than nothing."

"I got a busy day of appointments. Gotta run. Wish me luck, Geppetto!"

"Urchin."

Giovanni leaned on his broom as Perry jaunted west on Summer, back toward Chinatown. He was ragged, uncouth, dirty. Tough on the outside but good in his heart. Giovanni shook his head. These dangerous streets. Filled with traps for a young man like him. His old eyes heavy with sadness, he shook his head again and went back to sweeping.

"Mary, Mother of God, pray for him."

··········

Weasel had snot hanging outta his pointed nose. His eyes were sunk in and had black rings around them. He was twitchin', couldn't stand still, scratchin' his arms and his chest, fidgeting in the heavy morning mist. The damp cloud around 'em like a thick chilly blanket to Kujo, hiding the huge international airport a mile across the water, and even Fort Independence, which wasn't nothing but a quarter mile north on the causeway, and Head Island a quarter mile south. Water was moving under the bridge, but no other sounds hit Kujo, and he bet nobody else would be able to hear him and Weasel either. Most mornings, planes would be zoomin', and boats would be around close enough to see them, but this thick soup had everything shut down. It was perfect. It was like they were standing in a little room with white walls. The low bawl of a foghorn rumbled through the cloud from somewhere far away. Him and Weasel were alone, close and private.

"Weasel, where's the merchandise?" Kujo using his most patient tone.

"Man, Kujo, I'm tellin' you. I got rolled. You gotta believe me. I was headed for the place. Three dudes jumped me."

"You said two."

"It mighta been two, but it mighta been three, man. I don't know. It happened really fast."

"Shut up, Weasel." Kujo leaned over the bridge, looking at rushing mud-green water, a low waterfall twenty-five yards wide. The tide was rippin'. Pleasure Bay, the big half-mile diameter lagoon by Castle Island, was emptying back into the Atlantic. It'd be rippin' like this for at least three more hours. Throw a bottle in there right now, it might be ten miles offshore before the tide slowed down. Another six hours after that before the tide came back and hit high again.

"Weasel, you're killin' me."

"I'm sorry."

"Shut up. I already tol' you to shut up."

"I'm sorry. Please, Kujo. I'm sick, man."

"You're *sick?*"

"Yeah, man. You *gotta* believe me. You know I wouldn't be out here if I wasn't, in this cold, right after sunrise? Man, you *know* I'm sick. If I had scored last night, I'd be in heaven right now, sleepin' it off."

Kujo shook his head. "Everybody wants to go to heaven. What ever happened to personal accountability? Can you answer me that, Weasel?"

Weasel was shakin' his head, itching his legs now.

"Weasel, you bringin' shame down on me, man. You know that?"

"I—" Weasel snuck a look at Kujo, then at the pavement again.

"I got people to answer to, you understand?"

Weasel started cryin'. Kujo slapped him hard on the face, stinging his hand. "I said to *stop*." Pointing his finger at his face. Slapped him again, this time on the ear.

Weasel screamed, covering his head, jerkin' up and down like some kinda cheap battery-operated monkey.

"All right, shhhhhh. It's okay, Weasel. Come here, man."

Weasel gawked up at him scared, not sure what to do.

"Hey, man. I believe you. I know you didn't steal the merchandise. Like you said, you're sick, right?"

Weasel stopped crying, wiped a big string of snot across his sleeve.

"It's okay, Weasel. I'll work it out. I'll explain it to my people. Come here. I got somethin' for you."

Weasel was scared, hesitatin'. When he first took Weasel under his wing, he was a small-town kid runaway to the big city, never even smelled cannabis before. Now see him.

"Come on, Weasel. You sick, right?"

Weasel nodded, started scratching his arm again.

"Want to feel better?"

Weasel still looked unsure but nodded.

"Well, come here, man. I forgive you. I got what you need right here." He patted the big pocket of his heavy green army coat. "You want it or not?"

Weasel couldn't resist. He came over slowly.

Kujo reached out his long arm and pulled him in for a big hug. "Man, ain't I always taken care of you, Weasel?"

"Yeah, Kujo. I'm sorry, man."

"Let's forget about it. Let's get you feelin' better. I'll work things out, okay?"

Weasel buried his face in Kujo's chest, crying again. He was shakin' all over.

"Everything's gonna be alright, Weasel. You ready? You wanna go to heaven?"

"Mm-hmm," Weasel said through his sobs.

Kujo slid a six-inch blade between Weasel's ribs and yanked hard, slicing left to right.

Weasel made a funny noise and gaped up at him with his mouth and eyes wide open.

Kujo spit in his face and shoved him hard, Weasel gone over the rail backward. The splash was pretty loud. Weasel got swept under by the waterfall, and when he came back up to the surface, he raised one hand, like he was waving goodbye, sunk back down under the ripping current. Kujo flung the knife as hard as he could out into the Atlantic.

Kujo needed to pee. There's something really organic about peeing into the ocean.

·····•·····

It was still early. Perry peeped up and down Dorchester, being cool, hands in pockets, rolling a pebble back and forth with his toe. *Can't be too careful. Anyone finds your hiding place they'll steal your stuff.* Progress is hard to make. No way he was gonna let some fool thief him right back to where he started. Coast was clear, so he took the turn, headed for his secret spot. Von Hillern street was empty except for a little trash blowing along the edge, which was normal. Six hundred yards to the dead end, where the road ran into a clump of forest. Not a single person was around. At the dead end, he checked a last time, ducked into the trees, turned left toward the Metro tracks. The woods smelled cool and moist, the ground and leaves wet from a little rain or dew. When he got close to the Metro tracks, he went to a dense clump, pulled apart the scratchy leaves and branches and slipped in. He peered out through the heavy packed leaves. Nobody around. Invisible in here, he surveyed his secret spot with pride.

It took a week of hard work to carve out a clearing in the thickest part of the bushes and small trees. He went to the shopping cart, grabbed the snips from their spot, and scanned around for anything starting to grow into his space. As hard as it was to build this, he wasn't gonna let it grow closed again. Prime real estate and nobody even knew it was here. *You gonna be successful, you need a base of operations.* He clipped a few small branches and put the snips away. *Easier to clip a few each day so they don't close up the space and make you start all over again. You got to keep moving in life. Can't keep starting over, or you'll never get nowhere.* He stepped over to the shelf made of borrowed cinder blocks and boards, pulled back the wet plastic sheeting, and grabbed the box of heavy industrial-strength garbage bags. He pulled out two and put the box back on the shelf, changed his mind and grabbed a third. *It might be a good day. I can't afford to lose no revenue because I'm short a bag. Geppetto don't think I know what's up, but you can learn a lot from hanging around while the business suits talk. They waitin' on the bus, the crosswalk light, whatever, talking on phones, givin' away all kinds of secrets about how to run a business, get ahead in life. Stuff like return on investment, overhead, gross profit, and net profit. Not really clear on the difference between them last two, but I'll keep listening, figure it out. People see you, think you got nothing goin' on, and here in secret, you workin' a strategy, building a empire.* It made him smile.

The ground started shakin' and a Metro train went by, rumblin'. Perry could have almost reached out and touched it if he wanted to. The "T" trains don't travel too fast, but that's a lot a metal rollin' all at once. Some of the trains were slick and new, but this was an old one, beat to heck. Through the waving trees, he could see the old ratty cars swayin' and shakin' past, some bored passengers in there, but nobody could see him in here. In a few seconds, the train was gone, and the headquarters settled back down. A little distraction like that didn't faze him. *It's all about keeping yer eye on the critical path. That's the important stuff that's got to happen, no matter what, to get where you want.* For Perry, that meant gettin' up early, being first to hit the dumpsters, get the best of everything. *They call that market share. If you share the market with too many, you ain't gonna do too good, so you got to hustle, get as much of it as you can for yourself. And you got to make it look cool. The business types are always chillin', talkin' like they on top of it, when anyone's listenin'. But you hear two of 'em alone when a deal's going down, they scared as snot like everybody else. So, it must be important to not just do it but to also look good while you doin' it. Somethin' about a supply chain, which I don't have yet. Just me, hustlin'. But I got inventory.*

He checked the shopping cart over careful. Umbrella, window wash bottle, paper towel roll, garbage bags, couple different cardboard signs, extra clothes, his folded piece of frayed red cloth, some plastic in case it rained, folding chair, rope—*you never know when you gonna need some rope*—two thick sticks, just in case, and a little bottle of oil. He bent down and put a couple drops on each of the wheels. That front wheel was squeakin' worse and worse, and it was getting a flat spot. *Prob'ly gonna havta get a new cart, but that's a big risk. Gotta manage risk when you run a business. Keep to your critical path, without taking so much risk that you get busted, end up in the system. It's a lot easier to get into the system than to get out.* He'd seen a lot a guys, and girls too, get put into the system, and man, you are messed *up* then. Most of 'em got into the system by getting arrested. Perry was too smart for that. Manage risk. That was important. Think about the return on investment.

Dealers was all the time takin' risks, and big ones. They think its worth it, 'cause they have a huge return on investment. They get some product, step on it, make it ten times as much as they bought, and sell it for more than it's worth to the junkies who got to have it, and bam. Huge return on investment. But a lot of risk too. Dealers don't care. Not the big ones. To them managing risk means find some fool stupid enough to deliver your product. Let him get busted. Or popped and planted. He seen what happened to Bobby. A shudder shook him, remembering the terror on Bobby's face when he seen him in the alley this morning. And Kujo always on Perry trying to get him to jump in with the gang. *Screw that.* After Bobby got killed, Perry wanted nothin' to do with that business. He was too smart for that. *I don't need no help from nobody. I got my own thing goin' on.*

There's lots of ways to make a buck. Collectin' cans has basically no risk and a huge return on investment. Or ROI, same thing. *That's the way the suits say it when they bein' all cool.* Took him a while to learn that. *On cans, your ROI is total, cause there ain't no investment. Well, you have to buy the garbage bags, but one good day of divin' can get you enough cans to buy bags for a whole month, and sometimes you can get 'em on sale, maybe half price, or even two for one. Other than that, the only investment is time, and time is the cheapest thing anywhere. Time is basically free. Washing windshields has even better ROI, 'cause the time ain't nothin'. Usually, people pay you just to stop, get the hell outta their way. Holdin' a cardboard sign has no investment, and you can make a lot more money, but it can take all day, and it's boring. It's a good business model if you're old or sick. But if you're young, there's a risk someone will scoop you up and try to put you in the system.*

Should be past worryin' about that. The old man said Perry was twenty-one now. *But how's he know? Half the time he don't know what year it is, and even if he's right, he don't have no paperwork to prove it.* He used to. Dad had all the important papers in a cardboard case with accordion sides, but he lost it one night when he was on a binge, and they never did find it. Some bum probably hid it, his stash of toilet paper. Another train went whooshing past, rattlin' and clatterin', wind blowin' the leaves on the trees. Then it was gone.

Perry peeped through the bushes back toward the dead end, listened careful. Pushing the prickly branches aside, he stepped out of his hiding spot, pulled the cart out quick. He dragged it through the woods, checked for any people, dragged it out onto Von Hillern. He rolled the cart a few yards, went back to check his trail. He swished a branch across his back trail in the woods, moved a couple leaves that had broke off onto the asphalt and threw them over into the woods. He used his toe to sweep away some mud left from the cart's wheels. Headin' up toward Dorchester, he was making good progress, the street empty. *Wait. What is that.*

The back of a big four-door car with purple sparkle paint, dark windows and tall wheels. It was pulled over to the curb on the other side of the street, tail pipes smokin' a little. It was about a half block ahead. From between two buildings, a tall lanky dude with his back to Perry came out, headed for the car. *Kujo.* Perry would know him anywhere, even from behind. He had known Kujo most of his life, long as he'd been on the street. Seen him go from being a fun-loving kid, to a big bully, to a errand-boy for the thugs. Now he was blooming into a full-on criminal.

Kujo walked up to the car, and the back door opened. This big dude unfolds himself out of the back seat, a foot taller than Kujo, and about half as big around. He stood looking down at Kujo like a schoolteacher looks at a little kid. Perry was seeing the sides of both faces. Kujo held both his hands up, reached into his jacket, pulled out a envelope, offered it to the skinny giant. The giant glared down at him a second, snatched the envelope, gave a quick look at what was inside. He tossed the envelope in the car, started poking Kujo in the chest with a bony finger. His arms was about a mile long. Kujo steppin back, actin' like a whipped puppy, eyes down at the sidewalk, flinchin' from the dude's words. Perry'd never seen Kujo back down from nobody. *Who is this guy, that Kujo stands there about to wet himself?*

Perry knew he shouldn't be here but didn't have no way to disappear. This little narrow street, no side streets, the best thing was to just keep to his side and mind his own business. The skinny giant pointed his finger at Kujo's face, stepped up and put his chest almost against Kujo's chin. Kujo stood real still, looking away at the ground beside him. The giant said a couple more words Perry couldn't make out, turned to get back into the car. He stopped, staring across the top of the car right at Perry.

Perry froze. He was used to getting bad looks from people, but this was different. This guy wasn't lookin' down at him. It was like he was looking through him, his eyes all the way evil. Perry turned away, kept walking, made sure not to look back. He heard the big car moving up the street behind him. It pulled up beside him, tailpipes thumping a slow rhythm. It almost stopped, creeped along at the same speed as Perry's cart for a few seconds. He didn't look over. The driver slid his window down about halfway. That made Perry look. Dude pointed a camera, took about five shots of Perry, punched it, threw some gravel and they were gone like a flash of purple lightning.

Perry turned right on Dorchester, headin' up to West Fourth and into Southie. He had a bad feeling in his stomach. He'd been on the street long enough to know it ain't good to know other people's business. Especially the business of some giant so scary even Kujo won't look him in the eye.

....

"In my opinion," Professor Wilkes said, "the theory that makes the most sense is the Quantum Multi-Universe Theory. As to how the universes relate and either do or do not interact with each other, I think the jury is still out on that question." She took a sip of her coffee and sat it down on the dainty little table. She glanced around the small coffee shop, which was nearly empty.

"Your book is quite different from the genetics material I am used to reading," Professor Faulk said. It was a little beyond me. I didn't understand it." He was being kind. In truth, it sounded completely bonkers.

"*No*body understands! That's why it is fascinating," she said. "But it does go a long way toward explaining a lot of things that don't make sense if you try to reconcile them with more traditional constructs."

Professor Faulk studied her face. "In your book, you posit that every possible historical outcome has occurred somewhere, in some universe?" He asked.

"Well, that is the core of the Quantum Parallel Universe hypothesis. What I am suggesting in my book is that it may not be as simple as that."

"Okay, take me through it."

"Recall the experiment where you shoot hundreds of photons through a slit and produce the classic interference pattern. Bands of light and dark."

"Okay," he said.

"The results are counter intuitive. If you shoot an increasing number of photons through the slit, the probability of every location becoming a landing site should increase. The impacts should be random, and evenly dispersed. And yet, the probability of many of those landing sights are never realized. In fact, the more photons you shoot through the slit, the more strongly the alternating interference pattern of light and dark stripes is reinforced."

"And how does that alter your view of the multi-universe hypothesis?"

"I am suggesting that the idea of every possible outcome occurring in some universe somewhere may be an over-simplification. Just as not every possible impact site is realized, it may be that not every possible outcome is realized either."

"And the implications of that are?"

"I am positing that rather than every imaginable type of universe coming into existence, it is more likely that there are a great number of universes which are very similar, with only minor differences."

Professor Faulk shook his head. "Wow. This stuff is pretty out there."

"I invite you to do your own research on this. Multi-Universe Theory is hotly debated but is past the point of being someone's wild-eyed theory. Multi-Universe Theory is a mainstream concept at present. We're not talking about fringe science. You can find as many proponents of the theory as you can find detractors."

"I have a difficult time with this. It seems too speculative to ever be proven," Professor Faulk said.

"That is one of the major objections you hear. But this is an exciting time in science. The explosive growth rate of technology is making it possible to investigate things that could never have been examined before. For example, in 2010, they changed the speed of light, remember that?"

"I… sort of…"

"And in 2016, scientists at the Australian National University actually *stopped* two photons in a super-cooled cloud."

"I did read about that."

"They *stopped* the travel of light," she said.

"I know. It was pretty impressive, actually."

"Now, when you think about the fact that most of the equations that explain how things work in the universe include the speed of light as a 'known constant,' you begin to see how far-reaching this could be, as it continues to unfold."

"I do see," he said, nodding.

"We're talking about the outlier thought," Professor Wilkes said. "One radical question, 'is it possible to change the speed of light,' has produced an outcome. A new reality has emerged, and as a result, every theory about this universe, has been deflected off onto a new trajectory, different from anything anyone ever imagined before."

It was making more and more sense why her book sounded so crazy. She really did see the universe – universes, in a completely different way.

"So, hold onto your hat," she said. "In history there were times when this world was ready to receive certain information, and the information simply showed up. The time for the revelation of multiple universes may be close at hand."

"Hold on," Professor Faulk said. "how's that again?"

"The smelting of copper was discovered in multiple locations around the world at approximately the same time. Some people believe the same is true of smelting bronze. Calculus was simultaneously discovered by two different people, in two different countries. Charles Darwin and Alfred Russell Wallace both arrived at the concept of evolution through Natural Selection, independently, and at the *same time*. There are times when the world is ready for a new revelation, and when the world is ready, the revelation arrives."

"Wow," Professor Faulk said. "It looks more and more like an intelligent hand is involved…"

"No, that is not what I am saying," she said. "I am saying, the system in which we live is infinitely complex, and because it is so vast, random occurrences can unfold as if on a script."

…………

During that part of the day when the sky starts to look gray, colors fading, Guy told Wheels to pull the big black Lincoln to a stop a few yards back, pointing nose to nose with the sparkly purple Buick. Guy couldn't understand why these kids wanted to make their cars stand out with a sissy paint job like that. It ain't good for business to stand out. From the back seat, Guy watched the Buick's door opening, the tall thin guy getting out of the back seat and walking with long slow strides toward him. Punk's hands were in the pockets of a gray hoodie. Damn kids. Guy reached into his jacket and slipped his big cannon out of the shoulder holster and touched the muzzle to the base of the dark tinted window. The Punk stood there beside him. Let him wait. After maybe a minute and a half, Guy rolled his window down a couple inches.

"Kneecap, how about take your hands out of your pockets, real slow."

Kneecap slid his hands out slow, spread his ten fingers wide, palms facing the car. "Sorry about that, Mr. Big. I wasn't thinking. It's just getting a little chilly this evening, that's all."

"Yeah. Chilly. I understand. But people been shot for less. So next time, how 'bout keep your head in the game and your hands where I can see 'em. Show some respect."

"Yes sir, Mr. Big. I didn't mean disrespect. You know I'm your man."

"Apology accepted. Now what did you want to talk to me about?"

"I met with Kujo this morning to receive a cash transfer, and he was short."

"How short?"

"A courier lost a whole delivery. Thirty grams of gravel."

"You lost three grand?"

"Courier claimed he was rolled. Kujo fed him to the fish, said he's gonna make the money right. He raised half the money already. Says he'll get me the rest by next week."

"Sloppy. That's some amateur hour garbage, you know that?"

"Yeh. I do, Mr. Big. And I'm sorry about the delay. If Kujo don't come through by next week, I'll cover it."

"You'll cover it, alright. Tomorrow morning, right here, nine o'clock."

"Yes sir."

Guy held him a long time with his coldest stare. "Kneecap, I'm disappointed. I expect better from you."

"I know that Mr. Big. It won't happen again. I got the fifteen hundred right here in my inside pocket."

"Your inside pocket? What did I just tell you about showing proper respect?"

Kneecap didn't say anything.

"Wheels, get out and accept payment from this rookie operator, please."

Wheels slid his three hundred pounds out from under the steering column and went around the car, no jacket, shoulder holster showing a big cannon in broad daylight. "Put your hands on the hood."

Kneecap showed some frustration in his face, but he didn't say nothin'. He stepped forward, back the direction he had come and put his hands on the fender of the car, spread his legs wide. Wheels patted him down, took a butterfly knife out of his sock, and a snub nose .38 out of the back of his belt. He took an envelope out of Kneecap's shirt pocket and counted it.

"Fifteen hundred, Mr. Big." He stepped over and slipped the envelope to Guy through the window.

"Okay."

"Stand up," Wheels said.

Kneecap stood up, straightened his hoodie, walked back to the window and waited for Guy. He took his time scowling through the small slit above the dark panel.

"Kneecap, next time you meet me, use proper protocol."

"Mr. Big, you can trust me. I would never try-"

"Did I ask if I could trust you? People do stupid things. Follow protocol. You'll be safer that way."

"Yes sir."

Guy rolled the window down the rest of the way, let Kneecap see the muzzle of the cannon resting on the window frame, pointed right at him. He gave him a second to stare at it. "Alright. Wheels, give him back his personal property."

"Wait." Kneecap holding his hands up again. "I got something more I need to tell you, Mr. Big."

"What is it?"

"This morning, when I was meeting with Kujo, there was a witness to the transfer."

"You kiddin' me? What the hell is the matter with you, Kneecap? Your whole organization is falling apart."

"I'm gonna handle it, Mr. Big."

"Damn right, you are. So, you got two problems to handle. Somebody in your territory thinks they can hit a courier and make off with three large. You need to find out who that is. And who was the witness?"

"I got some photos in my back pocket. Its a young homeless guy."

SEPTEMBER 5

Anacette was working in the H&H conference room, located in the center of the penthouse suite. The suite was designed like nothing she had ever seen. The whole space was transparent. The interior partitions were clear Lexan, and the perimeter was hurricane-proof glass looking out over cityscapes on three sides, and a breathtaking view of the Atlantic Ocean to the East. The columns that supported the roof were ten feet high, wrapped in mirrors floor to ceiling, so they essentially disappeared. No matter which direction you faced, anywhere on the floor, you had awe-inspiring views.

Being in here was like walking around on top of a cloud or something. On the seventieth floor, mornings like this one, you really were looking down on the tops of clouds. The boss was standing with his slim back to her, hands in pockets, looking out toward the south, admiring the view of Pleasure Bay, visible sparkling through holes in a thick white blanket. Crazy architecture.

Anacette promised herself that when she got her degree, she was going to design awesome structures like this one. No run-of-the-mill utilitarian buildings for her. She was going to be the next great American architect, and she would spend her life designing signature pieces that people would talk about for a hundred years. She sighed. Someday. For now, here she was in her ridiculous French maid's outfit, wiping down the furnishings with a microfiber cloth in preparation for the meeting. She was kinda hot in the costume, but if her friends from the engineering department saw her, she would never live it down. She shouldn't wear it. Should have more pride. But the job paid double what most entry-level jobs paid, so she rode the elevators five days a week and prissed around with her feather duster like she enjoyed it. Tuition is not cheap. Another three years of night classes, maybe four, and she'd have something to hang on her wall that would open the doors she needed open.

It only took a second to wipe down the oblong mahogany table, and she started on the six high-end ergonomically perfect chairs. One day she was going to have a chair like this, and an office to go with it. Hire some meat-head body builder to wipe down the furniture. Make him wear a Chippendale costume. She turned her attention to the refreshment table and began arranging the pastries, drinks, and fresh fruit. She knew the same thing was happening in the other branch offices—in Corpus Christi, Chicago, and Los Angeles. At all the offices, the butter knives had gold plating, as did the coffee spoons. With a clean white cloth, she wiped each one carefully. Haruki didn't like fingerprints. The tiny cups were arranged neatly around the high-end espresso machine. With no apparent prompting, at 10:07 a.m. Eastern time, Pete and Lisa approached the conference room. Anacette held the door for them.

"Good morning."

"Good morning, Anacette." Pete touched her on the arm as he went by. He was kind of hot, but he was also married and had a kid. The large monitor near the ceiling came alive. It showed other young executives and their secretaries gathering in three other conference rooms exactly like this one. Lisa smiled warmly at her as she neared.

"How we doing today, Anacette?"

"Just fine, ma'am."

Lisa stepped closer and lowered her voice. "Honey, you don't have to be formal with me. You're doing fine. Hang in there. This place has big opportunities for you if you can make it through your rookie year." She winked. Anacette nodded and smiled. Pete was talking to the screen now, in a loud, confident voice.

"Shawn, did you send me those Cowboys tickets yet?"

Shawn, on the lower left corner of the monitor, shook his head. "Pete, get a map, okay? Texas is a *big* state, understand? I live way down here, by the water." He was pointing to an imaginary map. "Say after me: Corpus Christi. Got it? Dallas is way up there." Pete and Shawn both laughed.

"You're killing me, bro," Pete, pushing the narrative.

At precisely 10:13 a.m. Eastern time, Haruki turned away from the window and headed their way. She despised him. And admired him. There might be a lot of fish in the sea, but there couldn't be too many like him. He was one helluva specimen. Not married. He was tall but not too tall, and had the lean, muscular build of a guy who had studied martial arts all his life. Plus, he was stinkin' over-the-top rich. She stood as erect as she could, chin up, shoulders back, hands clasped behind her.

"Good morning, Haruki."

"Good morning, Anacette. Thank you for your help. Everything looks great. You can go start working on your filing now."

"Thank you, Haruki."

As she walked away, she heard his strong and friendly voice say, "Hey, Steve. How's that robotic lawn mower working out?"

....

Lisa booted up her tablet. Boston was the dominant image on the overhead screen, but each executive could see all the branches via the picture-in-picture windows in the lower part of the monitor. She watched Haruki turn to the screen with a big smile.

"Mary, did you do something different with your hair? I like it. Cute."

In Chicago, Mary blushed and looked down. Lisa narrowed her eyes. It was just an off-hand remark. He was being polite. Just like Mary to take it as a come-on. Lisa swiped her middle finger across her tablet to get ready to take notes. Haruki took a big breath, and with an expression of joy said,

"Well, shall we get started?" They all sat down facing their screens.

"I want to open this meeting with an important announcement." His sparkling eyes gave them his I've-got-a-secret look. "Whatever your plans are for Thanksgiving, cancel them," he said flatly.

All the faces on the screen went blank. Seeing him in profile, she could tell Haruki was giving them with his poker face. Then he smiled broadly.

"I've booked a small group of private islands in the Pacific, and we're all going to spend Thanksgiving *there*."

A little thrill tingled in Lisa's chest.

"The key employees at each of your locations are expected to attend. Each branch will have an *entire island* to themselves."

Gasps echoed. Lisa's heart fluttered. Thanksgiving on an exotic island with Haruki? An image of a moon-lit beach came to mind, two figures strolling close together, maybe their hands touching a little. To her surprise, a couple of people on the screen visually stiffened.

"I understand that Thanksgiving is traditionally a *family* holiday," Haruki conceded. "So, all of your families are *invited to come along.*"

All the faces were awash with shock and awe. *Fantastic.* All the others would be busy with their families, leaving Lisa and Haruki as the only two singles on the island. Pete broke her trance by raising his hand directly across the table from her. His face was clouded.

"Pete?" Haruki said.

"Thank you for your generosity. It is... *amazing*. But I have a significant problem. We usually host about ten people for Thanksgiving."

"Fine. Bring them."

"Really?"

"Really," Haruki beamed.

"Uh, Haruki?" Steve said from one of the small windows on the monitor. "I don't think I can make it. My wife has a big Italian family, and we've been selected to be the hosts this year."

"Bring them all to the islands."

"Sir?"

"I don't care how many. Thirty? Forty? It doesn't matter. These islands are small, but each one is a few square miles of pristine tropical beauty. And we've got the whole Pacific for our playground. There will be plenty of room for everyone."

"Haruki, I don't know what to say..."

"I understand. You're welcome. In fact, Shawn, Mary, all of you, bring anyone you want, and have your key employees do the same. Friends, families, anybody you would like to spend the holiday with. I'd love to meet them all. Local branch secretaries should send out formal invitations. Simply forward your guest lists to Lisa by the end of September so she can arrange for the amenities." Lisa made sure her face showed no trace of surprise.

Mary piped in. "Excuse me, Haruki?"

"Yes?"

"Some of the members of my family live kind of... frugal. They're simple working people, you know?"

Probably trailer trash, Lisa thought.

"We will not embarrass them," Haruki said. "I want them to have a once-in-a-lifetime experience. That week they will live as kings and queens."

"A *week?*" everyone said in unison.

"That's right." Haruki smiled. "A full week with your team on a private island. We are going to the Kingdom of Tonga, a collection of islands scattered across a large area of the Pacific Ocean. The islands we'll be on are uninhabited, but I'm arranging for you to be treated to a five-star experience, with private bungalows, luxurious linens, complimentary food and beverages, and world-class amenities."

What kind of amenities? Lisa wondered. Haruki was clearly enjoying watching them exchange surprised looks with their secretaries. It was starting to sound complicated. Was it going to be a working vacation for her?

"You can book massages, manicures and pedicures, facials if you want. I'll have scuba instructors. I can't wait to see what you think of this place. The water is so clear, you can see forever. There will be fishing guides, rowing instructors, and, in the evenings, you will be entertained by musicians native to the island chain, dancers, fire jugglers, the whole package. The Pacific Island food will knock your socks off. You and your teams are going to remember this for the rest of your lives."

The faces around the table were all beaming. Lisa's mind was racing. Did he already have all that lined up? He must, right? He must have someone providing local support for all those amenities. Surely, he wasn't expecting her to arrange all of that.

"Haruki, will I be booking commercial tickets?" she asked.

"No, ma'am. Each team will fly on their own private charter jet."

Lisa typed *BIG Jets. Capacity? Availability? Need Four.*

Haruki was still talking. "This is going to be lap of luxury. You are going to spend a full week in the Garden of Eden. I want you all to discover how it feels to be *truly* thankful."

They all started talking at once, like kids at a birthday party.

Haruki smiled and held up his hand. "Okay, team. Let's get to work. We've got to make enough money to pay for this thing."

Everyone laughed.

"Give me about fifteen minutes, and we'll begin the individual section head meetings, okay?" Everyone stood up, most of them swiping their phones to send text messages.

Haruki turned to Lisa, winked, and gave her a big smile. He was loving this. Nothing fired him up like making a big show, throwing money around, being the magnanimous Lord. But damn, he did have a flair for the dramatic. She had to give him that.

September 7

The sign on the building said *Life Choice League*. Beneath it, smaller letters said *If you love something, let it go.* Saturday morning, Father John, in the role of quarterback, huddled with his team. Eight-thirty, on the sidewalk in front of the bland structure, bricks painted with a thick beige paint, a six-foot wrought-iron fence separated them from the small parking lot.

"Okay, friends," John said, "time to share your artwork. Virginia, would you go first?"

Virginia was in her thirties—a beautiful young woman, one of the single adults in the parish, and a close ally to Father John. She held up a pink poster board sign mounted on a large paint-stirring stick. Block letters stenciled in pastel blue, outlined in dark blue, *CHOOSE LOVE.*

"I like it. Very nice, Virginia."

One by one, the others held up their signs.

LIFE will find a WAY

LOVE LIFE

LIFE IS LOVE

YOU ARE NOT ALONE

Next, it was Gabby's turn. One of the older members of the congregation, she was a pillar, still active as a senior, unfortunately not an ally to John. She constantly opposed his initiatives. The tension with her was causing problems for him in the parish. Gabby held up her sign—a large color photograph pasted onto black poster board; a human child chopped to pieces amid a pool of blood. John quickly pulled the poster downward so that the image was facing the ground.

"Get that thing out of here. I will not have St. Leo's associated with anything as ghoulish as that."

"How can you say that?" she asked. "*They* are the ghouls! I am merely exposing their evil deeds."

"It's not our job to expose their deeds. Our job is to expose the victims of this crisis to God's love. And to give them hope."

"Bah!" she grunted. "This is *war*!"

Father John took a deep breath. "Gabby, save those disturbing images for the lawmakers. Here, we are on a *rescue* mission."

She glared at him. The others were silent, watching the showdown. John inhaled and used his softest pastoral tone.

"Gabby, the Enemy's weapons are fear, anger, hatred, and guilt. If we fight the battle his way, we will lose. We have one secret weapon that will neutralize his entire arsenal. Our secret weapon is love."

Gabby scanned the other volunteers to see if she had any support, turned in a huff and headed toward her car. She turned over her shoulder, and said, "If you are too much of a coward to fight, we'll ask the bishop to give the job to someone else."

....

"Guy, was this really so important that we had to meet in person on a Saturday morning?" Pete asked.

"Well, that depends. I know it's important to Haruki. I don't know if that makes it important to you or not. What'd I do, make you miss a golf game or somethin'?"

"Guy, I don't want you to overreact to this," Pete said. "We're only talking about a small amount of money, and the homeless guy is too busy fighting off starvation to pose much of a threat to us."

"And that's your professional opinion, Pete? Applying all your long months of experience, that it?" His big, fat arms crossed over his barrel chest and keg-sized belly, giving Pete a sarcastic look. Pete despised him.

"I've been managing projects for Haruki for almost six years, Guy. Don't try to punch my buttons."

"Oh, zat right? Six years, huh? Whew-wee. I am impressed." His eyes narrowed, and his teeth clinched in a way that made Pete want to drop the discussion. "Big Guy" as he was known on the street, or "Mr. Big," as his subordinates called him, was as hard-nosed as they come. The last thing

Pete wanted to do was lock horns with him. He would have happily let this go. But he couldn't. He had to assert his authority. Otherwise, he'd lose his position, and how would he feed his family?

"Guy, listen to me."

"No, boy, you listen. I know you think you're somebody, but you better choose your words more carefully, or I might have to snap that little pencil neck of yours between a thumb and a finger. You hear me?" Pete lowered his chin, to hide his gulp.

"Guy, you've done your job by letting me know about the problem. You let me take it from here, and I might not mention to Haruki that you have a serious attitude problem."

"Oh, zat right. Let me tell you something, college boy. I was a lieutenant running these streets for Haruki when you had only been *alive* six years, get it? So, I'm tellin' you, one time only, you watch your punk mouth when you talk to me."

"Don't threaten me, Guy."

"I Just did. Now what exactly are you gonna do about it? Hmm? You're pretty cocky for someone who's a week away from being shark food."

"What is that supposed to mean?"

"It means that you are a soft little college boy getting ready to learn something hard about how the streets work. It might be a little different from how things worked in the dormitories. See, college boy, on the street, you run up a big gambling debt you can't pay off? People, certain people, might decide to cut their losses."

Pete swallowed hard. "What's that supposed to mean?"

"You know exactly what it means. You might be more valuable to certain people, as an example of what happens when someone don't pay. It's bad for business to have open accounts. They close your account, permanently, they send a message to all the other college boys out there ain't smart enough to figure out how the world works. That way, they at least got something for their money."

Guy's smug look made Pete's blood drain to his feet.

"See, little *Petey*, I've been around a long time. I have friends. I hear things. And I've seen a lot of hot shot punks who thought they had the world by the short hairs disappear into thin air."

"Who have you been talking to?"

"Or maybe they leave you all in one piece, disappear your sweet little family. There's things worse than dying, college boy."

••••••••••••

An hour later, Father John was waiting. God was going to do something today, but John didn't know what. His job was to pay attention and not miss God's leading. God is everywhere, all the time. But whenever two or more are gathered in His name, He is present in a special way. Scripture promises it.

A glint caught his eye. A man to his right across the street was shooting photos with a long lens out of a car window. Behind the glass lens the shutter opened and closed and the dark-tinted window raised to a closed position. Probably a reporter. Not a sympathetic one, or he would be over here interviewing the volunteers.

He heard brakes squeak behind him and turned to see a blue older model four-door sedan pull over to the curb a block up. A young African American girl got out of the car. The door slammed, and the car flipped a U-turn and sped away, muffler stuttering and puffing, leaving a cloud of dark smoke. The young girl stood motionless, looking around as though she were uncertain what to do.

John turned to the photographer again just as that car also pulled away. Strange. He glanced back to the young girl for a second, careful not to stare. She moved toward them but stopped, loitering at the end of the block. She kept looking toward them, and away. *She's reading the signs.* He started walking down the sidewalk, nonchalant. He was concerned she might bolt and run before he got to her, but she didn't. His clerical garb probably helped.

"Hi, I'm Father John. What is your name?'

"Elza Beth."

"Elza Beth, it's nice to meet you. Is there any way I can help you?"

She looked down at the sidewalk and shook her head.

"Elza Beth, I'm a priest, so I see people who are dealing with all sorts of life problems. It seems to me that you are struggling with something that's difficult. Am I right?"

She nodded her head, wiped away a tear and crossed her arms over her chest. She couldn't be more than fifteen years old. His heart went out to her.

"Have you talked with your parents about this problem you're having?"

A spark flashed in her eyes. "I can't talk to my mom about this."

"That must be hard." John kept his distance, not wanting to crowd her. "Not having anyone to talk to. It can be difficult." She was inspecting the pavement.

"Elza Beth, I would like to introduce you to a friend of mine. She's helped a lot of young women. You can talk to her about anything, and she won't be angry with you or pass judgment. Would that be okay?"

She sized him up for a moment. She nodded. John turned and motioned to a woman wearing a dark suit coat and knee-length dress who was talking with the volunteers. The woman nodded in response, said a word to the others, and walked toward them.

"Elza Beth, this is Sister Mary Frances. I know her well, and I know you can trust her with any problem you may have."

"Sister?"

"Yes, I'm a member of the Sisters of Saint Joseph. This Medallion I wear is to help people identify me as someone who is able and willing to help."

Elza Beth showed no sign of comprehension.

"It means I am a nun, sweetheart." She put an arm around Elza Beth's shoulders. "Let me buy you a soft drink and we'll talk, okay?"

Elza Beth nodded and began moving along with Sister Mary Frances. They crossed the street to a retro-looking diner fashioned after an old Metro car. As Elza Beth allowed Mary Frances to hold the door for her, John whispered an urgent prayer. The outcome of the conversation would produce either a life or a death.

·······•·····

Inside the diner, seated in a high-backed booth, Elza watched the nun order soft drinks and large fries. The nun was cheerful, upbeat, and talked with a lot of energy. She was pretty for a white woman, but she dressed like someone older than she seemed. Elza couldn't tell how old she was. A lot older than Elza, close to the middle part of her life. Maybe older than Mom, but not as old as Gramma.

"So, Elza Beth, what school do you go to?"

"You can call me Elza."

"Sure. What school do you go to Elza?"

The diner was really old. Like it came from a different century or something. Red plastic cushions in the booths, checkerboard pattern on the tabletops, black-and-white tile floor. A couple people sitting at the counter. One of them reading a paper, the other staring into a coffee cup like there were answers in there. The whole other side was windows, like looking out of a Metro train. "I kinda stopped going."

"Ah, I see. I understand that. Sometimes life gets in the way."

"What do you mean?"

"I mean life can be complicated. Sometimes things happen that we wouldn't have expected, and that can cause us to change our priorities."

"Sometimes things happen that shoulda *never* happened."

"That's true too." The nun said, her eyes fixed on Elza. "Like falling in with the wrong kind of boy?"

Elza turned toward the cook back there with a paper hat on. "I didn't fall for some boy."

"Do you want to talk about it?"

After a minute of silence, the nun said "Sometimes it helps to talk your way through your problems. It can help you see things more clearly."

Elza didn't know if she wanted to talk about it or not. She couldn't talk with any of the ladies at her school, and she sure couldn't talk about it with mom.

"Do you know any of the teachers over at Christ the King?" Elza asked.

"Christ the King High School? Is that where you went to school?"

"Well, do you?"

"I don't know any of the faculty over there personally. I do know the school has a reputation for working extremely hard to help kids get an even break in life."

"Yeah. They do. I'll give them that." She sighed.

"Then why did you quit going?"

"I *had* to. I couldn't face it. Didn't want to."

"The adults at your school don't know you're in trouble?" the nun asked. Elza shook her head.

"You said you didn't fall for a boy. What did you mean?"

Elza pushed her tongue against the back side of her clinched teeth. A tear slid down her cheek and she wiped it off with the back of her hand. It wasn't an easy thing to explain.

"Elza, I want to help you."

Elza checked out the antique soft drink signs hanging around, framed newspaper clippings of stuff that happened a long time ago. The people carrying signs across the street by the women's clinic were talking together.

"Elza? Please talk to me."

"What'd you say your name was?"

"Sister Mary Frances. But you can call me Mary Frances if you're more comfortable with that."

Elza shrugged. "I'm used to talking to nuns, Sister. I don't mind calling you by your real name."

"Okay. Any way you want it. Can you tell me what happened to you? How did you get into this predicament?"

She leaned forward and lowered her voice.

"By force."

"By force?" whispered Sister Mary Frances, leaning in. "You were raped?"

"Well, I don't know. I'm not sure if it counts as that."

"What do you mean?"

"He kept threatening me, telling me he would hurt my mom if I didn't."

The nun winced. "Oh no. I am so sorry, Elza. That was a terrible thing for him to do. Who was this?"

"My mom's boyfriend. This crazy white guy she brought home one night, named J.T."

The nun's face fell.

"After I let him do what he wanted, he told me he would kill Mom if I told her. Said he wasn't going back to prison."

"Oh, my Lord," the nun whispered. More tears were sliding down Elza's cheeks. She grabbed a napkin and wiped them away.

"Do you think he really would hurt your mom?" Sister Mary Frances asked.

Elza shrugged.

"Is he a scary man?"

"Yes."

"For someone who doesn't want to go back to prison, he is making very poor decisions," Sister Mary Frances whispered.

"He don't make decisions. He does whatever comes into his head without thinking about it."

"But he *did* think about it, to put pressure on you like that. He knows you care about your mom, so he used that love as a weapon against you."

Elza exhaled. "That's true."

"Is he the one who brought you here?"

"Yeah. He dropped me off a block away 'cause he didn't want nobody to see him. He gave me cash to pay for an abortion."

"He gave you money to pay someone to kill your child."

"This ain't my child. I didn't have nothing to do with it."

Sister Mary Frances was silent for the first time since they met. She took a sip of her soft drink, closed her eyes for a second. Elza was relieved after finally telling someone about it. Someone other than… him.

"Elza, he violated your rights and put you in a dangerous situation when he forced himself on you, and he's done it again, today. He has proven once again that he doesn't care about your safety. An abortion is not a simple procedure. It can be dangerous for the mother, and it is fatal for the child."

Elza traced her finger along a row of black and white squares. *The school chess club should meet here.*

"Elza?"

"Yes ma'am?"

"I need to tell you something important. It might be kind of hard to hear."

Oh, boy. Here it comes. The talk she was trying not to have with the people at school.

"This thing that has been pushed upon you is not your fault. It was wrong, and you are correct, it never should have happened."

"Thank you."

"While all of that is true, it is not the *whole* truth. The rest of the truth is that you are the mother of an innocent, vulnerable child."

"I ain't old enough to be no *mother*." Elza slapped the table, glanced quick over her shoulder toward the counter. She couldn't believe this woman was gonna put all that on her.

"I agree. And yet, that is what you are. There is nothing you can do to change that, now or in the future. You have to face that reality even though it is unfair."

"It *is* unfair. I didn't do anything to deserve this. I was working hard in school. My grades were getting better and better. I was going to start AP courses next semester, and I was definitely going to get accepted into a university."

"You're right. You don't deserve this. Let me ask you, why were you working so hard in school?"

"So I could have a decent life, get out of this stinking neighborhood, maybe be a doctor someday."

"Congratulations. You sound very mature when you talk about your plans for the future."

Each of Elza's hands only covered about four of the checkerboard squares. She wasn't mature. She was a young stupid girl, letting that creep put this over on her, mess up her whole life.

"When things are difficult," the nun said, "when times are hard, it's important that you try to be as mature as you can be, because big decisions can't be reversed. Each major decision will affect the quality of your life from this day, until you are very old. That can be either good or bad, depending on which way the decision turns out."

"What do you mean, good or bad?"

"Well, graduating a university is good and cannot be taken away. Once you've done it, it cannot be undone."

"Okay. And?"

"Aborting a child can't be undone either."

Outside, the people were standing in a circle with their cheerful signs. The priest was praying.

"You want me to keep the baby. I know that. All Catholics think everybody ought to keep every baby."

"I wish that were true. Unfortunately, this is a complicated issue, and not all Catholic people agree. People get confused."

"Confused how?" Elza asked.

"Most Catholics have a lot of empathy for people who are hurting."

"What's wrong with that?"

"Nothing at all is wrong with it. My heart is hurting for you, as it should be. I hate what has happened to you."

"Thank you."

"And I also know that you are not the only victim here. People focus only on the mother and lose sight of the other victims."

"My mom."

"Yes, your mom. She has made bad decisions and fallen in with a bad man, for certain. And her decisions have altered both of your lives and put you both in danger. But that isn't who I was thinking about."

Sister Mary Frances wasn't smiling, but her face was soft, like she was talking to someone she really cared about. It made Elza want to trust her. "The baby," she said quietly.

"Yes. *Your* baby. The baby God has entrusted to you, to take care of and to bring into this world."

Now Elza was crying more tears than she could wipe off, but she didn't make a sound. She wasn't about to start blubbering in public.

"Elza, if you go in that place, they will kill your child, and throw it in a dumpster, like a piece of garbage. The memory of this day will haunt you for all your life. You will be a victim of this as much as your baby. There will not be one life destroyed today. There will be two."

"It ain't fair."

"I know, dear. It truly isn't. But sometimes things happen to us that are not fair. It's the way of this world. All we can do is keep trying to live a good life and keep trusting that God will help us. Can you do that, Elza?"

Elza pulled a wad of napkins from the dispenser and held them against her face, the tears soaking in.

"Why do you want to be a doctor?" Sister Mary Frances asked. Elza was glad for a change of subject. She took a moment to wipe her face and eyes and took a breath.

"I want to do *good* in the world. I want to help people. Maybe save people's lives."

Sister Mary Frances was about to start crying too. "You sweet, sweet, thing." She reached for a napkin herself, wiped her eyes and blew her nose. Her eyes were shining with tears.

"Can you see the opportunity you have before you?" *How could this mess be called an opportunity?*

"Oh. You're saying I have someone I can save right here."

Sister Mary Frances smiled a big smile, wiped more tears, and nodded her head. "You don't have to wait for someday, Elza. You can save someone's life to*day*."

The checkerboard was blurry. The Nun was being true. Elza had to figure out how to do the good thing here, even though this wasn't her fault. The people out there were still praying.

"Will you help me?"

"Oh, yes, dear. Absolutely. I will help you. Many people will want to help you once you summon the courage to tell them what you've decided."

"Okay. But… If I do, how you all gonna protect my mom?"

September 8

Sunday morning, in the plush back seat of a Lincoln Town Car, Pete turned to his boss, dredging up his nerve.

"So, Haruki..."

"Yes Pete?"

"Guy mentioned there was a witness to a small money transfer this week. It doesn't sound like much of a threat. It was just a young homeless guy."

"Is that right, Pete? Are you basing that opinion on reliable information?"

"Well, a guy who lives outdoors on the street, I don't see him doing us any harm."

"Because he's homeless?"

"Exactly."

"Solving the homelessness problem is a top priority for me, Pete."

"Really? I guess I didn't realize that. What is it that drives your passion for the homeless?"

"Do you want the micro or the macro version? Homelessness is one of those issues that can be analyzed at the individual level, the community level, or on a global scale. It is a vexing problem any way you analyze it." As if on cue, a homeless guy pushing an over-loaded cart came walking along the street. That was an odd coincidence.

"I agree that it is vexing," Pete said. "But to make sure I'm on the same page with you, could you give me your analysis of the community level?"

"At the community level, homelessness is a type of blight, which, if left unchecked, will degrade the entire city."

"Oh." He had expected Haruki to say something about the suffering of the poor.

"The homeless scurry around in the shadows like an infestation of cockroaches. They crawl in and out of dumpsters, spread disease, scare respectable people."

Pete didn't know what to say. He kept his mouth from hanging open.

"The homeless bring down property values, accumulate garbage, which encourages further infestations, until the whole city is covered with bums, rats, and nasty insects. That is how the black plague was spread."

Out the window, the homeless guy wore a dark hoodie jacket, and over that, a tattered, filthy blue down vest. He had the collar of the vest popped up as a fashion statement. Dark sunglasses covered his eyes, and the way he carried himself, you would think he was somebody of status.

"You see that little cockroach over there?" Haruki said.

"Um, yes. Do we know him?"

"You tell me." He handed Pete a 5x7 photo. Same guy, a crystal clear closeup, maybe even on this same street. "Does that person look familiar to you?"

Pete was way behind the curve on this conversation. "How does he figure into this?"

"Well, that little roach is your witness. Not some beaten down old man, not a junkie. This kid has the hubris to think he can pull himself up out of the gutter and become something significant."

"That's admirable."

"No, that is *not* admirable."

"Oh. I'm sorry."

"That makes him *dangerous*. He considers himself an entrepreneur. An ambitious person like that, in possession of sensitive information, would be tempted to try to profit from selling that information."

"Oh."

"I talked to Guy yesterday. He gave me that photo. He's done his homework. There's more to that little roach than it might appear. He could become a thorn in my side."

"Is Guy running lead on this? I thought you liked to distance yourself -"

"Don't worry about how I interact with Guy. I have had a professional working relationship with him since you were in grade school. He is convinced this kid is a threat, and I agree with him."

"Oh. But-"

"But what?"

"It seems like a homeless person would want to avoid authority figures. It seems unlikely he would try to sell information." The homeless guy was moving past, not bothering anybody, pushing his heavy cart along like he was on an important mission.

"Thank you for sharing your *opinion*," Haruki said, a slight edge to his tone. "Get in touch with Guy. Do it in person, not over the phone. Let him know I told you I want this problem to go away. He'll know what you mean. We are going to solve this city's homelessness problem, and we're going to start with that little roach right there."

Harkuki's face was stern, as Pete waited for the next beat.

"Tell Guy to make it look like normal street violence. His people will know how to handle it."

Pete had a strong urge to protest. But what would be the use? In the end, Haruki would have his way. He always did. "Haruki?"

"Yes?"

"To be clear, you're saying, hypothetically..."

Haruki narrowed his eyes. "Hypothetically?" He turned toward the window for a second and back to lock eyes with Pete. "Hypothetically, if you have a particularly bothersome roach, there is only one thing to do. You crush him and toss him into a dumpster he'll never crawl out of."

··········

At a small wooden table in the kitchen of a Franciscan monastery, Father John Bianchi had a dreadful feeling of impending cataclysm. It was like standing under a blue sky, gazing at white clouds on the horizon, knowing that beneath those soft billows, in the dark shadows, tornadoes and lightening leveled towns and snuffed lives. John could sense a stiff, cold breeze coming, and it filled him with dread. His experience as a priest had taught him how to hold the face of a serene cleric even when he felt like screaming. He was doing it now. John stirred a bowl of clear beef broth and colorful vegetables. He could feel Father Alex's gaze. The kitchen was empty, the monks having cleared out a while ago, after the lunchtime bustle. It was larger than a home kitchen, set up for multiple cooks. Nothing fancy. Functional but spartan. The smell of the soup was present, but also vinegar from the monks wiping down the countertops and cooking surfaces.

It reminded him of his days in seminary, living in a community. That was a long time ago. Back when he first met Father Alex. John was nothing more than a kid then, full of awe and ambition. He spent eight years under Father Alex's tutelage, prior to ordination. Since John was nineteen years old, Father Alex had been his spiritual adviser. That's why he drove three hours from Boston on a Sunday to talk to his old mentor. Today's conversation held tremendous importance, possibly life-shaping importance. But John couldn't concentrate. The hair growing out of the old man's ears was distracting. Would his own ears grow hair like that someday? He didn't like the idea. At a time when the wisdom of age and experience should garner a person respect and admiration, the body goes haywire, doing all kinds of embarrassing things.

"So, John boy, what is going on with you?" the old man asked.

"Please don't call me that."

"Oh, come on, lighten up. I've called you that since you were in my Theology 101 class."

"I know, and all this time I've been asking you to please not call me that."

"Oh. I see." The old man looked down at the table for an instant.

Great. Now he had guilt over making Fr. Alex feel bad. It was meant to be a term of endearment, but he really hated being called that.

"Okay, John. Please forgive me for those offenses."

"It's no big deal. Forget about it."

"No, you don't get to do that. I've asked for forgiveness, and I meant it. Now you say…" Still the professor, prompting him, drilling him in the basics of sainthood.

"Now I say, 'Of course, Father. I forgive you.'"

"But do you mean it? Sincerely?"

"Of course, I do. I understand you meant no offense. It is forgiven."

"Okay. Thank you. What will I call you when I want to demonstrate that I'm fond of you?"

"How about John?"

"Boring."

"Sorry. It is my name. I like it."

"Okay." The old man sighed. "John it is."

"Thanks."

"Don't mention it."

There was a twinkle in the old eyes. The master toying with the student, putting him through the paces. He had been such a blessing in seminary when John was void of maturity but filled with zeal. John needed his help more now than he had back then. Now John had a *lot* of maturity, but zeal was in short supply.

"So, John, what is going on with you?"

"What makes you think anything is going on?"

"Well, for starters, if nothing was going on, you would have given an answer like, 'oh, not much,' or 'same ole, same ole.' Instead, you give me this kid-with-crumbs-around-his-mouth answer, like 'what cookie jar?'" He had hair growing out of his nose too. Long ones. Not gray, white. Long tufts of white hair.

"Well?" Father Alex said. "You drove three hours. Out with it."

John sighed. "Well, to be honest, nothing *is* going on."

"That's doesn't sound good. Tell me about it."

"I mean, I get up early, say the prayers of my morning office, go at it all day, and pray myself to sleep every night."

"Good."

"I'm giving it all I've got, but I am completely uninspired. Half my life has been poured into this vocation, and I feel... nothing."

The old man nodded his approval. He'd always liked it when students went straight to the point, with no tap dancing. John had been called down so many times that he knew tap dancing was a waste of time.

"How long have you been out of the seminary?"

"I was ordained fourteen years ago."

"Uh-huh."

"What do you mean, 'uh-huh'?"

"Well, you always were an overachiever. I shouldn't be surprised that you're a little ahead of the curve."

"I'm sorry, what curve are we talking about?" John asked.

"Oh, it's a theory of mine. More of an observation, really."

"Okay. Want to share it?"

"Well, I'm eighty-three years old. I've seen things. I'm a priest, so I have known a lot of people."

"Right. You have a lot of experience."

"Well, I have this theory. You hear a lot about the seven-year itch, how people get discontent about every seven years and want to change something."

"Okay, and your theory says?"

"I think the cycles are longer. I think the really big crisis points come about every fifteen years or so."

"Fifteen?"

"Sure. Think about it. A boy turns fifteen, realizes the world is not a simple place, and he goes through a crisis of sorts."

John nodded.

"He hits thirty, realizes he doesn't have it all figured out and isn't what he wanted to be when he grew up."

"Okay. I've seen that."

"Blink twice, the man turns forty-five and realizes that he's about to be fifty. He starts worrying and fretting pre-emptively. Wants to get ahead of the curve. Have you ever seen that?"

"Well, yes, I suppose I have."

"I know *I* have," Father Alex said. "In a marriage, a man realizes he's with the same woman almost twenty years and starts to panic. Starts wondering if he missed something, or if things couldn't somehow be better. Before long, the two of them are in my office, asking if their marriage was ever real."

"I've seen that."

"Same thing can happen in the years leading up to the twentieth anniversary of an ordination."

Bam. There it was. The punch line of the lecture. The old man really was good.

"Thank you, Father. But if I may ask, was there ever a time when you wondered if you were making a difference?"

The old man smiled. "You kiddin'? You mean other than this morning?"

A distant echo of the "Ave Maria" melody became audible from the hall outside. Someone was whistling those famous strains with a clear, resonant vibrato.

"No, I'm serious," John said. "Did you ever feel like that?"

"Did you?" Fr. Alex turning the tables on him.

"I... I feel like all I do is carry water and empty buckets, back and forth, till I find myself slipping in my own mud."

"Huh. That's pretty good, John b— Whoops, sorry. John. I like that image. You come up with that on your own?"

"Father, I'm really struggling here. Please don't poke fun at me. All I experience is drudgery, going through motions day after day, with no hint of inspiration."

The melody was coming nearer, a beautiful whistle, and in his mind, John heard the words. "Ahhhhhhh-ve Ma-reeeee-eee-ahhhh." It stopped him.

The old man stared at him, eyes a little narrow, like he was trying to read a book that was a bit blurry.

"John?"

"Yes?"

"You somehow miss that whole 'pick up your cross and follow me' bit?"

The tabletop was natural wood, pine slabs with a thick amber coating. The old man was right. Who was he to feel sorry for himself?

"What you're going through is not remarkable," Father Alex said.

"Boy, you can say *that* again."

"Huh. Funny. Keep that youthful wit. Now *listen* to me."

John looked up. The old man's eyes were focused, intense.

"Everybody goes through times when they don't feel inspired, John. It is part of the maturing process."

"Even you?"

"You think I got this far skipping through fields of daisies?"

It made sense that Father Alex must have struggled, but he had always seemed to be living a genuinely happy and holy life. It sounded like the whistler was right outside the door now, the crescendo soaring. "Blessed is the fruit of thy womb, Jesus," it sang, in Italian. A pang twisted in John's chest.

"Oh, excuse me," the whistler said, coming through the door with a brisk gait. "I didn't realize anyone was in here."

"Hello, Brother," Father Alex said.

"Hello." The whistler was wearing a simple brown frock, a rope belt at his waist, carrying an armload of fresh-picked carrots and radishes. John was grateful for the interruption. He took a drink of water from a simple clay goblet.

"I just need to put these into the crisper. I'll be out of your way in a moment."

"No problem, Brother. Take your time."

Alex smiled at John as the monk rinsed the vegetables and put them away. John inhaled deeply, rubbed his eyelids with his fingertips.

"Blessings, Brothers," the whistling monk said. "I'm headed back to the greenhouse." The strains of the Ave started up again out in the hall, and it made John take another deep inhale.

"You were asking?" Father Alex said.

"Oh. Did you ever wonder if it was a mistake?"

"What, my vocation?" Father Alex stared at him like he was deciding how much to say. "John, self-doubt is part of the human condition. Life on Earth is hard, no matter how you choose to live it. When the going gets tough, the weak side of our humanity wants to bail out, in any direction other than forward."

"I know. I understand it isn't very noble of me. I ..."

"What?"

He hesitated, took another sip of water. Father Alex's eyes were pale blue, set back beneath heavy white eyebrows.

"I don't know if I have it in me to do this much longer." There. Blurted out. See what the old man thought of that.

Father Alex nodded. "Did you know chickens are carnivores?"

"What?"

"Chickens. They're meat eaters. Did you know that?"

"Um... I... *might* have?"

"It's true. Omnivores, actually. People think of them eating only grain. But in fact, they eat bugs, worms, lizards, whatever kind of meat they can find."

"Oh." Maybe the old man had slipped off the rails for a second. It could happen at his age.

"In big chicken-production facilities, they snip the ends off of their beaks," Father Alex said.

"That sounds horrible."

"I don't know if it is or not." He shrugged. "Some people say it is like trimming a toenail or a horse's hoof. I don't know if that's how it feels to the chicken. But do you know *why* they do it?"

John shook his head.

"They clip their beaks because they are not only carnivores, but they're also cannibals. If their beaks are sharp, they will literally kill and eat each other. How is that for a new way of thinking about a chicken?" The old man smiled his mischievous grin.

"I have to tell you; I find that image disturbing."

It *is* disturbing. Now, imagine *this* scenario. A barnyard, just before sunrise. A low-lying fog. Smelly animal dung everywhere, the ground damp, hundreds of chickens standing in the semi-darkness, starving to death. The old chicken farmer, half-starved himself, gets up and walks out into the chicken yard wearing nothing but his boots, skivvies and a night shirt."

John didn't know what to say.

"One little chicken comes up to his bare leg, and thinks, 'You know, Farmer John is a good old boy, but I'm really hungry.' Maybe one little nip won't hurt. So, he pecks a tiny morsel from the farmer's leg."

"That's terrible. Spare me the visuals, okay?"

"Another little chicken, truly starving, thinks, 'Well, I don't need much, I'll only take a little snip.'"

"Lord have mercy."

"Exactly," Father Alex said. "Farmer John *better* be praying, because even though none of those little chickens really means him any harm, if left to their own devices, they will literally eat him alive." The old man was staring at him, waiting for him to catch up.

"Okay. Farmer John, Father John, I get it."

"It is what it is like to be a priest. We spend our lives caring for the chickens while we are slowly being pecked to death."

"Forgive me, Father, but that strikes me as a terrible way to view our congregations."

"John, when people come to you with their problems, with their pains, in their points of crisis, what is it they are asking from you?"

"Different things. It depends on the situation."

"Wrong." John almost flinched.

"They are all looking for the *same thing*," the old man said. "Think about it. What is it they need?"

John was starting to regret asking for this lunch. He had forgotten how much work it could be to interact with Father Alex. He took a sip of his soup.

"Come on, John. Stay with me."

"Sorry. I'm a little tired."

"I know you are, but this is important. What does a frightened person who is praying for a sick loved one need?"

"Healing?"

"Yes, healing, but how do they get that healing?"

"Through prayer?"

"Yes, of course prayer, but for that prayer to produce a result, what is required?"

"Faith?"

"Yes, faith. And what of a middle-aged couple, emotionally devastated, who is doubting their marriage?"

"Faith."

"Exactly. And the troubled young man who has lost his way and is seeking God?"

"Faith."

"And the old man facing death, racked with pain, afraid he can't get through the experience?"

"Faith."

"Faith is what *everyone* needs, John. It is the only thing that allows any of us to make it through."

John stopped to think about that. It might be true. There was certainly truth *in* it. The old man spoke again, this time in a softer tone.

"You say you don't like my image of your congregation as a bunch of cannibalistic chickens. I understand that. But these people you love, these chickens in your farmyard, are literally starving. They are starving for *faith,* and they all come to one person to find it. That person is you."

"The members of my congregation are very good to me," John said. "Almost all of them love me."

"They don't *mean* to harm you. They aren't even aware it is happening. All they know is that they need a little bit from you. A tiny bit of time, of energy, of emotional connection, but ultimately, what they need is a little bit of your *faith*."

"And I'm running low."

"Be honest. It is more serious than that. You are on the verge of starvation. And yet, out of a sense of duty, you wander out into their midst, completely unprotected, in your skivvies, so to speak." The old man's face was serious but filled with love and concern.

"That's one heck of a parable," John said. "I don't think I remember reading that one in the Bible."

The old man laughed a hearty laugh. "Don't you? It's in there, trust me."

"Yeah? Where is that?"

"The crowds were pressing in on Jesus so hard he had to go out in a boat to talk to them? There were so many people crowded around that he and the disciples couldn't eat or sleep? At every chance, he withdrew to deserted places to pray. It's everywhere throughout Christ's ministry. Who are we to expect anything better?"

John frowned. "You're right. As usual. But that doesn't inspire me. It only makes me more tired. Christ was fully human, but He was also fully divine. I am human only. I don't think I can do this."

"Without His help."

"Excuse me?"

"I don't think I can do this without His help. That's what you should have said. That would have been more accurate."

"That's just it. I don't feel like I *am* receiving His help."

"And yet you are. It is the only thing that has gotten you this far, and it is what will get you through this crisis."

"You sound so certain."

"I am."

"I wish I could have that much faith."

"It is what you came here looking for, isn't it?"

John paused, soaking in the irony.

"John, the married couple in crisis can make it through if they both give it everything they've got and sincerely seek God's help. The sacrament of marriage brings with it a gift of grace. But they will only make it if they don't give up. The same is true of the sacrament of Holy Orders. You will make it through, *if* you take care of yourself, take steps to replenish your supply of *faith*, and don't abandon the *path*."

"But shouldn't I be able to feel God moving in my life?"

"What about Saint Teresa of Calcutta?"

"What about her?"

"She went for years, *decades*, without any sign that she could perceive. And yet she changed the world."

"I don't think I could do that."

"You might have to, John."

··········

When Haruki dropped him off, Pete was deflated. He needed time to think and figure out his next move. He had underestimated the amount of sway Guy had. That was a mistake. And the big goon was right about one thing. Pete wasn't in any position to be throwing his weight around. The sand under his feet was shifting, and he needed to find some way to keep it from swallowing his whole family.

Peggy wasn't happy when he told her he had to come in to work on a Sunday. She thought he had a cushy office job and couldn't understand why he had to work unreasonable hours. She would never understand how much of a mess he was in. He walked into the parking structure and slowed to a crawl. There was a black SUV parked next to his car, and two big guys in tight shirts and sunglasses were leaning back against his trunk. Their huge arms were crossed over their chests, laughing, and talking to each other in Spanish.

Pete wanted to run, but he couldn't very well abandon his car. Best to act casual.

"Hey, Carlos, how can I help you guys?" He had their attention, frozen smiles, not laughing anymore.

"Mr. high roller. Mr. Romeo just wanted us to stop by and ask how you are doing."

"Okay, yeah, sure. I'm doing good. Taking care of some odds and ends. Putting things together."

"Oh, you're putting things together, huh?" Asked Carlos. "That's good." He turned to his partner. "Jose, putting things together is good, right?"

"Oh yeah, sure. It's very good. I'm sure that will make Mr. Romeo very happy."

"Yeah. I think you're right, Jose. Very happy." Neither of them was smiling anymore. Carlos raised one eyebrow, his face menacing. "It might not make him as happy as something else, like maybe twenty-seven grand of cold hard cash in a briefcase. That might make him even happier."

"And I'm going to get it to him," Pete said. "That's what I mean. I'm moving money around between accounts, taking care of the details."

"Moving money around between accounts, eh?" Jose asked.

"That's right. Tightening up the details."

"Oh, that's good. Very good," Carlos said. "Details are very important. Details like keeping track of dates, right? That kind of details?"

"Yes. Absolutely. I haven't forgotten the dates. I'm all over it."

"Oh, that's good. Mr. Romeo is going to be very happy to know that you are all over it. Because once you pay Mr. Romeo his money, twenty-seven thousand U.S. American dollars, we can all be friends, okay? Like we've always been. That's what we all want, right, Mr. high-roller?" Carlos had an intense look on his face.

"Yes, that's what we all want." Carlos stepped over and put a huge arm around Pete's shoulders, squeezed him in tight. Pete cringed.

"But, you know, Pete, if you *don't* remember the date, and you don't get Mr. Romeo his money when you promised? If it turns out you're not really all over it? Then..." He pulled his shoulders up into a big shrug. "Who knows... Bad things... Maybe your pretty little wife and your little baby. You know interstate ninety three?"

Pete was trying to maintain his composure, but he was shaking like a leaf.

"That big interstate, all that truck traffic, maybe your little family will be all over that."

Pete twisted his shoulders hard, tried to wriggle free from Carlos, but Carlos slipped his hands down and pinned his two arms behind his back. Jose slammed a big fist into his gut. All the air shot out of Pete's lungs, followed by a burst of vomit. Jose leapt out of the way, and Carlos started laughing. Jose got a terrible scowl on his face. "Did you try to puke on my boots, gringo?" He punched him hard on the side of the rib cage. That crunching sensation had to be ribs breaking.

Carlos said into his ear, "Pete, Mr. Romeo said since he has to wait, and can't enjoy his money until you pay him, he thinks it is fair you don't enjoy your pretty little wife till then either. Jose kicked Pete hard in the crotch, a big biker boot sending Pete into dry heaves. Carlos let go of him, and he fell down to all fours, hands in his own puke.

"You got five days, high roller. After that, we either gonna all be friends again, or you're gonna be a widower who ain't a daddy no more."

September 9

The next morning, seven hundred feet above the city, Haruki Yamamoto stood alone in the H&H penthouse suite. Looking toward the sunrise, he was enjoying the view of the Atlantic Ocean, the horizon curving like a giant bowling ball. He stood near the glass exterior, his hands in the pockets of his slacks, suit coat held open in the front, his dress shirt tucked in, as flat as the pane. One large cargo ship was approaching the port, another barely starting to roll up and appear over the horizon. Tiny little vessels were heading out, fisherman on their way to the Gulf Stream.

Gazing out from this vantage point allowed him to see everything below for miles while remaining invisible. From the outside, the hurricane-proof glass had the appearance of polished silver, so even a helicopter hovering nearby would not be able to see the man standing on the other side of the reflection. It made Haruki feel omniscient. Blue-gray cumulous clouds with golden tinges were dense, but some sunlight was penetrating through the interior, creating the effect of a bank of giant spotlights shimmering the water below.

He loved this office space. Natural light poured into the space every day from dawn to dusk. On overcast days, color-balanced LED fixtures above the ceiling provided a warm glow. So, no matter the weather, in here his ruddy complexion was that of a samurai warrior on the beach at sunrise. He did not need the artificial lighting effect this morning. This was the golden hour, the time when the dense atmosphere filtered the rising sun's rays and produced a flattering glow. He turned to his left and gazed at a mirrored column.

He smiled broadly, inspecting two rows of perfect teeth, brilliant white. He kept his thick black hair longer than typical for a high-level executive. With a finger, he flipped a stray lock away from his neck so that it joined the rest, lying over the collar of his suitcoat by two inches. His sideburns were trimmed down to sharp points, almost level with his ear lobes. The slightest touch of gray was apparent at the temples, giving him an aura of experience and wisdom. His carefully crafted image projected maturity but a youthful spirit and, more importantly, demonstrated that he had no one to answer to.

The new tailor was doing a fine job. This hand-stitched suit fit him so well, it appeared that he had given it no thought. He turned slightly to catch the reflection from the column behind him, so he could admire the shape of his suit in the back. Haruki turned slowly in a circle, admiring the views of the city. Even the receptionist at H&H had a better view than most C-level executives could hope for. A light beeping sound told Haruki that Lisa was on her way up.

To get here, a person had to change elevators on the sixty-fourth floor, using a key card that would alert the reception desk and security that someone was approaching. When that person got off the first elevator, two ex-Mossad agents hidden behind an ornate mirror checked them out. Someone who was not supposed to be here would never make it onto the second elevator. Nobody came to the penthouse uninvited, and few received an invitation.

Haruki stepped closer to the column in front of him and stared into his own dark eyes. They were nearly as black as his hair but lit with a striking internal fire. He practiced his expression of sincerity. Then fondness, then mischief, then mystery. He smiled again and practiced his playful expression. Slight laugh lines in the epidermis around his eyes really brought the effect to life. Few people put serious effort into developing control of the complex apparatus that moves the human face. Forty-three independent skeletal muscles, controlled by five sub-branches of the seventh cranial nerve, provided the capability for an almost limitless variety of expressions and sub-verbal communications. He gazed into his own eyes with empathy. With caring. Then with a slight hurt expression. Then with a stern, masculine warning. Then back to fondness, then genuine friendship.

Another series of beeps told him Lisa was rising in the second elevator. He moved through the space, perfect posture, past the elegant office furniture. Gray leather and dark mahogany. Graceful lines hinting of the orient, but simple, not intended to draw one's eye from the beauty of the surrounding vistas. He stopped near the north-west corner, gazing over the Back Bay neighborhood, toward Cambridge. A few seconds later, Lisa stepped out of the elevator. Haruki did not turn around, but her reflection was checking him out as she moved toward her desk. His physique was a powerful lure. He was gifted to a degree that few men would ever know. But he was not stuck on his looks. He was aware that he was handsome, but his physical traits, impressive as they were, could not hold a candle to his intellectual prowess. That was his real advantage.

He had everything a man could wish for. Money, women, and power came to him without any significant exertion. And yet, even with all of that, he never experienced real satisfaction. Within him was a constant gnawing. An insatiable appetite for more. An awareness of something he could not quite grasp. Haruki inhaled deeply through his nostrils, relaxing as he exhaled slowly. There were those who spent their time scheming and planning, stressed out, imagining themselves to be his competition. It was amusing. He was always twelve moves ahead of them, smiling as they busied themselves with bringing his plans to fruition. Here, at the top of the food chain, the top of the world, towering over everyone, he was where he belonged.

···········

Lisa could still feel every one of the hours she spent straining and sweating, carefully sculpting her figure. It isn't conceited to know you are beautiful if it is the truth. All the times she had a salad with no dressing rather than something more savory. Hours and hours spent going through style magazines. Her dark brown hair had just the right highlights, cut so that it seemed it was gorgeous by accident. She was careful not to over-do the makeup. Her face was that of an adult, but angelic. A lot of what she had was natural, she had to admit that, but she had worked damn hard to maximize it. Haruki might pretend not to notice, but he was watching her reflection in the glass. She went about her start-up routine fully aware he was checking her out.

Haruki had a strong voice, but he made it a point to be soft-spoken. She liked that. Strong, quiet, powerful. He didn't engage in idle talk, but when he did speak, his words carried more influence than the ceaseless prattle of all the other men. She had a mob of executives hitting on her, but none of them could ever hope to play at his level. Lisa had a plan, and she was executing it carefully. He was a man who could have anything he wanted. She intended to make sure he wanted her more than anything else.

She made coffee, booted up her computer, and spent a moment or two getting settled. He was leaving the window now, heading for his desk. Seeing him pick up a thick stack of manila folders and an ink pen and stroll toward her desk, sent a sizzle through her. He was pretending to be reading.

"Good morning, Haruki."

He turned from the folders and gave her a warm, caring smile. "Good morning, Lisa. How *are* you?" He was so sincere.

"I'm fantastic. How is your morning starting out?"

"I just witnessed the most fabulous sunrise. Really stunning."

"I'm glad."

He fixed his attention back on the manila folders, flipping through the top one, and continued to move closer to her. She started scrolling, feigning distraction. At the end of her desk, he pretended to fumble the folders a little, dropped his pen. "Lisa, would you mind picking that up for me?" he asked. A little obvious, but okay, she'd play along.

"Of course." She eased out of her chair and down onto her hands and knees to reach under the desk and retrieve it. She moved slowly, gracefully, stretching forward, giving him plenty of time to survey the shapely curve of her back. Her dress was form-fitting, hugging her across her hips. This was the moment all that work on the glute machines would pay off. She could feel him gazing down on her, in a crawling position at his feet. He was the kind of man who liked to be in control. She retrieved the pen and lifted it up toward him, being sure to lean forward a little as she did so.

"Wait," he said.

She stopped. His eyes moved across her, and from that vantage point, he had to be getting quite a view. She played innocent. "Yes?" Turning her face up toward him, now in a kneeling position.

"Take a close examination of that pen."

She focused on it, obedient, giving him plenty of time to look at her as much as he wanted.

"That pen retails for one hundred dollars." She gasped. It was what he wanted.

"I need you to find a place to buy them in bulk. I need about fifty units. I like to give them out as gifts to people who are important to me. That one is yours. You may keep it." She lit up her pretty face, giving him an expression that bordered on adoration.

"Thank you, Haruki. You didn't need to do that."

"Oh, but I did." He smiled warmly down on her. "You are a valuable member of my team, Lisa, and I believe in being generous with those who are loyal to me." He put the stack of folders on the corner of her desk, turned, and strolled back in the direction he had come. She watched him, remembering a nature show about deep-sea fishing, a great trophy marlin racing away from the boat, leaping and twisting, unable to shed the hook. He was gorgeous. He raised his voice so she could hear him as he walked away.

"Those files are the prep material for today's meetings. Please have Anacette re-file them. I've memorized what I need."

"Yes, sir." In the mirrored column, she admired the way her designer clothes moved with her body as she got up off the floor in her tight dress and heels.

"And Lisa?"

"Yes, Haruki?"

"Bring me a cup of coffee, would you, please?"

"Right away, sir."

••••••••••

Giovanni Gillespie unlocked his small store and rolled out a stand of magazines, papers, pastries, and coffee supplies. It was a simple brick storefront with large glass windows, showing display racks of books in plain view and a few small reading tables. He spent most of the day on the sidewalk, with the storefront as a backdrop. He picked up his old broom and started sweeping. His favorite part of the day. He loved smelling the fresh morning air. He loved the time to think, pray, and get ready to greet his friends.

"Hey, Mr. Gillespie, how are you doing this morning?"

"Good morning, Pete." Giovanni checked his watch. "You are early."

"Yeah, I… left home early to beat traffic."

"Early meetings today?"

"Well, to be honest, Mr. Gillespie, I needed some time to think."

"Pete, why you no call me Diz? That is what all my friends call me. You been coming here every day for … how long now?"

Pete crinkled up his brow. "It's been almost six years, Diz."

"Six years. It goes so fast, no?"

"It does. So… Diz. As in Dizzy Gillespie?"

Giovanni smiled. "My old Army buddy Delmond give me that name."

"Ah, I see. Clever. Hey, is the coffee ready?"

"Five more minutes. You got time to wait, Pete?"

"Um..." He checked his watch "Sure. I can wait. It won't bother you if I hang around?"

"No, no, no. I will enjoy the company. How is the family?"

"Okay, I guess. New baby, no sleep, work is kind of stressful. We're in a busy phase of life."

Giovanni nodded. The young business types were always under pressure. He'd seen it for years. The older guys, gray hair, softer around the middle, didn't seem as excited. Or they hid it better. "Look over the paper while you wait, if you want."

"Thanks, Mr. Gillespie. Diz. I like to save it, though. It gives me something to do on my breaks."

"I understand. Help yourself to a magazine."

"Thanks." Pete scanned the rack, picked up a magazine about money. "How long have you been in the news business, Diz?"

He leaned on his broom handle. "I started this business; I was twenty-two years old. After I got back from my extended vacation in the Far East."

"Vacation, huh?" Pete said.

"Yes, government sponsored. My travel agent, Staff Sargent Tasker, found me a deal I could no pass up."

Pete smiled and shook his head, opening the magazine. Just for a second, Giovanni was transported back. Three hundred sixty-five days. A long time to be in hell. Some people didn't believe in hell, but he did. He had seen it, and knew it could show up anyplace. Anywhere that had all the good killed out of it.

"I envy that," Pete said, not looking up. "Starting your own business right out of the chute like that and making it stick? Good for you, Mr. Gillespie."

"Ah, I got lucky. I had a VA Loan and a pretty good VA counselor. He pointed me in a good direction. I just kept going."

"Any regrets?"

Pete did not understand what he was asking. He was young. "There are always regrets, Pete. But don't spend too much time looking back at those. You might drive into the ditch. Best to keep your eyes on the road."

"That sounds like good advice. Do you have a family, Diz?"

Giovanni stopped sweeping. "When I was coming home from Vietnam, an angel appeared to me in an airport. The prettiest girl to ever grace God's green Earth. I was out of the jungle twenty-four hours only, and she had a glow around her, like…" He shook his head "We sat across the aisle on the plane, and by the time we touched down in Boston, it was… amore'. You know the song?" Pete grinned. "I married her as fast as she and her family would allow. The smartest thing I ever did." He smiled. "Maybe the only one smart thing I ever did." He gave Pete a broad grin and reached for the coffee pot.

"Diz, I don't mean to be insensitive, but… you're using past tense."

"Yes. Cancer. I guess heaven could not have her out on loan for too long. She was really something…" Giovanni started running out of words.

"I'm sorry. It's so hard to understand why things like that happen."

He nodded, handed Pete a steaming cup. "The mystery of evil. That is a tough one."

"So, you attribute it to evil?"

Pete's eyes were serious, deep green with little brown flecks. He was not being flippant. He seemed to be trying to figure something out in his own life. Giovanni decided to take his question seriously.

"Do I believe there are devils roaming the earth, meddling with people's lives?" Giovanni shrugged. "Bible says so. I never been so sure. I have seen a lot of evil, always in the eyes and hands of human beings. My Marissa getting sick? I don't think that was nobody's fault. People get sick."

"Diz, I'm sorry. I didn't mean to bring up a painful subject."

"Ah. That was long time ago. Mostly the pain is over. I have many happy memories."

"That's nice. Thanks. And for the coffee too." He held the cup in a salute.

Giovanni nodded. "If I could give you one piece of advice, would you want me to?"

"Sure, Diz. Please."

"Treasure family. While you so busy stomping grapes, be sure to set aside the best juices for your family. You'll be glad you did."

Those green eyes were full of questions or worry. Pete seemed sad this morning.

"You know, I'm glad I had a little time to visit with you today," he said. "I'm usually running through here as fast as I can go. You've given me some things to consider. I appreciate it."

"Have a good day, Pete."

"You too, Diz."

Pete walked east toward the Financial District. These young guys, feeling their way along, were living a life he never knew. Giovanni had grown up in a single year, in a jungle on the other side of the world. Pete was asking the right questions. If he dug for the answers, it would lead him in a good direction. But a lot of these young guys got lost along the way. Giovanni might not know where darkness—evil, whatever you called it—came from, but it did exist, and good people needed to beat it back with a stick at every turn. He swept his heavy broom across the stone pavers, clearing the way for his people.

Even here, this nice part of town, ruffians were trying to move in. Spilling out of Roxbury and Dorchester, young men mostly, united by ethnicity sometimes, and always by poverty. Strong and bored, they had too much energy and not enough dreams to keep them out of trouble. They should join the Army. That would teach them something. A few did, but most joined the gangs. They were turning the street into a jungle, filled with real danger. Stabbings, shootings, rape, robberies, and drugs everywhere. They banded together in packs for survival and had to constantly prove their toughness to climb the pecking order. You could almost smell the gasoline being poured onto the flames of crime and violence.

Perry. A good kid in a tough spot. The street people, with their tattered clothing and haggard looks, had fallen completely off the ladder, run over by the machine of success. They were the poorest of the poor, barely surviving, in constant danger of illness and hypothermia. And always the threat of violence. Somewhere in the distance he heard the familiar "beep, beep, beep" of a garbage truck making its rounds. Giovanni's heart twisted every time he thought about them. He wanted to give them a fighting chance. Was it because of guilt over things he had done in his youth? Yes, maybe some of that. But also, he could feel their pain. If you know pain, you feel it anytime you get close to it. His VA counselor called it empathy. Whatever you call it, it made Giovanni want to help people. By ten in the morning, he could help thirty or fifty people get a pleasant start to their day. It was a good reason to get out of bed.

Rich or poor, everyone was working hard, doing the best they could. But life was getting harder. Good news getting drowned out by the buzz of foolishness. Digital sewage flooding the world through earbuds on phones or tablets. Truth was not so popular anymore. The world growing darker and darker. The people who came to his stand came for encouragement. That was the real business. Serving up coffee and hope had kept him and his business alive over forty years, and it would probably carry him through his last fifteen or twenty. The same hope he served, served him. But Giovanni was no fool. He could feel the news business was dying.

....

Pete had a stomach full of butterflies as he walked into the conference room.

Haruki, on the far side of the room, smiled and motioned for him to close the door and have a seat. Haruki came over and sat on the corner of the conference table, looking down at him. "Are we making progress on the homelessness problem?"

"I… after we spoke yesterday, I started… doing some research."

"Research?" Haruki was surprised. "You know I don't want research. I want results."

"Well, sir, it's complicated."

Haruki had a winning smile that elicited a smile in return, despite Pete's nervousness.

"See, Pete? That is exactly what it is not. It is not complicated."

Pete wiped his smile away.

"The homeless are a blight on this city. In fact, they are a blight on the whole world. What do the homeless produce?" Haruki was serious now, almost hostile.

"They produce nothing. Yet they soak up unfathomable amounts of precious resources. Do you have any idea how many shelters, soup kitchens, and halfway houses there are in this city alone? Extrapolate that out to a global scale, and you have a crushing burden on a planet struggling to maintain viability."

"But—"

"But what?"

Pete reached deep down into the darkness inside, groping around hoping to find a shred of courage.

"C'mon, Pete. Talk to me. I want to hear what you think." He was sympathetic, almost smiling again.

"Those resources you mentioned. A lot of them are given *charitably* by caring people."

"Granted, a large portion of them are. But what could be accomplished if those resources were re-allocated to *productive* initiatives?"

Pete waited.

"And charitable donations aside, millions of tax dollars are funneled into taking care of the homeless, whether it be food, clothing, housing, or healthcare. And that is in the U.S. alone. Getting them off the street into shelters doesn't do anything. That only increases the burden on society. I want to get rid of them and clean up the streets. I want to start with that little roach I showed you. Do we have an understanding?"

Pete steeled himself, took a deep breath. "Haruki, to be perfectly honest, I'm finding this assignment to be..."

Haruki abruptly got up from the table and crossed the room, began serving himself a tiny cup of espresso. With his back still turned, he said,

"A friend of mine called me. He manages a certain casino. You know the one I'm talking about?"

Pete's stomach turned. "Yes, sir."

"You've had a run of bad luck, I understand?" Haruki returned to sit on the corner of the table again, closer than Pete would like.

"Yes, sir, that's all. Just a bad run."

He leaned forward. "Your private life is your business." His expression was serious, but not threatening. "I'm not one to pass judgment. All I have ever asked is that you refrain from activities that might expose this company to unwelcome scrutiny."

Pete nodded.

"What I'm saying," Haruki said, "is if you like to gamble, that's fine. But if you get in trouble, don't go to... let's say 'questionable' people to bail you out, alright?" His eyes were shiny black, deep.

Haruki's white tile floor didn't have a speck of dust on it. But Pete's life was a total mess. "I'm sorry. I didn't know where else to go."

"Pete, that is hurtful. If you get into trouble, *any* kind of trouble, you come to me. Understand?" Haruki's face filled with caring and concern.

"Of course. I'm sorry."

"No need to apologize. I have purchased your markers. Your debt to Romeo is cleared, and you are back in good graces with the casino."

"But… how will I ever pay you back?"

"With future winnings, how's that?"

Pete wasn't comfortable with the arrangement, but what could he say?

"Do you need any money to tide you over to payday, so your pretty little wife won't have to stress?"

Say no. Say no thanks. Don't accept it. "That… would be… great."

"Okay. I'll call and have accounting cut a check. We'll call it a performance bonus. You can pick it up when you leave for the day."

"Thank you, Haruki."

Haruki beamed. "You are welcome. I believe in rewarding loyalty."

"I'm speechless. You are the most generous person I've ever known."

Haruki waved his hand as though it were nothing.

…••••••••…

"How is Samantha?" Haruki asked. Shawn's face was pale, too gaunt for his young age. He was clearly exhausted.

"She's doing pretty well, considering. The pregnancy hasn't been easy. Honestly, it is kind of scary. Not much I can do about it." Four in the afternoon, just in from the airport, Haruki was sitting in Shawn's office in the Corpus Christi branch. They had the Lexan in opaque mode so that they could have privacy. "Well, listen, Shawn. I'd like to give you two a gift. I'm going to send over a friend of mine who is a real estate agent. I want you and Samantha to go house shopping. You're going to need more space with a little one coming."

"Haruki, thank you. But… I don't think we're prepared to take that step. Yet."

"Nonsense. *Carpe diem*. Let Samantha pick out the house, make certain it is in a neighborhood that will upgrade your circle of friends, and get the house under contract. I will provide a down payment in the form of a performance bonus, enough so that your mortgage payments only go up about ten percent. Maybe fifteen percent max."

"Wow. I don't know what to say."

"Don't say anything. Just sleep well, knowing your family is in good hands. You look a little tired."

Shawn smiled. "I guess I am, a little."

"From what I hear, pregnancy is tough for the mama and the papa both." Haruki smiled.

Shawn took a deep breath, shook his head. "It isn't easy. But it's pretty cool, really. I think we're closer than we've ever been."

"That's nice to hear. There is an important lesson in there for you, Shawn. Be sure not to miss it."

"Oh?"

"Have you ever heard of John Donne?"

Shawn's face crinkled a little. "I don't think so."

"I bet I can tell you who he is in five words."

"Okay."

"No man is an island."

"Oh, he wrote that?"

Haruki nodded. "I'm not a big fan of his work. He was a preacher, and... well, I think you know I'm not a churchgoer."

"Sure," Shawn chuckled.

"But those words contain a key to success in business, in politics, in social reform, even war."

"Really?"

"Absolutely. His words expose a deep truth about humanity. And a crucial vulnerability. There is no man who lives alone. All men gather into groups. It's in the DNA. Within those groups, lives are deeply intertwined. It's as though their guts are woven together."

"Wow. That's powerful."

"It is. Especially if you are trying to get something done. Knowledge is power, Shawn. Cultivate it. Hoard it."

"Yes, sir."

"For instance, in your challenging assignment with our friend in aviation?"

"Yes?" Shawn's squeamish response proved his recent failure was something he'd hoped they could avoid discussing—anymore.

"He is well-insulated, but one failed attempt doesn't mean defeat. He is a powerful man. He is a good test for your skills. Be patient. Take the time to set up the next salvo carefully. Learn about his organization, his circle, his group. And then, when you have him figured out, make your move."

"Yes, sir. I've been looking into it. I wanted to run something by you."

"Okay."

"His official headquarters is here in Corpus, since he started his business flying out of here, but most of his personal flights take off out of Boston. I thought he might be more accessible there."

"I leave that decision up to you. We have an established network in Boston. I'll get you some numbers. The key is that the work is clean, and untraceable."

"May I ask you a question?"

"Of course."

"Why are we interested in this aviation guy?"

"It isn't important that you know every detail. But consider this: Which is better, to do business with a company that provides nice charter jets or to *own* a company that provides nice charter jets?"

"So, you're saying we are laying the groundwork for a hostile takeover?"

"What I'm saying is, if you can't get to the pilot directly..."

"Yes?"

"Go after the people he cares about."

··········

After parking his cart at headquarters, Perry stopped at the edge of the trees to check for peepers, and headed up toward Dorchester. He had made it about halfway when he stopped cold. That big purple Buick from the other morning turned off Dorchester and was easing up the street. Only fifty yards away, moving slow, quiet, idling the engine. It kept rolling until it was almost to him and stopped. The back door opened, and the skinny giant stepped out, twice as tall as the car was. He headed around the front of the car, a big ball bat in his right hand. Perry's insides shrank. Even Kujo had cowered in front of this dude. Seeing his face this close, Perry understood why.

Perry started stepping backward. The dude was making big strides, coming right at him. It wasn't a time for acting tough. His eyes made it clear. Perry spun and sprinted across the street, into a parking area, toward the metro tracks. The fence by the tracks had razor wire on top. He ran along the fence, looking for a way over, got lucky. At the back of the parking area there was a gate that was locked but didn't have barbed wire on top. He grabbed the top bar, pulled himself up and over in one smooth motion, slipped a little as he turned toward the tracks. A metro train was rattling up the track, clacking loud, closing fast. He could hear the giant's feet behind, gaining on him. He was gonna get trapped between the train and this big lunatic with the bat. He heard the bat clacking against the metal, the giant climbing the gate. Perry gave it everything he had, a surge of superpower from somewhere, jumping several sets of tracks. The train was right there. He could see the driver's face, pure white, eyes terrified, shouting silent at Perry, reaching his hand up, blaring the horn so loud it made Perry's insides twist, but this was life or death.

He leapt as high and far as he could, all his strength, right into the path of the train. There was a great wind blast, the far corner of the car clipped his heel, spun him, bounced him off the side of the car, tumbling through the air, everything a blur. He tucked hard, spinning across the gravel like a soccer ball, heard a loud crack, his head against the last set of rails. The train brakes were squealing, the driver's reaction too late to matter. Behind him, he searched for the giant. There was houses on the other side of a fence. He was facing the wrong way. He glanced forward, from his belly, pushing up off the ground, orange sparks flying, the giant glaring at him through the windows of the screeching Metro cars. Perry got to his feet, took off running up the tracks, same direction as the train, trying to keep it beside him. Every step an ice pick stabbed in his heel, but he only had about thirty seconds to get lost into the neighborhood on the far side. If he didn't get enough of a lead, the giant would just run him down with those long legs. A big frame like that, he could crush his skull no problem, and Perry couldn't think of no worse way to die than being beat to death with a ball bat.

He sprinted 'til he came to a place that had a fence he could climb, vaulted over it, hit the ground running. A loud screech ripped just to the left of his head, and another one. *Bullets? You kiddin' me?* He didn't glance back. He found a cross street, turned right, left, right, then right again, doubling back, and another left. His lungs were burning, his legs couldn't go no more. The sudden burst of energy had drained him. He switched to sneaking. He moved as quiet as he could, heart pounding in his ears loud as a big drum. He ducked into an alley, hid every time he heard a car coming.

The giant wasn't playing. He already popped a couple caps, and besides, a big dude like that, swinging a long heavy club, he'd be dead in seconds. His lungs were burning. He could taste blood in his mouth. His breath coming in gasps, terror sizzling up his spine. He settled in between two green dumpsters, pulled his legs up in front of his chest, so nobody would be able to see his feet. He put his head down on his knees, but that made it hard to breathe. He laid his head back against the brick wall and sucked for air like his life depended on it. Where his heel got clipped was shooting pain, and soreness settling in all over from bouncing off the car and rolling across the gravel. He was lucky to be alive. But it had taken everything he had. He put his hand on the back of his head and found a pretty good lump coming up, but hardly any blood. He couldn't run any more. The only thing to do was hide till dark and sneak his way home super careful. If the skinny giant found him again, no way he'd win another foot race.

....

Bobby was staring down at him, kind of a blue-black light around him, standing in front of the dumpsters. Neither of them said nothin'. Bobby was really sad. Perry didn't reach out to touch him, didn't want a replay of that feeling. Bobby turned his head left, then right, then back toward Perry. Perry woke up with his chin on his chest, drool running out the side of his mouth. He wiped his face with the back of his hand, shook his head a little, to wake himself. That was a creepy dream about Bobby. He rubbed his hands over his face. The sun was gettin' low, but it wasn't down yet, so he couldn't have slept very long. He had slept hard, though. And he had all kinds of bumps and bruises from his close call with the train.

That giant. A shiver shook his whole body. He didn't have no idea how he was going to settle things with that guy. Perry wasn't dumb enough to go around talking about someone else's business, but the giant didn't know that. If Perry could just talk to him. But the giant wasn't interested in talking. He must have already decided he couldn't take a chance. For that guy, managing risk includes murder, looks like. Perry stood up a little, peeped both ways over the dumpsters to make sure the coast was clear.

He jumped up. A cramp yanked at the back of his right thigh, tying it in a knot. He stood, stretching his thigh until the cramp let go, then his arms and back. He figured he might be able to start sneakin' his way home if he was careful. He was getting hungry, and it would take a while to get there. No tellin' where the giant would be by now. He headed toward the end of the alley, had the impulse to turn and check his six, but he was afraid if he did, Bobby's ghost might be standing behind him. Perry hurried to where the alley met the street, quick glance both ways, then hurried out onto the sidewalk. He didn't want to run into the giant, but he really didn't want to walk down any more shadowy alleys, either. He had to figure this thing out. He couldn't beat the giant in strength. He was gonna have to outsmart him. Anyway you see it, this changed everything. Stayin' alive by selling cans was hard enough. But this problem with the giant was a whole other kinda thing.

··········

It had been dark for over two hours when Perry finally made it home. He hid a block away for thirty minutes, to make sure the purple Buick didn't cruise by. Shadows were moving and turning into shapes, playing tricks on his eyes. The last thing he needed was for the skinny giant to find out where he lived. At the same time, he really wanted to get into his shelter and turn on a light. Being in the dark was feeling super creepy. He got down on his hands and knees, pulled the plastic back, and crawled past the green dumpster into the shelter. He turned on the flashlight quick. *Man, that was a day from hell.* Trash days were always tough. But this was something completely different. Seeing the skinny giant talking to Kujo had been a bad break, but he didn't expect the giant to come after him like this.

It had started out to be a good day, for a Monday. Didn't make much on cans, but he got five bucks to stop washing a guy's windshield, so that made up for it. But making money didn't even seem important now. He had to concentrate on stayin' alive. His whole body hurt. He couldn't believe it. He got hit by a train. And lived to tell about it. If there was someone to tell. That dream about Bobby brought back all the creepiness of seeing him in the alley the other morning. *Bobby is dead, man. For reals dead. How in hell can he be showing up asking favors from me? And what does he need? If you're in trouble after you're dead, that's real trouble, man. The worst kind.*

The old man's spot was empty. He was lousy company, but at least if he was here, Perry wouldn't have to worry about him. And lousy company was better than being alone. Knowin' Bobby was in trouble made everything worse. And things was bad enough already. He opened a can of stew, warmed it up with the bluish flame of the Sterno can, and got out his white business papers. He turned to the page he had folded in half to keep his place, folded the packet back at the staple, and started readin'. There was lots of strange words in there, some of 'em was about a mile long. He didn't have it in him. He put the pages back away. All he could think about was the train, and Bobby, and that giant. How could he talk down that giant, without getting his head bashed in? And how do you help a friend who's already dead? He never heard of nothing like that. Ghost stories ain't real. But that was Bobby, for sure. And Bobby was completely dead. He seen him dead. He seen him put in the ground in a box. *What the hell, man?*

He leaned back against the dumpster and closed his eyes to rest a little, left the flashlight burning.

September 10

Perry was running again, all his might, a pack of wild hyenas yelping and howling, closing in on him from the north, and a huge purple giant with a big, spiked club lumbering toward him from the south. Every time the giant's feet hit, the earth shook beneath Perry's feet. He jumped as far as he could, but he was a fraction of a second late. He slammed against the front of the train, seeing the driver's shocked face through a shower of breaking glass. He bounced off the window, back first, head cracked against the tracks, train brakes screaming, horn blaring in a shower of orange sparks. He got halfway up, just in time to get slammed in the face with a big white light that woke him up.

He was gasping for breath, a shudder going through his whole body. He shook his head. Every morning he had to wake up scared to death. He was used to that. But this day wasn't the same. It wasn't just about starving or getting sick. He had that giant out there somewhere hunting him. What a life. Even on the best days he had to push back the feelings of hopeless, hustle all day, give it everything he had, then crawl back into the shelter at night with sore feet. But this... The rat was peering at him from under the dumpster. He put his hand in his pocket and pulled out a slice of apple. He held it out and stayed real still. The rat inched toward him, twitchy nose checking him out. The rat moved careful, then quick grabbed the apple and ran to the other side of the dumpster, nibbling it, and gave Perry a dirty look.

"Yeah, you're welcome."

Time to roll out and get movin'. Man, I could use a cup of Geppetto's coffee. His body was stiff and sore. *Got to push past the pain and go after the good stuff in life.* Would the giant be anywhere around here lookin' for him? No, that might be the bright side. The giant had found him over by his headquarters, a couple miles away. Maybe he wouldn't be lookin' for him over here. He would have to keep one eye looking for that purple car, but that left him one eye to look for any good stuff that might happen. I *can't just give up. Dad already did that. If I give up too, who will take care of Dad?*

September 12

Suits don't like to see street people hangin' around, so Perry always took his lunch early. No problem. He always started early, so lunch came early. He was parked under a big tree, cart pulled off to the side, kicked back in his folding chair, sippin' water. From where he was, he was kinda hidden behind the tree trunk, but could see up and down the street for a couple blocks. If it came down to it, he'd abandon the cart, and just duck and run. He dug into a brown paper bag, pulled out a tiny can. *So far so good.* He had made it to the headquarters and back with no sign of the giant, or the purple car. Still, just to be safe, he figured he'd keep the cart by the dumpster for the next few nights, steer clear of where he had seen the giant. It was a risk someone might steel some of his stuff, but that's better than the risk of meeting up with the giant and his big ball bat. He rolled the can around in his hand. One thing he had learned a bunch of times, *you can't stop going after your dreams just because stuff's goin' wrong. If I did that, I'd have gave up a long time ago.*

The best defense is a good offense. That's what the old man had always said. How could he go on offense against the giant? He couldn't whip him, that was for sure. Not even Kujo would try it. But how could he take him out if he couldn't fight him? The sky had some soft wispy clouds down low, and others, small ones, way, way up there that were fluffier. It seemed like the sky went up forever. His stomach was feeling a little hollow. The giant and Kujo was into something. Something the giant wanted to keep hidden so bad, he was ready to commit cold blooded murder. How about if he went to the cops, put them onto the giant? His blood ran cold. They found out he did that, they'd kill him for sure. He shuddered. But they was gonna kill him anyway. Wait. Did only the giant see him that morning, or did Kujo see him too? Kujo knew exactly where to find him, anytime he wanted. Was kujo hunting him too?

He had worked hard this morning, so he was thirsty. There was a little breeze, kind of a nip to it, but he'd warm back up when he started moving again. He popped the top off the little can, caught the smell of the mini hot dogs, slid one of 'em out, slurped the juice off it, popped it in his mouth. Squishy, but lots of flavor. Nice. He set the can on the arm of the chair careful, got a package of crackers outta his paper bag. Brown bag lunch. That's another business word he learned. Brown bag lunches are for goin' over strategy, planning deals, thinking things through. He had a lot of things to think through. How was he gonna deal with that giant? He needed to figure out what options he had. Better look at the balance sheet.

He reached into the pocket on his chest, fished out a little stubby pencil. He unfolded a piece of yellow notebook paper from his back pocket—two folds, each with a line in it, four boxes. At the top of the page on the left it said *money*. At the top on the right, *stuff to buy*. Under the fold on the left side, *expense*, and under the right side, *money to get*. The problem with looking at numbers on a page was, the numbers didn't always tell you everything there was to tell. He started chompin' on another mini hotdog, and a couple crackers. *Money*. Would that maybe work? Could he buy his way outa this? It was something to think about. He swigged some more water. The low, silky clouds was passing over, moving left to right. The high fluffy ones seemed like they was moving right to left. What would it be like to be up there, floatin' around? Two birds were circling, moving higher and higher, in the clear space between the two layers of clouds, gettin' so high they was only dots now. That would be somethin'. Giant couldn't touch him up there. He came back down to earth. *Nah. That envelope Kujo handed over probably had more money in it than I see in a year, and the giant wasn't even happy with it.* He couldn't buy him off.

In the *stuff to buy* square, he scratched out *garbage bags*, 'cause he already bought those and had plenty. What about a gun? If he bought a gun, he might at least have a fighting chance against the giant. Another thing to think about. He would have to see the giant before the giant saw him. Maybe park the cart in the street and hide. Get the giant to stop, step out in the open. He could raise enough money to buy a used gun. Maybe he should. But solving problems with a gun is the way of the gangsters. He wasn't a gangster. Didn't wanna be. Bobby had a gun. Look where that got Bobby. Even if Perry took out the giant, how many dudes are gonna pile out of that Buick and return fire? It would almost sure put an end to him.

Next item in the square said *plastic*. He had a big roll, prob'ly enough to make the shelter three more times, so he scratched that out too. The plastic wasn't bought, it was borrowed, so he had it hid at the headquarters. *That's what the biz types call maximizing profits. Gettin' stuff for free makes the money go further.* In the expense square, it said *land. That's a tough one. Land is expensive.* But if he was ever gonna build this business into something, he needed to own his base of operations. He could put up a fence, maybe even build some kinda shelter out of borrowed cinderblocks or wood. Stop worrying about people stealing his stuff. Have a good place to hide that was safe. Signs around town been sayin' *$150,700 per acre.*

At first, that sounded impossible. But he didn't know how much an acre was. Maybe enough for five or six houses, and he didn't need that much. His base of operations was only about six feet wide and five feet long, the way his boots measured it, so that was probably only a little bit of an acre. He put the end of the pencil in his mouth. He needed to find out more. *What actually is an acre? If you don't have a plan written down, you don't have no plan at all.* He'd heard that a lot. So, he went to the square that said *money to get* and wrote *land… $100.*

He had to look at that for a minute. *Whoa.* He reached into his vest pocket and pulled out a little plastic calculator that said *Plan the work, work the plan*—a treasure he found in a blue canvas bag outside a hotel once. The bag said *Seven easy steps to financial freedom*, and inside he found two full tablets of yellow paper, a bunch of white papers stapled together with business stuff printed on 'em, the calculator, and two pencils. This one was getting stubby, but he still had the other brand-new one at his headquarters, the end still flat. The business papers was hid, wrapped up in some plastic under the dumpster.

He punched in a couple numbers. Cans brought thirty cent a pound. 100 divide by 30. Equals 3.33. *Hmmm.* Didn't seem right. *Oh yeh. You have to put in the period.* He typed 100.00 divide by 30. Equals 3.33. *Huh. Oh, yeh, the period goes on the little number, not the big one.* He typed 100 divide by .30. Equals 333.33. *Booger noodles.* That couldn't be right. *That pounds? 333 pounds?* He wasn't sure it was right. Math stuff was super hard. *If I coulda stayed in school...* Sister Mary Frances, the best teacher he ever had, and the *last* teacher he had, was really nice, and she used to smell good too. It was so nice for her to stand close to him and ask him questions, give him little hints, her hand soft on his shoulder. Would he ever know that kinda closeness with a woman his own age? He would like to, someday.

A young mom came by pushing a stroller, a little baby inside. The baby was looking around at the world and smiling a cute baby smile. That'd be cool. Maybe someday have a wife, and a baby that would call him Daddy. Maybe after he got his business going. It was possible. He smiled at the young mom. She scowled, and hurried past. Maybe no woman could ever love him. *But Mom did. Sister Mary Frances did. But that was when I was little and cute. Plus, Sister was bein' extra nice to me 'cause she knew Mom had died.* She cried and begged Dad not to take him out to have him homeschool himself. Perry had cried too when nobody was around, 'cause he liked Sister Mary Frances. *She was a nice person. She made second grade fun.*

If he coulda got to some of the higher grades, he coulda learned how to use things like long division, nouns, verbs, and proverbs. *But – it don't help anything to wish for what ain't.* His home-schooling plan had been to pay attention to people who had been to school and pick things up from them. *It worked pretty good.* Ever since Mom died and he lost Sister Mary Frances, Perry had been working as hard as he could to take care of Dad, tryin' to put him back together. He used to try all kinds of stuff to see if he could get him to smile, but Dad never really did. Perry figured it was 'cause missin' Mom was hurtin' so bad. It hurt Perry all the time, missin' Mom, seein' Dad fall farther and farther down a hole and not bein' able to pull him out.

It made Perry want to cry, but cryin' wasn't gonna help, so he kept workin', and thinkin', and hopin' for things to get better. *That little baby was sure cute. Maybe bein' a grampa would make Dad smile. Ah well. Whatever.* He didn't want to think about Sister Mary Frances, or Mom, or babies no more. *That kinda thinkin' holds you down. You got to focus on the critical path.*

Buyin' the land was a big goal. Biz types called it a land *akwasition.* Sounded good. Like real important, which it was. And big, too. Maybe too big. *They call that a stretch goal. Less see. Can get maybe two hundred, three hundred cans on a good day, but they don't weigh nothin'. It would take forever to get 333 pounds.* Bustin' his butt, on a weekend he could make maybe five, ten bucks. *Wait.* He could figure it a different way. He typed 100 divide by .10, equals 1000. He stared at the number. *A thousand days?* His heart sank. *That would take forever. That'd be like, three, maybe four years.* He tried it again, without the period. He typed 100 divide by 10. Equals 10.

Ten days? He could have the money to buy his land in ten days? *Rot, that was nothin'. Too easy, really. Anyway, I prob'ly have almost half that much now.* He glanced around, made sure nobody was watchin', went into his pants pocket, pulled out a wad. He counted it quick. Ten, fifteen, sixteen, seventeen, eighteen… and a couple quarters.

He went to the *money* square and read 37. He put his wad away and punched his calculator again, 37 + 18. Equals 56. Huh. Hafta check back at corporate headquarters, count the coffee can to be sure that's right, but that said he had more than half already. He wasn't gonna go over by the headquarters, take a risk on a run in with the giant just to count the can. That could wait a while. Got to manage risk. It gave him some hope though. He could be ready in a week if he washed enough windshields. He fixed his mind he was gonna go for it. *Lunch break is over. Time to work the plan.* He tossed the little wiener can into the black garbage bag, put the crackers back into the brown sack, and folded up his chair.

Two cops, a tall one and a short one, turned the corner and come walkin' his way. His first instinct was to get his cart and get movin'. Or he could talk to them about the giant and kujo. It made him feel sick inside. That's a place, you go there, you can't never come back. Better think about it more. He pulled his cart onto the sidewalk and took off walkin', not giving those cops back there a look. He was gonna be alright. One week, he could buy his base of operations. He just needed to stay alive long enough.

··········

Perry kept checkin' his six o'clock, like dad taught him, make sure that purple car wasn't sneaking down the street. Ahead an old lady was sprawled out on the sidewalk. She had half-gray hair, a ragged old dress with pink flowers. First, he thought she was passed out, but when he got closer, she was cryin'.

"Ma'am, can I help you?"

She scowled up at him, almost stopping the cry in mid-bawl. "You got anything to drink in there?"

Perry's heart was gonna break. "No, ma'am."

"Got any money?" She sat up, her feet still wide apart on the sidewalk.

"I'm sorry. No, ma'am." He wasn't about to give her money to buy more poison.

She narrowed her eyes at him. "Yes, you do, you little brat. Give it to me."

It was time to move on.

"Wait!" she shouted, almost begging. "I'll do anything. I gotta have something. I'm sick. Please, what can I do?"

It was like lookin' at his old man. Made him wanna puke or cry, didn't know which. Maybe both.

"Hey, look here, Sailor," she said, struggling to her feet. She leaned her back against the wall, wiping the tears off, hand on her hip, trying to do some kinda pose. "Five bucks, anything you want."

What in hell was she talking about?

"I've been with lotsa men. I know how to make you feel real nice. Five bucks."

Yeh, definitely go with pukin'. He started pushing his cart.

"Two bucks, then!"

Perry didn't turn around.

"Wait! Lookey here!"

Perry turned around, and she pulled her dress up in front of her face, showing a big white belly and dirty underwear. Perry almost puked for reals. He took off as fast as he could push his cart.

Behind him he heard her screaming like the devil was comin' outta her, spitting every cuss word in the book. He checked his six again, and behind the lady, two blocks back, that purple car was crawling across West Fourth on a side street. He quick ducked down onto Pine Street, headed in the direction of the homeless shelter.

....

There was at least ten homeless people hanging around, and all of them peeping like crazy, trying to inventory his cart. He pushed it tight up against the wall, so he only had to defend one side of it.

A ragged voice behind him, heavy and deep, said "Hey, little brother, you got any shoes in there?"

Perry turned. A big man with super-dark complexion, white kinky hair, and a white beard to match, was wearin' a dark green button-up work shirt, pocket ripped half off. Over his shoulders, he had a sleeping bag draped, stained so dark you could hardly tell it was red. His dark skin was showing through the ragged knees of his old gray suit pants, the cuffs stomped through. His sneakers was stained dark, without laces, the fronts cut outta them so his toes could stick out the end. Old yellow toenails, long and gnarly, were showing through holes in his socks.

"Sorry, Pops. I ain't got any shoes."

The whites of the old-timer's eyes had turned yellow for some reason, and he was gritting his teeth like he was fightin' to keep from crying.

"I had any, I'd sure give 'em to you." *Poor old guy.* "I got some duct tape." He hoped somebody might be nice to his old man if they had a chance.

The old eyes, deep brown with yellow around them, looked sad.

"And cardboard. I got cardboard. We could put ends on your shoes that would be more waterproof than the rest of 'em."

The old man didn't speak, but he didn't leave. Perry dug in his cart quick and fished out a cardboard sign and half a roll of duct tape. He held them up, and the old-timer took 'em.

"You can keep those—in case you need to make repairs again later."

"Thank you, little brother," the old man said, quiet. "You a good man." He wandered off, shoulders sagging, feet sliding along the sidewalk.

"Hey, boy, you got anything in there to eat?" a burly red hair guy. Wide jaw, mean eyes. Not much older than Perry.

"They serve food right inside there."

"Man, don't sass me. I know what they do. I axed if you had any food in your *cart*."

A tall skinny white guy with a bald head and a tattoo that wrapped around and around his neck came up behind while the red hair guy was still talkin'. "You can wait in line like everyone else, Toad."

Burly dude turned around quick. "Man, Snake, I ain't talking to you. I'm talking to this fellah right here."

"Yeah, and I'm talking to you, *Toad*, and I said you can wait in line like everyone else."

The burly guy glanced up and down the lean frame, huffed off, mumbling.

"Thanks, Snake," Perry said.

"Man, no problem."

"His name really Toad?"

"Nah. He says his name is *Red. Red Dragon,* you believe that? I call him Toad 'cause I know he don't like it. He has a attitude problem I'm trying to help him with."

Perry laughed. “Man, you too much, Snake.”

Snake laughed. “I do what I can.”

“I appreciate it. Hey Snake?”

“Yeah?”

“How long you been working here?”

“I don’t work here, Perry. I’m just a volunteer.”

“You don’t get paid? Why do you do it?”

Snake shrugged. “This place, Miss Jasmine mostly, was really good to me when I needed it. Her and this place do a lot of good for a lot of people. So, I do what I can to help out.”

“Ah. Yeah, Miss Jasmine’s a good lady.”

“What’s happening, little bruh? Can I help you with something?”

“Maybe. I got two problems. First, you know a big purple car with glittery paint?”

“Big custom wheels, dark windows?”

“Yeh that’s it.”

“The crew that goes around in that car is bad news, Perry. You better steer clear from them. And if they offer you any favors, don’t take ’em.”

“Okay... I appreciate it.”

“Why you askin’ about that crew?”

“Ah, I don’t know. For some reason they seem like they’re chasin’ me.”

“Oh man, Perry. That ain’t good. Those guys are stone cold. If I can do anything to keep ’em off your scent I will, but you better get scarce.”

“Thanks, Snake.”

“What’s the second problem?”

“You seen my old man?”

“He gone missing again?” Snake shook his head. “That’s hard, Perry. I know you doin’ all you can for him.”

“Yeh, but he don’t much want help.”

“I hear you. I ain’t seen him, but I wasn’t around yesterday.”

“Could you check inside with Miss Jasmine? I don’t want to leave my cart unattended.”

“Smart man, Perry. These fools, some of ’em would steal you blind. Wait right here. I’ll check if Jasmine has seen him around.”

“Okay. That’s cool. Hey, Snake?”

“Yeah?”

“There’s a old lady over on West Fourth. She’s in real bad shape. Could you maybe have someone go over and check on her?”

"Perry, you alright, man. What you did for old Henry there, that was cool, bruh."

"Henry? That's the old man's name?"

"Yeah. He said he's passin' through. Came down from New York, trying to get to somewhere warm before winter hits."

"Man, sounds like a good idea. He's got a way to go, though."

"You know that's right. Perry, maybe you oughta head south too, with that crew lookin' for ya."

"Not really an option, Snake. I got the old man to think about."

"I understand Perry. I'll go ask Miss Jasmine about him. And thanks again for old Henry."

"No problem. Remember to check on the old lady, would you?"

"Yeah, man. We'll check on her."

"Thanks, Snake. Soon, okay?"

September 13

The next day, after the morning half of his loop, Perry took a few minutes to rest. He had spent the morning working the lower half of Chinatown, then hit the dumpsters of all the restaurants and bars in the Back Bay neighborhood. After lunch he would finish his loop through the top side of Chinatown and sell his cans at the recycling center at the end of West Fourth. That was off Dorchester, less than a mile from where he had the run-in with the giant. He didn't like that. But he had to sell the cans. He'd just ease his way over, sticking to side streets, hopefully be back home to the dumpster with the cart before dark.

This grassy bank, sloping away and down from Beacon Street, was a perfect place where he could see a lot of the park. *Why'd they settle on calling it The Common? Funny name for a park. Prob'ly named it a long time ago, people coming here hundreds of years.* In this spot, he could hang out under the trees and not bother anybody. His cart was parked just above him, on the other side of the iron fence. On either side of him there were two wide sets of steps, in case the purple car showed, and he needed to get away quick.

Temperatures were cool but turning into a nice day, a little blue sky, and sunshine. A soft breeze was moving through, bringing a sniff of the harbor with it. *Prob'ly be a clear night.* The grass would be under snow soon. It was a little brown, but still soft when he ran his fingers through it. Businesspeople strolled through The Common, some with sneakers, getting exercise and fresh air, some reading the paper. *Prob'ly huntin' for something to buy or sell. You hear suits talking a lot about buying and selling.* A girl was walking toward him, cute pink stocking cap with purple headphones over it. She wore a light jacket and tight-fitting exercise pants, stepping out with white and pink sneakers. Perry seen a doe deer cross The Common one time. Graceful, confident, her head up, slender neck moving as she walked. This girl was pretty as that, her head bobbing a little to the headphones. His heart twisted some. If he was clean, if he had nice clothes... If he did, he could go jaunting up beside her, maybe walk a little faster and smile at her as he went by. She scowled and turned her head away quick. He sighed. *Who am I kidding?*

Way down toward the middle of the park, a guy in a nice suit, talking on a cell phone, sitting on a park bench. An important dude, takin' care of important business. Dude was together. Had stuff cooking in his life, you could tell. A drunk came stumbling along the path, ratty clothes, stringy hair, crooked cap, bottle in a brown bag dangling from limp fingers. Green Army jacket, too warm for this nice day. Perry shrunk inside. *Dad. Don't do it. No, not that guy. Oh, c'mon, Dad.* But sure enough, he staggered up to the man, started pestering him, asking him probably for money, telling his same old sob stories or making up new ones. The together dude was trying to ignore him, but the old man was being pushy, asserting himself. *Jeez. Embarrassing.* Dad was getting more obnoxious, offended the guy wasn't giving him proper *respect.* He grabbed the nice suit by the sleeve and yanked. The cell phone flew across the path, the together dude come up off the bench, shoved hard, and Dad went rolling.

Perry jumped up, started sprinting. *Bum or not, nobody's gonna rough up my old man.* Dad sprawled across the path, started bawling and slobbering, reaching up toward the dude like he owed him a hand up. Together dude went over to his cell phone, picked it up, held it to his ear, stuck it in his pocket, miffed. He headed toward Dad. Perry was stuck running in slow motion. No way he could get there in time. The big suit leaned over Dad, shouted something that was drowned out by the wind in Perry's ears. Suit stomped the ground with his foot, turned away, then turned back toward Dad a second time.

Oh, hell no. "Hey!" Perry shouted loud as he could, still sprinting. Dude didn't hear. He was circling Dad, trying to decide what he was gonna do. Perry's heart was about to explode. Dad was completely defenseless, and this big suit was pissed. The suit shouted something again and stomped off. Perry coasted to a stop. He bent over, put his hands on his knees. The cool air was fire in his lungs, his heart pounding in his neck and ears. Dad was still down. A couple people were giving dirty looks, but that was all. Most people were ignoring him. Nobody cared about some old drunk. He walked over and squatted down beside Dad.

The girl in the stocking cap came in view and stopped, looking right at him. Her face was like an angel. Their eyes met. Hers were blue, deep, filled with… pity. And she jogged away. Perry got a lump in his throat. Watching Dad rolling around on the sidewalk, unable to find which way was up, slobbering pathetic, made him want to cry. He couldn't believe the great man he remembered from when he was little had been shrunk down to this. He had survived the war. It was love that destroyed him. He reached over and got the old man by the arm. "Come on, Dad. I'll take you home."

··········

By midafternoon, the wind off the harbor was cuttin' through the back of Perry's jacket, making him shiver. So much for the nice day. The embarrassing scene in the park made him feel like garbage and had wasted a bunch of time, but he was getting over it. Zig-zagging streets trying to manage Dad and a full cart to get him home wasn't easy. Dad kept wanting to stop and rest, a couple times tried to run off, bawling and threatening to kill himself. Aggravating.

It had *mostly* been a good day. He dropped three big bags of cans at the recycle and got nine bucks' cash. He already had eighteen dollars before that, so he was way ahead on his land akwisition. The breeze hit him again. *It'd be nice to get outta the cold for a little bit.* He kept checking behind him, to make sure the purple car didn't sneak up on him. So far, no sign of it. He hid his cart behind some junk cars next to the metro tracks. It was a risk, but he didn't feel like pushing it all the way back home to the dumpster. He started back the way he came, face into the wind now, doing a fast walk to get the blood moving. Pulling his shades up off his eyes, he set them on top of his head. He was scanning all the parking lots, trying to make sure the giant couldn't ambush him. He liked the cool look his glasses gave him, but with the sun behind the clouds, and everything all gray and winterish, they were makin' it too dark, and he needed to see. He went up Dorchester, left on West Fourth, heading into Southie. He zig-zagged over to Pine Street, turned right, coming from the opposite direction this time and went down to the shelter. Nobody hanging around outside today in this cold, breezy weather.

He went up almost to the door, but hesitated. Dad had warned him not to go in the shelters, "'cause you never know when someone's gonna scoop you up. Don't ask help from nobody, and you won't end up in the system." Dad had warned him that his whole life. He heard the door open.

"Perry? Is that you, little brother?"

"Oh, hi, Miss Jasmine. Yeh. It's me."

"Well, come on in, Perry. Get out of that cold."

Perry hesitated. Miss Jasmine went back inside a second, came out pulling on a jacket. She was a small woman, but her heart was big. She was always good to Perry. She seemed like someone he could trust.

"How you doin, baby? Is there anything I can help you with?"

"Nah."

Miss Jasmine had patient, gentle eyes.

"I'm kinda worried about Dad. He's gettin' worse."

"I'm sorry, Perry. You know how many times I've tried to help him. He's got a tough hide."

"You ain't tellin' me nothin'." A lump was rising in his throat. She laid her hand on his shoulder. A nice, close feeling. Not too many people touched him in his filthy clothes. If only things coulda turned out different.

"You sure I can't get you to come in outta the cold? We could get you into the system, maybe get you approved for an apartment. Prob'ly even help you find a job." Perry shook his head, lookin' down, tracing a line on the sidewalk with his toe. Dad had told him a long time ago, "if a thing seems too good to be true, it prob'ly ain't."

"Why not?" She sounded almost like she was begging.

"I do that, what's gonna happen to my dad?"

Her face went soft with kindness. She nodded slowly. "I understand. If you ever change your mind, we really can help. We've helped a lot of people find nice homes. Clean, safe apartments with locks on the doors. VA checks, disability checks, sometimes good steady jobs, a fresh start on life. You deserve a fresh start, Perry." Running from the purple giant made a fresh start and a door with a lock sound pretty good.

"Miss Jasmine? Was you able to help that old lady I told Snake about?"

"Oh, Perry. I meant to thank you for telling us about her. Yes, we got her, and she's in a clean bed. We're going to get her some help."

"Miss Jasmine? How'd she get like that? My old man's a drunk, but his sickness is really a broken heart. When Mom died, it was too much."

"It's almost never about the alcohol, Perry. Her name is Alice. And she suffers from a broken heart, too."

"Oh. I'm sorry to hear that. Someone she loved die?"

"Well... I can't really share her story. It wouldn't be right."

"Oh. Okay."

Miss Jasmine was hesitating, her brown eyes looking deep into his.

"But I can tell you *my* story." She zipped her coat up a little higher, turned her back to the breeze. "A long time ago, before I was a grownup myself, I became a mama. People told me the best thing to do was get rid of it."

"Get rid of it?" Perry repeated.

Miss Jasmine looked kinda sad.

"What, your *baby*?"

"Sad to say, but yes. It seemed like the right thing at the time."

"Oh, man."

"They convinced me it was my only choice."

"That's a pretty crummy kinda choice."

"As time went on, I started having a lot of problems," she continued. "My weakness was drugs. I fell into a dark place where I thought I wanted to kill myself. It took a long time and a lot of help from people who cared about me before I realized that it was the pain of that memory that I was trying to kill. The memory of what I did to my baby."

"I'm sorry, Miss Jasmine. I never knew." He couldn't understand how someone could ever hurt their own baby.

"It's okay. I can talk about it now."

He didn't know what to say.

"See, Perry, the Church knows that for every baby who is a victim, there is also a mama and a daddy, and both of them are victims too."

"That's pretty sad, Miss Jasmine."

"You're right, it is."

"Did you have some other babies later?" he asked.

She shook her head. "That thing I did when I was so young... it kinda mixed me up inside. Made it so I can't have babies. All I have is that one memory."

"I'm sorry. I didn't mean to make you remember all that."

"It's okay. Sometimes it helps to talk about it."

"I'm startin' to think I can't never have babies neither. It's a hard thing."

Her eyes looked at him like he was the only person in the universe. "Perry, you are too young to despair. All sorts of good things can happen if you give it some time."

"Yeh. But it's like you said, sometimes you get mixed up bad enough, you never can get better."

"But I *have* found a way to get better, Perry. I found a way to heal my wounds, and after a long time, I was even able to forgive myself for that mistake I made."

"That's nice, Miss Jasmine. I'm glad to hear it."

"And because I have that experience, I can help other people who are suffering with deep pain."

"You're a good woman, Miss Jasmine. All through. So… that's how you got to be like this?"

"I used to be like Alice. We're all just people, Perry. We're all hurting in one way or another."

He gritted his teeth and watched his toe trace the line. "Miss Jasmine?"

"Yes?"

"I appreciate you treatin' me like a real person. You always been good to me."

"I care about you. And Perry?"

"Yeh?"

"Sometimes things can't get better till you get to a place where you are ready to accept help."

··········

Walking toward Chinatown, Perry had a decision to make. If he went to the cops, they might start chasing the giant. That might keep the giant busy, leave less time for the giant to chase him. It was a dangerous plan, but he was running out of ideas. If he just kept runnin', the giant sooner or later was gonna catch up with him. Most of his mind was working on the giant problem. But some part of his mind must have been thinking about the weather because his feet took him back over by The Common, straight to the movie theater. On weekdays, when nobody wanted to go to the movies, they had cheap seats, showing old movies that everybody already seen. Two bucks.

Two bucks for a couple hours outta the wind. A big waste of money. But he was ahead. And he had worked hard today. And it was cold. But two bucks could buy tuna fish, or maybe a big can a stew. Or Sterno. He already had Sterno. And he had one can of stew already hid under the dumpster.

He still shouldn't waste the money. Should go home. Wouldn't be nothin' to warm up the stew, fill his belly, and slide under that Army blanket. Yeh. But a couple hours outta the cold would be pretty good. Before time to get under the Army blanket. He realized, if he walked into the cop station, told them about what the purple giant and Kujo had going, they would for sure take his name down and put him in the system. He gets in the system, he might never get out. He was gonna need to think about it some more. Until he made up his mind, he had to stay out of the path of that psycho giant. No way the giant would find him if he was hiding inside the movie theater. He went up to the window to the old guy, gray, kinda chunky, bored out of his skull, sittin' in a ticket booth in the middle of the day. The old guy gave him the look.

"I got money," Perry said. "Gimme a ticket to the three o'clock, a'right?"

"This isn't a homeless shelter."

"I never said it was. I said I got *money*. How 'bout gimme a ticket like you s'posed to?"

"I don't have to sell a ticket to anyone I don't want to."

"That right?"

"That's right."

"You got all them seats full up, you don't need my money?"

"What I don't need is you messin' up my seats with your filthy clothes. I got good payin' customers coming in later, and I don't want them getting no filth offa my new seats."

"*I'm* a payin' customer."

"With filthy clothes that'll mess up my seats."

He tried to keep calm. He really wanted to get in out of the wind. The old guy locked eyes with him in a staring contest. Wasn't goin' nowhere good. He really wanted to go in. Better save the pride for a warmer day.

"Look here." Perry pulled a rolled-up garbage bag out of his jacket pocket. "I got this. See? Contractor strength. I'll put it over the seats, you won't never know I was here. And you'll have my two bucks."

The old guy looked at him, at the bag, then at the two bucks. He pushed a button and spit out a ticket. Perry took the ticket, wanted to yell back some cursing at the old jerk, but he didn't. Instead, he went inside. The warm smell of popcorn greeted him. He gave the guy his ticket and went to the third theater on the right. He went down to the middle of the empty theater, slipped one garbage bag over the seat back and laid another one across the seat cushion. He eased into it. Man, it was like heaven. The theater was warm and there wasn't no wind. This would be perfect if the old man was here. That put a sick feeling in his gut. He shook his head. *He's better home sleepin' it off.*

His old man taught him the trick of goin' to the movies to get warm back when he was little and hadn't got strong enough to take the cold yet. Days when he'd be so cold, he was cryin.' Nobody never gave the old man flack at the ticket window. Not because his clothes was clean, but because he basically scared the livin' snot out of 'em.

It didn't matter what the show was. They was only there to get warm. Dad usually never watched the movies. He mostly just always slept. Or sometimes he would sit and cry, tryin' to be quiet about it, but Perry always knew. He couldn't count how many hours he sat trying to hold his dad tight enough that he wouldn't fall apart. He had did his best, but it didn't work.

There was commercials, pictures to make you wanna eat popcorn, candy, soda pop, different stuff, but it was all way expensive. No, just the movie. The commercials would be over soon, so he focused on the floor. There was a lot of popcorn down there. When he was little, he used to eat the popcorn off the floor. Dad would have a fit though, so he quit doin' it.

A few short snips of other movies, some exciting stuff, one he'd already seen, a couple he hadn't seen, and one looked crummy. About a man hooked on drugs, let his life go to hell. Tellin' his wife he needed his medicine.

Perry didn't need to see that one. He already lived it. Gotta have the medicine. That's when they stopped goin' to the movies. When the old man had to spend all the money on medicine. If the more medicine you take, the sicker you get, that ain't no kind of medicine. That's poison. Take enough poison, it'll kill you. That was his fear his whole life. That his old man's medicine would kill him. It had took a lot longer than he thought it would.

The movie started for real, the theater came to life with huge sights and sounds. All that was going on there, he'd like to understand how they did it. He'd like to go up in that room, where the projector was, and see how they run the movies, but they'd never let him do that.

The sound was his favorite part of going to the movies. The sound was so huge, it shook yer chair, and it didn't seem to come from nowhere in particular. It was like the sound was everywhere. Like you was in*side* the sound. How did they do that? It was like magic or somethin'.

This was a movie he'd seen before. About the Atalian Stallion. Perry liked it because it was about a loser who figured out a way to win. That was the best kind of movie. There was a lot of stupid movies out there, but this one was for *real*. In one of the later ones, the old man who used to be a boxer said, "It ain't about how hard you can hit. It's about how hard you can *get* hit." Maybe the truest words any movie ever said.

That's what this first movie was about. The underdog showin' he can take a beating, the worst the world can dish out. Just by doin' that, he turned ever'thing around. Got the girl, the big house, lots of friends, money, *and* respect. He got a whole new life. It was a awesome story.

The warmth of the theater was rolling over him in waves, startin' to seep into his hands. He unzipped his jacket, closed his eyes for a second, and decided to keep 'em closed and listen to the big sounds for a couple minutes. The theater went dark, sounds slipping farther away, mixing up with other sounds, in and out of dreams. Dreams of winning. Of having a girl, and a big house, and some babies, and friends, and his old man safe, and healthy, and dressed real nice.

••••••••••

Snake pulled his jacket off the peg and called out. "Miss Jasmine? I'm taking off, okay?" From the kitchen, he heard her.

"Thank you, Snake. I'll be right behind you. I'll shut off the lights and lock up."

Snake turned to go but stopped before he got to the glass doors. The purple Buick Perry had asked about was sitting beside the curb outside, dark windows up, a little fog rising out of the tailpipes. Snake turned back toward Jasmine, and hesitated. He pushed the door open, stepped out into the brisk air. He stood on the steps and zipped up his coat, taking his time. The passenger door on the far side opened, and a gang banger with a blue bandana on his head got out, came around the front of the car. Snake started to go to meet him, but he already had the high ground, so he stayed on the steps. Dude started out friendly.

"Hey, cuz, how you doing today?"

"Alright. 'Sup?" Snake was ready for anything.

"I'm looking for my little brother. Maybe you've seen him? He pushes a cart, a hoodie with a down vest?"

"Hmmm. Not sure. I don't think that's ringin' any bells. What's your brother's name?"

"Name's not important. I'm sure you musta seen him."

"You're sure, huh?"

The guy's eyes narrowed. "I know he's been around here. How about don't insult me by acting stupid?"

Snake gave him a steady stare. "What's your business?"

"*My* business, that's what. You trying to start some trouble?"

"No, man. I wouldn't think of it. I just don't think I can help you."

"No?"

"No."

"How 'bout Miss Jasmine? You think maybe she could help me? Maybe I'll go in and talk to her."

Snake shifted his feet, put himself dead center in front of the doors, got ready. "We're closed."

"Oh, this isn't a good time?"

"No, it isn't."

"Maybe you'd rather I come back later and talk to her? Maybe some time when you're not here?"

"You don't want to start down that road, brother, believe me."

"That a threat?"

"No, man. I don't make threats. Bad for bizness."

"Yeah, it is."

Dude was young and lean, but hard. He had that street cred look about him. *Wonder how many people are in the car behind those dark windows?*

"I tell you what," the guy said. "I don't want to take up any more of your time. I'll just come back later when you're not here. I'm sure Miss Jasmine will tell me what I need to know."

"How you know Miss Jasmine?"

"Oh, I remember her, trust me. I used to come here for lunch back before I became successful. I always thought she was real fine. Don't you think she's fine?"

Snake gritted his teeth.

"Don't worry about it," the guy said, turning to go. "Me and my crew will come back later and pay Miss Jasmine a nice long visit."

"You don't wanna do that."

"Huh. How you know what I want and what I don't want?"

"You seem like a smart man."

"Yeah, well, that's one of us, string bean. You're seemin' kinda stupid, thinkin' you can protect Miss Jasmine with tough words. You can't be around to protect her every minute. We gonna find out what we need to know, one way or another way."

"Miss Jasmine ain't got nothin' to do with this. You leave her out of it."

"That's up to you cuz. You don't want to tell us where to find that kid with the cart? We'll find out another way. The fun way. I bet before we done visiting with her, Miss Jasmine'll be more than happy to tell us what we want to know." He was already half-way around to the passenger side.

"Wait." Snake said.

"Yeah?"

"He sells cans over at the recycle, off Dorchester. His name's Perry."

"See? That wasn't that hard, was it?" Guy smirking. Snake wanted to slide over that hood and break his neck.

"I find out you been back here to talk to Miss Jasmine, it'll be the last thing you ever do."

The guy was looking over the top of the car, grinning. "Well, something's gotta be the last thing, don't it? That might not be a half-bad way to go out, you know? He winked at snake, flipped his middle finger up at him, dropped his grin into a scowl that lasted a couple seconds. Then he got in the car. Snake glared at the black windows while the car slowly inched its way down the street, crawling, till it turned right and disappeared.

···••·•••··

After leaving the theater, Perry wanted to go home, get outta the wind. He didn't wanna fool with Kujo. But when he got over by the Chinatown Metro station, here Kujo came, jaywalking toward him, with his punks right behind. Perry stopped, put his back to the wall, sizing him up with a wary eye. He was about to find out if Kujo was with the giant in huntin' him.

"Hey, what up, P-dog? What you got shakin', little brother?"

"Hey, Kujo. What's up?"

"Business, man. Business. What about you? Gotta career takin' off yet?"

"Yeah, man. I'm makin' a career outta stayin' outta jail."

"Aww, spit. Perry, you a pussy." Kujo's sidekick, Kilo, giggled, like that was clever. "You still think you can be a good guy and live on these streets, dawg?" Kujo asked. "These streets is *ugly*. You know it. Why ain't you carvin' out a piece of the action for yourself?"

Kujo was lookin' down at him. *Would the giant leave me alone if I joined Kujo's crew? Nah.*

"I see you," Kujo said. "You're resourceful. I could make a spot for a man with yor skills, feel me?"

"Yeah, I feel you. Like Bobby, huh? Big man on the block, only now big man's dead. What good that's doing Bobby now?"

Kujo glared. "Man, you better watch yor mouth about Bobby. I don't wanna hear you say his name ever again, you hear me?" A stiff finger jabbed into Perry's shoulder.

"I don't mean no disrespect to Bobby. He was my friend. I just think it was a waste, that's all I'm saying."

"Man, you better stop *sayin'* and start *listenin'.* I tol' you not to say his name, and you just said it again. You some kinda stupid or somethin'?"

"I can say his name if I feel like it."

"That right, pussy-boy?" Kujo's eyes narrowed. "Try it. Say it again."

Behind Kujo, Kilo and the whole gang was payin attention, things startin' to get interesting. Kujo's dark eyes were daring him. He could say it. He should. For Bobby. Kujo don't own Bobby's name.

"You don't want anyone sayin' his name, 'cause you want everyone to forget."

"Man, what the hell you talking about?" He turned and looked to see what his dawgs was thinkin'. "We never gonna forget our own. You the one forget what happened."

"I remember. You sent him out, he got ambushed."

"Yeah, Bobby got ambushed, that's true. By Lizard and Flint. Big tough men. You heard anything from either one of them lately?"

"No. Guess not."

"That's right. Cause they stone cold dead. Nobody forgot about Bobby."

Kilo reached around Kujo and tried to slap Perry across the face. Perry slipped it, and Kujo spun and punched Kilo so hard, his feet flew out and the back of his shoulders hit the pavement. Kilo lay there blinking at the sky. Kujo pointed down at him.

"Man, don't you *ever* reach around me and start somethin' before I tell you to." He turned back to Perry. "See that? Kilo's my right hand. If I'll do that to him, what I'm gonna do for *you,* you think?" Perry gave him his best stare. He only wanted to get home. Kilo was getting up slow, dusting himself off.

"You got anything more you wanna say about Bobby?"

Perry hesitated. He didn't want to get punched in the face. He didn't want any kinda trouble. But he needed to stick up for Bobby.

"You want everyone to forget that he died for *nothin'*."

Kujo shoved him hard, both hands in the chest. Perry cracked his head against the brick wall. Dude was strong, turning into an animal. He should punch Kujo for that. He didn't feel like it though. Not with five or six dudes standing backup. Even if he did handle hisself okay, they'd kick the livin' slop out of him. He spit on the sidewalk instead.

"Pussy-boy, you 'bout to run outta chances," Kujo said. "It ain't *safe* to be out here alone. A dude by hisself could run into trouble. Maybe even get hurt, feel me? Better think about it, man."

Kujo knocked the wind out of Perry's chest with a huge forearm, on his way by. Kilo laid a crisp backhand across his cheek as he passed. Three or four of the other boys pushed and elbowed him. The last one, the youngest, named Clevon, looked back and grinned, sliding his finger across his neck. Perry took a quick step toward him, and the boy turned and ran to catch up with the group.

That kid Clevon was a punk. But that don't make him wrong. This rot with Kujo wasn't goin' nowhere good. Like he needed that on top of his problem with the giant. An icy breeze hit Perry in the face. Time to get home and settled in for the night, before that purple car spotted him. Prob'ly gonna be a long one. His coat couldn't have hung no heavier if his pockets was full of bricks. His shoes was made of concrete. With more weight than he could carry, Perry started off toward home.

....

Perry turned a corner, almost ran into a creepy-lookin' dude. The guy stared at him, dark eyes peering from deep sockets. A bleached skull with a little skin stretched over it. A few hairs still hanging on. He was skinny, like a black suit draped over a skeleton. His shiny head leaned forward, like the skull was barely hooked on, about to topple off. He had a thick Bible in his hand, long ribbons dangling out of it. He pointed the Bible at Perry like it was a weapon.

"I been watching you."

"Yeh? So?"

The dark eyes were judging him up and down. Same look he always got from everybody. Time to move.

Dude stepped in front of him. "You are on the path to perdition, young man."

Dude didn't seem that much older than Perry, so the *young man* thing was kinda aggravatin'. Perry side-stepped, but the dude stepped in front again.

"I am here to save your immortal soul." Perry glared at him, but the dude didn't budge.

"You must stop being evil, and start being nice to people. You're running out of time!"

That was the same thing Kujo had said. "You threatenin' me?"

"It is not my place. But I see the path you are on. Your life is filled with hatefulness. And sin. And debauchery. If you continue this path of anger and hatefulness, Jesus is going to come like a thief and cast you into eternal darkness."

"You threatenin' me with *Jesus*?" Perry couldn't believe it.

"The King of the universe is a jealous God who gives no mercy to quarrelsome servants."

Perry shook his head. "Man, get the hell outta my way. I've heard enough of you." He pushed past the bag of bones and started moving toward home again.

"If you reject me, I will shake the dust off of my feet and leave you to your own demise!"

"Good," Perry called back over his shoulder. "Leave me however you want. Just leave, that's all."

• • • • • • • • • • •

Dad was gone again when he got back. That was aggravatin'. It was like he was *tryin'* to make it harder than it had to be. It was gonna get cold tonight. Cold for reals. And it was almost for sure going to rain. People don't think you can die when the temperature's above freezing. But you can. Perry had seen it happen to street people more than once. Perry was sittin' against a couple folded newspapers, insulation between him and the chilly dumpster, holding the flashlight, the plastic shelter flapping some but keeping the wind off him—mostly. He was s'posed to be reading a page of business stuff. Through the fog of his breath, the words weren't makin' no sense. It might be time to fire up the sterno, cook some stew.

Where was the old man tonight? Hopefully he'd found a place to hole up so somebody didn't find him froze stiff in the morning. *Popsicle*. A dark thought. He didn't laugh at it, but if things was different, it mighta been funny. Strange, how your brain will sometimes spit out somethin' weird like that. The old man always talked about growin' up in Georgia, where it didn't never snow or hardly even freeze. Said he left to come up North to get outta the summer heat. Garbage. It'd be nice to have a little summer heat right about now. There was a noise outside. The plastic canopy lit up, like daylight. He dropped the flashlight quick and hustled to open the flap and crawl out.

The alley was filled with a bright, white fog. In the middle of it was the outline of a lady, surrounded by a warm halo, holding her arms out to him. Was she real or some kinda vision? His heart stuttered a little.

"Mom?"

"Perry?"

He recognized that voice. "Hey, Mrs. Ming. What's cooking?"

"Perry," she said. "You silly boy. Always make joke. Come here." She gestured for him, holding out one of them food boxes with more than one compartment. It was warm in his hands and smelled crazy good.

"Man, Mrs. Ming, you the jazz, you know it?"

She smiled big at him, old eyes crinkling around the corners. "You be safe, Perry. You keep eye *open*."

"Thank you, Mrs. Ming. This food's gonna hit the spot." He opened the flap and crawled back into the shelter, tied down the corner, wrapped the wool blanket across his legs, blew hot air onto his hands, and opened the container. Steam rolled off all kinds of good food, a feast. Plenty for two if the old man was here. He'd save some for when Dad came back. In this cold, it would keep, no problem. He could wrap dad's blanket around it, so the rats couldn't get it.

Mrs. Ming with her funny talk, givin' him a hard time, but she cared about him. *Keep eye open*. The plastic tarp over his head sloped a little from the dumpster to a stack of pallets, pretty good at making water run off. The plastic tarp walls were pretty good at keeping the wind out. The refrigerator boxes did pretty good at keeping the cold of the asphalt off him and Dad. It was a pretty good home, built with his own two hands.

"These are my *digs,*" he said out loud. "What bad's gonna happen to me *here*?" Just at that moment, the flashlight flickered, and plunged the shelter into darkness.

September 16

Beep! Beep! Beep! Beep!

The unmistakable sound of the garbage truck making its rounds. He hated Mondays. His old man was snuggled up to the dumpster. He must have stumbled back home some time while Perry was makin' his morning loop through lower Chinatown.

Perry was ready for the garbage truck. The appliance boxes were stowed in the corner of the alley, folded flat and leaned against the brick wall. The newspapers carefully stacked in front of them, and on top of those, the two Army blankets. The plastic was untied from the dumpster, neatly folded, tucked over all the other parts of the shelter, and rope was tied snug around the whole package, holding it together. All he needed to do was get the old man up and out of the way. When Perry wanted him home, he was gone. When he needed him out of the way, he wouldn't budge.

"Dad! We gotta *go*. This is *trash* day. The garbage truck's coming to empty the dumpster." Nothin'. Not a movement or a sound other than soft snoring. He stank like vomit and whiskey, which was his usual, but Perry still hated it. That poison bottle had taken a proud man and shrunk him down to… well, this.

"Dammit, Dad. Get the hell up. We got to go. Otherwise, I'm gonna leave you, and you can get run over by the garbage truck. Come *on*!" He kicked his shoulder.

"Hey! Whathehell!" His eyes were out of focus, wildly looking around for the attacker. He found Perry and focused on him with a mean glare. With his palms on the dumpster, he tried to get up, but fell against the green steel, hitting his cheekbone with a grunt.

"Dad! We gotta *go*!"

"You li'l thit! I'll theath you thum…"

Perry reached down to grab him by the arm, and he lunged, big fist looping wildly. Perry easily evaded the punch, and the momentum carried the old man around in an arc to fall on his back on the wet asphalt. Sprawled flat in the grime of the alley, mouth wide open, he was snoring again. Perry picked up the Army hat and dropped it over the wrinkled face. He stood and stared down at him, shaking his head.

"Respect, Dad. I think you was gonna say respect."

He slumped down to a squat with his back against the end of the dumpster. He searched for the blue sky. Up, up, up the tall brick prison walls surrounded him. Dark clouds hovered, menacing. He breathed in deep and closed his eyes. The smell of musty bricks, wet asphalt, the dumpster, vomit, and stale whiskey. Cold metal against his back chilled him. He opened his eyes again as a few raindrops streaked down toward him.

"God, if you're so good, why does slop like this even *happen*?" he asked.

Laughter echoed from the wide end of the alley, mocking him. Two young women—slender, pretty, dressed nice, dainty little umbrellas, chatting and laughing, hugging and waving as they separated—heading off to find even *more* success. He banged the back of his head against the steel dumpster. The dull gong sound echoed down the alley only to be swallowed by the bustle of the street. The beeping of the garbage truck was coming closer. He rested his head against the cold steel, blinked against large drops of water hitting his face. The echo of a nursery rhyme from his childhood came slithering forward in time, bringing with it a creepy, haunting irony.

It's raining, it's pouring, the old man is snoring.

••••••••••

Monday afternoon, Haruki was staring directly into the conference room camera, projecting his serious business look toward his subordinates. "I want to go over a procedural question Shawn has raised. Shawn? Please share your question with the group, would you?"

"Yes, sir. My question was about resource allocation. On tier-one projects, what percentage of the budget should be allocated for contract labor?"

"That is a thoughtful question," Haruki said.

Shawn smiled.

"But it might not be the most *insightful* question."

The smile faded.

"I suggest you start by asking whether it is appropriate to allocate anything at all for contract labor."

They all listened carefully.

"When dealing with tough people—those of hardened character, or those with hardened security resources—you may need to utilize professionals. Contract labor. But when you are dealing with average citizens, especially people who see themselves as virtuous, that is not a good investment."

He paused. They were completely silent.

"You need to be students of human nature. People who think they are good and upright have a need to prove it to themselves by passing judgment on others. To be certain they are 'good,' they need to find others who they can label as 'bad.' Are you tracking with me?"

The four of them nodded.

"Okay. That trait—that self-righteousness—is the best weapon in our arsenal. Their need to feel superior is more powerful than anything else we have." He could tell he had their attention. He continued, "Do-gooder people, so-called 'holy people,' will take care of all the dirty work *for* you if you give them even half an excuse. There is nothing they want more. If they see a chance to attack someone over a perceived moral failure, they will pounce like wolves on a wounded animal. This makes your jobs easy. There is no reason to get involved directly and expose our operation to scrutiny."

"Thank you for the clarification," Shawn said.

"And remember," Haruki went on. "We are under no time pressure. Allow things to unfold." He smiled broadly at his employees. "We are not playing whack-a-mole."

The execs laughed, and he laughed with them.

"What we are playing is a careful game of chess."

They all nodded.

"That hate-filled Church teaches there are seven deadly sins." Haruki shrugged. "I prefer to think of them as the seven *lovely* sins. They are some of my personal favorites." The four section leads grinned broadly at him and at each other.

"Listen, the takeaway from today's meeting is this: I want you to do your work with soft hands. Gentle coaxing and nudging only. Instruct your people to do favors, make allies. Occasionally, have them whisper that one of our targets has committed a lovely sin. Do this, and the target's own friends will bring down more hatred on their heads than we ever could. Keep your hands clean, smile, and watch them destroy each other."

··········

Sr. Mary Frances stood upwind from Elza's mom while she had her smoke. They were out in front of the superstore, about one hundred and ten feet from the entrance, as required by the store's policy on employee smoke breaks.

"Jeneane, Elza asked me to tell you she's sorry, and she loves you."

"You know where Elza is? Have you seen her? Is she okay?"

"Elza is fine. She's safe, with people who care about her."

"I care about her. How come she didn't come home, or even call me?"

"She's afraid of your boyfriend, J.T."

"What's he got to do with it? Did he try to hurt her? Is that why she ran away?"

"I will fill you in on every detail, but I don't have time right now. Are you safe at home?"

"Why wouldn't I be safe?"

"Elza is afraid J.T. will be angry with you because she ran away."

"Oh. Yeah, he's angry alright. But I told him I didn't know where she is, and he believed me."

"And for that reason, I am not going to tell you where she is today. But I want you to know she is safe."

"Okay. I appreciate that."

"I need your help. We need to protect Elza from J.T."

"Why? Did he try to hurt Elza?"

"Elza has information about something that could get J.T. sent back to prison, and he knows it. So, Elza is not safe."

"He's been watching me. I see him outa the corner of my eye. He might be watching us now. He's been real nervous."

"I bet he has. But don't ask him any questions or accuse him of anything. As long as you don't know anything, you're safe. I need you to get me some samples of his DNA. Can you do that?"

"DNA? Like what? Did he kill somebody or something? Lord have mercy. If anything happens to Elza Beth, I'll just die."

"Together, we're going to make sure no harm comes to her. Can you get me some hair samples in an envelope? Maybe from a hairbrush? Or maybe off his clothing or his pillow?"

"The man sheds like a wild dog. I can get you all the hair you want."

"Okay, bring an envelope with you to work tomorrow, and I'll meet you here to pick it up."

··········

The cart weighed a thousand pounds. Perry kept lookin' behind him, trying to spot the purple car before it spotted him. This was the most risky stretch, this busy street. But there wasn't no other way to get to the recycle. That lousy front wheel. The oil had limped it along for a while, but the thing was wore out. Perry figured he put eight or ten miles on it every day, and a lot of those streets were kinda rough. He was going east on West Fourth. He had almost made it to the 93 overpasses, just past Pine Street, where the big homeless shelter was. He woulda liked to stop and ask if anyone had talked to the old man, but he couldn't 'cause the cart was about to self-destruct. Being out here on this main road made him feel exposed and vulnerable, and he was moving like a turtle.

That front wheel was screeching like an angry bat. It was making him more and more fed up, sweat beading on his forehead and running down under his shirt. His wrists, back and shoulders ached from pushing. Next to a big high-rise, he stopped on the sidewalk and squatted down to look at the bad wheel. His heart sank. The flat spot on it had made it hard to push for a while now, but that wasn't the problem today. The metal pin that ran through the wheel had wollered out the hole so the wheel could flop back and forth like it was drunk. Sitting still, it was leaning hard over toward the other wheel. He had at least another mile to get to the recycle and sell his cans. How was he gonna make that? He was stuck. He couldn't leave his cart here in this public place. It would for sure get stripped clean.

You can't buy a shopping cart. You got to borrow one. Stores ain't too happy about that, so its risky business. He would have to walk the streets at night, hoping one got left out on the edge of a parking lot. No tellin' when he would be able to find that. Might be a day, might be a week. He couldn't make no money if he didn't have a cart to move his business. Sweat ran into his right eye, salty and burning like fire. He gritted his teeth, wiped his hand across his wet face, onto his jacket. There wasn't no choice. He *had* to keep going. This business was all that was keeping him and Dad alive. Across the street a dude standing at a gas pump, was starin'. Even from here, he could tell the dude was judgin' him.

"I can do this," he said.

He put his fingers over the cold metal wires on the front of the cart and started yanking with all his might. The cart wobbled ahead a few inches at a time, trying to go sideways instead a forward. He gave it one extra-big yank, feet slipped on a couple pebbles, concrete jarred up through his backbone, as he pounded his butt down hard on the pavement. A sharp pain shot through his hand and his ankle at the same time. He checked his hand first. A nasty slice deep into his palm, from that broke weld on the cart. It was bleeding good, running down toward his fingers, his palm full of it, a big mess. He pulled his pantleg up and checked his ankle where it slammed into the bottom bar of the cart. Skin scraped off, red dots starting to ooze out. He gritted his teeth.

Two young guys in dress shirts and nice pants stopped talkin' long enough to walk around him, giving him a look like he was messin' up their day. He got up, dug out a paper towel and some black electrical tape, made a hand bandage to catch the blood, and limped to the back of the cart.

If I can't pull it, I'll go back to pushin' it. He started pushing with everything he had. The cart wasn't going to budge.

"Oh yes, you *are*!" Perry shouted.

His feet slipped out backward, his forehead cracked hard against the metal handle, and his shin scraped over the jagged edge of the curb.

"Dammit!"

Blood trickled down off his forehead, into his eye, making him squint and makin' it hard to see. He could feel the give-up building in him. But he *couldn't* give up. Wasn't nobody else gonna take care of the old man. He had to make this *work*. He had to make it to the recycle and sell his cans.

"Okay, God," he said, lookin' up at the sky with one eye open. "I admit it. I can't do this alone. Is that what you want me to say?"

Dude at the pumps was lookin' at him like he was crazy. He held his hands up to the sky and shouted. "Why ain't you helpin' me? What'd I do wrong? I got giants chasing me? Gangs coming at me? Now the cart's falling apart? You *know* I got to take care of Dad." He didn't hear no answer, which didn't surprise him.

He sighed. The busted wheel mocking him, feeling the lump raising up on his shin and another one in his throat. He wiped his sleeve across the blood in his eyebrow.

"God, I give in, okay? I need help. Send someone to help me." Nothin' happened. The only thing he could think of to do was pick up the cart and carry it. But he couldn't. It was way too heavy.

"But I can carry one *end* of it," he said. "God, c'mon, man. Help me carry this thing." He went to the front of the cart, cleared the pebbles outta his way with his toe, got his legs under him good, reached back, and lifted with his strongest muscles. To his surprise, the front wheels came up off the ground easy. There was hope. He started forward. The back wheel dropped off the curb, throwing the whole load sideways, weight slamming over, taking Perry with it, down with a hard sideways fall off the curb, crashing his shoulder into asphalt. A car swerved around, close, honking, then hit the gas.

Perry lay there stunned. He was blinking, blood from his eyebrow had his eye full. The blue sky was a purple haze. He could feel blood trickling into his ear, his palm sticky with it, shins banged up, everything throbbing. More cars swerved around him, honking, shouting cusswords.

"Filthy bum!" an old man shouted out his car window.

Perry didn't even try to get up. After falling the third time he was done. He was too beat up. Defeated. It was more than one man could do alone, and he wasn't getting no help. Lying in traffic, he was just like his old man lying on the sidewalk. A wave of shame and frustration rolled him. He heard footsteps approaching. His brain told him to get up and run, but his body said no. The preacher's skeleton face blocked out the purple sky, lookin' down at him with a half-snicker.

"Now do you believe you need me? Now are you ready to listen to my message?"

"What *is* your stinking message?"

"You have been living a life sin. A life of anger, and hatefulness. But I am here to save you."

Perry breathed out through his nose. "Save me how?" He struggled to sit up. He heard the low thump, thump, thump of tailpipes coming toward him.

"Get the *hell* outta the road, moron!" a guy shouted as he gunned his engine.

"I'm bringing good news." The preacher pointed the Bible at him again.

Perry closed his eyes, wishing the dude would disappear. When he opened them, he was still there, ugly as ever. Seein' him through the bloody haze made him look like the devil himself.

"The good news," he said, still leaning over Perry, "is you don't have to live like this."

Perry squinted up at him.

"You can live a better life, but only if you choose to."

"*Choose* to?" The fight was coming back into him.

"Yes. The life you live today is the life you created for yourself. If you want a better life, you must change your ways."

"Yeh?" Perry tried to get his leg out from under the cart. "Change my ways how?"

"You must stop taking the easy way. Pull yourself up out of this gutter, go make something of yourself. Stop being *lazy*. And start being nice to people."

"Stop being lazy?" Perry kicked the cart off his leg and rolled to his hands and knees. Another car zoomed past.

"That's right, brother," the skeleton preacher said. "Jesus says in Scripture, 'You must pick up your cross and follow me.'"

"Pick up my *cross?* You want me to pick up my *cross*?"

"Yes, brother. Pick up your cross and follow *me*, and I will show you the way to *Jes*us."

Perry was so mad he couldn't talk no more.

"Pick up your cross, brother."

"You wanna see me pick up my cross?" Perry asked, finally on his feet. "Well, look. Here's a piece of my cross right *here!*" He slung a can of mini wieners and bounced it off the skeleton's skull as hard as he could.

"Shit!" shouted the preacher.

"How 'bout *that* for a cross?" Perry asked.

Dude wasn't so smart now, duckin' and coverin'. Perry picked up a big can of stew. "Here's another piece of my cross right *here*!" He bounced it off the side of the skeleton's rib cage.

"Jesus is gonna get you for this!"

"Yeh?" shouted Perry. "You go back to hell. I don't want nothing to do with *your* kind a*jesus!*"

He picked up a can of green beans, and the skeleton took off running, headed for the overpass. Perry slung it as hard as he could. It flew long, just over the skeleton's shoulder, and busted into a million beans on the sidewalk in front of him. The skeleton started slipping and sliding, arms flailing like a first-time ice skater. He almost went down but kept on running. Perry huffed through his nose. He set his feet and turned the empty cart right side up. People was still honkin' and hollerin', but he didn't care. *They can all go pound sand.*

He threw the spray bottle, newspapers, cardboard signs, pieces of rope, two big bags of cans, his umbrella, his spare clothes, his old red cloth, his folding chair, all the canned food, flashlight batteries, couple good sticks, and the rest of the bizness into the cart. He went around front and stood with his back to it. He half squatted down, and grabbed the wire with his fingers, as low as he could reach.

The sky directly above him was blue with some hazy clouds. He closed his eyes, took a deep breath, and stood up, lifting the front wheels off the ground. He started forward in the street, against the traffic, dragging the heavy load. His heels hit the bottom bar about every other step, and the wires were digging into his fingers, but he was at least moving. Only one more mile to go.

Up the street, the skeleton creature was in the shadow of the underpass, still running at a full bone rattle, Bible ribbons flapping in the wind.

·····•·•····

The hunting party came up from the south, off Essex Street. They usually hopped the Metro Orange Line at the Roxbury Crossing station, where Tremont runs into Malcolm X Boulevard. They got off at the Chinatown station on Washington. It was the same way Giovanni came and went every day to get to his store, a half dozen blocks north of the Chinatown station. It was late in the afternoon. Five young Hyenas, males, prowling like they didn't know what they were looking for, like they'd know it when they saw it. Crud. First thing they saw was Giovanni.

Monday evening, most of the business workers already cleared out after a hard day. The street was empty now. He picked up his broom and started sweeping, sideways to them, keeping them in the edge of his vision. The alpha, a big boy named Kujo, was in the lead. Four others moved in a loose fan-tail formation behind him. That punk Kilo was like a shadow to him. All of them strutting, pumped up on adrenaline or something worse. This the same crew always giving Perry a hard time, wanting to jump him in. They were getting stronger and more cocky. Trying to claim the Financial District as their turf. Getting a reputation, building fear, and liking that.

"Yo, G-dawg, what's *up*?" Kujo asked, loud, eyes dark with intimidation and meanness.

Giovanni stopped sweeping, still standing sideways to Kujo. "How can I help you young gentlemen?"

They all laughed, punching each other on the arms, shaking index fingers and thumbs like mock pistols, having a good time.

"I don't know, old man. What you *got*?" A little snear there.

"Same as every day, Kujo. Coffee, donuts, reading materials. Would you like a cup of coffee?"

"Coffee? Yeah, old man, sure. We take some coffee. Right, dawgs?"

They all parroting Kujo, they gonna do whatever he say, follow his lead.

"Help yourself." Giovanni wasn't gonna turn his back to them.

"Help yourself? Hear that, dawgs? He says help yourself. We can't insult the man, can we?"

Ice dumped into Giovanni's veins. They no gonna stop with making noise this time. They already past the edge. Kujo picked up a magazine, glossy cover, four wheelers. Six dollars merchandise. He fanned through the pages, tossed it in the gutter. They laugh, like he's clever. Next, he does the same thing, a fishing magazine.

"Hey, old man," Kujo said. Serious, smile gone. Mean, hard eyes. "Where you keep the cash, old man? We gonna need some cash." He reached for another magazine. Giovanni placed the broom handle across the top of Kujo's wrist, pressed down.

"Coffee only."

Kujo's eyes fired with violence. "Old man, you must be crazy, touching me with that little stick." He grabbed the thick broom handle.

Giovanni let him get a good hold. He planted his feet, made Kujo pull against him. When Kujo tugged hard, he thrust it toward him, stepped into it, pushing Kujo off balance. He made a little circle with the end of the broom, pulling Kujo toward the gutter, and brought the stick up under his chin, hard. Crack!

Kujo cursed, let go of the broom, trying to catch his balance. Giovanni grabbed the broom firm, like a bayonet, stabbed the end of the handle hard into his jaw, knocking him clean off his feet, down to the sidewalk. Kujo rolled over onto his hands and knees in a panic, trying to get up.

Giovanni swung the broom handle in an arc, brought it down hard with both hands, dropping his weight onto the base of Kujo's skull. Someone grabbed Giovanni from behind, pulling him away. He shoved with all the strength his legs could produce and snapped his head back. A soft nose squished flat against the back of his skull, and the person groaned and let go.

He turned to face them as one of them side stepped, two of them caught the attacker, a kid named Kilo. He bent over, cursing, catching blood in his hands. The other three hesitated. Kilo stood upright, wiping blood off his face. Giovanni showed them the stick.

"Don't."

But they did, lunging forward as one. Giovanni stepped to the side, brought the stick down hard on the back of Kilo's head, sent him reeling forward to the ground. The second guy got behind him, grabbed for a headlock. Giovanni put his chin down, pinned the attacker's arm to his own chest, dropped to one knee and bent low. The thug flew over him, slammed down hard, half on top of Kilo, half on the sidewalk. His face filled with pain, air knocked out of him, eyes wide.

Kujo was back up, he and the other two jumped, hands, feet, everything tying up Giovanni. Blows started coming in. Hard, young fists not aimed well, but some landing. Giovanni struggled to maintain balance, tried to stand back up, but someone got their feet tangled in his legs, and brought him down backward to the pavement. A blur of kicks and punches. Shielding his head, catching it in the ribs and back mostly. One of them leaned in too much, Giovanni got him by the throat, squeezed hard. Good hold but left one side of his head unprotected. Kujo's hard blows cracked against his skull, lights blinking.

"Old man, you a fool." Kujo's voice. "You gonna die over a few bucks cash."

Giovanni rolled, knocked one of them off his feet. He heard other blows and grunting. A second Hyena went away, peeled off, an arm across his throat. Giovanni heard a loud crash, the newsstand. Kujo was still on him, punching hard and fast.

Giovanni was covering best he could, eye swelling shut, when a streak came from the side. Kujo grunted and flew away sideways. Kilo sent one sloppy kick past Giovanni, hurried to help Kujo. That left only two, one he had by the throat. The other got up from the sidewalk and jumped on him, riding piggy on his back, not doing harm but holding on. Giovanni shoved the throat down onto the sidewalk, pressed hard. The eyes bugging, fear and panic. He pressed until he heard gurgling. He released, lunged backward, smashed his back against the brick wall. The air went out of the little piggy as he dropped off. Over in the gutter, someone down, three of them kicking him.

"Perry!" He was curled up, blows still getting in. Two steps to the newsstand, reached behind the counter, pulled out the snub-nose, and fired it into the sky with a loud bark. The kicking stopped. The attackers all staring, eyes wide. He leveled the pistol, both hands, at Kujo and started gliding forward, knees and elbows bent.

"You die in three seconds. Three..."

As one, they backed away, hands up.

"Two..."

"Old man, you the one took this all sideways. We were just having fun."

"I see you my side of street again, you catch a hot slug instead of broom stick. You run now, and no come back."

"Old man, you—"

"One!"

The three spun and ran, the other two slipping along the wall, trying to stay invisible, as far away from Giovanni as they could. He glared at them, and they also broke into a stiff run. When the group was a half block away, they slowed and started trying to strut again, limping, tails between their legs, whimpering Hyena pups now. A moan from behind him. Perry, shoulders on the curb, head hanging into the gutter, was trying to get up.

"Easy, son. Easy." Giovanni got to his side, cradled his head. "Take it slow. Let's see what hurts. Can you move your legs?"

"Uh. Yeah, I think everything works."

"Good. Take a second before you get up. You had one helluva fight." He cradled Perry's head, helped him turn so he was lying straight on the edge of the sidewalk, one arm in the gutter.

He grabbed some papers off the sidewalk, rolled them up, and placed them under Perry's head. "What hurts first?"

"Ooh. Ribs."

"Next?"

"Head's pounding pretty good."

"Look at my eyes, Perry."

Perry squinted up at him.

Giovanni realized the sinking sun was behind him. He moved to cast a shadow on Perry's face. Giovanni pulled one eye open with a thumb and finger, then the other one. The pupils were different sizes. "You probably have concussion, Pinocchio. Did not think they could hurt that wooden head."

Perry laughed, winced, and held his ribs. Blood showed in the corners of his mouth.

"You gonna be okay, Master Perry. Old Giovanni gonna make sure of it."

"Thanks, Geppetto."

"You lie here and rest. I gonna close up shop, and we go to hospital."

"No." Perry tried to sit up, winced, lay back down on the sidewalk. "Can't go to the hospital, Geppetto. Hospital means questions, questions bring cops. Nothing good."

Giovanni hurried about, limping, wiping blood off his face with his handkerchief. The newsstand was smashed and couldn't roll, so he left it cock-eyed across the sidewalk, newspapers and magazines fluttering in the gutter and across the street. The street was empty up and down, them Hyenas not coming back for another attack. Yet. He took the cash box from behind the counter, stuffed the snub-nose in his belt, tossed a couple bundles of newspapers into the storefront, and locked the door. Back at Perry's side, he supported his back to help him sit up.

Grunting and groaning, they got him to his feet, the two of them limping across the sidewalk. Giovanni helped Perry sit against the brick wall, went back to the wrecked stand, found a cup, poured what coffee hadn't spilled, and grabbed a donut. And a wad of paper towels. He handed the donut and coffee to Perry and started wiping blood from his face with paper towels. Nasty gash over his left eye, probably opened by a boot. He pushed hard on it, making Perry groan. Another smaller cut on his cheekbone, not as deep.

"I think you gonna be okay, Perry. You tougher than you look."

"Huh."

"You wait here. Giovanni be right back." He took two steps away, came back, put the snub-nose in Perry's hand.

Perry questioning him from down there on the sidewalk, one-eyed.

"It's double action. Point and squeeze. Got it?"

··········

Giovanni was limping pretty good as he headed off down the street. Perry squinted at him, seeing blurry through one eye barely. The old man was tough as *hell.* Never seen *anyone* fight like that. *Who woulda thought old Geppetto knew how to handle hisself? Gotta watch these old men. Sometimes they surprise you.* Perry half smiled, his fat face stretchin'. His little Rocky dance in the alley. *Welterweight champion uuuuh the werrrrrld.* He was exactly like Rocky. Beat to slop but alive, and that counts same as a win. A few minutes went by. He let the bricks hold him. Nothin' to do but wait through the pain. The coffee was hot and it helped. Burned a couple cuts inside his cheek. Perry was tired, closed his eyes to rest. Didn't eat the donut. Better to save it for later.

"Oh, my God!" a woman exclaimed.

He opened his eye. A pretty young woman stood a few yards back, mouth hanging open. She was terrified, tears in her eyes. Perry hid the snub-nose under his leg.

"Oh, my Lord, what have they done to you?" she asked.

Perry tried to speak, but nothing came out. After staring for a second, the woman hurried over to him and knelt down right there on the sidewalk. She reached into her purse and pulled out a nice cloth hanky. Real careful, she held it up so he could see.

"I'm not going to hurt you." She wiped his face real soft, cryin' the whole time. Made Perry wanna cry too. No stranger ever been that nice to him.

He was embarrassed. He smelled bad. *How can she be like that to me? Me all filthy and bloody? How can she be like that?*

She was really cryin', like he was her close friend or something. She kept wiping his face, stroking his hair, sayin', "Oh, my Lord. Sweet Jesus. Oh, my Lord."

Didn't make no sense to Perry, but he was about to go lights out, so he couldn't ask no questions. A car pulled up. Yellow. Giovanni got out, left the door open, started toward Perry.

"Is he going to be all right, mister?" the nice young woman asked through tears.

"Thank you for your kindness, miss. God bless you for it. I gonna take him and get him help." Geppetto started tugging, trying to get Perry to his feet.

Oh, man, it *hurt*. "No, Mr. G. No hospital."

"No hospital, Perry. Giovanni gonna get you somewhere safe, where you can rest and heal up. No hospital. Don't worry."

·····•·····

It had hurt like hell getting into the cab, but the seats were so soft and rich, Perry couldn't believe it. He had forgot what the inside of a car was like. The cab started moving. It was quiet, soft, and safe. He was drifting into a nice memory. Mom's smiling face, buckling him into a kid's car seat.

"Sing a song of six-pence, pocket full of rye…" She was always singing back then. "Four and twenty black birds baked in a pie…" And smiling. Dad, a big man, turning and smiling at him from the front seat. "How you doin' back there, sport?" Perry smiled. Hadn't heard that nickname in a long time. Ancient memories. A hospital room, the smell of medicine and cleaning stuff, quiet machines beeping, Mom in the bed, Perry sitting beside her, playing with plastic dinosaurs on the small table. Dad asleep in the chair, hand on the bed. Even asleep, he looked sad. Sometimes he cried. Mom was sick. She wasn't singing no more. She coughed a lot. Dad opened his eyes, they were filled with tears.

"Perry."

"Yeah, Dad?"

The pain started coming back. Ribs, head pounding.

"Perry, wake up." Geppetto was shaking him. "We're here."

"Whaa?"

The cab. Oh. Right. The big rumble at the newsstand. Crud, lost that fight bad. Almost died. Fear started to rise. *They were getting ready to curb stomp me to death. Geppetto stepped in and saved my scrawny butt.*

"Good old Geppetto," he said.

"Come on, Perry. We gonna get you cleaned up and get you some rest."

"Geppetto, you seen my old man?" Geppetto's eye was swollen half shut.

"Today? No. Not today."

"I got to go find him, Giovanni. I got to warn him to watch out."

"No. Sorry, Perry. I don't know where to find him, and we got to get you fixed up."

"Gotta… find… him. Might be in… trouble…"

"First we get you put back together, then we find your dad."

Perry walked into the lobby on his own steam, but barely. Everything hurt. Legs shaky. Giovanni was doing only a little bit better. The place was fancy, Even had carpet. Too good for his boots. The guy behind the glass window gave them a dirty look.

"We need a room. With a kitchenette," Mr. G said.

"We do not have a kitchenette. We have a microwave."

"In the room?"

"Yes, in the room. And a little fridge, holds a couple six packs."

Perry lost interest in their conversation, lookin' around to see if there was some place to sit. There was a couple chairs, but he was covered in grime and blood, figured the guy would have a fit. He didn't want to look weak, but man, he really needed to sit down. He leaned against the door frame, tried to look casual.

"Is he alright?" the man behind the glass asked.

"Yeah, he will be. Some punks jumped him, roughed him up. He gonna lay low here, get stronger."

"They going to be coming here to find him? I don't want any trouble."

"No, they from over in Roxbury. I don't think they find us here." *Geppetto don't know about the purple car.* Geppetto slid a few bills under the glass into a little metal bowl. The man grabbed the bills, slipped a key back.

"End of the hall, turn right, third door on the right. One forty-two."

"Thank you."

The man pulled down the plastic door to cover the opening, turned away to watch little ants playing soccer on a tiny television. The walk to the end of the hall was *long*, every step a struggle, stabbing pains making it difficult to breathe. Vision was going blurry, head blowing up like a balloon. Finally, they turned right, found 142, and Giovanni opened the door.

The room had a perfume smell. Strong, like trying to cover up something else. Should get some of that for the dumpster. There was two beds side by side, Giovanni motioned for him to sit on the one closest to the door, helped him lie back. *Oh, man, the ribs are freakin'.* He struggled against stabbing pains when he tried to lift his legs. Geppetto lifted his legs up onto the bed. Perry lay still, exhausted. Oh, man, he'd forgot how nice a bed could be. No pebbles, no dampness. Soft on top of soft. He heard Giovanni moving around, shuffling things, and opened his eye a little. Geppetto was at the door.

"Perry, I taking the key with me. Anybody knocks on this door, it is not me. Do not open this door for nobody, understand?"

"Mm-hm." Way too tired for chit-chat. Mom was really pale and weak. Her hair almost gone, so much older now. She used to have pretty hair. Barely a few silky strands left, and even they were sick. She tried to smile, but she was too tired. Perry knelt on the bed, looking down at her.

"I love you, Mommy."

She nodded, raised a hand, and let it fall on his knee.

His tummy hurt. "Wake up, Mommy. Don't go to sleep."

"Baby, I'm just… so… tired."

Over in the chair, Dad sound asleep, pale, starting to be sick too. Perry's tummy hurt for Mommy and for Daddy. He lay on his side, curled up beside Mommy, trying not to cry.

"Perry…" It was Mom's voice, but with a funny sound to it. "Perry, wake up, son. I brought you ice."

He opened his eye to find Giovanni standing over him. Ice wrapped in a towel.

"Hold this on your eyebrow. Bring down swelling."

He nodded, put the towel gently on his pounding eyebrow. The cool towel soothed the burning, the stretching skin. Soon the ice was cooling his face, the bone cold underneath. Perry was busted up inside and out. But that wasn't the worst thing. The worst thing was thinking about the future. His life was a living hell already before all of this. Now that giant was out for his blood, and how was he gonna get by with the Hyenas hunting for him every minute too? And they know where he lives. His heart stopped.

Dad's out there…

··········

"Mary, could you please come in here?" Haruki said into his intercom. At the far corner of the office space, Chicago branch, through several transparent walls, Mary closed her laptop, grabbed a tablet, headed his way. Everyone else was already gone, only he and Mary left here burning the late-night oil on a Monday.

The top executive here in Chicago, Mary was a strong and capable advocate for their cause. In her college years she emerged as an exceptionally bright student with almost limitless potential. Until her sophomore year when her future was put at risk by an unwanted pregnancy. Had she been forced to raise that child, she probably would not have achieved the same level of success in the business world. Now a mature woman in her late thirties with a strong business savvy, she had an unbeatable passion for the work.

She poked her head in the door. “Yes?”

“Sit down,” he said with his winning smile. “I would like an update on our progress with the Life Choice League.”

“It’s going well.” She smiled, easing down onto the couch. “The number of people we’re helping shows a strong upward trend. The buffoon who blew himself up in front of the Dallas clinic last month provided a great PR boost. Polls show public opinion swinging strongly in our favor. Donations from private individuals are up, and for the time being, nobody will dare challenge our government funding.”

“That is good to hear. Improving the quality of life for at-risk young women is important work. If these young ladies stay in school and become doctors, lawyers, and political leaders, rather than being chained to a baby carriage for eighteen years, everyone wins.”

Mary nodded her agreement. Her strongest motive was the gratification of knowing how many people she was helping.

“On top of that, we are protecting millions of unborn children from the misery of living life as an unwanted child. Most of these pregnancies would result in a child destined to spend their life incarcerated. It would be inhumane to allow them to suffer poverty, rejection, prostitution, and addiction, only to be put to death later by the state.”

Mary appeared to think about this, a fresh angle on the issue. She probably had been attractive once. Reasonably so, anyway. But life had not been kind to her. The trauma of a long chain of failed relationships had taken a toll, both physically and emotionally. Too bad, really.

“How are the secondary revenue streams doing this month?” Haruki asked.

“Tissue sales are stronger than ever. We’ve signed agreements with two new laboratories, here locally. The public is getting used to the idea. We expect the sales of organs and tissue to be normalized in public opinion within a couple of years, and at that point, those revenue streams will skyrocket. It's good to know that someday all of this could result in curing some problematic disease." She paused.

"What is it?" Haruki asked.

"There is only one concern..."

"Yes?"

"These court challenges. Some of them will be hard to defeat."

"Mmm. Yes, I've been tracking that. Mary, I want you to increase your networking efforts. Concentrate on women in positions of influence. We need powerful allies to maintain our momentum. The stakes could not be higher. Specifically concentrate on those who are passionate about the environment. In the broader picture, we are saving the planet by reducing excess population."

....

When Perry woke up, he didn't know where he was. Inside a room somewhere. A soft place. A beam of light cut across the carpet from an open door. He blinked, waiting for things to make sense. He tried to sit up, but a dagger stabbed deep into his ribs. Oh. Now it was coming back. The rumble in the jungle. Head pounding, face stretched and throbbing, ribs totally wasted. *Giovanni—what did he say?* "Don't open the door for nobody." *Yeah. A motel room, right? With ice.*

The towel was wet, water trickling down his neck. He rolled onto his side, pushed off the mattress, his feet falling to the floor. Excruciating. Sitting, head spinning, fingers gripping the blanket to keep from falling. Not green wool blankets. Soft, sissy blankets. A person could get ruined living like this. *None of these people know how soft they have it—they think life is hard.*

A folded pair of pants and a shirt, underwear, socks, even sneakers were on a table. All brand new. Like from a store. A piece of paper with big letters in black marker. Perry squinted past his puffed-up nose to read *FOR PERRY*. Giovanni—old man full of surprises.

He took a deep breath, braced himself, and pushed off the bed to stand. "Oh, man." He shuddered. Even the shudder sent stabs of pain through him.

A mirror was in front of him, over a sink, and a long narrow countertop made of plastic stone.

"What you lookin' at?" he asked.

The guy in the mirror was at least ten years older than Perry expected, and his face was busted *up. Garbage.* His shirt was stained almost solid red from blood, his hair matted with it. He stepped forward, leaned toward the mirror, turned on the light to see better. *Jeez. What a gash. Jerks. I'd like to catch any one of them woosies alone. Three on one, big tough men, right? Slop.*

Staring at himself, he had an urge to shout "*Ay-driennne...*" to see what it would feel like. But he didn't have the energy. To his left was a little bathroom. *Hot water? Whoa. What would that feel like? When was the last time he had a shower? At a truck stop. Maybe a month ago? Water was cold. Can't forget that.*

He limped forward, reaching from counter to doorframe to wall. Turned on the water, fiddled with the knobs to figure out how to make it hot, turn on the shower.

He struggled back out to the mirror, inspected the damage s'more. Hurt like hell. Lot of blood in there but all the teeth was still connected. Lips swole and cut up, but that'd go down. The two big face cuts though. They was gonna leave marks the rest of his life. The mirror started to fog over, the image of the busted-up kid fading.

A pale-faced dude with a skin-and-bones face appeared, staring over his shoulder. He spun, but there wasn't nobody there. He keeled over. *Damn ribs.* He turned back to the mirror. His heart was beating fast, like when he seen them bum-rushing Geppetto. He took a breath and let it out. With the skeleton dude gone and the fog getting thicker, the face of the busted-up kid was less scary. He started to wipe the glass but - it didn't matter.

The beat-up kid disappeared into the fog. He shook off the memory of the skeleton face and struggled the two steps back to the bathroom. Standing outside the plastic curtain, one hand on the wall, he let the steam surround him. Steam filled the room, rolling out the bathroom door. He stood inside it, like a moist, warm cloud. It was like being on another planet. Maybe another universe. That would be nice. To be in any universe but this one. He put the lid down on the toilet, sat down careful, trying not to tweak the ribs.

The steam grew thicker and warmer, moist, warm air in his lungs, wet gathering on his face, damping his clothes. He didn't think. He sat in the white cloud and saw his vision blur as the tile floor faded away. Cloud above, cloud below, even cloud inside. Lungs full of it, warm all over. He didn't want it to never end.

This place—this cloud—Any way I could just stay here? Warm, safe, no danger, no fear, no nothing. Only the cloud. He tried to remember if he had been here before. *Like maybe a long, long time ago? Or was it a dream I had?* It was too familiar to be his first time. It was like he belonged here.

Images of childhood began to pass through the cloud, weaving in and out of the whiteness, like gray horses galloping through fog. The cloud swirled and rolled, stirred by the passing images but not interrupted by them. Faces. Mom, Dad, the boardwalk, a boat, a car, catching a ball, finding an egg, running with a kite, all within the cloud.

A lady high on a hill, surrounded by a bright mist, sun behind her, hard to see. She was reaching out toward him. *Mrs. Ming? No. Maybe Mom? Could it be?* He started toward her, but she held her palm up like a traffic cop. He stopped. It wasn't Mom. It was someone like her though. She kept her hand out and shook her head no. He was trying to figure out why, when she called out—a gruff voice—"Perry!"

···········

He woke with a start, Giovanni's face coming at him through the cloud.

"Perry! You okay, son?"

"Uh-huh."

"Come on. We gotta get you fixed up. I brought medical supplies. You still in the old clothes? You all wet, but no take the shower? You okay, Perry? You with me, boy?" His face concerned, his eye swollen bad.

"I'm okay, Giovanni. Really tired and sore."

"I know you sore. We gonna fix you up. We gonna set you good as new again."

"Giovanni?"

"Yes?"

"Before the fight, I was lookin' for something..."

"For what?"

"I... I can't remember... Seems like I always been lookin' for something."

"Perry, look at me. You okay, son?" Peering into his eyes.

"Yeh, Giovanni. I just need to remember...Giovanni, you ever seen a ghost?"

"Perry, why you keep asking me that? Are you okay, boy?"

"Giovanni, I think there might have been a ghost in here when you was gone..."

"I going right now to call a cab, and we go together to the hospital."

"No. I can't go to the hospital. Too many questions. Too many cops. I'm fine, Giovanni." Talking made his face hurt bad. Squinting at Giovanni like Rocky after Apollo.

"All these years, you never call me Giovanni. Something is not right with you. We going to the hospital."

"I said *no*!" The ribs ripped at him, doubling him over.

Giovanni looked at him steady, seein' if he meant it. "Okay, no hospital. We stay here."

"No. I got to go home."

"You *cannot* go home. Those Hyenas will come back and kill you for sure."

"But I have to..."

"You *cannot*. We stay here tonight, rest up, and get stronger. Tomorrow, we talk and make a plan. We decide what to do after you have sleep and food."

A loud knock on the door made them both jump. "It's okay, Perry. I think I know who it is." He went to the door and pressed his eye to the peephole. "What you want?"

"Delivery for Mr. Gillespie, room one forty-two."

Giovanni turned back from the door, smilin'. "You going to like this." He opened the door and took the most delicious-smelling Chinese food that ever filled up a motel room. He paid the delivery man and relocked the door.

"Chinese?"

"Yeah. You no like Chinese?"

"I really like it. But ain't you Atalian?"

Giovanni laughed.

"You think I only eat pasta and meatballs, eh?" He hurried to prepare a feast on a paper plate.

Perry was starvin'. When Mr. G handed him the plate, he started shoveling the noodles and vegetables. Made his mouth hurt, but ah man, the taste was something else. As he shoveled, he was trying to tell Geppetto how much he liked it, but it was mostly coming out as grunts and noises, tangled up with the food and his puffed-up lips.

"Boy, you eating like there is no tomorrow." Geppetto was smiling, then it was like he had a bad thought or somethin'. The old man's face turned white, and he sat down like he was wiped out. He sat there starin' at the floor.

Perry kept on shovelin' the noodles. Tomorrow or no tomorrow, stuff tasted good, man.

··········

Giovanni sat in the chair, looking at Perry, who was snoring. The boy cleaner than he'd ever seen him, new clothes, down to the stockings on his feet. The new shoes were beside the bed, and an ice pack rested on carefully applied butterfly sutures. The boy in a real fix. Nowhere to go, and the Hyenas know where he stays. They not used to people standing up to them. They not going to take a beating like that without striking back, especially from this scrawny street boy. Perry streaking in from the side, taking out Kujo in one shot, knocking him to the curb. What a sight. Perry had him, little fists flying, the bigger boy covering up. Until the others jumped him. Giovanni gulped, a stab of fear cutting him. *This boy risk his life to save mine. I will not abandon him. I gonna take care of him and take care of those thugs—for good.*

He reached into his pocket and pulled out his flip phone. Not fancy, but smart enough for him. He did not want to wake Perry, so he went into the bathroom and closed the door. He closed the lid on the commode, sat down, the plastic lid flexing under him, picked out the keys one at a time. 4-1-1 SEND. After a moment, a little musical chime sounded, then a woman's voice that was very cheerful. Because she a recording.

"Your account will only be charged after a number is provided. Say yes to confirm that you understand."

"What? I will be charged for getting a number from information?"

"I'm sorry. I didn't understand you. Say yes to confirm that you understand your account will be charged when you receive a number."

"Oh, for Pete's sake. Ye—"

"I'm sorry. I didn't understand you. Please try your call again."

"No! Don't hang—"

"Goodbye."

"Stupid machines."

Thick fingers punched the tiny little numbers on the phone. 4-1-1 SEND!

The musical chime, the same female recording. "Your account will only be charged after a number is provided. Say yes—"

"Yes."

"—to confirm that you understand."

Silence.

"I'm sorry. I didn't understand you. Say yes to confirm—"

"Oh, for cryin' out loud! Yes, dammit!"

"—when you receive a number."

"Yes! Yes! *Yes*!"

"Okay. Next, say person or business."

"It is not a person or a business. It's the police department, you stupid machine."

"I'm sorry. I didn't understand you. Please say person or business."

Grrr. "Business."

"Okay. What city?"

"Boston."

"Okay. Please say the name of the business you are trying to reach."

"Police Department."

"Okay. I heard you say police department. Is this an emergency?"

"I sure hope not, or everybody dead already."

"If this is an emergency, please hang up and dial 9-1-1."

"This not an emergency! Don't hang up!"

"Are you still there?"

"Yes!"

"Okay. Here is the non-emergency number for Boston Police Dispatch."

Giovanni panicked. He didn't have a pen and paper ready. "Wait!"

"The number is 555-372-4245. Would you like for us to dial that number for you? Please say yes or no."

"Yes!"

"Okay. Your service will be billed one dollar and fifty cents. Please hold."

"One fifty? To have a machine connect a number? That is ridiculous!"

"Okay. You will be connected momentarily. Have a nice day."

"Dispatch."

"Hello? Is this police department?"

"Yes, sir. This is Greater Boston Dispatch. How may I help you?"

"I want to report a gang attack."

"Sir, is this an emergency?"

"No, this not an emergency. It happened a couple hours ago."

"Why are you just now reporting it?"

"A boy was hurt. I had to get him to safe place, so they not come back."

"I understand, sir. Are you in a safe place now?"

"Yes, we in a motel, over in Cambridge, ten miles from where attack happen."

"You said this was gang related. How many people were involved in the attack?"

"Five."

"Okay. Do you want to file a report?"

"Yes. I want to file a report of attempted murder."

"What is your name, sir?"

"My name Giovanni Gillespie. I own Gillespie Periodicals, on Summer Street, Financial District."

"And where did this attack occur?"

"At my store. They bust up my newsstand."

"They broke into your store?"

"No, my newsstand was broken *up*. Threw my papers and magazines all over the street, tried to get my money box, but Perry stop them."

"Perry is a witness?"

"No, Perry the victim. He save my life, and they almost kill him for that. He is a good kid, and no deserve what he got from those Hyenas."

"Is the victim in need of medical attention?"

"Yes. Yes, he is, but he will no let me take him. He is a stubborn boy, very tough. He live on the street a long time, understand?"

"Were there firearms involved in the attack?"

"No, no firearms. Well... I had mine, and they lucky this not turn out different."

"Sir, where are you currently?"

"I *told* you. Perry and me in a motel. We over at the Daze Inn, West Soldier's Road, Cambridge."

"Sir, would you like me to send over a squad car so that an officer can take your statement and file a report?"

"Yes. I want to file a report. For attempted murder."

"Yes, sir. Tell it to the officers when they arrive. How can the officers find you?"

"Ask the man at front desk to call me. I no want them to come to the room. They wake Perry and get him upset."

"Yes, sir. I will dispatch someone as soon as possible."

Giovanni sat back against the tank of the toilet with a sigh and put the little phone in his pocket. Now we gonna see. Nobody will call the cops on those punks because they are afraid. But Giovanni is no afraid of punks. They should be afraid of Giovanni. We gonna see how they like to have all their names in a police report. We see how they like Giovanni pressing charges. Those punks are not so scary. What they gonna do?

....

The man behind the glass gave Giovanni a dirty look when he came into the lobby. Two uniformed officers waited—a big dark-skinned guy, NFL build, and a small female, military type.

"Hi. I am Giovanni Gillespie. I called the police station."

"Good evening, sir," the male cop said in a deep rumbling voice. "Are you the Giovanni Gillespie who runs the periodicals store on Summer Street in the Financial District?"

"Yes."

"Do you have ID on you?"

"Yes." He pulled out his wallet and handed him the card.

The big cop looked at it, at Giovanni, and back at the ID. "Hold on a second, sir." He triggered the mike on his collar. "Dispatch, Unit 1-2. We have a positive ID of missing person Giovanni Gillespie. He called in a report of gang activity. We're going to take his statement. You can cancel the all-points."

"Two beat cops discovered your broken news stand" the female cop explained, "They sent out an all-points bulletin, reported you as a possible endangered person, a victim of assault."

"Are you a victim of assault?" the big officer asked.

"Yes. Five little punks try to rob me, but I cracked them good. They were beating me, but Perry tackle them off me, and together we sent them running. I want you to put down that the attackers ended up victims. We flog them good. Big tough Hyenas ran off whimpering liked whipped puppies."

Both cops laughed, exchanging glances with each other. Giovanni was not laughing.

"Sir," she said, "maybe we will write this up as a gang attack, attempted robbery. Maybe not include all those details. Did they show or threaten the use of a firearm?"

"No. Physical violence."

"So strong-arm robbery. They busted up your news stand. That's destruction of private property."

"Yes."

"Did they threaten you?"

"Yes. He say he gonna kill me."

"That's assault. With intent. Those injuries on your face, did they strike you?"

"Yes."

"That's battery. What did they do?"

"They were all on me, punching, kicking, like that."

The female cop looked up at the male cop. "High and aggravated?"

The male cop nodded.

"Perry came and tackled Kujo."

"Wait," the NFL cop's heavy voice said. "You *know* the individuals who attacked you?"

"Yes, and I know their moms, most of them. They could have been good boys, but they decide to be gangsters instead."

"We're gonna need those names." He rested his hand on his holster.

"I give them to you right now."

"Who is Perry?" The female cop glancing up from her notepad.

"Perry is my friend. He save my life. Those Hyenas should go to jail for a long, long time."

"What is Perry's last name?"

"Hmmm." Giovanni was embarrassed. "All these years, I never know Perry's last name. He just Perry to me. Or sometimes Pinocchio." He chuckled.

"Pinocchio?" she asked.

"That's a joke between us. Perry is a good, good boy."

The two officers looked at each other.

"We're gonna need to find Perry's last name," the big one said. "Is Perry in the system?"

SEPTEMBER 18

"Eddie, let's make our way over to Summer Street, see if Giovanni is going to open today. I'm anxious to get firsthand intel on this gang activity."

Typical Wednesday morning. Two cops wearing thirty-pound duty belts, strolling to no place in particular on sore feet.

"More like anxious to be the first hand on one of those pastries with chocolate frosting and Bavarian cream," Eddie said.

"Funny, young man. Talk to me in ten years. You won't be as fit at this age as I am."

Eddie rotated his shoulders side to side, twisting at the waist, feeling a nice stretch in his back, his lats and his abs. "Okay, old-timer."

"What was yesterday, upper body day?" Bert asked.

"Yeah. I'm a little stiff, but I feel solid."

"Yap. Me too." Bert rapped his knuckles on the Kevlar vest that covered his torso.

Eddie laughed.

He was a good kid. He took the razzing like a man. He'd do okay, you give him time. "Did you read the report?" Bert asked. "Sounded like things were dicey. Diz says five of 'em were on him, including that big punk Kujo, and out of nowhere comes that scrawny street kid Perry, mows 'em down, takes over the fight."

"Go figure, right? You never know who's who until it hits the fan. I'd a figured that kid for the cut-and-run type."

"I'll tell you this, Eddie, if they were givin' it to Diz, they were gettin' some back. That old man's got steel."

"Really? Seems like a nice little old man to me."

"Eddie, that 'nice little old man' was stompin' the jungle in 'Nam when he was nineteen. Never talks about it, but sometimes you can see it in his eyes. I wouldn't mess with 'im."

"Serious? At his age? Maybe when he was younger. Memories ain't exactly concealed weapons."

"Oh, zat right?" Bert gave him a scowl. "Where were you at nineteen? Probably wasn't even weaned yet."

"Screw you. Don't pull out that been-there-done-that bull with me. You never been in combat either."

"Come talk to me after you have fifteen years lockin' horns with hardened criminals. Tell me about it when they give you a first-year snot nose for a partner."

"Screw you," Eddie said. "You really stink for a partner, you know that?"

"Ha! Noted."

"Hey, look at that." Eddie pointed. "There's Giovanni, sweeping the sidewalk, same as always."

"Told you. Man's got steel. He filed that report, called out those thugs by name, went right back to sweepin' the sidewalk. Showin' them the finger. Not too many like him anymore."

"Hey, Diz!" Eddie shouted.

Bert didn't shout but he raised a hand.

Giovanni looked up and smiled. "Hello, friends. How are you today? Like a cup of coffee?" His cheerful demeanor didn't hide the dark subdural hematomas on his face, the bulging lump under his left eye, or the rigid, careful way he was moving the broom.

"We're glad to see you here," Eddie said. "You had us a little worried." He was young and idealistic, and he cared more than was good for him. Time in grade would probably take that outta him. Usually did.

"To be honest, I was a little worried too," Giovanni said. "Thank you for filing that report, getting people searching for me."

Bert nodded. "Something was up. You left a helluva mess behind, and that wasn't like you."

"I had help making that mess." Big smile, like they were talking about a bunch of beer cans or something.

"We figured that out. We found blood spatter here on the sidewalk, there on the curb, a smear of blood and hair, scrapings of epidermis mixed with blood. Over there, next to the wall, pooling blood."

"Also, boot prints with blood, headed off in that direction," Eddie added. "We preserved the scene, got the techs down here, had 'em collect samples of everything, took a ton of photos, sent a bunch of stuff off to the DNA lab."

Bert, serious now, said "Diz, when we get the results, we can crossmatch all that evidence, corroborate your testimony, and we'll have 'em by the short hairs."

"I think most of that DNA gonna belong to me and Perry. To get *their* DNA, you have to scrape my *face.*" Diz being funny. *His defense mechanism. Inside, he must be so steamed he could choke the life out of those punks. And he's probably scared.*

While Eddie was talking, Bert tried to imagine what that must feel like. Served time as a warrior, seen people killed—enemies and friends, probably had killed people. Then worked as a productive, law-abiding citizen for forty years, only to have punks bum-rush you and try to stomp you into the sidewalk.

"Bert," Giovanni said.

"Yeah, Diz?"

"Perry save me."

"Yeah, read that in the report. That surprises me. Kid seems shiftless."

"No, no, no. Perry is good boy. You see him in dumpsters, in parks, walking the sidewalks? You think he is up to no good. But that is *not* Perry. All day every day, he watches out for his old dad. Working hard, raising money, gathering food. He *never* thinks about Perry. Only about his old dad. Perry has taken care of his dad many years. He protects him. And now he came and protected *me.*"

Bert thought he heard a little choke in that last part. "You guys got to watch out for Perry," Giovanni went on. "Keep a sharp eye. Those thugs hate Perry with a powerful hate. Why? Because he is so *good.*" He was gritting his teeth now. "He is good, but they are evil. Please, you gotta keep an eye out for Perry!"

Poor Diz was about to break down. The situation was serious. Kids these days were mixed up in all kinds of criminal activity, and if pushed, they could turn lethal. They had to do something for Perry, and for Diz. The old man stood up to the bangers, and there was a price to be paid for that. *But not on my watch,* Bert thought.

"I hate like hell that this happened to you, Diz." His throat tightened up, and he gritted his teeth. "Of all the people I know..."

"Ah. Not a big deal." Diz wiped his sleeve across his face. "They just punks. I seen worse." He looked down the street, like it was a thousand miles long, then shook it off and smiled at him. "I got some of those Bavarian Crème pastries. Want one?"

Eddie chuckled. "Yeah, Bert. Want one?"

"Shut up, Eddie."

A flashy Buick with purple metallic paint rolled by slow, big over-sized wheels and tinted windows.

••••••••••

"Apparently," Pete said, "the… uh… protesters…"

"The protesters what?" Haruki interrupted.

"They intercepted a young girl and dissuaded her from going into the clinic."

Haruki's jaw muscles flexed. His look made Pete want to wilt. "That priest. I've lost patience with his interference. I'd like to rid the world of him and all of his kind."

Pete stood still.

"Did your guy get any useful photos?"

"There's one attractive woman. The priest seems to have a soft spot for her. He got a couple shots of them standing together, in conversation."

"That's it?" Haruki asked. "One of his parishioners is attractive?"

Pete shrugged.

Well, keep an eye on it. All we need is the *appearance* of impropriety."

"Yes, sir."

Haruki shook his head. "They had it right in the Roman era. They knew how to deal with the Christian rabble. I wish I could do that for this Bianchi character. I want his head on a pike." He turned back toward the window. Pete hesitated, searching for the right words.

"Won't that bring down all kinds of unwanted attention?"

Haruki faced him, and the look in his eyes was so angry, it made Pete's heart stutter. Haruki was used to getting what he wanted.

"You cannot touch him yourself," he said in an even voice. "Piking his skull is not an option, but maybe you can arrange to have him thrown to the lions."

Pete stood still and waited.

"Draw him out. Continue to put temptations in his path. Tempt him into sin, especially sins of the flesh. Document that, and his friends will destroy him for us."

Pete liked the idea, but… "But what if he *doesn't* take the bait?"

Haruki gave a mischievous smile. "Never be caught with a single plan. If you box him in with a beautiful female, he will almost certainly fall. For all his pious pretense, he's only human. Even if he rejects the bait, he is *still* doomed. Hell hath no fury like a woman scorned."

September 19

Kujo had seen the old cop around. Him and that baby po-po walked a beat over by old man Gillespie's stand. They were a pair, this one tall and lanky, the young guy short and stocky. Kujo yawned and stretched, showed the cop he was good and bored. Thursday afternoon. Maybe take a nice nap.

"Come on, Kujo," the old cop said, slouching back in his chair, actin' like he was riffin' with a buddy about a football game. Man, cops are all the same.

"We've got you cold, man. Only chance you got is to talk to us before one of your crew does. We've got them in separate rooms, sweating 'em out."

Kujo slouched back more, folded his arms across his chest, fists under his arms, showing off his tats, getting his biceps to pop. He gave the old cop the stink eye.

Cop leaned forward like he was gonna confide something top secret. "I've got to tell you, that young boy, the little cute one? He seems about to cry. He's gotta know prison is going to be rough for him. How long you think he can hold out before he gives you up?"

Kujo blinked slowly, let his eyes open only halfway. Playin' it cool, knowin' the cop had truth, but also knowin' he was full of spit, like all cops. Same lies, same angles. Divide and conquer. Dude in need of new material.

"I wanna report a crime."

"Yeah? What crime is that duckweed?"

"Assault. And I know the attacker. That mean old Italian, Gillespie."

Old cop turned sour. "That right?"

"Hell yah. He beat the spit out of me with a broom, tried to kill me. He'd a done it if my bros hadn't jumped in."

"Watch yourself, punk."

That hit the nerve. Kujo Kept pushin' buttons, see if he could get the old cop to do something stupid.

"How you think I got these bruises, huh? You didn't even ask me about that. You see this lump on my jaw? He almost knocked my teeth out, the big ones in the back. That old man's crazy."

"Okay, you want to play that way? Fine. Let's get your statement. We already read you your rights. You telling me that you're waiving your right to remain silent?" Cop took out his notepad like that was s'posed to be scary.

"Hell yah. That old man's gotta pay. Streets ain't safe with crazy old geezers runnin' around tryin' ta kill people."

"Okay, saggy britches. Give me the scoop. How did this assault happen?"

"I'm telling you straight, man. The five of us, out cruisin', lookin' for something to do. We see Mr. Gillespie and say hello, like we always do."

"Uh-huh."

"He offers us a cup of coffee. We say no thanks. I seen this four-wheeler magazine looked interesting, so I picked it up, see if I might want to buy it. Being distracted, talking with Mr. Gillespie, I accidentally dropped it. Be sure you get that. *Accidentally.*"

"Yeah."

"Yeah. Old Gillespie cops an attitude, like 'Hey, punk. You gonna have to pay for that.' I say, 'Mr. Gillespie, how'm I gonna pay for it? I'm gonna need cash for that.'"

Cop was *really* glaring.

"Next thing I know, he cracks the back of my hand with that broom stick. I'm like 'Hey, old man, you must be crazy, hittin' me with that stick.'"

"Zat right?" Cop was steamin'.

"It's right. I grab the stick, try to take it away from him, in *self defense.* That's when it happened. He got this crazy look on his face, like a stone-cold killer, I swear. I think he might've been having like a Vietnam flashback or somethin'."

"I don't believe you."

"I don't *care* if you believe me, man. I'm telling you, I tried to grab that broom *after* he already hit me with it. Be sure you get that part. *After.* And when I acted in my own *self-defense,* he pulled out some crazy ninja spit and starts pashing the tar out a me and my boys. I'm tellin' you, man. That old geezer is *dangerous*. You should have him behind bars, 'fore he hurts someone."

The old cop stood up, wiped his hands across the front of his shirt like to smooth out wrinkles. He walked slowly around the end of the table, come to stand right next to Kujo. One big fist on the table, the other hand clinched the back of Kujo's chair, leaned in with his coffee breath, close enough to bite. He prob'ly wouldn't risk a lawsuit. He did, Kujo would own 'im. He had to know it. It'd be worth takin' a beatin' to get this old hard-nose cop off the street.

"Now you listen to me, you little snit," the old cop said. "I know exactly what happened. We've got witnesses, DNA evidence, photos, all of it. No number of lies are gonna get your scrawny little backside off, you understand me?"

Kujo was a little scared, but not that bad. "You collected DNA at the scene, right?"

"Bet your butt we did."

"You find skin, hair, blood over on the curb?"

"Not sayin' we did, but so what?"

"So that DNA gonna come back and prove that it was *me* gettin' grounded and pounded on that curb. Look right here at the back of my head. That look like a match to you?"

The old cop seen it and looked sick. That bad scrape on the back of his head would fit the physical evidence. His story had just enough truth that it might fly. DA might flop, and this cop's whole thing fall apart.

Cop screwed up, hesitated a little too long. Tipped his hand. Kujo had 'im on the ropes. "Hey, man. Are you listening to me, Robocop? I wanna press charges. I want that old man brought in. And I want a *lawyer*."

"Now you're a victim, but you want a lawyer?"

"Yeah, man, 'cause I can tell I'm being railroaded. You tryin' to hang this on me, but I'm the *victim*. You a *dirty cop*, with your hands in the attacker's donut box. I seen you a hundred times, him bribing you with donuts and free coffee, knowin' someday he'd need you, and that day is here." Kujo stretched out and screamed right in his face, "I want a freakin' lawyer, and right *now*!"

Cop gritted his teeth. Had to pry his hand off the back of the chair. Kujo could tell he wanted to up-end it, dump Kujo on his head. But he wasn't gonna do it. The cop was at a disadvantage. He had to play by the rules.

Instead, cop stood up very slowly, both of 'em havin' a starin' contest. Cop's face twitched, made him blink a little. He walked slowly to the door, not making a sound. He opened the door, playin' it cool, stepped out, and slammed the door so hard it almost broke the glass.

Kujo flinched, then threw his head back and laughed loud. The old cop had to be able to hear him all the way down the hallway. "Bring him in, Robocop! You *know* you gotta do it! Go get the old man and bring his b'hind down here. *You hear me, Robocop*?"

September 20

"Are you freaking kidding me?" Bert said.

He couldn't believe what he was hearing. Three o'clock Friday afternoon, and his whole week was going to hell. The assistant DA was a beautiful young thing, slim and pretty. Eddie was about to slip a disc, he was puffing his chest out so hard. Thumbs in his gun belt, not able to breathe. *C'mon, Eddie. Focus.* She was easy to look at, could've been in television, but he would trade her, without hesitating, for a warty old troll who would prosecute violent criminals.

"You telling me that you're not going to prosecute these thugs? What's gotta happen before they become a big enough deal for you? You gonna wait till they kill somebody? They almost did the other day."

"Officer Strickland, I understand your frustration. I really do."

"Oh, you do? Do you walk these streets every day, watching this district go down the toilet, filling up with drugs, prostitutes, punk gangsters coming up out of the rough neighborhoods?" He glared at her, daring her to answer.

She didn't.

"Every time you let something like this pass, it makes them feel bullet-proof. You make me cut these thugs loose, it won't be long before someone gets killed, and that blood, missy, will be on your hands."

"Don't you point your finger at me, and *don't* talk to me in that condescending tone. Look what you've brought me: DNA and crime scene photos all proving that these punks got the fluff beat out of them by an old man and a scrawny homeless kid. How is a jury going to see them as a danger to society? You bring me five witnesses that all say the old man struck first, with a deadly weapon, threatened to blow their brains out, and actually discharged a firearm."

Bert gritted his teeth. There was a smudge on the toe of his right shoe.

"You're lucky I haven't been ordered to prosecute the old man. Felonious assault? Reckless endangerment? Discharging a firearm within city limits? Littering? *Those* charges I could make *stick.* Do your *job,* Officer Strickland, and give me something to work with. And don't *ever* come in here with that sanctimonious attitude again!"

Crud. Bert's eyebrows were blocking the top part of his view, but he could see her. She was impressive. One twenty soakin' wet and putting him in his place without a flinch. It was true. They had nothin'. Nothin' to charge the thugs with, and nothin' to protect Perry or Diz.

"I'm sorry, miss," Bert said. "I was outta line."

Her eyes burned hot holes in the back of his Kevlar vest as he opened the door, slipped out.

Eddie turned back, stuck his head in, said real sweet like, "You have a nice day."

Once he got out in the hall, Bert slapped the back of his head. "Shut the hell up, Eddie."

•••••••••••

"He's threatened to kill the girl's mother if she cooperates, and the mother is still living with him," the detective said. It was 5:15 pm, the DA's office was supposed to be closed by now.

"The girl is fifteen?" the assistant DA asked. Her brow was furrowed as her eyes moved back and forth across the page in the file folder.

"Yes, fifteen years old, six weeks pregnant."

"The paternity test is conclusive. No wiggle room there. I think you've got him."

"I hope so."

"Is the girl …" She flipped a page "Elza Beth, is she safe?"

"Yes, she's got a room at House for Life. She committed to their two-year program."

"Okay. This loser has two felony sexual assaults already, so if we put him away, he's gone for good. For the sake of this young girl and her mother, we've got to make sure every 'I' is properly dotted."

"Understood. This one is pretty cut and dried. She's underage, and he's the biological father. Even if we can't prove first degree rape, we've got him on statutory rape. And we've got the science to make this stick. Juries love DNA."

"The girl's testimony would be helpful."

"In open court? Can't you find a way to avoid that? No way we want to make this young woman look this guy in the face. That would be cruel and unusual."

"I agree. I'll see what we can negotiate with the judge. Given her age, and her vulnerable state, he might accept a deposition."

"A written deposition would be best," the detective said. "Relatively painless."

"Written would be most *comfortable*. Video would be best for nailing down a conviction."

"Maybe in a closed court? Protect her identity? This guy is a thug, and he's got to have some rotten friends who would do his dirty work for a couple rocks of crack."

"You're probably right about that. We'll do everything we can. We need to convince the judge to deny bond. Let this guy rot in a cell for a few weeks before we depose her. I want to give time for the baby to start showing. Get that on video."

"Remember, we're not protecting just the girl. The threats were against the mother's life."

"Right. Another reason to justify denial of bond. Is there any indication this guy's connected?"

"I don't think so. He's just a lowlife."

"Like I said, we'll do all we can. But the most important thing is to get this creep behind bars. I'll get you the paperwork. You go get the scumbag off the street."

••••••••••

"Pride, avarice, envy, wrath, gluttony, sloth, lust," Father John said. "The Church tells us that these are the seven deadly sins." He had hoped that opening would grab them, and it did. Every face was turned toward him, except for one young mother who was desperately wrangling a child, trying to get her to be quiet. These First Friday gatherings were becoming popular. An evening Mass and a devotion to the Sacred Heart of Jesus, followed by a simple meal. The sanctuary was almost full.

"So, what has this to do with us?" he asked, pausing for effect. "In a word… everything."

The sanctuary was quiet. He could hear the baby in the back sucking on a bottle.

"How many of you know your current weight, within a few pounds?"

Most people raised a hand.

"Okay, good. Put your hands down. Let's do another survey."

People looked intrigued.

"How many of you have a health club membership?" John raised his hand.

People looked around at each other, a few of them putting hands up.

"Good. Keep them up there. How many of you have a schedule of walking or other exercise you do for your health?"

More hands went up.

"How many of you count calories, or avoid specific kinds of food or drink for your health?"

Now at least three-quarters of the congregation had a hand in the air.

"How many of you intend to make lifestyle changes soon, or know that you should?"

The rest of the hands went up.

"Look around you. Virtually every person in this room has an awareness of specific things they need to do for their physical health." People were looking around, hands in the air. "If you can name the seven deadly sins from memory, keep your hands up."

Almost all the hands dropped.

John smiled and motioned for the few remaining hands to be lowered. "I think you see my point. We are keenly aware of our physical bodies, and we know what we need to do or not do to maintain our health. But we don't even know the *names* of the things that are deadly to our spiritual life."

Silence. The baby must have fallen asleep.

"Our souls are eternal. For better or for worse, we will live forever. Doesn't it make sense to spend time becoming familiar with what we need to do to stay healthy spiritually?"

Heads nodding. Good.

"Pride is the capital sin that undergirds all the others. Pride is when we try to play God in our own lives. We know what God wants. When we do what we want instead, that is sin. And no matter what sin we are committing, the sin of pride is present." John could tell they were thinking about what he was saying. They were a great community. He loved them, and he wanted to help them. "Listen, friends. I invite you to ask yourself honestly, which of these sins have wormed their way into your life. Spend time with that question, and you will find all seven have at least appeared as temptation, and some may be present in your daily thoughts and actions."

That produced furrowed brows. A few faces turned downward. He allowed quiet to fill the room.

In a loud voice, he counted them off on his fingers. "One, pride: trying to play God. Two, avarice: an inordinate desire for wealth or possessions. Three, envy: longing for what someone else has. Four, anger: embracing a feeling of hostility toward another. Five, gluttony: eating or drinking to excess. Six, sloth: laziness in matters of the spirit. Seven, lust: an inappropriate desire for sex, especially when it treats another human being as an object. There they are friends." He held up seven fingers. "The top contenders on evil's leader board."

He kept his hands up for a while, rotating a little so every person in the room had a chance to see and think about them. When the echoes of his voice had fallen away and the room was utterly silent, he lowered his voice and said, "There is a darkness in this world that invites you to embrace your destruction." He scanned the congregation, trying to touch eyes with every person.

"Please, please, do yourself a favor. I beg you, don't cooperate with evil. Seek out and *eradicate* these deadly sins in your life."

The whole congregation was looking at him gravely.

"I have good news for you," he said, smiling. "For every deadly sin, there is a lovely virtue that will banish it. I want you to know the names of the seven deadly sins, but don't fear them. Instead, cultivate the virtues that will flush them out of your life forever. You will find a list of the seven lovely virtues on the inside cover of this week's parish bulletin. Read them. Pray about them. Post them on the side of your computer monitor. Make a stand against the powers of evil. Be bold in your faith and be not afraid."

Father John paused a moment to let it sink in. "May God bless you, in the name of the Father, and of the Son, and of the Holy Spirit."

He returned to his chair, sat quietly for a couple minutes, and prayed. He prayed for his people. And he prayed for the strength to heed his own advice.

••••••••••

"I tol' you, we got to get strapped, and right now too." Kujo said. Clevon's little face was blank, eyes wide. "Li'l bruh, that's the last time that old man gonna get the jump on me like that. An' I tell you what else, that pussy Perry got to die for blindsiding me. And you gonna be the one gets ta pull the trigger. This a big opportunity for you."

Clevon gawked up at him, shaky but keepin' it together pretty good. "I ain't got no gun, Kujo."

"Don't worry about that. I'm a show you where you can *steal* one."

Now the kid looked like he was gonna puke. It was a big step. "Listen, little cuz. You the smallest. All you got to do is skinny through a window, open the door, and I'll come in and get you yor gun. Nothin' to it."

Watching those little feet wriggling through the window, Kujo was kinda nervous. Long as the little puke got the door open and didn't make no noise, it'd go fine. The old man had guns in the house, and he had soup supper at his church on Friday nights, according to what he was sayin' at the barber shop.

The boy hit the floor with a thud, friggin' clutz. A crash, like a big silver platter rolling around and around put his teeth on edge. Send a boy to do a man's job, this's what you get. Good thing the old geezer wasn't home. Kujo stood by the door, heard a click, and pushed against the door, knocking the kid out of the way.

"What the hell's the matter with you?" he hissed.

"I —"

Kujo put the palm of his hand over Clevon's face and shoved him aside.

The lights came on.

"What the hell?" Clevon didn't hit the wall, so how —

"Freeze."

The old man was behind him, starin' at him over the top of a pistol. He didn't shout it like they do on TV. He said it cool, with ice around the edges.

"Front sight."

"What?" Kujo said.

"Front sight. That's where I want you to look. Right here, on the end of my barrel."

Kujo looked. Jeez, that was a big barrel.

"See, my son's a Marine. He taught me to always say that. It helps me remember how to aim before I shoot someone. Front sight."

"Hey, man, hold on. There's a misunderstanding here."

"Front sight. Keep staring right here. Don't twitch. You either, little guy. No sudden moves. I might accidentally squeeze. Front sight."

"Spit! Stop sayin' that, all right? Nobody gotta get shot here. We'll just leave."

"Don't. Move. A muscle. You move, I'm gonna shoot you. Look at the size of that bore. That's the size hole this bullet's gonna make goin' in. This is a .357 Ruger Blackhawk. It's a magnum. That means it has a lot more powder behind it, but I bet you already know that. It will make a hole four times that big coming out. Unless it shatters a bone. Front sight."

Kujo was thirsty all of a sudden, and when he tried to swallow, the two sides of his throat stuck together. It made him cough. He started to raise his hands very slowly. Nobody tol' him to. But it seemed like a good thing ta do.

"My son is an expert marksman. He can put fifty rounds through a hole no bigger than a silver dollar. Front sight. It is impressive to see."

The hell this old geezer talkin' about?

"But I'm not nearly that good. For me, fifty rounds would be a lot bigger pattern, like maybe the size of your heart. Front sight."

"Spit, man. That's enough, a'right? What do you want? I already said we'd leave."

"Front sight."

"Stop sayin' that!" Kujo was startin' to lose it, right when he needed to be cool. Spit!

"Front sight. It don't work like that. See, this's my home. My castle. You broke in, violated my sacred space. If I let you go, you might decide to come back sometime when I'm not expecting it, like you did tonight, and I can't afford to let that happen. Front sight."

"Man, what do you want from me?"

"I want you to get down on your knees reeeal slow. Front sight."

Kujo needed to pee bad, but the guy wasn't gonna push pause to let him go.

"On your knees. Now. Front sight."

Kujo froze. It could be a bluff. He pulled his eyes away from the barrel. Hard to do, man, that big bore starin' at him. The old man's eyes were green and brown mixed. Did he really have it? Was he really stone cold as he was lettin' on? He looked like just a regular guy. Like old man Gillespie. These old guys, man, you never know. Sometimes they spend their whole life gettin' dumped on, by the time they get this old, they already taken all they gonna take.

"One time I worked with a guy," the old man said. "An ex-con, nice fella. He shot a guy with a .357 like this one, tried to kill him, but he didn't know how to aim. Front sight. He missed. All he did was blow the guy's arm off."

"Jesus."

"Are you prayin'? You *should* be prayin'. I don't want to think you're using my Savior's name in vain. Front sight. Not in my house, my sacred space. Front sight."

"Jees —"

"Aht. I told you about using that name in disrespect."

This man was crazy. *Scary* old cuss. Shoulda made the kid come in, get the guns hisself.

"Now, son. I asked you nicely. Get down on your knees. I'm not gonna ask again. Front sight."

If it was me, I'd a pulled the trigger by now, Kujo thought. He could feel the night air breezing in the open door behind him. Maybe this old geezer was fulla spit. Dive backwards, roll across the grass, be gone before the old man knew what happened. *Maybe.*

Clevon started to sniffle. *Are you kidding me?* Kujo turned, half a mind to back hand the snot out of him.

"Don't do that," the old man said. "Look right here. Front sight."

The big barrel, front sight steady and true, pointed right at his chest.

"I'm going to give you a three count. Front sight. If you are not on your face, with your hands behind your head, I'm going to shoot you. Front sight. You will die. Do you understand clearly what I am saying to you? Front sight. Nod if you understand."

Kujo was nodding. *Jesus, don't let this crazy old bastard kill me*, he prayed. Why you always need to pee at times like this?

"Front sight."

This was really happening. He was gonna die, or he was going to jail.

"One."

I'm going to jail for sure.

"Two."

Ah, hell no. No, I'm not.

"Three."

He shoved Clevon toward the old man, dove out the door. The cannon went off, the kid screamed, cannon went off again, a screeching sound ripped over his head. *Spit!* He was up and running, two doors down, ducked between houses, over a couple fences, gone. Kujo started laughing so hard, he didn't think he could stop. He kept running and laughing. Man, he needed to pee. He didn't stop. Didn't want to. Running meant he was alive. But he would have to stop soon. He needed to pee bad. He was kinda sorry Clevon didn't make it out.

··········

"He was always such a good boy, Father," Isabella said.

"Yes, he was. He was very good. We all loved him." Father John's plate of pasta alfredo was cooling. It would be inappropriate to take a bite right now.

Isabella pulled a hanky from her purse and blew her nose as daintily as she was able. "Father, why would God allow this to happen? Why didn't he cure my boy?"

An ache in his sternum. There were no words that would take away her pain. "A day will come when you are reunited with your son. Maybe then you will understand this. Until then, be patient, and know that God loves you."

"I'm struggling to keep from *hating* God. I worry that I may go to hell for that, and never see my son again."

He held her gaze. "Isabella, could you ever banish your son to hell?"

"No!" She looked up at him, shocked.

"God loves you more than you love your son. Can you imagine that?"

"No."

"And God understands your pain. He will not reject you. You *will* see your boy again. I know that is true."

She sighed. "It seems so unfair. How will his wife raise those little children? How will they make it in the world without their father?"

John's heart dropped an inch. "It does seem unfair. We cannot understand these things, but God has not abandoned your family. One day, you will understand these things and more. Hold onto your faith, Isabella. Talk to God, be honest with Him, even in your anger. He can handle it."

A young woman walked in, three toddlers trailing her. She had clearly tried to get herself together before coming here, but she looked beaten, exhausted.

"Oh, there she is, Father. I've got to go." Isabella got up and hurried to them without glancing back. She scooped up the youngest child and put an arm around the young woman. Three other ladies hurried over, hugged the young widow, and led the children by the hand to a table with open chairs. Father John was proud to see how his little flock was ministering to this hurting woman. The ladies hurried to bring plates of food, beverages, and desserts, hovering to make sure the bereft family had everything they needed. Tragedy brought out the best in them.

At the far end of the room, rectangular tables were piled with home-made breads, soups, and desserts provided by the parishioners. The large room was crowded with round tables, conversation circles, where members visited and shared their lives as they ate. He watched as members went to and from their chosen places, chatting with friends, thanking the volunteers who were serving. Teens moved about the room with pitchers, offering refills of tea, juice, or water. Others picked up unwanted plates or napkins and took them to the trash bin.

To his left, a young couple holding a tiny baby glowed with pride as gray- and silver-haired seniors stopped by to coo at the child and compliment them on her full head of beautiful copper-colored hair. To the right three women were talking, friends for decades, sharing their concern about an absent friend who was deteriorating with a terminal disease. In front of him, a table was filled with young adults laughing about their college days and discussing the ups and downs of trying to start their careers. At another table were retired men discussing lawn mowers, fishing trips, and grandchildren. A little farther away, an engaged couple was talking with a pair of newlyweds, discussing wedding plans, cake designs, and guest seating strategies. Off to the side was a round table, low to the floor with tiny chairs around it, where a group of children were busily working on masterpieces in the coloring books provided.

John smiled. He was tired. But he was also *happy.* A young teen fitted the opening of a balloon on a rubber stem at the top of a helium cylinder. The gas transformed a scrap of latex into something that made the eyes of children and seniors glow big and their mouths open in wonder. The child waiting clapped and jumped for joy. The young volunteer smiled and continued filling. The balloon grew larger and larger, stretching, expanding, to the point where John was afraid it would burst. Here, surrounded by his people, his heart felt like it would burst from joy and love. What a life this was. Exhausting. At times he simply could not continue. And then an experience like this one would fill him with gratitude.

Father, he prayed, *thank you for this. Thank you for my vocation, for this parish you've entrusted to me. I promise you, Lord, I will persevere. I will care for these people.*

"Father John, may I refill your juice drink for you?"

He turned. "Oh. Hi, Virginia. I thought the teens were supposed to be covering refills."

"They've been working so hard, I thought I'd give them a break. So?" She held up the pitcher with a cute little waitress pose. She was such a warm spirit. One of the really special people in the parish.

"Sure, why not. Thank you."

She poured blue liquid over ice, her eyes sparkling. She curtsied and walked away. She was something. Sweet, kind, clever. And cute. It was a mystery how she could still be single.

....

"Freeze!"

"What the hell?" Kujo turned to look over his shoulder, still peeing on the man's boat.

"Hands in the air! Now!"

Freaking cops. Always got to be screaming, barking orders.

"Hey, man I gotta put away my joint."

"You put your hands in the air or it ain't gonna matter."

He raised his hands. This trash starting to get old. Twice in one night? First the old geezer, now these cops. *People gonna havta quit pointin' guns at me, or someone's gonna get hurt.*

"Yes, sir, Officer." Kujo turned toward him, flexed his abs to push out another squirt. "You wanna come over here and tuck it in for me?"

"Put away your junk." The cop said, disgusted. "And then get your hands behind your back."

"What's the problem, Officer?" he asked, zipping up.

"You're vandalizing private property, that's what."

"You kiddin' me? That all?"

"That and public indecency."

"Man, that's dumb. That ain't no vandalism. That pee gonna dry before you can even get your cuffs out." Ah spit, he should'na said that. Now he *was* gettin' the cuffs out. Gonna show how important he was. Spit!

"Put your hands behind your back. You're under arrest for vandalism, public indecency, and anything else I can think of. Want to try for resisting arrest?" Daring him. Dumb freaking cops. Like anyone cares about being run in for taking a leak. Judge gonna bust his b'hind for wastin' the tax-payers' money.

"Man, you interrupted me mid-stream. I hope I don't have to take a leak in the back of your car."

"You do that, see what happens."

Kujo sat in the squad car, eyeing the old man staring out the window of the house. Kujo wanted to flip him off, but he was cuffed, so he stuck his tongue out and slid it across the window, giving the guy an evil stare, grinning, chomping his teeth at him.

"I be back!" he shouted against the window.

••••••••••

The coffee was bitter and cold. Eddie gulped it and made a nasty face. "There's something not right about that punk."

"Oh, you think so?" Bert being sarcastic as usual. "That will go down as one of your most piercing insights."

"Screw you, Bert."

"Crimenintly, Eddie, you must be a superhero. Under your uniform, I bet you're wearing red long johns with a big white 'O' stitched on the chest. Captain Obvious."

Eddie took another slug of the lousy coffee, chewing the grounds.

"Why do you always have to give me a hard time?"

"Why do you always beg for it?"

"Screw you."

"Captain Obvious. King of the snappy retort." Bert laughed.

Eddie grunted under his breath and pretended to be absorbed in the paperwork on his desk. "This thug gets picked up for strong-arm robbery and felonious assault, gets off without prosecution by a miracle, then gets scooped again the same day he's released 'cause some law-abiding citizen don't appreciate him taking a leak on his boat. Something's not right with him."

"You're not wrong, Eddie. The kid has problems. And there's more here than we can see. But we'll get him. All we need is one good break."

The squad room door opened, and Mazy walked in. She took two seconds to assess the whole room, made a beeline for them. She was the scariest woman Eddie had ever seen. Built more like a man than a woman, except in the chest. She walked like a linebacker cutting up field. Far as anyone knew, she didn't have emotions, or a sense of humor either. But she was a helluva cop.

"What're you two sissies doing sitting around in the squad room? Don't you know there's a crime wave out there?"

"Hey, Mazy," Bert said. "What's shakin'?"

A different woman, that might've gotten a chuckle out of the guys, but not with Mazy. They were all secretly afraid of being the one she finally beat the tar out of. It would ruin a guy's reputation. Well, except that the beat-down would come from Mazy. Nobody's gonna laugh at that.

"We scooped up a fifteen-year-old kid a little while ago. Citizen called in a 10-62 Code-1 B&E. We get there, this old man is literally sittin' on this kid, who's crying, the old man giving him the sermon of his life."

Eddie cracked up. "Man, I wish I coulda seen that."

"We get more into it," she said, "It wasn't a laughing matter. This boy got boosted through a window to open the door, and a big guy, complainant says six-four, comes in with intent of burglary. Boy says they were hunting for firearms."

Bert shook his head. "Used to be these kids were stealing bicycles."

"I know, right?" Mazy said.

"They find any firearms?" Eddie asked.

"Oh, yes." She gave a big smile. "Old man showed 'em his .357 mag, stuck it right in big man's face."

"Oh, man," Bert said. "Bet that got his attention."

"It did but get this: the big guy tosses the kid in front of the muzzle and escapes."

"Sounds like the boy might be hanging around with the wrong friends," Bert said.

"Where's the kid now?" Eddie asked.

"We got him downstairs in interrogation. He's got a welt looks like the complainant's hand on his cheek, and snot all over his face. That, and gunshot residue."

"GSR? On his *face*?" Eddie said.

"Yep. Old man pulled the trigger, trying to take out the big guy. Barely missed killing the kid. The round went into the wall above the door."

"Hoooo." Eddie shaking his head.

"Second round went out the front door, skipped off the lawn, and we haven't found where it ended up yet. I hope we don't get a report of a guy dead in his living room, shot through his recliner."

"The homeowner wasn't bluffing, huh?" Bert said.

"Well, he was, and he wasn't. He was pissed. But he didn't want to kill anyone. He talked to the big guy a long time before the shooting started. Goin' on and on about how his Marine Corps son taught him to shoot to kill. He was doing a lot of posturing, sounds like."

"He didn't learn *that* from the Marine. Those guys don't posture," Bert said.

"Complainant was trying to get control of the situation, but I think he was out of his league. He wanted big guy to kneel and submit, but big guy decides he'd rather sacrifice the kid. Real humanitarian."

"Any chance I can have a chat with young junior?" Bert asked.

"You can get in line. Captain says nobody talks to him till a social worker and a public defender are present. Till then, the boy's sitting in a room snotting on himself."

"I hope he's thinking about that sermon he was getting when you walked in," Eddie said.

"How about the complainant?" Bert asked.

"Oh, I'm sure *he'll* talk to you. He's livid. He'll tell his story to anyone who'll sit still for it."

Eddie nodded. "Text me the address, would you, Mazy?"

"That's *Miss* Mazy to you, young blood."

"Sorry."

"I'm giving you flack, Eddie. Lighten up. I'll text it to you in a second."

Bert was chuckling, enjoying this. What a Jerk.

"You have any idea who this big guy might be?" she asked.

"I have a hunch it's the same Neanderthal we've been tracking."

"Kujo."

"Yes, indeedy," Bert said.

"That's why I stopped in. It sounds right. This guy was real cool under pressure. Wasn't his first time starin' at a muzzle. And he didn't give a pig's *slop* about the kid he brought with him."

"That's Kujo, all right," Bert said.

Eddie snorted. "I bet we see a different side of him if we get the kid to turn state's evidence."

"Don't hold your breath. That kid is scared out of his skin." Mazy said.

"And for good reason," Bert said. "Turning states evidence against Kujo would be a life-altering decision."

"Life or death," Eddie agreed.

Bert shook his head. "These poor kids join the gang to get protection and end up a target. What a mess."

"Bert, you know anything about Kujo's whereabouts?" Mazy asked.

"Yeah. Downstairs in holding."

"Really?"

Bert grinned. "Yep. Citizen dropped a dime on him for taking a leak on his boat."

"What a loser," shaking her head.

"We figure that should hold him for about ten seconds," Eddie said.

"We need to get over there and talk to that complainant that took a shot at him, see if he'll come pick Kujo out of a lineup," Mazy said. "He does, we've got him."

Bert nodded. "We'll get him. It's only a matter of time. I just hope we can get him off the streets before people start dying."

··········

The smell of smoke and wet charcoal was everywhere. The house was lighting blue, red, blue. White strobes flicking, smoke and steam rising from black siding. One whole side of the house was burned, shrubs turned to little collections of naked black sticks. Bert stepped over the thick hose, sloshing through the puddles, feeling the sod give beneath him.

"Hey, Chief," he said to the firefighter. "What's it look like?"

"What do *you* think it looks like?" He gestured toward the charred siding. "Unless this house spontaneously combusted, someone tried to burn the old man out. See the eaves? Another ten minutes, the roof would have caught and the whole structure would have been compromised."

"Arson."

"Sure looks like it. We'll wait for the official ruling from the investigators, but there wasn't any lightning tonight, and siding doesn't light itself."

"Thanks, Chief."

"I hope you catch the skunk, Bert."

On the far side of the street, past the fire vehicles, a squad car was lit up, sitting quietly, two men standing by the front grille. A uniform and a civilian. Probably the homeowner.

Bert started sloshing toward them. "Evening."

"Good evening, Bert," the uniform said.

"I'm Officer Strickland. Are you the homeowner?"

The old guy nodded, stoic, but shaken.

"Any idea who did this?"

The old guy shook his head.

"You had a complaint here earlier tonight, didn't you?"

The old man stared at him.

"You had a B&E, right?"

The old guy looked at the other uniform.

"Breaking and entering," Bert explained.

The old guy looked down and away.

"We think we might have gotten lucky and picked up your burglar on an unrelated charge. We'd like for you to come down and see if you can identify him."

The old guy looked at his feet, shifted his weight left and right, shaking his head. "Probably no good. It was a confusing situation. I don't think I could identify him."

"From ten feet away?"

"It happened fast. The lighting wasn't the best. I was kind of in shock, probably. I don't think I'll be able to remember anything."

"In your initial report, you said you turned on the light."

"Maybe. I… can't say."

"You can't say?" Dammit. Bert could feel everything slipping.

"Look," the old man said, "I don't want any trouble. I'm just trying to live my life here."

"You don't want any trouble?" Bert pointed a thumb over his shoulder. "Looks like you got trouble whether you want it or not."

"Maybe."

The old guy wouldn't make eye contact, focusing everywhere else. "Look, I understand. This is intimidating stuff. But you can't play nice with these people. Why did you invite them into your home in the first place?"

The old man's eyes flashed. "I didn't invite them. They broke in through a window!"

"Exactly. See what I'm getting at? For whatever reason, these thugs have targeted you. You are in this soup whether you want to be or not. The only question is, do you want to be in it alone or would you like help from us?"

The old man's eyes were a pale blue, steady, something in there that hadn't been said yet. "Sometimes it's better not to poke the tiger, even if he's in a cage," he said.

"I understand. But let me tell you something about this particular tiger. He likes *older* people. People past retirement age, or anyone who's defenseless. You're not his first victim. And you won't be his last. So, ask yourself, who do you know who is your age that is better prepared to deal with this thug than you are? Maybe a little old granny who lives by herself?"

"Look, I didn't ask for any of this."

"And neither will the next victim, or the one after that. Someone is going to die. Do you want that on your conscience?"

The old man glared at him. "You really going to make me the bad guy in this?"

"No, not the bad guy. The coward that let the bad guy get away."

The old man grit his teeth. "I'm not a coward. I have a sick wife upstairs, confined to bed. I almost" His voice broke. Bert shouldn't have gone at him so hard. "I almost lost her tonight. In *a fire.* How could I ever live with that? I don't have the luxury of being the city's superhero."

Bert had a sinking feeling; He might have underestimated that punk. If Kujo could organize this fire while he was still locked up, what could they expect when he got sprung?

He could see the future. Blue lights and yellow tape. A scene of violence. Death.

SEPTEMBER 21

Bert hated to start this conversation.

"Good morning, officers. Would you like a cup?" Giovanni asked.

"No thanks, Diz. This isn't a social call, old friend. We've got important business to discuss."

"Oh? What has happened?"

"Nothing. But we're having a problem with those punks who attacked you. Turns out that leader, Kujo, is a little smarter than he looks. He outmaneuvered us with the DA."

"He did what? How he —"

"He waived his right to remain silent. Spewed like a broken fire hydrant, all lies."

Diz looked at him, questions in his eyes.

"It wasn't a surprise that he lied. But we underestimated his lying skills a little. He knows how to put in enough truth to make his story sound solid. So, I need to ask you a few questions."

"You asking *me* questions?"

"That punk's pulling some antics to make our lives difficult. Listen. Officially, we should invite you down to the station to take your statement, but we'd rather do it here, if that's okay."

"Sure, Bert. That is okay. I tell you anything you want."

"Good. Eddie, get your notepad out. This is an interview with Mr. Giovanni Gillespie, owner of Gillespie Periodicals. And Eddie?"

"Yeah?"

"Anywhere I say Diz, you write down Mr. Gillespie. In case I forget. Got it?"

"Yep. Got it, Bert."

"Okay. Mr. Gillespie, last Monday you filed a police report about an altercation that occurred at your newsstand. You stated that a gang of five young men attacked you. Is that correct?"

"Yes. They came from Chinatown, hunting for trouble."

"Explain what you mean, they were hunting for trouble."

"They always hunting for trouble. Usually, I give them free coffee and they go away. That day, it was different. They no gonna go away. They want money. They demand cash, like I told the other officers. I say no, I not gonna give you no cash. Coffee only."

"What were their words exactly, when they demanded cash?"

"Kujo say, 'We gonna need some cash.'"

Eddie looked up with a raised eyebrow. Bert frowned. "What happened before he said that?"

"Before that, he take a magazine, throw it in the gutter. He grab another one, throw *it* in the gutter. That's twelve bucks my money in the gutter. I offer them coffee like always, but he say, 'No. Where you keep the money? We gonna need some cash.'"

"Ok, Di — Mr. Gillespie. What happened next?"

"He grab another magazine. I am sweeping the sidewalk, like always. When he grab a magazine third time, I laid the broom stick on top of his hand, told him no."

"See, Diz, that's a problem. You can't touch someone with a dangerous object. That's called battery. He said you hit him with the stick."

"Yes, I did. I cracked him good. But that was after. I told the other officers this already. The DA no believe Giovanni?"

"Mr. Gillespie, please go back to the part where you laid the stick on the back of his hand. Are you sure you did not hit him?"

"It was no battery. I was protecting my merchandise, my business. But the boy got really mad."

"Eddie, strike that. Don't write down 'boy.' He is twenty-two years of age. Legally, that is a man."

"Got it."

"Now, Diz — Mr. Gillespie, after he got really mad, what happened?"

“He said he gonna kill me. I believe him. He had that look in his eye. I seen it before, you know? He try to take the stick from me, to hit me with it.”

“Hold on. Eddie, make sure you get that. He was genuinely afraid for his life. Okay, go on, Diz. What did you do then?”

“I gave him the stick. Pushed him off balance and cracked him a good one. After that, I don’t remember details. It happens very fast. They were all on me. Kujo said 'Old man, you gonna die for a few bucks cash.' If Perry had no come along, I would be dead.”

“And where is Perry now? We need to talk to him. The punks have five who say you initiated the assault, and they were acting in self-defense, trying to save Kujo.”

“I have Perry in a hotel to keep him safe and give him time to heal up. He was beaten bad.”

“They say you threatened to kill them. Say you pointed a loaded handgun at them. Is that true?”

“Yes, that is very true. I did. They were all on Perry, trying to kill him. I gave them three counts before I start shooting. It was no bluff. That is the only reason they left. I did it so I could take care of Perry. He was hurt bad. I had no time to mess with those punks.”

“Okay. There’s another problem, Diz. Those punks were arraigned this morning. The judge imposed a stiff bail for Kujo’s release, but if I had to guess, I’d say someone will put up that money. We have reason to believe somebody with resources is protecting him. He’s going to be set free. You’re going to be in danger. You might consider closing the shop for a couple days.”

“No! I will no close up shop. I been running this shop every day for forty years. Those punks are no going to be the end to Gillespie Periodicals. No. I no close, no way.”

“Those punks are trouble,” Bert said. “I mean real serious trouble, Diz. They’re gonna want to make an example out of you.”

“If they do, I’ll —”

No! Absolutely do *not* tell me what you’re going to do. That would indicate premeditation, understand? You must choose your words carefully. And watch your back. And be prepared. Stay prepared. For anything. Understand?”

“I understand.”

"We're going to do what we can to keep an eye out for those punks. But we can't keep Kujo in jail, and we don't know who else might be involved. There's no way to know what they'll do when he gets out, but you should assume they'll be coming for you and for Perry."

....

Jack Thompson — street name J.T., — woke up at his ol' lady's house in Roxbury feeling like he'd swallowed a pee-stained carpet. His head was splitting open on the top, and the daylight was so bright, it practically seared his eyeballs right out of his skull. He squeezed his eyes shut, rolled off the bed, and groped his way along the walls. Two door frames would get him to the kitchen. His hands led the way along the vinyl countertop, found the sink, turned on the faucet, and scooped a hand full of water. He swished it in his mouth, spit it out, wiped some on his eyes, trying to get them unstuck. Still too damn bright in here. He made his way to the fridge, groped around on top, but didn't find what he was looking for. He opened his eyes, desperate measures. The top of the fridge was all cleaned off.

"Oh, hell," he growled. "Where did that damn woman put my bottle?" He started a frantic search. Under the sink, in the drawers, knocking stuff over, to see the back of the shelves in the pantry. Nothin'. *Damn* it.

"She must be trying to kill me. She's gonna regret that when she gets home from work." He punched the fridge, left deep knuckle dents in the soft metal skin. He slapped a chair over on its back, swept his arm across the table, cleared off the butter dish and the little flower vase, enjoyed seeing them shatter. Served her right. Nothin' he could do but go get another bottle.

He went back into the bedroom, started digging through her drawers. Rosary beads, prayer book, couple old photos, one of her and the kid's old man. He spit on that one and stomped it on the floor. He stood there hurting, trying not to lose it. There had to be some cash in here somewhere.

He looked at the closet, started ripping the clothes off the hangers, checking all the pockets, checking shoes, throwin' each empty shoe at a picture on one of the walls. Her old hag of a ma, her dead dad, her piece-of-trash sister. Elza's fat baby pictures.

Finally, he hit the jackpot. In a plain-lookin' pair of shoes, stuffed into the toe, a roll of bills. He kissed it and shoved it into his pocket. He found a shirt crumpled beside the bed, slipped his big feet into his shoes and went to the front door.

Damn. Cold this morning. He went back in and grabbed a coat, headed for the liquor store. He stuffed his hands in his pockets.

A few steps down the sidewalk, a guy comes up and gets in his face.

"Jack Thompson?" Ah crap. Had to be 5-0. J.T. adjusted his hand in his pocket. "Says who?"

"Jack Thompson, you're under arrest for —"

He swung his knife at the cop's face, missed, did a backhand slash at his throat. Cop was fast. J.T. turned to run, but someone took his legs out. He hit his cheek on the sidewalk, the lights flashed. A heavy knee-drop in his back took his breath out, and the cuffs cut into his wrist.

"Jack Thompson, you are under arrest for sexual misconduct with a minor and conspiracy to commit murder."

"Ow! easy, man."

"We're gonna add to that assault with a deadly weapon and resisting arrest. Your lucky day today. You have the right to remain silent. You have the right to an attorney."

J.T. couldn't believe he was hearing this garbage again. That little brat, *Elza.*

"You boys go ahead and have your fun," J.T. growled. "No way you're ever gonna be able to prove anything."

··········

Deputy Carter stood in the waiting area of Boston Police District A-1 beneath a sign that said *Post Bail Here*. A young clerk sat on the other side of a thick Plexiglass window, chit-chatting with him while working at a computer screen. It was boring duty, but she was a cute young thing and helped the time pass with pleasant conversation.

A prostitute came in. She looked like one, anyway. They were coming and going from here more and more often, usually escorted by deputies or officers. This one came in alone. She had a lean body, a hefty rack half hidden by a hot-pink top that was not much more than an elastic band, and a stole of purple fur over her shoulders. Her blond hair was teased up into a high pile on her head with a purple skunk stripe. She had an anorexic waist and had stuffed her round hips inside a blue super-mini skirt that barely covered her bizness. Her tight-fitting pink stockings disappeared down into six-inch red heels.

The way she entered, she knew her way around. Her perfume was so heavy you could smell it ten feet away. She came up to the window like she owned the place, smacking loud on chewing gum. “You people got Kujo locked up in here?” without even glancing at Carter.

The clerk looked her over. Carter hated to see that the prostitute was not much older than a girl. Her face betrayed a lot of wear and tear.

“We have a Kojo Robinson,” the clerk said, staring at the screen.

“Yeah, that’s him.” She blew a bubble and popped it loudly.

“Charged with breaking and entering and destruction of private property. His bail is set at five thousand dollars.”

“That right?” she asked, a smart, sarcastic tone. “Well, sweetie, that’s how much I happen to have right here.” She pulled an envelope from somewhere under the fur stole and tossed it into the tray at the bottom of the Plexiglass. Her eyes met Deputy Carter, said “screw you.”

He gave her a bored look and watched the clerk open the envelope.

“Five thousand cash?” she asked.

“Good for you, sweetie. You can count.”

“Settle down, little sister,” Carter said.

The clerk pulled up the appropriate screen on her computer. “Who should I say is posting bail?”

“Santa Claus. No, the tooth fairy. How ’bout that?”

“I’m sorry, miss. I need a name.”

“Yeah? Okay, say Jones. Mrs. Jones.”

“And your relation to the suspect?”

“Put down no.”

The clerk stared at her.

She glared back. “We finished, baby 5-0?”

Carter wanted to snap cuffs on her and put her in the back with the others.

“He’ll be processed out shortly.”

“You gonna give me a receipt, sweetie pie?”

The clerk slid a receipt through the window.

The young girl walked out, throwing her hips side to side like someone would wave their middle finger.

Carter went to the glass door. She walked down the steps with that same sassy attitude. A long black Lincoln Town Car with tinted windows was idling at the curb. The window opened a crack, but she blocked his view, leaning toward it. After a couple seconds, she stood up and headed down the sidewalk, stuffing something into her halter. The Town Car sped off. He couldn't see the plate number.

··········

Perry was going crazy. He barely had enough room to pace.

"Don't go out for anything, Perry. Those thugs will be hunting for you." That's what Geppetto had said.

He was right. They would *definitely* be hunting for him. And Geppetto didn't even know about the purple giant. But none of that was going to change. And that wasn't the worst thing. Dad was alone. How long had it been? He hadn't seen him the morning of the big rumble, and they had been hiding here for four or five days, maybe more. Seven days? Dad had disappeared before — on a binge, sleeping it off somewhere — but he was never this long on his own. He couldn't take care of himself. There was a trench in the carpet the shape of an "L," worn by his restless feet. Left to right in front of the big window, turn, walk past the end of the beds to the door, turn around, do it again. Boring. The perfume was stinking after almost a week, no air. Unbelievable. He was homesick for the dumpster. No sounds in here. Like being underwater or something. Unable to breathe, held down to the bottom by an invisible chain.

One thing was sure. Sooner or later, if Dad was still alive, he would stagger back to the dumpster. He had always done it, and prob'ly always would. The giant with the purple car didn't know where they stay. Unless Kujo told him. The Heynas knew. They had to be really pissed. The giant wouldn't know who Dad was if he saw him. But Kujo would. They would wait, and watch. If Kujo couldn't get Perry, he would go after the old man. Perry had responsibilities. Couldn't hide here safe while Dad was out there unprotected on the streets. Geppetto said the Hyenas was in jail, but soon as they got out, they would come. They find the old man asleep by the dumpster, no tellin' what they might do. He kept walkin' the L, thinkin'. Geppetto was doing everything he could, but nothing was changing the truth. There was another fight comin', this one for keeps. This was life or death, them or us. He had to find a way to win. Without him, Dad would be completely alone in this world.

"Screw them." That was it. His decision was made. He grabbed some motel paper out of the drawer, one of the pens with it. In big letters, clear as he could, he wrote:

THANKS FOR EVERTHING, G. GONE TO FIND DAD – Perry

Hiding time was over. Dad was in a war when he was this same age. Now it was Perry's turn. He put the motel key with the note, walked out of the room, and closed the door.

....

"I know this seems like a long walk," Perry muttered to himself, "but this ain't that much farther than you walk every day, making your rounds."

It sure seems a lot farther, he thought.

"It only seems farther cause you're all busted up. Quit bein' a sissy and keep walkin'." He was lookin' over his shoulder about every ten seconds. He was way far away from where he had the run-in with the giant, but cars can cover a large area. he didn't need the guy to accidently catch him out in the open like this. *It ain't just the battle damage, it's also 'cause I'm worried sick about Dad. For all I know, he might be dead already.*

"It don't do nobody no good to be thinkin' stuff like that. Shut up and keep walkin'." He was carrying the weight of the whole world on his shoulders with every step. Geppetto had picked that hotel 'cause it was far outside the Hyenas' range. That was good thinkin', but it wasn't outside the range of the purple Buick. And today that distance was a problem. The afternoon was gonna be over before long, and Perry had to get to the dumpster, in case Dad came home. He had a bad feeling in his stomach, like it might already be too late. He had some cash, but not enough for a cab ride this far.

Perry was better off now than right after the rumble, but his ribs were still jacked, and his face had turned weird purple and blue colors. A lot of the swelling had gone down, but out here in the autumn nip, he was still a long way from being right. He had aches where he didn't even remember getting no injuries. As he struggled along, he held his thumb out. It was a long shot. Not too many people willing to pick up hikers these days, crime was so bad. But Perry had to cover a lot of ground in a short amount of time, so it was worth a try.

Cars zoomed by, one after another. His heart started pumpin' when he heard one slowing down, almost matching his speed. He turned to see the purple car, but it was a cream-colored luxury model, with three ladies inside. They was all looking him over careful. The car pulled over ahead and stopped, started to drive off, then stopped again, like they couldn't make up their minds. Perry couldn't hurry if he wanted to, so he kept steppin', doing the best he could. When he got beside the car, the two windows on his side rolled down.

"Young man are you okay?" the woman in the back seat asked.

Perry didn't feel like talkin' to no one, but he needed a ride. "Yes, ma'am. I'm trying to get to Chinatown. Any chance you can give me a lift?"

The one in the driver seat was shakin' her head and givin' the evil eye to the one talking to Perry. As he got closer to the car, the woman in the back kind of gasped.

"My Lord, what happened to you?" The women were dressed fancy, like they had been to a nice restaurant or a party or something. Even with his new clothes, Perry knew he looked terrible but couldn't do nothin' about it. He stood there.

"Are you the victim of a crime?" the woman sittin' beside the driver asked.

"I was tryin' to help somebody and caught the worst of it."

The one in the back seat got tears in her eyes. "You poor thing. How can we help you?"

"We can't help him!" the one in the driver seat blurted. She started to roll the vehicle. Perry took a step back.

"Lina!" the woman in the back shouted. "You can't leave him here. *Look* at him." The one on the front passenger side seemed like she was gonna cry too.

"Young man," the driver said through tight lips, "I'm sorry. I really am. But you understand we cannot pick up a strange man, especially one who has clearly been involved with violence."

"Lina!" The woman in the front passenger seat sounded like she was scolding a kid. She started digging in her purse, which got Perry's attention. She pulled out... Oh. A Kleenex. He was thinking she might give him cab fare. When she blew her nose, it was clear they was wastin' his time.

"Listen," he said. "I appreciate you stopping. But you cryin' over me ain't gonna help." He didn't know why, but it kinda irritated him. He started to walk, and the car moved ahead a little, stayin' with him. He stopped again. "I know you feel sorry for me. That's 'cause you think I'm different than you. You think this can't happen to you. But you ain't no safer than I am.

Nobody in this messed-up world is safe. You wanna cry over someone, cry over your own selves. You gotta live here, raise your kids here. Cry about that. The way things been goin', my troubles gonna be over soon enough."

••••••••••

"I give you extra twenty dollars if you get me through this traffic," Giovanni said. Without a word, the cabbie punched it. As soon as he found out those gangsters were out of jail, Giovanni stowed his rolling stand, locked the storefront, and hailed a cab. The cabbie had been crawling along, while Giovanni's mind raced. How was he going to keep Perry safe, with the Hyenas back out on the street? He had to warn him. Now the cabbie was swerving between cars and trucks. It was frightening, holding tight to keep from sliding side to side, but Giovanni had to get to Perry before the Hyenas did, or the boy would be dead for sure.

••••••••••

Perry waited until the foreman locked the chain on the big construction gate. He was across the street chillin', a normal kid wastin' time. Foreman didn't even notice. Couple minutes later, Perry checked up and down the street, crossed to the other side, grabbed the links with his fingers. As soon as he pulled, his ribs kicked the air out of him. He let go, bent over double, waited until he could breathe. Not a good day for fence climbing. He had to get in though. And he had to get in *now*. Dark was comin', and there wasn't no time to waste. He walked along the fence, looking for a weakness. Near the corner was a place where it looked like a truck had backed into the fence. The pole was bent, straightened kinda, and the fence wired back together. He looked both ways, untwisted the wire, loosened the chain link enough that he could squeeze through.

Once inside, he saw a stack of cinder blocks. That would work. Too heavy, though. Couldn't lug those all the way back to Chinatown. A stack of two-by-four lumber under a plastic sheet. Same thing. They would work, but no way to carry 'em. Hmmm. A bunch of wood concrete forms stacked up. Could build a good little shelter out of those, but no time for that. There. A bundle of rebar hooks, each as big around as his pointing finger, long as his forearm, bent over close to the end to form a four-inch spike.

He found one that would slide out of the bundle and inspected it closely. Both ends had been chomped off by a big pinching machine, leaving two razor-sharp ridges. He turned it around to hold the long straight end, waved it to see how it felt in his hand. A little heavy but... nasty. Exactly what he needed.

He raised the hook up and smashed it down on a bag of powdered concrete. It buried the four-inch spike of the hook all the way in. *Yeh! That'll work.* He quickly pulled three more out of the bundle and slid 'em up inside the sleeve of his jacket. He heard something and crouched down.

··········

Giovanni could feel the presence of the large Chinatown Gateway looming to his left, as he stood on the sidewalk outside the narrow end of Perry's alley. He put his back to the cold brick wall. Up and down the street as far as he could see, it was clear. The last thing he needed was to get caught in this dank alley with a pack of those Hyenas. Not too many people walking the street. He could probably get in and check on Perry without any trouble. Unless the Hyenas were already in there waiting.

Giovanni put his hand in the pocket of his jacket. His training kicked in, the snub nose grip becoming part of his hand, index finger straight along the barrel above the trigger guard. The hefty little piece was a comfort. If the Hyenas came here, to Perry's alley, they'd be out for blood. He was not gonna play with those punks this time. He drew a deep breath and exhaled. A car rumbled down the street, slow. A big flashy Buick with glittery purple paint. It had tinted windows, so he couldn't see who was inside, but he had seen that car before, somewhere. It wasn't the Hyenas, because none of them even had a car. He stood casual, waited for the car to rumble on down the block, and turn right.

One last glance up and down the street, he slipped the snub nose out, held it against his chest, pointed to his left. He rolled over his left shoulder, the pistol still against his chest, but pointing into the alley. A quick peek around the corner, and then back. Didn't see any movement. He glanced up and down the street again, another peek into the alley, a little longer this time. No movement. It sounded empty. He stepped around the corner into the dim interior, both hands on the pistol now, in front of him in the low ready position. His hair was standing on end. A familiar rush.

Adrenaline. Shaking with every step, he moved into the narrow passage, raised both hands in front of him, the pistol leading.

He called in a harsh whisper, “Perry?”

Nothing.

He approached the shelter. The canopy had collapsed on one side. Perry had not been here, and most likely neither had his dad. Giovanni lifted the flap and peered inside to be sure. Nothing. Footsteps behind him. His heart flip-flopped as he spun. Two figures coming toward him from the large opening of the alley. He stood, bringing the gun up.

“Diz? Is that you?”

Giovanni exhaled a big rush of air. “Bert? You trying to give me a heart attack?” He slipped the pistol into his pocket.

“Sorry. You asked us to keep an eye out. We were on our rounds; thought we’d swing by. What’re you doing?”

“Perry is missing. I can no find him anywhere.”

“Oh, hell,” Bert said. “Kujo made bail three hours ago.”

··········

Perry heard the pipes first. The sight of the purple glitter stopped his heart. The giant, slow rolling his crew car along beside the construction fence, for sure looking for Perry. There was the low rumble of the pipes, and a thumping noise from the music inside the trunk. How had they found him? His body was coiled to take off running, but he fought the urge. He held still behind the concrete bags. This was crazy. If they made a movie out of his life, nobody would believe it. Some poor homeless dude being chased by a pack of wild hyenas and a big purple giant. He wished he was watching it on the big screen at the theater, instead of being trapped here in the middle of it. He hardly breathed until he heard the thumping music fade away down the street.

Quick as he could, he limped across the site to the foreman’s stand. A rough plywood table with a tilted top for layin’ out blueprints. Underneath, a little shelf for holding the prints, a tape measure, a couple markers, a ruler, and... jackpot. A roll of duct tape. He stuffed that into his jacket and headed for the messed-up corner of the fence. Two seconds he was back outside. Ten more, he was ducked into an alley and began a zig-zag path home, moving fast as his jacked-up ribs would let him. His mind was racing. He was weak and trembly inside.

"God," he whispered, "I know in all these years I ain't talked to you much. An' I know I was prob'ly wrong to try to do things my own way. But – please don't let the Hyenas come tonight. Please don't make me go through this. And keep that damn giant away from me." He didn't expect much to come from that. But one thing was for sure. If Dad came home tonight, he wasn't gonna be alone. *Yeah, Dad, I gotchew.*

"God," he said under his breath, taking another run at it. "I know you could keep this from happening, and I wish you would." Each step was painful, the dread building in his gut. "If there ain't no way for me to get outta this, at least help me get through it. Please let me be one of yours. *Please.* I ain't got nowhere else to turn."

··········

Perry was going over and over it, trying to figure out how he got in this mess. He wasn't never looking for trouble. He was always doing the best he could. It ain't like he wasn't trying to live right. But everything had fell apart completely. All he ever wanted was to take care of Dad, and God never lifted a pinky finger to help him with that. For all he knew, Dad was already dead. Alone for seven days? Nobody to protect him? A lot of bad things can happen on the streets in seven days. The old man couldn't protect himself, that was for sure. He had to get to the shelter, and soon. He wanted to stick to the alleys, but it was taking too much time. He decided he would have to risk taking a more direct route. Perry peered both ways at the end of the alley, and turned the corner, sticking to the inside of the sidewalk, close to the building.

He was so focused on his thoughts, he missed the familiar thumping rhythm, until he saw the purple streak go past and screech to a stop. Perry froze in his tracks. The back door opened, and the giant popped out, bringing his ball bat with him. Perry couldn't move. He was stuck to the concrete. The giant was only a few steps away, started to raise the club, when a loud metallic "Blat! Blat!" noise made Perry jump. A black car screeched brakes, front tires sliding, hitting the curb behind the Buick. The giant jumped sideways, like he thought they were coming up over the curb. In front of the Buick, a white SUV, blue stripe down the side and light bar on top screeched nose to curb, pinning it in. The giant looked behind him at the Boston city police cruiser, beside him at the black unmarked car, then at Perry, trying to figure out what was going on.

“Drop the weapon!” The gun was already out of the holster, a tough lookin’ guy in street clothes leveling it at the giant. Two uniforms jumped out of the white SUV, pointing handguns at the windshield of the Buick, shouting “Out of the car!”

Perry was still frozen. He couldn’t believe what was happening. He heard the wood bat hit the sidewalk and roll, saw the giant raising his long arms about ten feet in the air.

“On your knees!” a second plain clothes guy coming around the door of the black unmarked. Three guys were sliding out of the Buick, hands raised, looking back and forth between each other, the cops and their guns, the back of the giant. Nobody knew what to do, but the cops. They were pretty clearly working a plan. Perry didn’t dare move, with all those guns pointing around and all the shouting going on. In a couple seconds, the whole crew was in cuffs, mean looking guys with tats and piercings, stripped of their weapons, not saying nothin’. Leaning against the side of the Buick, at gunpoint, they all stared at Perry. The giant was kneeling on the sidewalk, a street clothes cop pointing a gun at him from a couple feet away. His eyes were as mean as any Perry ever seen. The other guy in street clothes came over to Perry, holstered his weapon in his armpit. Perry was hoping none of the stolen rebar pieces would slide out of his jacket.

“Where did you get those bruises? Did these guys assault you?”

“No... No sir.” He said it loud, so everyone could hear.

“If you want to press charges, nothing will make me happier than filling out the paperwork.”

The giant was glaring at him with death in his eyes.

“No, sir. I don’t know who that is.” Perry made sure even the furthest dude could hear him.

“It really looked like he was getting ready to assault you with a deadly weapon.”

“Nah, I don’t think so... I never seen him before.” Nearly shouting it.

“You sure? He can’t hurt you now.”

“I’m telling you man, I don’t know him. I couldn’t tell you his name if I tried!”

Cop looked disappointed.

“Hey, Adams, check this out.” One of the uniforms over by the Buick, the trunk lid open. “We hit the jackpot, boys.” With a blue doctor’s glove on, he held up an assault rifle, showed it to the other cops, then puts it back, pulled out a shotgun with a short barrel. "We must have fifty weapons in here."

"See?" The cop talking to Perry again, like they were friends. "We've got these guys on illegal trafficking of firearms. They aren't going to be able to hurt you. If you testify against them, we can make sure they go away for a long time, and nobody will get hurt. We have an opportunity here, you understand me?"

"Mister, I tol' you already, I don't know those guys. They ain't nobody to me."

The cop stared at him, a long, disappointed look. "Okay."

"Can I go? I gotta be somewhere."

"We need you to make a statement."

"I can't make no *statement,* man; I don't know what's going on. I was walking along minding my own business, cops started falling out of the sky. That's all I saw."

The cop breathed a big sigh. "Alright." He hesitated a second, wanting to negotiate some more. But then he said, "You can go."

"Thanks." Perry squeezed his arm tight against his side to keep the rebar from clanking, made a wide path around the giant, could feel him glaring, but didn't look over. He didn't look at the crew either. All he wanted to do was put distance between himself and that mess, as fast as he could. Now it seemed like his body was loosening up. He was able to walk a lot faster than he could before.

••••••••••

Giovanni reached into his pocket and found his key ring. The first day he held those keys he had been so proud. He was young then, full of bright dreams, his fresh, lovely bride holding his arm. The neighborhood was just as bright and full of promise as the young couple. The solid click of the knob, and the heavy cluck of the deadbolt unlocking were so familiar. Her face beaming up at him as he carried her over the threshold in his arms. A slow-motion movie, a soft and muted glow, captured forever. Their dreams had not lasted too long. They only lived together ten years before his sweetheart got sick and left him for better shores. Coming home had not been the same since.

Not long after that, drug kings took over and the neighborhood went down the toilet. But Giovanni was still here. Same routine every day, coming home to an empty house, thirty years. Inside the narrow foyer, he slid the bolt back into place, hung his coat on a wooden peg, and gently placed his keys into a porcelain bowl. Tuscany. A little shop in Florence. That was where she found that little bowl. The excitement in her young pretty face, holding it to show him. He smiled, his fingers lingering on the glaze, beginning to show faint lines but still smooth. He stepped out of one shoe, then the other, and slid them under the half-round table against the wall. The house used to be full of life.

He paused to look at a photo of a furry face, touch the small wooden frame, the name *Dandy* burned in one night ten years ago. Wood smoke curling up to his nose, the sound of a tear sizzling when it hit his old wood burner, blurry eyes making it hard to see. The "Y" was a little crooked. Good old Dandy. Immortalized in the photo, that smiling face, tongue half out, sparkling eyes. So happy to see him come in the door. His tail, sweeping the floor so fast, quivering with excitement, hardly able to wait until Giovanni got his shoes off, his warm furry back so grateful for a little pat. Dandy bounding with excitement, leading the way to the kitchen, stopping to look back, his eyes saying "Hurry!" At the counter, Giovanni shook a box and brought out a treat shaped like a little bone.

He shook his head. With his hand on the refrigerator door, he peered in, eyes roving over neatly stacked leftovers from several dinners. He sighed. Maybe later. He closed the door and went to his old chair in the living room. It was a good chair, real leather, an investment made decades ago, now soft with the wear of time.

"Buy quality, and it will last," Marissa had insisted, not allowing him to choose the lesser, more affordable version. He settled in. It was a great chair. The greatest. Hers, soft fabric with a straight back, wings at the top, silent beside him. It was turned slightly toward him so the wings could not hide her pretty face. She sat smiling, humming quietly, working on a beautiful needlepoint scene from the Tuscany region of Italy. A beach on the island of Elba, where they spent their honeymoon. Up on the wall across from him, above the piano that used to sing such beautiful melodies when she touched it, Tuscany was more beautiful than when she first finished it. When the thread was new and the colors more vibrant. The piano had been silent a long time. Giovanni sighed.

He closed his eyes. She was like a child, dragging him along, unable to contain herself. Her awe at the famous pieces of art, the ancient architecture, and her reverence in the holy places. She was young then, exuding life, beyond beautiful, a miracle of God's creation, never seen before and sure to never be duplicated, if the Lord waits a million years to come back. She was the one and only. He placed his hands across his chest, holding the memories, and allowed himself to fall into it deeper, the realities of today dropping away, drifting into a blissful world he knew was only a dream.

··········

Perry didn't think the Hyenas would be coming tonight. He *knew*. And when they did, they'd mean bizness. No smart remarks, no struttin'. This was gonna be a night for pain and blood. His stomach turned. *Where in hell is Dad?* He was pretty sure he was gonna vomit. Perry closed his eyes, breathed deep. He shuddered.

"God, if there ain't no way to keep them Hyenas away from here, please, please don't let Dad come home tonight." If Dad showed up here, he'd prob'ly be dead by morning. This slop was going down, and there was no getting out of it. Got to get *through* it. He had never been so alone. Or so afraid. He had nowhere to run or hide. He had to make his stand. They wouldn't be expectin' that. The element of surprise was the only element he had. He was gonna make it count. He untied the plastic canopy and folded it back outta the way.

He pulled the new hoodie Mr. G had bought him over his head and hung it on the dumpster. These were the nicest clothes he ever owned. A brand-new white hoodie, a nice heavy one with purple at the cuffs and pull strings. He looked down at his brand-new denims, his new shirt, and the first pair of new shoes he ever had. It didn't seem right, having these fancy clothes here in this filthy alley. *Ah well, nothing to do about it.* He started wrapping the long part of the rebar with duct tape, got it on there good and tight. He pulled up his shirt sleeve and laid the cold bar along the back of his forearm and hand. A few inches of the long part sticking out past his fist, the hook, pointing down over the ends of his fingers. Perfect size. Starting at the elbow, he fastened wraps of tape around his bare forearm and the rebar every couple inches. At his hand, he wrapped several wraps around between his thumb and pointer, like a boxer taping his hands, making the nasty hook a part of him. He made a fist. The tape gave him somethin' to grip, but still allowed him to use his fingers if he wanted to. He was shaking but not from the cold. He grabbed another hook in his hand, held it up, and admired it. He was a weapon now. He taped another hook on his other arm. He started to think he might have a chance to survive. He couldn't whoop 'em, but he might be able to scare the hell out of 'em, get 'em to leave.

The only way to do that would be to take out Kujo. Whoop the big dog, the little puppies might run off peeing themselves. He pulled his shirt sleeves down, hid the rebar, all except the hooks. With a broken bottle, he started cutting the green wool blanket in half. He wrapped his forearms with the thick wool and covered them solid with duct tape. He slipped the hoodie back on. The sleeves were snug, barely fitting over the wool blanket and rebar. Pretty good armor. If Kujo pulled his knife, at least Perry would have a fightin' chance.

He dug in the dumpster, found a half dozen bottles, went to the entry of the alley, started busting them on the ground, kicking the chunks of glass around to cover as much alley as possible. He scattered a bunch of empty cans. If he was gonna survive this, he had to know they was coming before they got here. Walking back to his spot by the dumpster, he realized he shoulda got a helmet. Where could he get one? Steal it off a parked motorcycle? If he had thought of that while he was out. No time now. The darkness was here, and he didn't want to get caught out in the open. He had to fight outta his corner. Nothin' harder to fight than a cornered animal.

He imagined himself as a tiger, shoved into a corner, huge claws lashing out, teeth bared. *Let 'em come. Let's get this over with.* He positioned himself in the shadow of the green dumpster, steel protecting him on one side, solid brick wall on the other. *No way out. Got to go through.* He kept talking himself up. Gettin' ready. His heart was pounding. Sweat was pouring off his forehead. He put his head behind the dumpster and puked so hard his ribs about collapsed. The pain left him breathless.

"God, if you're listenin', I'm begging you, man, please keep them Hyenas outta this alley. I know you can if you want to." Wasn't no way to talk God into nothin', so he added, "But that's up to you."

Getting ready, on top of all that walking, and the puking, was exhausting. He had did all he could. He laid the two extra rebar hooks beside his legs and settled in to wait. Had to rest a little and catch his breath. Had to build up his strength for the fight. The broken glass was glinting on the asphalt. It was the best early warning system he could think of. He had to be quiet. Had to surprise them. He closed his eyes.

••••••••••

Pop-pop-pop. Pop-pop-pop-pop. Automatic weapons, somewhere close.

Diz was sweating, flinching from the sound of gunfire. Then silence. Face pressed hard into the wet grass, the heat and humidity pressing down on him. He hissed his buddy's name,

"Delmond!" Heard it echo off the walls of the empty room and woke up, breath quickened, heart pounding. It was dark. The Tuscany artwork was barely visible through the gloom. Giovanni blinked. *What is happening?*

Pop-pop-pop.

He spun his head toward the door. This… not Vietnam. And not a dream. He froze for a moment, wondering if it was safe to move. He slipped his hand under the shelf on the coffee table and found the .45 cal Colt 1911 semi-auto, heavy and cold. He jacked a round into the chamber and laid it across his chest, his trigger finger straight along the barrel. After a second, he got up, crouching low, started moving quietly, using the two chairs for cover. He listened.

Sounded like people shouting, maybe a block away, outside. Down the short hallway to the living room, moving with purpose, doing the combat glide, knees slightly bent, pistol up, double hand grip, peering across the front site as he moved. He was surprised how unsteady he was. His body used to be a machine. His old legs not in shape for this anymore. He approached the living room from the left, used the barrel to move the curtain an inch, peered out. The street empty. He listened again. Silence, then a car roaring toward him, a police squad car flew past, passing from right to left, lights flashing, no siren. Far away, he heard a siren begin to wail. Quiet at first but getting louder. Soon, lights from the ambulance, engine roaring, same direction as the squad car.

Through the peep hole, the world looked warped, the handrail on the darkened stoop wrapped around a tiny center. Nobody out there. He unlocked the door with a solid clunk. The pistol was heavy against his leg. His other hand on the doorknob, he shook his head. His neighborhood turning into a jungle. His heart was thumping. He cracked the door. The shadows beside his front stoop, left and right, both empty. *Where is the shooter?* He would be running and hiding, evading the police. Or, he might have been driving by.

At the end of the next block, the ambulance, two cop cars parked haphazardly, strobing colors lighting up the street and the windows, where other neighbors were peering out. Seeing their world turning blue, white, blue. He shook his head again and went back inside. Locking the bolt and the knob, he carried the pistol back and put it under the same shelf, close at hand, always ready. He sat down. His little house. He was glad Marissa was not here to see what their beloved Roxbury had become. His guts turned to a knot. His little business, his street-side newsstand. Perry was out there somewhere, beat up, alone, defenseless, those thugs hunting him.

He pulled Perry's note out of his shirt pocket. The big letters again filled him with dread. His plan was to pick up Perry at the dumpster and bring him here until they could figure out what to do about the Hyenas. But he could not *find* Perry. He had to honor Perry's heroism, his own promise of what he would do if the Hyenas came back. The world was getting darker and darker, his life path returning to where it had begun, in jungle warfare. He didn't want it then, and he didn't want it now. *But what you gonna do?*

More cars roaring past, the colored lights flashing off the dark walls of his empty home. Giovanni gritted his teeth. He could not let Perry go through this night alone. But it wasn't safe for an old man to go out after dark. He grabbed the pistol from under the table, stood, tucked it in his belt, headed for the foyer. Putting on his jacket and his shoes, he worked on a plan. If he could make it to the Metro terminal, jump the Orange Line, he could probably make it through Chinatown to Perry's secret spot. Sleep by the dumpster all night if he had to. Be there if Perry came back, no matter what. Them Hyenas show up, looking for war, give them what they wanted. Outside, the air was cool on his face. He was walking as fast as his old legs would take him. Already his breath getting short. Fear stabbed into him. He was not sure if he could make it back in time. He could not walk fast like he used to. A dull pain radiated from his chest down into his arm.

··········

Dad was walking on tiptoe, careful moving a dry leaf so it didn't make sound. Rigid, like a hunting tiger, he slipped his foot down and turned and motioned for Perry to do the same. Perry tried moving a twig, snapped it, clumsy, sounded loud as a cannon. Dad was disappointed. He shook his head, pointed at Perry's feet, and placed his finger across his lips.

"Shhh."

Perry tried again with a leaf this time and did better. Dad smiled broadly and gave him an up thumb. They both carried make-believe rifles, hunting their way across the big backyard. Mom stepped out onto the deck.

"Perr-rry!"

Dad gave the *shh* signal again. Perry froze, not even peeking her way.

"Where's Perry? Perrr-rry! I can't see you anywhere! I can't hear you either!"

Dad and Perry exchanging mischievous smiles. Dad winks.

"Perrr-rrry."

"Perrr-rrry."

Something not right. Her voice now sounding harsh, raspy, like when she was sick.

"Perrr-rry." Her pretty face turned into the face of a snarling hyena. "*Perry*!"

A hard slap on his face. His eyes flew open wide, a bright light shining, Kujo's menacing grin bent close over him.

"Where's yor old bodyguard, Perry? Not here tonight?"

Perry's heart froze. He blinked, looking past Kujo. Four other silhouettes, standing tall against the distant streetlight. Bats. *They have ball bats.*

Blam! Perry struck hard and fast with a balled-up fist, forgetting the rebar hook that stuck out in front. The hook crushed into Kujo's face, standing him up and sending him reeling backward. Perry was a tiger, quick to his feet, lunging forward, punching and raking with the rebar hooks, fighting for his life. Kujo was screaming, stumbling backward, trying to cover, but he had no way to fend off a tiger.

Crack! Something loud across the back of Perry's head. The alley turned end over end, he spun to find who was on him, Kilo swinging a ball bat from high above. Perry rolled and heard the bat hit the asphalt so hard it made Kilo grunt. He swung the rebar hook and ripped at the back of Kilo's ankle. Kilo screamed in pain. Perry yanked, dug the hook in deep, and Kilo went down hard on his back, his head a loud crack against the asphalt. Another bat, this time crushing Perry's busted ribs. Perry heard a terrible sound. A wounded animal. A dog hit by a car. The sound gave him chills. It took a second to realize that he was the one who was making the horrible sound.

"Oh, God!" He tried to get up, but lightning struck the side of his face. A bright flash and a hard crack sent him flying backward. He lashed out at the darkness, swishing empty air.

"Steal his fancy shoes!" one of them shouted.

He didn't want them to take his new kicks. He tried his best to fight back, but his busted ribs, and there was three of them. Two of them grabbed the rebar hooks and yanked his arms out straight. Laying flat on his back, no way he could overpower both, his insides on fire from the busted ribs. He could barely breath. That punk Clevon started untying his shoes. Perry kicked, slid one across his face. Clevon grunted and laid over sideways. The two pinned his arms down by steppin' on the rebar hooks. "Get 'em, Clev!" one of them shouted.

Perry threw another kick at Clevon, barely missed. The Hyena on the left stabbed the end of his ball bat hard into the palm of Perry's hand. He screamed as bones snapped against the cold rebar. The other one thought it was funny, so he slammed his bat down into the other hand. Perry didn't care about the shoes no more. He quit fighting. But they was having fun, so they kept driving the ball bats into his hands again and again. Perry could hear the terrible screaming, but it was like someone else was doing it.

God wasn't coming. This wasn't going to be over till it was all the *way* over. It hurt so bad. The pain of the beat-down, but knowing God wasn't gonna do nothing to stop it hurt even worse. Perry was alone, completely abandoned. He gathered all his strength and shouted up at the black sky, "Oh, God! Why ain't you been helping me?"

"Nobody's gonna help you, P-turd. It's just you and us," the one on the right said.

"Where'd you get them fancy new clothes, pussy-boy?" the one on the left asked.

Perry couldn't even speak. He wanted to leave, be somewhere else.

"So now you better than everybody else in them fancy clothes, zat right?" the one on the left snarled.

Perry looked down at his new hoodie. It was half red now, spattered and stained with a bunch of blood, his and Kujo's.

"Strip him!" Kilo's voice, growling somewhere close. He was still down, sounded like. "Strip him naked!"

Perry wanted to fight but couldn't. They was jostling him around, yanking his hoodie, then his shirt off his busted ribs, over his mangled hands, his pants over his bare feet. Finally, they tore off his underwear, cackling like wild hyenas. Clevon wrapped his pant legs around his ankles, holding his feet together, so he couldn't kick no more. Then he picked up his bat and swung it like a golf club, crunching the bones on top of Perry's bare feet. He lay there completely naked in front of them under the huge black sky. The cold steel of the rebar throbbed against the back of his hands. All he could hear was a high-pitched ring and his killers laughing so hard. Kilo was there beside him, on hands and knees, holding a shining knife blade up to his face.

"You think you gonna cut me and get away with it?" His face was filled with pain and anger. Perry felt the knife stab deep into his side. He gasped for air, his mouth gaping open. Kilo pulled the knife out, and Perry felt warm blood gushing over his bare skin. Kilo side rolled away from him, and went back to groaning.

In the black sky was all the pain and sadness of his whole life, all the times people laughed at him and looked down on him, and he was never as rotten and ashamed as in this minute. He wanted it to be over. He couldn't keep from crying. "God," he cried, "please come get me."

One of the laughing boys said, "Listen to him! Fool thinks he's talking to God!"

"I'll show you God," another one said.

Perry's head got struck by lightning again. It was over, finally. He was glad. It got darker, and quieter.

Dark.

Silent.

Still.

··········

Perry was staring down, seeing the alley below. A mess. Kujo against the far wall, crying, cursing, twisting and rolling on the ground. Kilo rocking back and forth, holding his ankle, trying to stop the bleeding. Three other Hyenas in a circle, kicking and stomping what looked like a big white bag of trash. Kicking and kicking and swinging the bats. They were laughing hard, slipping in pools of dark blood and broken glass.

Perry climbed higher, up out of the alley. It didn't matter. It had nothin' to do with him. He turned away. *Ooh, look.* A soft glow rising above the tall buildings. He wanted to see. He rose higher, over the tallest buildings, till he could see it clearly. Prob'ly the most beautiful moon ever was rising full out of the harbor. The water shimmered, a slight breeze brushin' his face. Man, refreshing.

A soft light soaked a sleeping city. He was fresh and happy. *Everything* was beautiful. He wanted to get closer. He started moving toward the glowing silver disc, gliding weightless, floating on top of the beauty. Or in it, sliding along above the sparkling water. Ahead, feathery clouds were on the horizon. Cotton candy, drifting silent across the face of the moon. Perry was drifting too. Silent, smooth, no hurry. But he did want to see where he was going.

....

Mr. Ming, owner of Mings' Wings, Chinatown, ran respectable American business. He was talking to customer, nice American man, come in almost every night. They talk about how much he and Mama Ming work very hard, together put daughter in university, Texas AM, far away, and she not very good at writing letter or calling. He wonder did they do right thing, sending her away? Maybe better she stay here, cook wings, go to school nights. Many good schools in this city. Why Texas? She want engineer degree. Mama Ming, say she apply the institute, good chance she get in. She have good grade, very smart, they like Asian girls, the institute. She say, "No, No, No. Texas."

"Why Texas?" the customer asked.

"I don't know." Ming almost always thinking of his daughter, Ju Min, as he worked. He picked up two large bags of garbage, pushed the back door open with his foot, and heard shouting and laughter. He drop bags. Many people fighting in alley. Three on ground, three standing. They standing over someone, kicking, not with skill, kicking like thugs, ball bats too, someone getting bad beating, very bad.

The three attackers did not see him coming. He took three running steps, leapt into air, and planted a steel-legged sidekick on the center one, between big one's shoulder blades. Big one flew forward like missile, over the body on the ground, landing face first on the pavement, leaving opening between the other two. They turn toward each other, Ming cracked them both with hard backfists. They no kicking no more. They both stumbling back, cursing. He stand over the one on the ground, see if any of them come back. Only one did.

A ball bat in one hand, he swing like American baseball sucker going after high ball, head level with much force, not accurate. Ming turned, grabbed the arm above the wrist, twisted his hips, shoved a stiff arm in attacker's chest, easy and relaxed. The attacker's weight and momentum carried him away in a wide arc. Attacker flew six, eight feet, crashed hard on the asphalt, and skid more. The fall was executed poor. Ming had the ball bat in his hand, handle up, big club pointing down, beside his leg. He turned and looked at the other attacker, who changed his mind, dropped his bat, and ran out of the alley. Nobody coming. Fight over.

One very bloody boy slumped against the brick on right side of alley, moaning. One lying on back, cussing in English, bleeding bad near ankle, one on left side of alley, trying to get up after the hard fall but collapse back down. The other one, curled up in fetus position, completely naked, half covered in blood, lying near Ming's feet. The one they were kicking, not moving at all.

Ming squatted down and turned him a little to see his face. "Perry!" It was the poor boy who live by the dumpster, the boy always take care of his father. Oh, this terrible. "Perry!"

Perry flopped like wet dish towel. Mr. Ming hugged him around the shoulders, pulled him up against his chest, shouted in Mandarin, "Mama Ming! Call 911! They've killed the boy who lives in the alley!"

••••••••••

Perry let the warm mist engulf him. Steam was all around. The mirrors would be starting to fog. He sat inside the mist—the warm, moist cloud. It was like bein' on another planet. Maybe another *universe.* The steam grew thicker and warmer. Wet, warm air in his lungs, drops began to gather on his face, damp his clothes. He didn't think. He sat in the white cloud and let his vision blur. *There isn't no tile no more.* Cloud above, cloud below, even cloud inside, lungs full of it. *I don't want it to never end,* he thought. *This place—this cloud—it'd be nice to stay here. Warm, safe, no danger, no fear, no hunger, no nothing. Just the cloud.* He tried to remember if he had been here before. Like maybe a long, long time ago? Or was that in a dream?

It was too familiar to be his first time. It was like he belonged. Scenes of his childhood passed through the cloud—gray, grainy images, moving pictures, old silent films. Little short videos of another time, weaving in and out, like gray horses walking in fog. The cloud swirled and rolled, stirred by the passing images. Mom, Dad, the beach, catching a little fish, sitting in a blanket tent, running with a kite. Each image appeared and disappeared—once gone, forgotten—the next taking its place, and then only the wispy cloud again. Through the mist, he saw a bright light, far off. The shape of a woman moving toward him, a halo around her flowing dress. The light so bright behind her it was making her hard to see. She called to him, her voice like music.

"Mama?"

He had missed her so much. The light was bright, she was smiling, young, beautiful. He narrowed his eyes. It was either Mama or someone who was a lot like her. She was close now, her face surrounded by a bright glow. Over her shoulder the sun was makin' it so bright, Perry squinted his eyes almost shut. He couldn't see her face, and he wanted to see her so bad. Her soft voice said,

"You must find the path, Perry."

"Can you stay with me, Mama?"

"No, love. I must go."

"Please don't go. I love you, Mommy."

Her smile was as bright as the glow. "I will always love you, Perry."

"Mama, I want to go with you!"

"Where I am going, you cannot go. I'm sorry it is so difficult, love. I will pray for you. Now, and in your defining hour. Find your path, Perry. It is important."

The glow got brighter and brighter till it washed over her, and he closed his eyes. The glow slowly faded, and when he opened his eyes, He could see a vast landscape of clouds, some of them low, around his feet, but in the distance, large ones, rising like mountains. It was beautiful. *Heaven.* He turned to look behind him, and nearly jumped out of his skin. The dumpster. The green dumpster, and his shelter tied to it. It was here. He couldn't believe it. He had a sick feeling. *Why in the hell is the dumpster here?* He turned again and looked around at the cloudscape. *This don't make no sense.* The fear was back. The terrible, paralyzing fear of seeing the hyenas in the dark alley with the ball bats.

Most of his life had been spent not understanding stuff. He hated that feeling, but this was the worst feeling ever. It wasn't like not understanding math, or big words. This was like not understanding anything at all. *I died, right? I floated away. The scene in the alley was ugly, and I was floating above it. I left that grungy alley and the stink behind. I'm supposed to be free now, ain't I?*

One time when he was sleeping in the alley, laying on his side, something was crawling up his back, inside his shirt. He didn't know what it was, but he could feel tiny little legs touchin' against his skin. Little light soft legs. Maybe a giant roach. Or maybe a big spider. It took everything he had not to jump and scream, but he was afraid if he did, whatever was crawling on him, would bite him with some kinda poison. This was like that. The terrible thing crawling up his spine was an idea. More like two ideas, crawling across his skin side by side. One was the idea that he had died, which was for sure, and the second was the idea that he wasn't in heaven. The dumpster proved it. *There ain't no dumpsters in heaven. There's supposed to be mansions.* But all he got was the same old stinking dumpster. *You kiddin' me?* He heard a man's deep voice, soft but strong next to his ear.

"Perry."

Through the mist, a figure far off, coming toward him. The cloud was glowing bright around the figure. Even from here, Perry could see that it was a tall man, stooped shoulders, sleeves rolled up at the elbows. A familiar form. He was still far off, but the gravelly half - whisper right next to his ear gave him chills.

"Perry, where are you?"

"I'm here."

"Where is here, little brother?"

"Henry?"

"Perry. Where is here?"

"I'm in the cloud."

"Good. Good man. You are safe here, Perry. Can you feel that you are safe?"

"Henry, is that you?"

Now his face was close, smiling. The bright white fog around them was close too. Henry's dark complexion, his white teeth and white kinky hair, his grizzled beard, the torn pocket on his dark green work shirt.

"Henry, its been so long. Has it? Or—" Henry smiled wide at him, nodding.

"It's okay, little brother. Time is different here. Long time ago, tomorrow, right now, are all the same."

Perry looked more closely, feeling suspicious, confused.

"You ain't Henry. You just *Like* Henry." The old man smiled a warm smile.

"I suppose I am."

"But you don't *talk* like him."

"Would you be more comfortable if I did?"

Perry paused for a second.

"Or maybe you'd like me to talk like your friend Geppetto?"

"Naw, that'd be creepy." The old man tilted his head back and laughed hearty.

"I wouldn't want to be *that.*"

Perry looked at him, the bright white mist of the cloud moving between them in swirls. His old eyes were twinkling.

"Can I help you with something, little brother?"

So mixed up. Everything jumbled. Memories, dreams, thoughts, all flowing together.

"I was looking for… something."

"What was it, Perry? What were you looking for?"

"I… I don't remember… I'll think of it."

"Was it important?"

"Yes. *Really* important, I think."

"It will come back to you. Important things always do."

Perry scowled. "Why do you look like Henry?"

"Maybe you have it backwards. Maybe Henry looks like me."

"Huh."

"Who do you think I *should* look like?"

"I don't know. I just wondered why."

"Wondering is good. It opens the mind. Keep wondering, little brother."

Perry liked this old man. Seemed like a good dude, like old Henry from the shelter, but different. Happier. His ragged old suit pants, ripped knees with his dark skin showing through. Everything around him was all soft, and misty, with a glow to it.

"Perry, I wanted to thank you for helping me out with my shoes." He picked his foot up out of the cloud, to show his old dirty sneaker, nice cardboard and duct tape toe added to it, and a duct tape strap across where the laces were supposed to be.

"Yeah, no problem. Turns out I didn't need that cardboard no more anyway." Perry looked at Henry carefully. The old man was really happy, relaxed as could be. He was glad that Henry wasn't sad no more. Which was another thing that didn't make sense. If it was Henry, that would mean Henry was dead. Did Henry even *know* he was dead? He didn't act like it. But Perry didn't think it was really him.

"Where's your sleeping bag?"

"I don't need it here. The weather in this place always feels just right."

"Okay. What do I call you?"

"Hmm." The old man cradled his chin between his thumb and his index finger. He smiled.

"I like Henry. You can call me Henry."

"Okay, Henry. Whatever you want."

"You want me to call you Pinocchio?" He was grinning, eyes full of mischief.

"Why would you do that?" Perry asked.

"Because of your friend at the news stand. Giovanni. That thing you do — Geppetto, Pinocchio — is funny. Creative. I like that. It makes me smile."

Perry looked into his brown eyes, clearer now than before. Trying to figure this thing out. He seemed alright. But strange too. He was just hanging out, smiling at him.

"I like it when people smile." Perry said.

"So do I," old Henry fixing the roll on one of his dirty sleeves.

"There used to be a lot of smiles." Perry sighed. "Not so much no more."

"Ah. I understand, little brother. How does that make you feel that the smiles have gone?"

"Angry, I guess. Cheated maybe."

"Yes, that is true. You are a good man, Perry, and honest. It makes me proud of you."

"Nobody is proud of me."

"That is incorrect. Giovanni is proud of you."

"Even my *dad* is ashamed of me."

"Do you really think so?"

"Yes."

"Is he? Why do you say that?"

"I see it in his eyes. When I look at him, he is ashamed."

"Ah. I think that you are correct. But is he ashamed of *you*? Are you sure that is what you are seeing?"

Perry peered into the cloud beneath his feet. Wisps so soft that even a breath made it flow and roll.

"Maybe not. Might be somethin' else."

"Like what? Why do you think he is ashamed?"

Perry tried to sort through the confused images and emotions. White and gray images, vague, fading in and out. Another little movie started, down by his feet. This movie had sound. Dad was drunk, as usual. A 12-year-old Perry was sitting on the wet asphalt, his back to the dumpster.

"I'm just sayin', Dad, maybe you should ask for help."

"Shuddup! Don' thew look ad me when I'm thalking thoo you!"

Perry remembered the smell.

He kicked Perry with a drunken foot, barely able to keep his balance. It didn't hurt. Not his body, anyway.

"Dad, I just want to know, what are we *doing*? How are we going to fix all this? I think we should go talk to someone at the mission and get you some help."

"No! No help! Thath the rule! What I thay goth, and I thay no!" Dad got a strange, disconnected look on his face. "Ath long ath you're living in my houth..."

Sitting by the dumpster, looking up, Perry saw tears come to the old man's eyes. The corners of his mouth flinched, kinda jerked down. He wiped his old Army jacket across his eyes and staggered off.

Perry looked up at Henry, water in his own eyes blurring the cloud.

"He's ashamed for me to *see* him?"

"Yes, Perry. He is not ashamed *of* you. He is ashamed in *front* of you."

Perry was so *tired*. He closed his eyes to think about that, falling into the cloud, moving toward a deep sleep. The brightness began to fade. His eyes flickered open for a second, the cloud rolled and swirled. Old Henry was gone.

SEPTEMBER 23

Perry woke up. Everything hurt. A pebble under his left shoulder blade was the worst. He rolled onto his side, away from the pebble. A bird was chirping somewhere far away, echoing into the alley. *What day is it? Sometime last half of September, right? Is this trash day? Trash day is awful. If you don't take down the shelter, old man Ming will come out and chew you out, throw all yer stuff away, make you start all over.*

Starting over...

That thought was strange for some reason. He opened his eyes. Under the dumpster, two beady rat eyes were staring back at him. He put his hand in his pocket and pulled out a slice of apple. The rat sneaked toward him, then quick jumped back, hissed, and bared his teeth. It moved on, in search of something else. *Searching... searching for what though? Searching for something that's missing.* Perry couldn't put his finger on it, but he could feel it. No, not *it,* really. More like the place where it *otta* be, but it wasn't. He listened. No snoring. No mumbling or moaning. *Where in hell is Dad?* He turned his head and looked up. *No plastic canopy? Weird.* There was a stack of pallets but no plastic. A big wash tub from a restaurant sitting on top. Everything was wet from last night's rain.

Wait a second. He couldn't remember no rain last night. His clothes was damp, like from dew, but not wet. He concentrated hard. He couldn't remember last night. At all. Or yesterday. Or— He sat up quick, forgot the wash tub, hit his head. The pallets rocked and the tub of water gushed down on him.

"Aww, slop!"

He tried to jump up. Feet tangled in the pallets, he fell over on his side, shoulder pounding the pavement, soaking himself head to toe in the water, lying in a pile of cold trash goo where his home should have been. He fought himself free, shook off the water, soaking wet in the alley, freezing, blinking at where there wasn't no shelter. He gasped in the cold morning air.

"Cussit!" He shuddered. "Where in hell is Dad?" Dad hadn't never been on his own this long. *The streets are so dangerous. No way he can defend himself.* A terrible feeling started seeping into his bones, like the morning cold. Not much chance Dad would even be alive when he finally found him. He stood looking at the blue dumpster, shivering and blinking.

Wait.

Blue? Why blue?

Why the stinking dumpster is blue? It's always been green.

He spun quick to look around, and the alley rocked hard to one side. The tall brick walls started tipping side to side and began to spin. He grabbed the dumpster and placed his feet far apart for balance, a terrible pain in his insides. A bad muscle cramp in his guts. A surge of hot, nasty fluid shot up out of his stomach, like a water cannon, dark green liquid jetting out between his lips, splashing off the blue dumpster. *Nasty!* He started to catch his breath, but it happened again, and again one more time. He clung to the dumpster for dear life, bent over at the middle, his legs shaking.

Like a newborn baby deer, shaky like that. And a old man, about to die. Both at the same time. After a little while, the alley settled down and he got his balance. He stood up slowly.

"Oh man." He wiped his mouth, spitting out the nasty taste. His whole body was shaking. He held onto the dumpster a little longer, to make sure the alley wasn't gonna act up again. He stood, and carefully turned. The back door to Ming's Wings.

Okay, so it's the right alley. What in hell?

He had a creepy feeling, like someone was watching him. The alley was empty. Everything but the dumpster seemed normal. He shook again, starting to shudder from the wetness and cold. *Man, I could use a cup of Geppetto's hot coffee.* He started makin' his way out of the alley, moving his arms around, trying to shadow box a little, but his heart wasn't in it. *"Welterweight ... aw, screw it."* Walking was hard enough without all that.

He got to the end of the alley, still a little freaked. Peered around the corner, looking both ways. A creature with a face like a skeleton almost ran into him, stopped him in his tracks. With wild, wide eyes, the creature said in a strange voice,

"Just because you're good doesn't mean you're safe."

Perry narrowed his eyes at him. Shivering, sick, and weak, he took off walking. He didn't want to talk to that guy. He made his way past the Chinatown Gate, mind clouded, trying to understand. The skeleton creature followed right behind him. Perry growled over his shoulder at it.

"Leave me alone."

"The place you don't want to be is alone. You need a friend."

Perry started across Essex, cutting diagonally to get to Lincoln. The guy followed him, talking almost right in his ear.

"You need me, man. I'm trying to save you."

"Go *away*." As he walked up Lincoln, the creature followed him.

"Without me, you are doomed. You hear me? Dooooomed!"

At the corner of Summer, Perry spun and was about to smack the dude, but there wasn't nobody there. Down the block, there was Geppetto, sweeping the sidewalk as usual. The sign on his storefront said *Gillespie's Fine Periodicals.*

Fine periodicals. Perry had to think about that one. *Geppetto gettin' a little snooty. Wonder why he changed the sign?* He headed toward Geppetto, tryin' his best to hurry, needing to move to stay warm. Still shaking. Really no way ta look cool when your freezing your butt off.

"Hey, Geppetto! Morning!"

Geppetto looked behind himself, like there might be someone else there, and turned back to Perry with one eyebrow raised.

"Good morning, young man."

"Young man? What's wrong with you, Geppetto? Them Hyenas rattle yer head a little?" It was tough to act all cheerful when you was so sick you might die any minute. Geppetto's forehead was crinkling.

"You all wet. You must be cold. This morning very chilly. Would you like a cup of coffee, on the house?"

"Uh. Yeah, Geppetto. On the house. Sure." *What is up with Geppetto?* The old man poured, handed Perry the cup.

The coffee hit the spot. He sipped it, holding the warm foam between his frosty fingers, shifting his weight from foot to foot. Geppetto was starin' at him. He was still weak and shakin' from pukin', but also from the wet clothes. He needed to figure out a way to sneak over to his headquarters, dig in the cart, and change into something dry. How could he get over there without running into the giant?

"Geppetto, have you seen my old man?" Geppetto was concerned.

"Nobody on the street so far this morning but you. Are you okay young man? You white as a ghost."

Perry did his best to laugh at that, but the words struck terror into him.

"Geppetto, did you see that creepy dude like a skeleton lurking around this morning?" Geppetto looked worried.

"Young man, you have me confused. My name not Geppetto. I am Giovanni. Giovanni Gillespie. See?" He hooked a thumb over his shoulder, pointing up at the sign.

"Yeah, got yerself a new sign, huh? I like it. Gives the joint class." Geppetto was lookin' more worried by the minute. You could see it in his face.

"Not a new sign. Same old sign, almost ten years. You okay, son? Can I help you?" That creepy feeling was getting stronger, really uncomfortable.

"No, Gep—uh, Giovanni. I'm cool. I'll catch you later, a'ight?" He started moving down the sidewalk, feeling Geppetto's eyes on his back. He turned to look over his shoulder.

"Hey, and thanks for the coffee."

Normally he would walk five or six blocks down into Chinatown, start checking out the newspaper machines, see if any were left unlatched. Today, he turned right at the first street, Essex. Once around the corner, he stopped, stood against the bricks, letting the morning sun shine on him, hoping it would warm him up. His heart was pounding in his neck, his legs still trembling.

"What in hell?"

It was all he could think to say. This was the weirdest day ever. The bricks looked warm in the morning sunlight, but they were freezing cold. The breeze wasn't much, but it was chilling his wet clothes, sucking the warmth out of him. And that feeling of being watched again. He turned, and his whole body went rigid. It was a big blue Buick, sparkle paint with tricked out wheels and dark windows. Barely moving, rumbling slow. When the Buick got right next to Perry, the back window slid down, and Perry's insides knotted up. It was the giant. The giant in the back seat looked right at him. He gave him a stare, but it was like he didn't recognize him at all. He slid his window back up, and the car eased on down the block.

As the Buick was turning a corner at the far end of the block, the skeleton-faced dude popped out, peering at him around the corner of the bricks. Today wasn't the first day he'd seen that face. But where? A chill rattled the bones in his spine. It was the skeleton dude from the mirror in the hotel room. *Was it? How could it be? How could that be the dude from the mirror?* His legs started to wobble again. He checked his six, which was clear. When he turned back, skeleton dude was gone. Nothin' was makin' sense. The giant seen him but didn't recognize him. Geppetto didn't know him from Adam. And the dumpster and the Buick had both turned blue. Perry had hair standing up on his neck.

"Aw, slop." He was shivering so hard his teeth rattled. *What kind of messed-up day is this gonna be?*

··········

Perry had to shake it off. That's what Dad always said. *When something is buggin' you, shake it off.* Like a boxer goes to his corner to shake it off after he gets his bell rung. *Yeah. That's it. Go to my corner.* He had warm dry clothes at his headquarters.

I get there, I'll feel better. He wandered along, tryin' ta figure things out. Creepy feeling wouldn't go away. *What's with Geppetto? And the Giant? And the blue dumpster? And who is that creepy skeleton dude? And where in hell is my shelter? Or Dad?*

He used to play a game with Dad before Mom died. Perry would jump up and down on the bed, and when Perry's feet hit, Dad would yank the covers, rip his feet out from under him, and he'd hit the mattress hard and fast. They'd both laugh till it hurt. This was like that, only on concrete.

The streets were going by, nothing standing out, kind of a blur. His head was full of confusion. Everything all mixed up, out of focus, thoughts and memories tangled, couldn't tell which was which. Almost only shadows, like gray horses running through fog.

"Hang on. What?" He stopped. The creepy feeling was up to eleven. "What kind of a weird thing is that to think? Gray horses? In *fog?*" He turned to see if anyone heard him. Nope. Street was empty. One suit walking a half block away. Perry headed on up the street. That creepy feeling was driving him nuts. He wanted to run but if he did, something would chase him. But what? What would chase him? Creepy. *Really* creepy. *Something is missing here. This is not the whole picture. What's missing? Why can't I figure it out?*

Instead of winding up at his headquarters, he found himself standing on the grassy knoll overlooking The Common. Weird. Above, a few cars moved along Beacon Street, a couple people on the path, only the serious walkers on this chilly morning. He sat down, scooted lower on the hill, tryin' to get out of the wind a little. The grass was wet, but so was he, so...

Down in the park, a suit came walking up the path. He was talking with his hands, gesturing like there was someone could see him. One of his hands was holding a folded paper, the other a phone, his ears stuffed with those blue tooth bud speakers. Early to be that into it. Most people sucking on the first cup of coffee, praying for a caffeine jolt. Perry Shivered.

Wait. That's the suit that knocked Dad down and yelled at him. Maybe he has seen Dad again, can tell me where. Perry started toward him. It was a long shot, but he needed answers. He stuffed his frozen hands in his wet vest pockets. The chances of finding Dad alive were getting less and less. He knew it, but he didn't want to believe it. The man stopped and stood in front of the same bench. How could he talk to the suit when he was on the phone? It didn't go too good when Dad tried it.

Before Perry could get there, another suit walked up. This guy was wearing a long coat the color of a young deer, some kind of soft material. Perry shivered again. Man, nice coat. Prob'ly warm as hell. Prob'ly cost a ton. Guy stopped, fist-bumped the other suit. Must be buddies. Perry slowed, feeling cautious. He moved a little to keep from turning to ice. Something familiar about the guy with the long coat. Salt-and-pepper hair, beard cut short. He turned sideways for a second and Perry stopped. *Something about that guy's face. The cheekbones maybe?* It was like Perry had seen him before. Perry was walking slow, sneaking'. Wanting to see without being seen. Like a magnet was pulling him toward the suit. He wanted to walk right up to him. *Better not. Better hang back. Suits can be twitchy. Never know what one might do.*

The dude by the park bench finished his call, plucked out the ear buds, left 'em dangling around his neck. The two suits talked for a minute, pointing at the paper, shaking their heads, laughing. They shook hands, and the guy with the long coat walked off, heading away from the water, toward the Business District. Perry let him go a ways, then started following, hanging back, watching him close. The more he watched the guy, the more he was convinced he had seen him before. Trying to get closer, he blew his cover and the guy seen him. Soon as he did, the guy turned, and started walking right at him, like gonna start something. Perry took off as fast as he could.

The jacked-up ribs made it tough, but it was time to get outa there. Suits can be dangerous.

....

"Diz, I'm sorry. This is wrong. Should've never happened." Bert and Eddie stood in the hospital waiting room like statues, their hats in their hands, looking very uncomfortable. Through his tears, Giovanni could see that this was hard for Bert. He was thankful to have his old friend here at this terrible time. He felt big tears run down his face. He didn't care. He was a worn-out old soldier, no fight left. He was sure this grief would finally kill him. The waiting area was designed to be a comforting place. To Giovanni, it was as dark and dank as the catacombs.

"We're gonna make sure these punks pay, Mr. Gillespie." Young Eddie trying to fix things with words. He just young. Did not understand this thing is so big, it can no be fixed. Bert knows, though. He stands pat, does not say nothing. Bert was hurting with him. Eddie was a good boy. He would learn, like every warrior and every cop has to learn. Giovanni barely nodded at Eddie, then turned to Bert.

"I had him in safe place. He should have stayed at the hotel. He should have waited for me. I told him how dangerous it was. I told him he could *no* go home. I *told* him."

Bert laid a big hand on his shoulder.

"He ran away, Bert. Ran away just like Pinocchio."

Bert and Eddie exchanged glances. Bert gave a little shrug. Giovanni did not have energy to explain. He could not stop crying. Did not want to.

"This terrible, terrible thing happen to such a good boy."

"I know." Bert was wise from the street. He understood there were no words.

"He saved my life. I swore I would not let nothing bad happen to him. I *swore* it!" he punched his boney old fist into his other palm.

"You did the best you could, Mr. Gillespie." Eddie said. "Sometimes you can't help these street people. They lead a hard life."

Bert gave Eddie the shut-up look.

"He was so young," Giovanni said. "*Too* young." For the thousandth time, the young face looked up at Giovanni with eyes that could not focus. Holding him in his arms, he could feel him slipping away. Giovanni looked at his hands, soaked in blood, the green Army shirt turning black with it. Delmond's breath coming in gasps.

"Diz, I can't. It's too soon, Diz. Help me." His body went rigid, he coughed, blood gurgled out of his mouth and his chest, then he relaxed. No sound, no struggle. Only bird calls echoing through the silent jungle. Echoes of life in this far-away country filled with death. Giovanni started to sob. "No, No, No. Stay with me, Delmond. Stay with me."

"Diz? Diz! C'mon, Diz." There was terror on Bert's face. He grabbed Bert's arm and yanked.

"Get down, Bert!" Bert here in the jungle? No, not the jungle. The hospital. Not Delmond. *Perry.*

"Oh God, no. Please, not Perry." His body collapsed, shaken by uncontrolled sobbing, lying on his side on the waiting room sofa.

September 24

Across the fine linen and crystal, Haruki's associate, Jason was well-groomed, genteel, his mannerisms refined, as you would expect from a person who had made his way to the top rungs of society. With his light brown hair, his baby face, he appeared younger than he was. Magazines said he was one of the younger billionaires to come up through traditional business, excluding the Silicon Valley millennials. He was worth a little *less* than one billion, according to Haruki's research, but still, his holdings were impressive.

"So let me understand this clearly." Jason stalled his fork two inches above his plate. "Your foundation is setting aside land reserves, with the express purpose that future generations will *not* be able to enjoy them?"

"With the express purpose that untouched wild areas will still *exist* during the time of future generations," Haruki said.

"So, the concern is for future generations of humans, or for the future of the planet?"

"The planet. The way humans proliferate, their future generations are going to take care of themselves."

Jason shook his head. "I don't know..." Haruki wiped his mouth on the linen napkin. He put on his sincere, caring expression.

"How many acres of land are covered by your manufacturing facilities around the world?"

Jason scowled. "What are you getting at?"

"Oh, nothing at all. I'm only curious. It seems likely an operation of your scope might occupy a large footprint on the planet."

Jason looked back down at his plate.

"There comes a point," Haruki went on, "as a corporation reaches a certain size, it becomes important to keep an eye toward public *perception*."

Jason took a sip of wine, fixed on Haruki with his blue eyes.

"Is this conversation turning adversarial?"

"Oh, I certainly hope not." Haruki donned his concerned look. "I would hate to see that happen. I think you might be misinterpreting what I *said*."

"Well, clarify for me, would you?"

Haruki switched to his innocent look. "I only meant that if a high-profile journalist ever did an environmental exposé, revealing the negative impact manufacturing has on the planet and how little some mammoth corporations give back, it would be unfortunate if *your* company's *name* came up."

Jason's eyes narrowed. "What do you want?"

"You own sixty-five thousand acres of virgin timber in Montana, correct?"

"My ranch?"

"The concept of a person owning a piece of the planet was baffling to the indigenous tribes when the Europeans first started confiscating large tracts of America."

"You want to take my *ranch*?" Jason asked.

"Not take it. I am asking you to donate it, out of the generosity of your heart. Out of your concern for the good of the planet."

Jason shook his head again. "I don't believe this."

"It would go a long way to insulate you from any negative press that might someday come up. Hypothetically."

"You are a ruthless thug, you know that?"

"Me? How can you *say* that?"

"You're a criminal. An Eco terrorist."

"I've already donated more land than that."

"I read about that. Seventy thousand acres of alkali flats, test wells full of poison water, and not a single tree on it."

Haruki nodded. "Valuable land, and I don't take a single penny in salary from the foundation. This is strictly a philanthropic endeavor."

Jason exhaled. "If I do this, I can count on you 'insulating' me from any negative press?"

"I will be your strongest advocate."

Jason frowned and looked at his watch. “I really must be going. I’ve lost my appetite. I’ll have my attorney draw up some paperwork.”

Haruki stood and extended his hand of friendship. “Thank you, Jason. That is *such* a generous offer.”

“Don’t mention it.” He gave the hand a single brusque shake. “Seriously. Don’t. Ever.”

September 27

Where the heck is this? Perry wondered. *And how did I get here?* The place was old, like the whole town was a museum. He could see water glistening in the moonlight far down at the end of the street. He could smell salt in the air, but this wasn't Boston Harbor. It was a different place, warm and humid. Empty streets, somewhere he'd never been before. He hid in the shadow of an alley, trying to get his bearings.

Footsteps echoed off old brick walls. The streets here was made of big round cobble stones. From the shadows, Perry could see two people coming toward him. He squinted to try to make them out. A big guy and another guy who was kinda small. They came to an old-timey streetlight, and Perry got a jolt. It was that same suit, from the park. He wasn't wearing the long coat on this warm night, but it was the same face. Same short beard, same duded up hair, nothin' outta place. The suit spotted him. Perry shrunk back into the shadows, stood real still.

"Hey, son. Let's cross over to the other side, shall we?" the suit said.

The little guy is the suit's son. What would it be like to be the son of a dude like that? The kid grunted, and they crossed to the other side of the street. *Kid prob'ly don't even know how good he's got it. What a idiot.* Perry kept watching 'em, moving along behind, stayin' hid. Something about those two. Both seemed familiar. But from where? He couldn't place it. He seen the suit the other morning in The Common, but he was sure he never laid eyes on that young guy. Perry sneaked and ducked along, finding chances to watch 'em without them knowing he was there.

They went into a hotel, a bright-lighted lobby, real fancy. A guy out front in a uniform helpin' people outta their cars. Nothing like the hotel he stayed in with Geppetto. Once they was gone, Perry didn't know what to do. Heck, he didn't even know where he *was.* A window curtain moved and caught Perry's eye. Second floor, in the middle, there was the suit, peeking out. He let the curtains go closed, but he was still there, Perry was sure of that. He shrunk into the shadows.

An old-timey carriage clattered by, fancy, shiny and white like Cinderella might ride in. Big horse hooves clopping loud on the stones. A dude in a top hat, high on the driver's seat with tuxedo tails dangling. Behind him, a pretty young woman in a wedding dress, and a young guy in a white tuxedo. They was kissing so much, they prob'ly didn't even notice when the horse stopped to do his business in the middle of the street. Perry turned away. He didn't wanna watch them makin' out. Nothin' like that ever gonna happen in his life, he was sure of it. He heard the carriage clop away. He couldn't feel no worse. He could smell the stench from the dumpster on his clothes. His hair was oily. He smelled something else. There was a big puddle and a pile left by the horse. That's what he felt like, right there.

He heard a little noise and turned. A bright flash, the crack of a bat. He was on the ground, and they was on him again. He started fighting for his life, and then stopped. His old man's face, white teeth gritted, snarling, fist raised, ready to blast him again. The old man froze, and his mouth dropped open.

"Jesus, you're just a kid."

Perry was so freaked out he didn't know what to say. His old man dead and come back again, but this time as a rich man with perfect teeth and a full head of hair? He had the same scowl and the same punch though. Damn, Perry's ears were ringin'.

"You're dead!" Perry shouted.

The old man looked even more surprised. Perry had to get outta there. He started floppin' and kickin', anything to get away before another punch landed. When his old man let up a little, he twisted free, rolled out of it, and took off as fast as he could, with his busted-up ribs and a brand-new shiner. Behind him, he heard his old man's voice. "Hey, come back, kid! I'm not going to hurt you. I only want to know what's going on!"

SEPTEMBER 28

Father John was walking across the lawn, toward the church building, when he heard the squeal. Two young children, running across the grounds in jubilant terror from their dad, who was pretending to be a dinosaur. It stopped John in his tracks. The beauty of the scene transfixed him. The dad caught the children and hoisted them up, one onto each of his shoulders, roaring loudly. Giggling, they hugged him, smothering his cheeks with rapid-fire kisses, until he was laughing so hard, he looked like he might drop the children.

The dad seemed to sense that their private moment was being surveyed and stopped, looking up. Seeing Father John, he smiled and put the children down. He nodded to John, who waved and gave his best smile of approval. But inside John's heart was breaking. He would never experience such a moment. He could never have his own children, or even interact with children in such a carefree way. Some would think it inappropriate. Somewhere those children had a mom who probably loved the dad as much as they did. She probably hugged him at the door, kissed his cheeks.

Stop. He dared not go any farther down *that* road. Not in his current weakened state.

··········

Moments later, seated in the small room as he was every Saturday, Father John switched his focus and readied himself to administer the sacrament of reconciliation. A soft tap on the door, and—

Oh.

Virginia stepped in. Her graceful presence made the room seem softer. John smiled and invited her to sit in the chair across from him. He might not have eaten enough lunch. He was weak and hollow. Virginia had been a good friend for several years. She had a charming gentleness about her and was pious in her faith. She was a good listener, and he had seen her put the needs of others before her own time and time again. She was also physically beautiful. Whenever she walked into his field of vision, he had to force himself to turn his head and focus on something else. She was magnetic. Today, he forced his eyes to remain above her dimpled chin. Her beautiful lips, with perfectly applied lipstick and liner said,

"Forgive me, Father, for I have sinned. It has been six weeks since my last confession."

"May the Lord be in your heart and upon your lips that you may truly and humbly confess your sins: In the name of the Father, and of the Son, and of the Holy Spirit. Amen."

"Thank you, Father John."

"It is the Lord who extends the grace of this sacrament to you, Virginia."

"I know, Father. But still, thank you. I have been having a terrible time. I believe I have committed the sin of lust."

John's throat was dry, and he swallowed. "You are not sure?" He reached for his glass of water.

"I don't know. That one has always been confusing to me. In the Catechism, I read that the sin of lust is a 'disordered desire for or inordinate enjoyment of sexual pleasure.'"

"Good for you. Kudos for going to the Catechism during your examination of conscience, and even more so for memorizing that."

"But, Father, it only confused me. That first part, an inordinate desire, I am guilty of. I have been out of college ten years and have never had a full adult sexual experience with a man. So yes, I do have an inordinate desire for that. God help me, I do." She was about to break down. It was difficult to hear such intimate things from a woman. Especially *this* woman. It was a time to tread carefully.

"It sounds like you are truly repentant. Are you?"

"If I am guilty, yes, I am."

"There is that doubt again. Tell me where that is coming from."

"From the second part of the definition. It says, 'Sexual pleasure is morally disordered when sought for itself, isolated from its procreative and unitive purposes.'"

"That's correct. Why is that causing you trouble?"

"Because I *don't* seek sexual pleasure only for itself. I *want* those unitive and procreative purposes, Father, with all my heart. I *want* to be united intimately with a man. With one man, for life, and I want to bear his children. I want to snuggle under the covers, to become one, to be intimate and wake up to chaotic breakfasts with toddlers. I want to have quiet evenings flipping through old family photographs as we grow old together. That's why I can't figure out if it is a sin."

That stab of guilt again, remembering how he had envied the man with the two small children, and the thought that there must be a wife somewhere. Boy, talk about being convicted. And *weak*.

"How does this question come up, Virginia?"

"In dating. I keep going out with men, each time hoping *this* one might be *the* one. Some of these guys have been amazing. Handsome, sweet, caring. I have been strongly attracted to several of them. Almost more than I could resist." Father John decided not to reach for the water glass again.

"And what is the result?"

"The result is, the guy always makes his move, ready to take it to the next level, and I have to push him away and tell him that I am saving myself for marriage."

"Good for you, Virginia. That takes a lot of courage and spiritual fortitude."

"And I never *hear* from him again."

"Oh. I see. That must hurt."

"Yes, it does hurt. I am struggling mightily, Father. I've been patient. I've prayed so much, and God has not shown me the path. I'm so tired of waiting."

"I understand," he said. "Assuming there are elements of this which *are* sinful, are you truly sorry?"

"Yes, Father. Truly."

"Then God will forgive your sins. And He will give you the grace to continue. Might I offer you a word of counsel?"

She nodded. "Please do. I'm desperate."

"Stay the path, Virginia. As a priest, I have heard many times the wrenching pain suffered by women who gave themselves away, hoping to endear themselves to men. I can tell you; it is not a fair bargain. The gift you have is precious. Once he has harvested that gift, the man has no compulsion to be loyal, or even friendly to you. The only thing that would compel him would be his own spiritual purity."

Eyes down, she gave a slight nod.

"If he has any spiritual purity, he will *cherish* the decision you've made. You will become much more valuable in his eyes. He will gladly wait with you. Each of these men who did not call you back after learning of your virtue, was confirming for you that he was not the one."

She was touching her eyes with a dainty handkerchief. Soft linen brushing her long, pretty lashes. *What kind of fool would walk away from a woman like her?*

"For your penance," he said, "I want you to spend an hour in the presence of the Holy Eucharist, meditating on the humility and obedience of our Blessed Mother. Also, during your adoration, thank the Holy Spirit for giving you such clear signs that none of these are the man you are looking for."

"Thank you, Father." She began to emit quiet little sobs. His heart twisted like a dishrag being wrung out. He had the impulse to give her a hug. But he could not. Absolutely not. Even though that's what she needed, pastorally. Even though it was what *he* needed. No. It could not happen. A shiver crawled up his spine. He shook his head, adjusted himself in his chair, and prayed aloud in a strong voice,

"God, the Father of mercies, through the death and resurrection of his Son has reconciled the world to himself and sent the Holy Spirit among us for the forgiveness of sins, through the ministry of the Church. May God give you pardon and peace." Making the sign of the cross over her, he said, "I absolve you from your sins in the name of the Father, and of the Son, and of the Holy Spirit."

··········

"Hello?"

Just moments after Virginia left, the voice sounded like a young person. Normally only elderly people used the confessional behind the screen. And it was unusual for *anyone* to speak in full voice in a confessional.

"Hello. I am Father Bianchi."

"Hello, Father Bianchi, name's Perry."

"Hi, Perry. Are you here for confession?"

"What's that?"

"You're not Catholic?"

"I s'pose so. My old man told me I was baptized when I was a baby."

"Ah. I see. Welcome, Perry. I'm glad you're here."

"My mom was a real churchgoer, according to my old man." The slang dialogue confirmed that he was young, and the slight odor coming through the screen hinted that this young man might be homeless.

"Your mother is no longer with us, Perry?"

"Nah, she died when I was a kid. Been just me and Dad since."

"I'm sorry to hear that. It must've been difficult."

"Still is. Difficult every day."

"I believe you."

There was a long pause.

"What'd you say yer name was?" the young voice asked.

"Father Bianchi."

"Can I ask you a question?"

"Sure."

"Why are Catholic priests called Father when they ain't allowed to have no kids?"

John smiled. He liked this kid already. Direct, inquisitive. "You can call me John if you would be more comfortable."

"Yer name's not Bianchi?"

"Yes, it is. John Bianchi."

"Oh, okay. Cool. Thanks."

"No problem, Perry. Can I ask you a question?"

"Sure, man. Shoot."

"Is there a particular reason you stopped by to talk to me today?"

"Why can't I see you?"

John laughed. "Well, Perry, you opened the door on the left. That little booth allows you to remain anonymous. If you had opened the door on the right, you would be sitting in the same room I am."

"Little choices make a difference, huh? There's nowhere to sit in here."

John laughed again. "Would you like to go out and come through a different door? Start again?"

"Do-overs? Those allowed in religion?" This kid was a riot.

"That's pretty much all we do here, Perry. Come on in. Let's have a chat."

The kid opened the door, stuck his head in, curious.

John stood and extended his hand. "Hi, Perry."

"Hey, John. Nice to meetcha." Hard, bony little hands, strong. "Kinda cool in here. A candle, couple soft chairs, nice. I like it way better than the little booth with nowhere to sit."

John smiled. He wasn't really a kid, more like a twenty-something, clearly carrying a lot of mileage. He looked like he had been roughed up.

"Have a seat, Perry."

"Naw, thanks. These clothes are kinda dirty."

"The chair's got leather upholstery. Don't worry about it."

"Yeah? Cool." He sat, relaxed into the soft leather, stretched his legs out, filthy boots scraping on the oriental rug. His eyes went from point to point. The icon of St. Leo, the small crucifix made of bronze, the wooden fish symbol, the table with the pitcher of water, the candle, the box of Kleenex.

"Wow, this is a nice place. This where you live?"

"Uh, no. I have another place… near here. This room we use for visiting with people who want to talk with a priest."

"Wow. Nice."

"So how are you doing, Perry?"

"Me? I'm all right, I guess."

"You seem like you could deal with about anything and still be doing all right."

"Yeah, I s'pose. Old man always said that you gotta roll with the punches, ya know?" He held up bony little fists in front of his face, rocked side to side slightly, demonstrating what he meant. Perry's hands were stained dark from the street. The cuts and bruises on his face indicated it hadn't been long since his last fight.

"I do know," John said. "I boxed a little in high school."

"Fo' real? Check that. A boxing priest. I'm gonna call you K.O. for short."

John laughed. This kid was sharp as a tack. "I never said I was any good at boxing."

Perry grinned. "Hey, man, that name can go either way."

John laughed even louder. Amazing, this kid. Probably never seen the inside of a ring. He had the look of a street fighter. No ref, no bell, just fighting to stay alive. His eyes were dark, deep, but there was a goodness in them. An innocence that belied everything else about his appearance.

"So, K.O. Mind if I call you that?"

How could you not smile at this kid? "You can call me whatever you like, Perry."

"Cool. So, K.O., what's the thing with God?"

"Excuse me?"

"I mean, what's He all about? What's He up to? That's why I stopped in today. I got some questions about how this all works."

"Those are big questions," John said. "Can you be more specific?"

Perry looked at him, a little suspicious. "Tell me about this confession thing."

"That I can do. Confession is one of the seven sacraments of the Church. Do you know what a sacrament is?"

Perry shook his head.

"A sacrament is a physical sign of a spiritual grace that is happening in the life of a person. Something that would be invisible if it weren't for the sacrament."

"Huh?"

"Your baptism was a sacrament. It was a physical sign. The priest poured water over your head and said, 'I baptize you in the name of the Father, and of the Son, and of the Holy Spirit.' He also anointed you with the oil of chrism. He lit a little candle from the large Easter candle and gave it to an adult to hold for you. Those outward physical signs were part of a ritual, making a hidden spiritual reality visible to everyone who was there. Together, the ritual and the hidden spiritual reality make up the sacrament."

"What was the invisible thing that was happening?"

John smiled. "At the moment of your baptism, a mark was placed on your soul, which can never be washed away. It says that you belong to God. We call it an indelible mark."

"Huh. Can't never be washed off, huh?" He looked down at his hands.

"Never."

"What about all the *bad* shit people do? Oh, sorry."

"That's okay. An excellent question. This room, the cubicle next door, are spaces set aside for people to come receive another sacrament, called the sacrament of reconciliation."

"Reconciliation..."

"To be reconciled?"

"Like patching things up?" Perry asked.

"Yes! That's it exactly. Patching things up with God. People come here, talk about things they've done that they regret, and ask to be reconciled to God."

"So, before they come in here, what happens to the little delibal mark?"

"The *in*delible mark is always there, Perry. Once baptized, you *always* belong to God. Nothing can change that, no matter how badly you mess up in your life. If you return to Him, He will never reject you. Do you understand?"

Perry's dark eyes were peering into him, searching. Was he going to pass the inspection?

"That's pretty crazy sh— I mean stuff, K.O."

John smiled. "It really is. And it's true. Scripture tells us, in the Gospel of John, that God says, 'No one will ever steal you out of my hand.'"

"That's *crazy.*"

"Yes. And remember I told you of the oil of chrism? That is to represent the spiritual reality that you have been anointed, in God's kingdom, as priest, prophet, and king."

"King? I don't feel much like a king."

"It's hard to understand, Perry. Give it time. All we can do is try to learn from each day. The important thing to remember is that God is right here with us, cheering for us, while we are struggling and learning. He gives us the freedom to do whatever we want, but His hope is that we will choose to be with Him."

"Tell me more about that part."

"Which part?"

"That part about choosing who you gonna be with."

"Ah. Well, it's like you said. As humans, we all mess up. We do bad things. But even when we mess up, we can, at any minute, make a choice to turn and find God."

"Where do you *go* to find God?"

"He's usually standing right behind you."

Perry scowled. "I ain't never felt Him there."

"He is there. But sometimes we don't feel Him because other things are stealing our attention."

"Yeh? So how you s'posed to get where you can feel Him?"

"That is not a simple question," John said. "I guess I would say that it starts with the priestly office."

Perry was staring at him again.

"You were anointed as priest, prophet, and king, remember? The priestly office is about learning to offer right praise."

He shook his head. "I don't get it. Right praise? That don't mean nothing to me."

"People worship money, power, fame, even pleasure. These are examples of false praise. The only right praise is that which is directed to God our Father. If you want to learn to feel God's presence, I think it starts there."

He still looked confused.

"Perry, you told me you've had hardships. But have you ever had a moment when you were genuinely happy?"

He paused for a moment. "Yeh, I have. A lot of times when I see little animals, like rats or birds, that makes me happy."

"Rats?"

"Or squirrels. Once I seen a deer walking across The Common like she owned the place. That made me happy. Sometimes I'm happy just to see the sunrise. Or to get back home to my shelter safe."

"Those are great examples, Perry. When you feel that joy, that is a small experience of God. He is love, and from that love comes joy. When you feel that, whisper 'thank you' to Him for the thing that made you happy, and for that feeling. That would be a good example of right praise."

Perry's brow furrowed. After a moment, he looked up. "Father John, this was cool. Can I come by and talk to you again sometime?"

"Sure, Perry. Every Saturday afternoon I'm right here to help people be reconciled to God. I would like to talk with you again."

Perry stood up, so John did also.

"I'll stop by again some time."

"Cool, Perry. Until then,"—Father John held his hands up in a boxing posture— "keep rolling with the punches."

"Yeh, man. Count on it."

"And don't forget about the indelible mark. God is with you."

••••••••••••

Later that evening, Virginia sat brushing her dark hair one hundred strokes, as Mother taught her. The three-panel vanity mirror was lighted with a soft glow.

Life is so strange. It drags and lags until suddenly you realize it has fled, and there is nothing left but a trail of regret and tears.

The specter of a gray-haired spinster appeared in the glass, then vanished. How and why would God have it this way? One can aspire only to holiness, forsake all the world's allure, and come up empty. Others compromise, cheat, and acquiesce to the ways of the world, and end up with everything. In the center mirror, her face was almost perfectly symmetrical. Her complexion was nearly flawless, and her deep blue eyes had a nice sparkle to them. In the two side mirrors, her profiles were nearly identical. Her lips were full and graceful. Her cheekbones were high but soft. She was a beautiful woman. A lot of good it had done her.

Every woman wants to be beautiful. Many chase after it their whole lives, but not her. This was the way she had been created. When she was a little girl, she heard a lot of comments about how cute she was. People were drawn to her. Later, the boys started paying attention to her. She never tried to use that or take advantage. At an early age, she had made a promise that she would live a pure life. By the time she made it to high school, that decision started causing her problems. When the other girls were talking about their first sex experience, or their hundredth, she felt awkward. They picked up on that and began to tease her, as if something was wrong with her. Mom said they were jealous because she had been the first to blossom and was blessed with a beautiful woman's body.

In the high school locker room, she hated to drop her towel to shower. She could feel their narrowed eyes roving all over her body. You would expect that to be something you could outgrow. But at parish gatherings, she still sometimes got that look from the wives—and a different one from the husbands. It was such a mess.

She laid the hairbrush down and walked over to the full-length oval mirror. Gazing at her figure through the long silk negligee, she moved her hands gently over her front to smooth the fabric and set off a little tremble. She turned to one side and then the other. She turned to look over her shoulder at her shapely back. She was a woman in her prime. Her body was round where it should be and pointy where it should be. In the mirror, for a moment, she was on the bed with a strong, gentle man, kissing, moving into an intimate embrace. She shook her head and turned away.

Even with Zumba, spin classes, and Pilates, how long could she sustain this? How long would it be before the good looks began to fade and the firm body began to droop and shrivel? How would she find a husband then? Did God really gift her with all of this only to have it wither on the vine? It seemed impossible. And yet, home alone on a Saturday night, she was without a single viable prospect.

Father John was so compassionate. He understood the depth of her pain, she could tell. His empathy was like a soft embrace. With a hollow in the pit of her stomach, she went to her bed and knelt on the floor. She wanted a relationship *so bad. Father, why can't I find a man like Father John? It isn't fair that You have taken him to be a priest. There are so few good men. Show me, please, what am I supposed to do?*

SEPTEMBER 29

Sunday morning, Father John stood at the doorway after the early Mass. This was a great group. The early risers. The dedicated Catholics. Or the ones who wanted to get it over with, have the bulk of their Sunday free. Probably some of each.

Nearly everyone waited their turn to say hello on their way out. For most, it was only a friendly greeting or a handshake. A few wanted to tell him about a big event that happened the past week — sometimes good, sometimes bad. He listened intently to each one. He genuinely cared for them. He never brushed off anyone who had something to tell him.

"Oh. Hi, Virginia." It caught him off guard. He hadn't seen her in the line.

"Good morning, Father," she said. Sweet. "I wanted to say thank you."

He was not certain what she was referring to. He searched those deep blue pools.

"Thank you for being such a wonderful priest, for giving your life so generously."

He was at a loss. She grasped his hand in both of hers and gave it a little squeeze. Her hands were soft and warm.

"I will be praying for you, Father."

"Thank you." As she walked away, he noted a look that shouldn't have been there. A little too much affection in the eyes. A certain sparkle. It bothered him.

"Good morning, Mrs. Mackernary," he said.

"Father, I'm going to be praying for you too," she said, with a grin. He smiled.

"Thank you. I can use all the help I can get."

•••••••••••

Wow. The old man could pack a punch. Perry carefully touched the lump under his eye. Dad always had a mean haymaker, but he was usually so drunk, Perry could get mostly outta the way. But this new version of the old man, damn. He was fast—and silent. Perry was on the ground before he knew the old man was there. He stopped. How could the old man *be* there? All duded up like that? Perfect hair? Perfect teeth? How do ya grow back hair and teeth? He never heard of that before, nowhere. Didn't make no sense.

The only way it could make sense, is if the old man died and went to heaven. That had to be it. But... this grungy city? Trash in the gutters? Pawn shops and subways? Streets all cracked up? Scaffolding on the buildings? This is *heaven*? This is some strange kind of heaven. A working girl on the corner was smiling, waving at cars going by. She spotted Perry and took a couple steps sideways, too good to be seen close to him. *Wait. Hookers in heaven? Okay, maybe. But working in heaven?* He shook his head. *No way.* He came to a corner and stood waiting for the light to change.

His heart stopped. Across the street, the old man and the younger guy he called "son" standing sideways to him, getting ready to cross the street to the left. The younger guy turned and faced him. Perry froze. *What kinda weirdness is this?* He was lookin' across the street at a mirror. The dude looked just like him. He tried to blend into the crowd. They didn't see him, he didn't think. Maybe. Perry crossed the street and walked right by where the two went, without lookin' their direction. He was scared the old man would sneak up from behind him again, but he didn't want to start nothin' by eyeballin' him.

Huh, look at that. Stars stuck in the sidewalk, with people's names. Hey, these are movie stars. He had seen some of these people at the movie theater. Perry took a little peep over his shoulder. He wasn't in the mood for another punch in the face. *Who goes around heaven punchin' people in the face? If anyone would do that, it'd be the old man, that's true. But no. No way. Working hookers, and the old man punching people in the face? Nope. That settles it. This ain't heaven. Wait.* It hit him again. His stomach turned. *Really? I died, and I didn't go to heaven? Fa' real?*

October 1

"When I saw him on The Common, I thought he was a street kid wanting to mug somebody," Deuce said. "Then I thought he might be trying to give Peregrine a hard time."

D.M. had cold steel eyes. It was like staring into the bores of two blued muzzles. The occasional glint like a Maglite on steel. Deuce knew him forever, still couldn't get used to those eyes. This diner was low-rent, blue collar, but Deuce liked it. It had character. Red vinyl cushions, black-and white tiles, and a checkerboard pattern on the tables. Like stepping back into the 1950s. D.M. listened without expression. He was a good guy, a buddy from the old days in the Corps, the first pilot Deuce hired when he started his charter company.

"Since this damned accident with Mac happened, I've —"

"That wasn't any accident. They tried to take you out, Deuce. Someone used a hacksaw to cut halfway through the lower control arm."

"I *know* that."

"But you're asking for security for Peregrine?"

"Because of what happened to Mac. I can't have something like that happen to Peregrine."

"Do you think he's a target?"

"Well, I did. But when I confronted the kid, he threatened *me*."

"What did he say, exactly?"

"He said, 'You're dead.'"

"And you let him get away with that?"

"No. Not really… Well… Yeah. I did. I was so shocked, he squirmed loose and got away."

"Are you sure this kid is part of it? Is he a credible threat? I mean, he's a street kid, and you're… well, you're you."

"I know. But this isn't an ordinary street kid. He's working for someone."

"So, you *do* think this is connected to the attempted hit. Does he look like a pro?"

"No, you're not listening to me. He looks like a street kid. You know, like… homeless."

"Must not be working for anyone who *pays* very well."

"Look, in Boston on Thursday, he was shadowing me during my morning walk on The Common. I confronted him in Charleston on Friday evening in an alley, and I gave him a shiner. But I wasn't the first. His face was busted up already. On Saturday, Peregrine and I fly to New Orleans, and I see him hanging around in the French Quarter. On Sunday, we're out in Los Angeles, and he's loitering on the corner of Hollywood and Vine."

"You're sure it's the same kid?"

"I'm telling you, the same kid, same busted-up face."

"Okay. So what?"

"So *what?* You tell me. How does a street kid get from Boston, to Charleston, to New Orleans, to LA inside of a week? I mean, we're flying the G5 and he's pacing right with us. This thing is bigger than this kid. I don't know who's coming at me or why, but there's something strange going on here."

"Hmm," D.M. said. "After what happened to Mac, I would have to agree. We need to post security on your jet. Nobody goes near it unless they're part of your team. Wait. What if the saboteur *is* someone on your team?"

Deuce rubbed his temples with his fingertips. "I don't want to even think that."

"I can have someone travel with you and look for a chance to nab the kid."

"D.M., I don't want *someone.* I want *you.*"

"Deuce, I understand you're concerned about this. But I've got a business to run. Today I have guys on mission in five different countries. That takes a lot of management. I don't stand security details anymore."

"Are you friggin' serious? This is my *family*. My mechanic is in the hospital hanging by a thread, and Peregrine and I have picked up a tail. I want you to travel with us until we can resolve this thing. I'll pay you whatever you want. For Pete's sake, the jet's got wi-fi. You don't even have to be out of touch. Run your business from the lounge of the 550."

"You drive a tough bargain. But I need a lot more than wi-fi."

"Add in any expenses you can dream up."

D.M. was staring at him.

"I'm serious. Pull out all the stops. I want this thing to go away. And I don't want Peregrine to know about it."

"He already knows what happened to Mac."

"He doesn't know details. He only knows there was an accident."

"You don't think he'll suspect something, me tagging along?"

"That's one more reason it's got to be you personally."

"Fine," D.M. said. "I'll call your bluff. The fee is ten thousand a day, plus I need to set up a situation room with SATCOM in the G5, and I don't stay in anything less than four stars."

"Ten thousand? That sounds a little mercenary."

D.M.'s eyes narrowed. "Supposed to be some kind of a joke?"

"Forget it," Deuce said. "I want results. I don't care about the cost."

"Fine. Next time the kid shows up, I'll snag 'im and find out what's going on."

"No, I want you to bring him to *me.* I want to talk to him."

"How 'bout I talk to him, and tell you what he said. That way, you don't take a chance of getting your hands wet."

"Hold on. I don't want you to *hurt* him. He's a kid."

"You mean he's a minor?"

"No, he's not a minor. He looks a few years older than Peregrine, but to me he's a kid."

"So, he's in his twenties. You better smell the coffee. I've seen twelve-year-olds take out Humvees with RPGs. Twelve years or fifty, you eat an RPG, you're the same kind of dead."

"I *know* that. I only want a chance to look this kid in the eye. Something about him."

"You said it wasn't about the kid," D.M. said. "said yourself he's a surrogate. Powerful men like you have powerful enemies. If you drag me into this thing, you gotta respect my experience. I'm not interested in being part of your amateur hour."

"Give me a break, D.M. I'm not a babe in the woods. Be serious."

"I *am* serious. Life and death. Whoever these people are, they don't play. They flat out tried to *kill* you. It was a fluke that they hit Mac instead. I'm the one spotted your roadster in the bottom of that ravine. From the air it looked like a crumpled soda can. Its some kinda miracle Mac's still alive."

"Fair enough. But could we at least *try* letting me talk to the kid? It's my funeral."

"You don't know that," D.M. said. "Might be mine, might be Peregrine's. Ask Mac what *he* thinks about that."

D.M. stared at him until Deuce nodded. "These things don't unfold on a script, Deuce. Once it starts, you got no idea where it will end up until you're on the other side. If you *make* it to the other side."

"I know that. All I am asking for is one chance to figure out what we're into. Put the kid in front of me in one piece. If things seem hinky, you take us to the next level."

D.M. was not the same guy Deuce knew in Officer Candidate School. At OCS he was a fresh-faced kid. Now he had several small shrapnel scars, leathery skin and deep lines forming a permanent look of concentration. He also had a tat of an M-4 assault rifle pointing down one forearm, an upside-down K-bar knife tat on the other. Inside his half-unbuttoned shirt, you could see a part of his older tat. He got that one right after The Basic School. Against protocol, D.M. wandered away from the TBS graduation party, showed up the next morning with a permanent necklace of low-hanging barbed wire, three large hand grenades hanging from it, tattooed to his chest. Deuce thought he was crazy. Now there was also barbed wire at his wrist. A woven charm bracelet in dark red ink. Rusty barbed wire with tiny gray skulls hanging. D.M. was eccentric, but he was a good friend, a man with a sharp and unflinching understanding of the world.

D.M. let out an exasperated sigh and shook his head. "Okay. But if my spidey sense gets even a hint of this thing going sideways, I won't ask your permission to escalate." He held up a fist, showing the charm bracelet tattoo. "I've lost enough people. You got a death wish, you're on your own."

"Just give me one chance to talk to him *before* you do anything… enhanced." D.M. held up a single finger. "One chance."

"Fine."

"One last question."

"What?"

"Does this 'kid' as you call him, look like he might be capable of operating a *hacksaw*?"

October 4

Two days later, D.M. came in with the kid from the alley, half dragging him, half shoving, his fist pushing his shirt collar, his big hand clamped on his elbow. It was Deuce's lunch appointment. Great.

"In Jesus' name, D.M., what part of 'I don't want him harmed' did you not understand?"

The old warrior delivered him to the booth, pushed him down with a decisive whump, stepped back, and looked at Deuce.

"Not a scratch on 'im. Trust me, he's been enough trouble to have earned some. I kept it civilized."

Deuce shook his head. "I forgot to factor in your skewed perspective."

"I'm executing the plan exactly as discussed," D.M. said.

"You can leave us. I'll let you know if I need you."

"Fine by me."

The glaring kid across from Deuce was obviously livid. Not helpful, as conversation starters go. "I'm sorry about all that," Deuce said.

The kid ground his teeth. A wave of confusion swept over Deuce. Sometimes counterfeit "relatives" crawl out of the woodwork when word gets around that you have money. But this kid -in broad daylight, he could be Peregrine's cousin. Or *brother*. The family resemblance was uncanny. He looked anorexic, his skin was rough, he had fresh cuts and bruises, and old scars. But his facial features... This kid was a dead ringer for Peregrine. Deuce regretted the ugly purple shiner he had added under the kid's eye. He began mentally going back over his wild oats period. Any chance there was a son out there he didn't know about? Was this about a paternity action? No. Nothing came to mind. He would remember, wouldn't he? Besides, this kid was such a dead ringer, he would have to have the same mother as well. After serving as a USMC captain, Deuce didn't scare easily. But this – this was creepy. Sitting here under the piercing stare of this street kid, was freaking him out.

"You alright, Mister Faulk?"

"Yes – I'm fine. How are you?" *The kid knows my name.*

"It's just that you look a little freaked. Like you're seeing yer own face starin back at you or something."

Crap. There it is. It must be about paternity.

"Hey, let's stop conning each other," Deuce said. "What's this all about? Why not come right out with it?"

"What is *what* all about?"

"Listen, kid. You've been shadowing my son and I all over the U.S., so don't act like you don't know what I'm asking."

He shrugged. "I don't have any answers. I'm not in charge of this thing."

"So, you admit there is someone else pulling the strings?"

"Hell yeh, there is. You think I chose to be in this mess?"

"What kind of mess is it you think you're in? Believe me, if you don't come clean, it can get worse."

The kid scowled. "Now you gonna *threaten* me?"

"I'm not threatening you. But that guy who nabbed you? He's a serious man. He's been all around the world, making people's problems go away."

"You hired a *hit man*? Jeez!"

"Not a hit man. A bodyguard. But he takes our safety seriously. He will take decisive action to get to the bottom of this. Do you understand me?"

"You hired a bodyguard slash *hit* man? Who the hell *are* you? I don't even *know* you. Am I that scary to you?"

"The question is, who the hell are *you*?" Deuce said. "Answer that and tell me who is bankrolling you, and we won't have any further problems."

"What? Man, I look like I got a bankroll to you? You think I like dressing like this? I'm trying to figure out the hell is going on, just like you."

Deuce paused. Nobody would dress like that, *live* like that, if they had financial backing. He didn't only *look* homeless. He *smelled* homeless.

"Look, son. How about give me your name. Let's start with that."

"Don't call me that unless you mean it."

"What?"

"Nothin'. Fergit it. Listen. I'm not gonna tell you my name. You gotta figure it out. Shouldn't be hard for a man smart enough to wear them kinda clothes. When you got it figgered out, let me know and we'll talk. Until then, how 'bout keep yer goon offa me. I ain't done nothin' to you." The kid slid out of the booth and limped off without looking back.

Crud. So much for getting to the bottom of it. The kid really didn't seem dangerous. If there was a powerful enemy at the helm of this, wouldn't there be demands? What a mind twister. The kid's familial looks were haunting, and he did seem confused. But those were the only things strange about him. Well...that, and his ability to teleport across continents.

D.M. was going to have a fit, and he was going to want to escalate.

October 5

Another Saturday morning, Father John was casually walking back and forth in front of the Life Choice League building. God would do something here today. In the meantime, he was keeping his distance from the ladies. Each time he looked their direction, Virginia was staring at him, and she would smile. It was awkward. He didn't want to hurt her, but he could not let this get out of hand. A familiar figure was moving along the opposite side of the street.

"Perry?" he called out.

When Perry looked up, John waved. Perry cocked his head a little, checked for traffic and headed across the street.

"Hey, Father John. How's things going?"

"Everything is fine. How are you?"

"Ah, you know." He shrugged. "What are you doin' here, Father?"

"I'm here with a group from the church. We're trying to keep young girls from making a mistake they can't reverse." Perry looked confused.

"Young women come here looking for help, but they end up suffering terrible harm. So, we try to convince them not to go inside."

"What kinda harm?"

"This is a place where they kill unwanted babies."

He winced. "Oh. I know about that. Man, that's a bad thing. I have a friend who hurts real bad because of that."

"All women who go through with it do, but only after it's too late. So, we volunteer our time to try to rescue women. And babies."

"That's a really good thing to be doin', Father John. I don't see why anybody would wanna hurt a baby."

Sister Mary Frances approached, and John turned to introduce them.

"Perry, I want you to meet a friend of mine."

Perry's face drained of color, and it looked like he was fighting a sob.

"Sister Mary Frances?"

"Why, yes," she said.

"You two know each other?" John asked.

"Sister, don't you remember? It's me, Perry."

Sister Mary Frances looked perplexed. "Hi, Perry. Can you remind me how we met?"

"Second grade?" Perry hinted. "You was my teacher?"

She glanced at John, then back to him. "Perry, I'm honored to meet you ... but I never taught second grade. I am a teacher, but I taught high school my whole career."

At that, Perry seemed to shut down. He dropped his eyes and took a couple steps back. "I... musta had you mixed up with somebody else. I gotta go. I'll talk to you later, Fr. John." He took a couple steps, then looked back. "Sister, it was really nice to see you."

He was slouching more than usual, dragging his feet, till he turned a corner, disappearing past a row of blue dumpsters.

October 7

"Hi, Perry. How have you been?" Father John asked.

Perry was sitting on the brick wall of a raised plant bed. The church plaza was empty on this weekday.

"Hey, K.O. What's up?"

"Did I see you in Mass last Sunday?"

"Yeah, I was there, in the back. Went in through the side door."

"I thought that was you."

"You wasn't sure? On account of I'm blendin' in with all the *other* homeless people comin' here?"

John smiled. "Yeah, that's it. So… how was that experience for you?" The cool color of the autumn sunlight was not flattering. Perry's skin had a leather quality, as well as the old and new injuries from fighting. Sad to see on a young man.

"It was alright. Been a long time since I was at a Mass. Last time I think I mighta been colorin' in a book 'stead a listenin'."

John chuckled. He took a seat on the planter, careful not to invade Perry's personal space. "Were you listening this time?"

"Yeh."

"Did you hear anything interesting?"

"Yeh. I heard it kinda different since things are different now."

John nodded. "That's how it works, Perry. The same readings take on different meanings, based on what you are going through at the time. Holy Scripture is fascinating that way." He breathed deep of the fresh autumn air, looked around at the deciduous trees, the few dry, crunchy leaves on the ground. One more good frost, they'd be coming down like a colorful blizzard.

"K.O.?"

"Yes?"

"What's the communion-a-saints?"

John smiled again. "So, you *were* listening. That's good. The Communion of Saints is the entire community of all people alive now, and who lived in the past, who have dedicated their lives to serving God."

"Alive now, and was alive *before*?"

"Yes. It takes a minute to get your head around it."

"So, like you and me now, we're doing that?"

"Uh. Well, yes, anytime two or more are gathered. Sure."

"So, a community. Like a town?" Perry asked.

"Well, maybe more like a group. A private club."

"I ain't got no experience bein' part of a private club."

"Are you sure about that?"

Perry's eyes narrowed. "This a quiz?"

John chuckled. "No, not a quiz. But let me ask you, have you ever been somewhere where people who live on the street gather?"

"You mean down by the rail yards, under the interstate, where people light fires in barrels and stand around ta get warm?"

"Yes, exactly. When you were there, standing around the barrel, there were probably people you knew and some you did not know, right?"

"Yeh. Some I seen around, some not."

"And yet, I bet you could sense that you all had certain experiences in common, is that right?"

A brisk gust swept the plaza. It didn't seem to even register with Perry.

"Well, yeh. You been on the street a while, you've had a bunch of experiences. Like bein' ripped off, or beat up, or turned away, or looked down at."

"Exactly. So even though you don't know everyone there, you all have common experiences. You belong to a *community* of people who live on the street."

"Huh."

"Everyone in that group understands things that other people who have not had those experiences would not be able to understand."

"Yeh. That makes sense. So that's the kinda community yer talking about with the community-a-saints?"

"Yes. The word we use is the *Communion* of Saints, but it means the same thing."

"That's kinda interestin'. A group with people who are alive and people who are already dead?"

"And they all gather together, drawn by a certain force."

"What kinda force?"

"Well, why do homeless people gather down by the rail yards?"

"For light, and ta stay warm."

"That is why the Communion of Saints gather as well. We gather together, seeking light and warmth. Down at the rail yards, the light and warmth come from fire barrels, but with the communion of saints, the light and warmth come from… any guesses?"

"From God."

"Yes. We all gather around the light and warmth that comes from God. The people who have already gone ahead of us are in God's presence. Because God is everywhere, we are also in His presence, especially when we gather at the Eucharist."

"The big circle a bread you held up."

"Yes, we elevate the Eucharist so that all who are gathered can see. It is a powerful moment. Remember, a sacrament is an outward sign of an invisible grace that is happening."

"Yeh, I remember that."

"The Eucharist is a powerful sacrament, an outward showing of the spiritual fact of Christ's real presence."

"His presence," Perry said.

"Yes."

"Like in, He's really there."

"Yes."

"In the piece of bread?"

"Yes, in all the pieces of bread that have been consecrated on the altar, even though it still looks like bread."

"Prayed over? That what cons'crated means?"

"Yes, prayed over, in a very special way."

"That's some crazy stuff, K.O."

"It is, Perry. But Christ Himself instituted that sacrament and commanded us to continue to celebrate it whenever we gather as Church."

Perry looked at him for a long time. John pulled up his coat collar to shield his neck from the cold breeze.

"You ain't kiddin' when you say it takes a minute," Perry said. "I can't really get my head around it."

"That's okay, Perry. It is a challenging mystery. Even the people who walked with Jesus here on Earth had a tough time accepting it. He said, 'This is my body, this is my blood.'"

"You talkin' 'bout the wine?"

"Yes. Even when people were walking away from Jesus because of that teaching, He never wavered. He never softened it. The sacrament of the Eucharist is a great gift to us from God. A way for us to be in direct communion with Jesus Christ Himself."

"That word again, only now you're using it different."

"Communion. Being one. One with the saints, one with Jesus. One with each other, in the body of Christ."

Perry nodded a few times. "I'm'onna have to think about this some."

....

Perry found himself standing in the opening of an alley in a part of town he never went to. He didn't know how he got there or why he was there. That was the aggravatinest part about all this. Never knowin' what was comin' next. Then he spotted the suit. The old man who wasn't his old man, but still was. He was standin' at the crosswalk checkin' his watch. It was weird how he kept showin' up places at the same time as Perry. It couldn't be no accident. Not this many times. The lady in the light had said "find your path." Whatever Perry was s'posed to do, this suit was a part of it. He was sure of that.

The old man went inside the sandwich shop, bought a couple sandwiches, went and sat by a big window, starin' out at the street. The old man might have seen him, so he ducked back into the alley. But the old man kept starin' down the street, opposite where Perry was, so maybe not.

Old dude acted nervous, checking his watch every ten seconds. Must be late for something. But no, 'cause he had two sandwiches right in front of him and he wasn't touchin' 'em. The old man's ears perked up. Perry followed his eyes and ducked back farther into the alley. It was the guy. The son. The same one that was with the old man in all those cities. That's who was late. Walkin' along like he was in a dream, not seein' anything around him. Perry couldn't help starin', even though it freaked him out.

The guy looked exactly the same as Perry. Except he was rich, and soft, and spoiled, and wore fancy clothes. He didn't look like he ever had a hard day in his whole life. Like he never been in a fight, or went hungry, or was ever cold, or was ever looked down on by nobody nowhere. It made Perry mad.

All those years, I took care of the old man. And where did it get me? It got me killed, that's where. And now, in this new place, whatever this is, all these blue dumpsters everywhere, the old man is a big shot. And now that he's a big shot, he acts like he don't even know me. That's bad enough. Now I find out he has another kid he calls son, who's as much a big shot as he is. And where is good old Perry? Perry is out. Out in the cold, out in the stink, out of luck, out of ideas, out of time.

While they chewed on their sandwiches, he chewed on all that and got madder and madder. Finally, the guy got up to leave. The old man hugged him. Actually *hugged* him. The son came out, walked right by Perry like he was invisible. *This ain't right.* Right there, he decided. He wasn't going to sit still, and take being treated like this. He was gonna confront the old man.

....

Deuce watched the homeless kid glare at Peregrine until Peregrine passed him and then turn this way. Deuce focused on his phone as if he was checking his messages. In his peripheral vision, the kid walked across the street, headed straight for the sandwich shop. The bell told Deuce he was inside, but Deuce didn't glance up. The kid walked right up and stood by his table. Same ratty clothes, same smell, same busted up face.

"You in heaven?"

"What?"

Typical of this kid. No foreplay. Right to the pointed questions. Insane questions. Deuce looked at him for a moment, gestured for him to sit down.

"You heard me. Answer the question." The kid slumped into the chair.

"Well, that's a funny way to put it, but if you want to speak in metaphors, yes, things are actually very good for me."

"You got it made."

"Most people would say so, I suppose."

"Yer rich."

"Everything is relative. But yes, I am very fortunate."

"Then why am I still here in these rags?"

"Uh... I'm sorry, I don't think I understand. What are we talking about?"

"We *talkin'* about why you got all this and I still got *rot.*"

Deuce gave him a stern look. "I don't know what this is. I have been trying to understand. What do you want?"

"That guy, you call yer son. Who is he?"

Deuce searched his eyes, trying to read what was beneath the words. "That guy, as you call him, *is my son.*"

The homeless kid seemed to choke on that. "And where's he live?"

"I'm not going to tell you that."

"What does he do, how 'bout that?"

"He is a professor."

"A *professor*?"

"Yes, a college professor."

"Of course, he is. That's just *great.*"

Deuce was disoriented, lost in the trees. "Young man, this guessing game is tiring. Whatever is on your chest, I wish you would just say it."

"Yeah? Well, how 'bout this. You the worst old man *ever.*"

Oh God. There it was. He finally said it.

"You never did *slop* for me when you were alive, and you still doing nothing for me now that yer *dead.*"

"What?"

"Screw you, man." The kid stomped out. Was he almost in tears? *That* was disturbing. Deuce had been through all kinds of dangerous situations, but this kid... Deuce's hands were shaking. He pressed them flat against the cool tabletop. D.M. was right. You never know. He was beginning to think the kid was harmless, but it turns out he is a mental case. Maybe schizophrenic? And he's angry. That presents a whole *different* set of security problems. Deuce was going to have to be careful how he broke this news, or D.M. might decide on his own to take the kid out.

··········

"I don't understand how it happened," Perry said. He was sitting in front of his dumpster, cloud billowing around him. "Or why. I died tryin' to take care of him, and I spose he drank himself to death. He gets to go to heaven, and I'm still in hell, just like I always been. I never thought heaven and hell would be in the same place. I'm still here stinkin', while he has everything he could ever want, including the son he always wanted. He's living a life I coulda never *dreamed* for us, and he can't even remember my name. It's like I don't exist."

"Are you sure that is what you are seeing?" Henry asked. He was sitting relaxed, arms folded, strong dark forearms below the rolled-up sleeves, one ragged pant leg bent across the other, swirling the cloud with his patched-up tennis shoe.

"No, man. I'm not *sure.* I'm not sure of *any*thing. Nothings makin' *sense.*" Perry swatted at a wisp of cloud with his hand, came up empty.

"What are some other possibilities? Can you think more broadly?"

"More broadly? What do you mean? Why do you havta talk in riddles, Henry? Can't you just help me? Can't you just tell me what to do next?"

"I am helping you, little brother."

"No, you're not."

"I am."

Things couldn't be no weirder. "Okay, yeah. You are. And thanks for that. But I need more than that. A *lot* more."

"Be patient, Perry. Allow things to unfold."

"Man, that's what I been doin' all my *life.* That's how I got *inta* this mess."

"Things may not be as bad as you imagine."

"Oh, yeah? Less see. Mom's dead of cancer, ol' man's drunk hisself to death… lived my whole life under the stink of a dumpster… that it? No, another thing… Got my brains bashed in with ball bats, now I'm floatin' around in hell like… I don't even *know* what."

Henry looked at him, patient, his nice, calm look.

"This ain't my imagination. My life sucked. And this, what come after my life, sucks *worse.*"

Henry looked at him kindly. "I have a suggestion for you."

"Okay."

"Next time you see Father John, ask him to tell you the story of poor Lazarus and the rich man."

October 8

The next morning, Perry found hisself somewhere he'd never been before. Again. It was like a park. Not huge, like The Common, but a good-size piece a grass. Walking paths crisscrossing, and people hurrying between tall buildings. A lot of strange stuff here. On one end of the grass, a pile of twisted steel beams was bent and folded over. 'Stead of hauling them off, someone painted them red and left them right there. Someone musta give the pile of junk iron a name, cause a little stone with a metal plate told what they named it and who left it there, like you would see on a statue. But it wasn't no statue. They shoulda painted it green. At least then it would blend in. As it was, it stuck out like a big sore thumb. If they took all that to the recycle, they could get quite a bit.

Most people were carrying books, dressed in nice clothes, but not like the suits downtown. A lot of these people were young as Perry or younger. A few geezers mixed in, but not too many. In one place, a wide set of steps was wrapped around so it was half a circle. Trees was growing right up out of the steps. Someone shoulda plucked those when they was little. Behind that, tall buildings like stacks of kids' blocks that might fall over any second. Weird buildings. Perry realized what this was. This was the institute where suits went to be trained. The way things been happening, he figured he was gonna see the professor show up any minute. Maybe he could finally figure out what was going on. Probably better act to casual, just let it happen.

He went almost to the end of one of the paths and stood by some trees. A cool breeze came across the grass, refreshing. A dude came walking like he was lost in another world, head back, eyes half closed, barely payin' any attention. It was him. The guy. The professor. When he seen Perry, he stopped, fancy shoes skiddin' on the walking path. The professor looked like he was gonna bolt, but he pulled himself together and came on. Perry stepped out onto the path and blocked his way. The professor froze again.

"What's yer name, man?" Perry asked.

The guy's mouth went slack, like he'd been slapped. Then he bucked himself up and says real snooty,

"I am Professor Faulk. I am on faculty here at the institute."

"Faulk, huh?"

"Yes. *Professor* Faulk. Is there something I can help you with?" The guy was so soft it was embarrassing. Trying to act tough, but Perry could tell, first sign of trouble, he'd wilt like a flower.

"Don't you want to know who *I* am?" Perry asked.

"Should I?"

"I think maybe *so*." He took off his stocking cap to give the spoiled kid a better view. "Take a good look at me, man. Do I look familiar to you?"

The professor's face went whiter than it already was. His mouth trembled a little.

"Kind of freakish, isn't it?" Perry was startin' to enjoy this.

"What… what is this?"

"What kind of professor *are* you?" Perry demanded.

"Wh-what do you mean?"

"What do you *teach*, man?" *Jeez. Stupid.*

"I teach mostly two-hundred-level courses, but my field of research is genetics."

"Genetics? No snot? Wow. Check that out." Perry spit on the sidewalk.

"Is there something you want from me?" the professor asked, shaky. "I need to be somewhere—"

"Oh, zat right? Gotta be somewhere, huh? Well, that makes *two* of us. I'm trying to get somewhere too. And you should care about that."

"Should I? How so?"

"Man, don't you *recognize* me?"

"I've seen you around. You've been following me, but I don't believe I've ever met you before."

"Man, look me in the eyes. Don't you see it? The eyes of the *soul*?"

The professor met his eyes for about a second, then shifted away. He looked like he was gonna be sick. The professor was actin' so scared, Perry figured it would be fun to mess with his head a little. He started actin' real snooty, mocking the professor. He figured out too late he shouldna did it. He laid it on too thick. Before he could get any answers from him, the professor freaked out, took off runnin' back where he came from.

....

"Haruki, sorry to interrupt, but do you have a second?"

"Yes, Pete. Come in." Haruki closed a file folder on his desk. "I read an article about a young homeless man who was killed in an alley. Apparently, it was random violence."

"Yes sir, I read about that."

"I like it when things are tied up neatly, with a bow on top."

"Thank you, sir."

"I read an unrelated story, about a crew of gang members who were arrested with a trunk load of firearms."

"Oh. Yes Sir."

"I thought to myself, that is sloppy. Something must have gone wrong in the handling of that crew."

"I'm sorry sir."

"And now the threat exposures are multiplied as a result."

"Yes sir. I am working on it."

"Working on it?"

"Yes sir. I'm working with Guy to help him handle it."

"Pete, I pay you very well to manage things for me. It is not good form to come in here and blame subordinates for your bungling."

"Yes Sir. I will handle it."

"I would expect so.

October 9

Father John smiled when he smelled the buttered popcorn. Whenever he walked into a movie theater, that aroma took him back to his childhood. He loved the movies, especially thrillers. He always had. It was a captivating medium that could transport him far away to places of excitement and intrigue.

A small girl, maybe seven years, was negotiating with her mother to get a box of candy. The glass display was positioned precisely at eye level for a child. The girl was losing, so she was resorting to attrition warfare, taking down each of her mother's nerves, one by one. John smiled and checked his watch. Ten minutes until the show starts. *Should have gotten here earlier. Oh well, it will be okay.* He didn't like to miss the previews because they helped him choose which movie to see next.

The girl working the concession spilled a large tub of popcorn, had to stop and clean it up. *It will be okay. She's doing her best. Four minutes until the show starts.* Finally, it was his turn. He ordered an extra-large buttered popcorn and an extra-large soda. He promised himself he would make up for it later. Fast walking to the previews was a start. He gave his ticket to the usher, who directed him to theater number four. He was barely going to make it. As he arrived at the door, a young woman ahead of him held the door open for him.

"Oh. Hi, Father!"

"Virginia." He stood there blinking, hands full of junk food. She smelled nice and her smile was engaging. Over her shoulder, the dark theater loomed.

"I've been *dying* to see this movie, Father. What a surprise to bump into you here." Her smile was so sincere, and...

"Um. Yes, that is a surprise," he said.

"I'm here alone. Do you have a seat yet?"

He peered past her into the dark theater. "Um. Actually, I… forgot something… that I meant to remember. At the concession…"

"Really?" She looked at his extra-large popcorn and soda.

"Uh-huh." He turned and headed back to the concession as fast as he could go.

············

Father John sat through the credits at the end. Amazing. Hundreds of people poured their talents, hopes, and dreams into the production. Yet almost nobody stayed to read their names. Out in the corridor, he dropped his half-full bucket of popcorn into the trash bin. He scolded himself. A touch of gluttony there. He hated to waste the popcorn, but it would be worse to finish it. He wiped his hands with a paper napkin and headed for the door.

Overall, a disappointing evening. The movie was marketed as a thriller, a conspiracy story about an attack on the Vatican. They gave away all the surprises too early, so it wasn't really an edge-of-the-seat experience. And they applied a load of negative stereotypes to the Church. Oh well. Time to get home and close the day. He opened the door to a breeze of cool air, and a familiar scent.

"Hi, Father."

"Oh. Hi, Virginia."

"How did you like the movie?"

"I would say maybe a six or seven. How about you?"

"I was disappointed. A cast like that and they couldn't make it thrilling? I give it a three," she said.

"I agree that it wasn't the acting. It was bad writing."

"Exactly," she said.

"Well, good evening, you two," a sing-song voice behind him said. "Small world, isn't it?"

John turned. "Gabby. How are you?" Her ironic grin was accusing. She was glancing back and forth between him and Virginia.

"Did you two enjoy your evening out?"

"We were just discussing that," Virginia said cheerfully.

Gabby looked from her to him. "Well. Don't let me intrude. I've got to run."

"Nice to see you, Gabby," he said, trying to mean it.

She glanced back over her shoulder with a smile that said "Gotcha."

His heart plunged. On the far edge of the parking lot was a dark sedan with tinted windows. The window raised when he looked at it.

"I've got to be running, Virginia."

"Where did you park?"

"I'm sorry. I'm short on time. I really must go."

"Okay, Father. It was a joy to see you, as always."

It wasn't her smile that bothered him. It was that look in her eyes. He turned and walked into the darkness.

October 10

The next morning, after daily Mass, Gabby, Betsy, and Liza huddled in the corner of the front vestibule. Father John could tell they were gossiping. He had been working with each of them, trying to help them understand how harmful that habit is. He had better engage and break up the party.

"Good day, ladies," he said, as cheerful as could be.

They fell silent and faced him. Oh. This must have been some good gossip.

"Are you ladies waiting here for something to start? I don't remember seeing any small group meetings on the calendar."

"No, Father. We're talking," Gabby said.

"Ah, I see." He kept his tone cheerful.

"It *is* okay to visit a little after gathering for Mass, isn't it?" Gabby asked.

"Of course. Community building. Very important."

"Thank you, Father." Gabby turned her back to him as though that finished their conversation.

"Be sure your words are building the community *up*," he said with a big smile. "We don't want our words to tear the community down, do we?"

The three of them glared. It might be worse than he had imagined. He turned to go and a twist in his stomach told him what they must be talking about. He faced them again as if he had remembered something.

"Oh, I almost forgot. Gabby, last night outside the movie theater?"

She gave the ladies a knowing look.

"You left so quickly; I didn't get a chance to ask you what you thought of the movie."

She hesitated. “Truthfully, I thought it was trash. Like most movies, it did not place the Church in a good light.”

“I see.”

She smirked. “What did you and *Virginia* think?”

“I wouldn’t go quite so far as to call it trash,” he said, “but I didn’t think it was very well written. After the movie, when I bumped into Virginia *outside*, she said she had a similar impression.”

“I see.” Gabby glanced at the other ladies again.

“Do you often go to the movies alone, Gabby?” he asked. Her eyes narrowed.

“You *were* there alone, weren’t you?”

She pursed her lips.

“It’s nothing to be ashamed of. I was there alone too. I go to the movies to relax. I was surprised to bump into *two* of my church sisters outside after the movie.”

"That *is* a surprising coincidence.” Her tone seemed to imply “if true.” That annoyed him, but he had pushed it as far as he could without sounding defensive.

“Well, you ladies have a nice day.”

Father John left the church and headed across the campus to the office building. There was no winning with Gabby. The wedge between them grew deeper with every interaction. In the end, people were going to think what they wanted to think. His conscience was clear. A little twinge tweaked him. Hmm. What was that there for? No need to dwell on it. He’d done nothing wrong.

....

Later, Perry was hiding behind a big elm tree, watchin’ the door of the church office. After about a hour, Father John came out, headed over to the church. Perry *had* to talk to him. After a minute, he followed and opened the door. He sneezed loud to make sure Father John would know he was comin’.

“Hey, K.O.?” he called.

Father John came out of the room where he kept the priest robes, holding some papers.

“Yes, Perry?”

“Who’s Lazarus?”

"Lazarus?" Father John glanced into the room like he wanted to go back in there, then he took a breath and smiled. He motioned for Perry to follow him as he headed for the reconciliation room. "Lazarus was a particularly good friend of Jesus. Have a seat. Have you been reading about him?"

"No, just wonderin' about him. What's the story with him?"

"Well, there are a few places Lazarus is mentioned in Scripture. He had two sisters, Martha, and Mary. The family was special to Jesus, and they were among the first to realize something powerful was happening with Him."

"Yeah? And so?"

"Well, one day Lazarus became ill, and his sisters sent word to Jesus to ask Him to come save Lazarus."

"Save him how?"

"Jesus was both God *and* man, so He had the power to heal anyone He wished. Martha and Mary had *seen* Him heal people. Naturally, they wanted Him to heal their brother."

"And He did it?"

Father John shook his head. "No. He was within walking distance, but He didn't go to Lazarus right away. In fact, He waited for several days."

"What? With His buddy in trouble, needin' His help?"

"Yes. But not because He didn't love him. He waited because there was a bigger purpose for this illness, and He needed to let things unfold."

"Bigger purpose?"

"Perry, there are things in life that are bigger than we are."

"So, you mean Jesus had a plan, and Lazarus had to take a hit so the plan could play out."

"Well, may…be…?"

Perry scowled. "I never knew Jesus was like that. I know a dude who's that way. Kujo had a plan to make a name for hisself, so he sent Bobby to do a thing, and Bobby took the hit. So Kujo's big man on the street but Bobby's dead."

"No, Perry. This was not like that at all. Jesus didn't inflict Lazarus with the illness. I don't think so anyway. Well, maybe He allowed it to happen, but…"

"Sounds pretty much the same to me."

"It is *not* the same."

"Kujo wasn't there when Bobby needed him, and Jesus wasn't there for Lazarus. Same thing."

Father John sighed. "Perry, listen to me carefully. God is not like anyone you've ever met. He is our heavenly Father. He loves everyone. He would never allow someone to be hurt to better Himself. Understand?"

Perry looked up at the crucifix. "You say so."

John sighed. "Let me tell you the rest of the story."

Perry shrugged.

"Lazarus got very ill, and in fact, he died."

"Like *Bobby*."

"Well... anyway, once Lazarus had died, Jesus went to him."

"That don't make no sense."

"It *does* if you allow me to finish the *story*. Lazarus was dead, understand? He was dead and buried. He had been in the tomb for three days."

"Don't get much deader than *that*, man."

"Exactly. And when Jesus arrived, Mary asked why he didn't come. She said, 'If you had been here, my brother would not have died.'"

"I think she's right, He as powerful as you say."

"Yes, that's the human way to think about it. But do you know what Jesus said?"

"What?"

"He said, '*I* am the resurrection and the life.'"

"Resurrection?"

"Yes, resurrection is being raised from the dead. He called Lazarus' name, and Lazarus came walking out of the tomb."

"No *kiddin'*?"

"No kidding."

"So, Lazarus was dead, and now he's alive again?"

"Yes. Through that event, Jesus demonstrated that He had the power to defeat even *death*."

"Whoa. I never even knew that could *happen*."

"With God, all things are possible, Perry."

"Where's He live?"

"Who?"

"*Lazarus.*"

"Well, he's not *still* alive."

"He's dead *again*?"

"Well, sure. Everyone's got to die sometime. But that's not the point of the story —"

"Way I see it, point is, don't matter how it happens, you dead, you dead for good, right?"

"Well… uh…"

October 11

"Good morning, Haruki, I have some good news about the priest, Bianchi."

"Please tell me you have gathered some damning evidence we can use."

"Well, no. Not Damning. But we're making progress. Our guy got a few photos outside a movie theater. Most of them have him talking to two women, one of them older, but there are a couple, where he and the pretty young one are alone."

"That's it?"

"A priest, talking alone with a pretty young woman outside of a movie theater. The shots look pretty good."

"It sounds skimpy. If it were a motel, it would be better. I need you to work harder on this. Waiting for some relationship to run its natural course could take forever. Or, it could amount to nothing. I need him out of the way. He's disrupting important initiatives."

"You want him to... go away?" Pete asked.

Haruki scoffed. "I don't want him taken *out*. The world doesn't need another martyr. I want him to be ruined, and I want him to *suffer*."

Pete waited.

"Destroy his reputation. I want you to make sure every seed he ever planted withers and dies along with his career."

Pete hesitated before speaking. "So... when you say suffer..."

"Scandal, Pete. Get some professional women involved if you have to. I want him brought down in flames, and I mean soon. I'd like to see him burn in hell, but for now I'll settle for seeing him burned alive on the front pages of all the papers."

. . . .

What a day. John was tired, and demoralized. Maybe some fresh air would help. He stepped out of the rectory, dressed in civilian clothes. He didn't feel like being visible tonight. He just wanted to blend into the fabric of society and have some time for himself. Friday Evening, there was an easy bustle in the city. People moving around, but for pleasure, not business. John needed some rest and relaxation. He decided he would allow himself a nice long stroll in the crisp air. It would be good for him. Maybe do a little window shopping, and relax. He found himself on Washington, looking through the window of a jewelry store. It was a strange attraction, considering he didn't wear Jewelry. He wondered how many young couples had stared through this very window, eyes glittering as they looked over the sets of wedding rings. He could imagine their hearts filled with love and excitement, running headlong after dreams of a life filled with marital bliss. Another experience he would never know. In the window, he saw the reflection of a young woman standing on the street corner at the end of the block. Her back was to him, and all her clothes fit her as though they had been sprayed on. He only allowed himself to examine her form for a second. Maybe two.

OCTOBER 12

Fr. John was moody today. Sitting in the little confession room like he did every Saturday, he looked grumpy around the edges. What makes a priest grumpy? Seems like they'd be too holy for that. Perry had been excited to tell him what Henry said, but when he did, K.O. didn't like it.

"Tell me more about the cloud." Father John said. He hadn't bothered to light the candle today. That was different.

"I already *tol* you. I can't explain it more. I was hoping you could explain it to *me*."

"I don't know that I can do that, Perry."

See, grumpy. Right there, the corners of his mouth, and the way his eyes drop down to the floor. Wonder what's up with that.

"But K.O., all I'm askin,"

"Don't call me that."

"What?"

"Please don't call me that. I'm not in the mood for it today."

Woah. *Really* grumpy. Never been like this before.

"Everything alright, Father John?"

"Everything is fine, Perry. I just don't feel playful."

"Sorry. Didn't mean nothin' by it. I thought it was, you know, kind of a secret handshake we had."

Father John sighed and looked up at Perry, but in a weird way. Like he almost didn't want to look at him. Maybe tired of seeing him?

"You want me to go and come a different time? If you do, that's cool, ya know?"

"No, Perry. I do not want you to go. What was it you were going to ask?"

"It's all right. Nothin'."

Father John sighed. "Look, Perry. I'm sorry. Please understand that a priest is only a human person trying his best to do a difficult job. Okay? Can you cut me some slack and accept my apology?"

"Sure." The room was different without the candle lit.

"Thank you."

"Father?"

"Yes, Perry?"

"What do you know about angels?"

That made Father John smile a little. Must like angels. "I'm going to be perfectly honest with you. I've read a lot about them, and I find them fascinating. The concept, I mean. One of my favorite mysteries."

"They for real, then?"

"Oh yes, I'm convinced they're real."

"You ever seen one?"

"No. But I would *like* to."

Perry paused. He wasn't sure if he should say it. "I'm not sure... but I been thinkin'... maybe I have."

"Have what?"

"I been thinkin' maybe the old dude in the cloud is a angel."

Father John was starin' at him with a weird look.

"Only not with wings and all. Just like... you know, undercover, dressed up like a normal dude."

Father John opened his mouth like he was gonna ask a question, but he didn't.

"Do angels ever go undercover like that? You know, how sometimes cops try not to look like cops?"

Father John smiled a little, but looked kinda sad, too. *Weird.* He was off his game today, for sure. Maybe not grumpy. Maybe just sad.

"Perry, the Bible has multiple stories about angels disguising themselves as normal people and walking among us."

"I *knew* it! Old Henry *gotta* be undercover. That's what it is. Awesome. Thanks, Father John." *What? Now he's grumpy again. Man, dude is hard to figure. What ya think will make him happy makes him sad. Or grumpy. Can't tell which.*

"What makes you think he is an angel, Perry?" Serious, like throwin' out a challenge.

"Well, he's smart. Not that regular Henry ain't smart, but this dude's different. *Really* different. Like he knows stuff — stuff that nobody oughta know."

"You're talking about the man who comes to you in the cloud?"

"Yeh. He comes and goes. Can't never tell when. Sometimes he's there, sometimes he ain't."

Father John was slumped into his chair, folding a church bulletin into something. Maybe one of them fancy animals like a bird. Maybe... Nope, just a ordinary paper airplane. He tossed it across the little room straight into the corner. It fell to the floor with a crumpled nose, and he sat there and stared at it. Woah. Father dude was not hisself today.

"Father John, you mad at me?"

"What?"

"Are you like... steamed at me or something?"

"No, Perry."

"I say somethin' wrong?"

"No. Look, I told you, this job can be frustrating. I'm doing the best I can."

"No problem, Father. You doin' good. Your tryin' to help me, and I 'preciate that."

"Thank you, Perry." Still grumpy. The way Dad is when he can't get a drink. Perry studied Father John carefully. He was back to staring at the crashed airplane. Yep, he needs *somethin'*. It aint a drink though. But he needs something he can't *get*. And it's hurtin' him, like it hurts Dad to be without booze. Man, that's awful, ta see someone suffer like that. Someone you'd like to help but can't. They go without that thing they need long enough, it starts to make 'em sick. Seen it many times, but not with Father John. Some kinda strangeness goin' on.

"Father John, you believe me?"

"What?"

"You think I'm lyin'? I know I been tellin' you some crazy stuff. You think I'm makin' it up?"

Father John sighed. "No, I don't think you're making up *any* of it. I can tell something dramatic is happening in your life."

"Oh. And you ain't mad at me?"

"No, Perry. Please stop asking that. Believe me. I'm not mad at you."

"You ever had anyone else come in here and tell you stuff like this? Anybody ever talk about the white cloud before?"

The priest shook his head, frowning. "I've never heard anything *like* it, to be frank."

"Is somethin' wrong with me?"

Father John took a deep breath, sat up straight in his chair. "Look, Perry. God comes to us as He chooses. How and when is not up to us. We can wish, we can pray, we can work. But God will not show up on command. He is God. We must accept that, even if we wish it were different. Sometimes you can go for years and do everything you know how to do—feed the chickens, lay yourself out as a sacrifice, give up the nicest things in life like family, and love, and closeness, and intimacy, and in return you might get nothing but silence, you understand? You *cannot* rush God, Perry. You might as well accept that. It is just the way it *is*. Who are we to question, if God doesn't come talk to us or even send an angel with a little encouragement? It is out of our hands!"

Whoa. Father John be trippin'. Perry sat still. *Pretty sure Father John ain't talking about Perry's problems no more.* The priest was staring, blinking. Forehead crinkling up like he was confused. Another big, heavy sigh. Father John came half outta his chair, reached for the paper airplane, slowly crumpled it, quiet, and carefully dropped it into the trash bin. Like... gently. Making a show of being in control. But he ain't in *no* kinda control, that's for sure.

"Perry, I owe you an apology. I'm not myself today. I'm sorry."

"It's okay, Father. We still cool. You wanna tell me what's up?"

He smiled. A real smile this time, but tired. "Let the student be the teacher for a bit, huh?"

Perry grinned his broadest. "Sure, why not. Give you the day off."

Father John chuckled. *There he is. K.O. comin' up off the ropes, makin' his comeback.*

"Perry, I don't want to neglect to answer your question. Something strange and unusual is happening in your life, would you agree?"

"Man, you ain't *kiddin'.*"

"Well, God is with you, wherever you are. Remember we talked about the indelible mark you received at your baptism?"

"Yeah, man, that's some crazy sh—stuff."

"It really is. God doesn't want you to be taken from Him. Jesus tells us clearly, if there are ninety-nine loyal sheep staying close to him, He will abandon them all and go into the wilderness to search for a single sheep who has lost his way. If something unusual is happening to the lost sheep, He might need to do something unusual to save him. Understand?"

Perry nodded. "That's crazy."

"Yes, but that's our God. Would you like to know what I think is happening to you in the cloud?"

"Yes, Father. I would like to know that."

"I suspect… I could be wrong about this, but I have a sense that the cloud experience you keep having, is God trying to reach out to you. He is trying to find you, Perry, because you've lost your way."

Perry tried to talk but he couldn't. It was like those words had zapped somethin' in his voice box and knotted it up. The dampness of the cloud moved in around him. He tried again, but nothin'. Father John started getting blurry, and when Perry blinked, water ran down his face. He had to get outta there. He stood up, but Father John beat him to the door and blocked the way. Then, a total unexpect, he threw his arms around Perry, like a boxer tying up his opponent so he can't fight no more. That clean black shirt was pressed against his filthy, stinking rags. It didn't seem right. Perry knew he wasn't worth all that.

October 14

Across the street, the professor dude and some older woman disappeared into a coffee shop. As usual, Perry was trying to figure out where he was and what to do next. He couldn't go in that shop. It was one of them kind that charge like six bucks for one cup of coffee. Perry couldn't believe people would pay that. He could go to the movies three times for that much. Besides, Geppetto gave it away free.

The professor and the older woman came out, sat at one of the tables. Traffic was blocking his view mostly, but he was catching peeps between cars and trucks. They was leaning across the table, their heads close together, like they was talking about something they didn't want nobody else to hear. It would be nice to know what they were sayin'. Rich people talked about interesting stuff sometimes. But not always. The professor looked this way and his eyes met Perry's. They both froze. Wasn't nowhere good to hide here, out on the sidewalk like this. Perry wanted to run, but he didn't.

The woman spun around and looked right at him. His stomach dropped a couple inches. *Crud.* She jumped up from the table and headed toward him. Perry took a couple steps back. He didn't like suits, and especially women suits. They was super unpredictable. She stepped right out into the traffic without lookin'. *See? Crazy woman.* Cars started screeching and swerving. There was a loud crash and the woman screamed, but Perry didn't see what happened. He was makin' tracks as fast as he could down a side street, runnin'.

•••••••••••

Father John was exhausted. He had never been so tired. He arrived at the meeting center at nine Monday morning. He was anxious to spend time with his brothers. It was a jovial atmosphere, everyone greeting and catching up, some of the people he only saw a few times a year. He had been looking forward to this retreat. An annual event, a few short days to gather with his brother priests and rest.

His brothers were as diverse as any group of men would be. Maybe more so. But the one thing they all had in common was their love for the deep and perplexing call to the priesthood. They looked forward to sharing the common joys and sorrows of this life they had chosen, or rather had chosen them. Nobody else could really understand. Like any group of human beings, occasional friction was inevitable. Sometimes there were misunderstandings, pettiness, and even betrayal. But what held them together was more powerful than the dynamics that might try to pull them apart.

John relished the chance to catch up with his young friend Bob. Right after Bob was ordained, he had been assigned to the parish where John was Associate Pastor. That was five years ago. Despite being ten years younger than John, Bob had a maturity about him, a strong sense of human dynamics. Sometimes John was shocked by the insights that could come from the young man. He arranged to sit with him at dinner.

"Whoever was in charge of getting the caterer did a good job this year, didn't they?" Bob being his usual cheerful self.

"Yeah. Fish, right?"

"Hah! John, you reduce everything down to the base. I believe this is Kerala Fish Moilee. It is a dish thought to be of Portuguese origin. I believe this is the Indian version."

"Spicy. With vegetables."

Father Bob was smiling. "Yes, *spicy. With vegetables*. Very astute. Did you pick up on the coconut?"

"Is that what that is?"

"Yes, John. Coconut is a key ingredient."

Most priests have a special area of interest, a way of expressing their unique God-given gifts in the context of their ministry. John's was his love for astronomy and cosmology. Bob's was the culinary arts. Good for him.

It made him a more interesting person. But in the final analysis, it was still fish any way you cooked it.

"John, how are you?"

"Oh, I'm fine. You?"

"John, you look tired. Everything okay? Been to the doctor lately?"

"The doctor? No, I don't have time for such personal luxuries."

"Brother, when going to the doctor feels like a personal luxury, it might be a sign your life is out of balance."

"You think so? I don't know. There are millions, probably billions, who never go to a doctor in their whole lives, birth to death. It *is* a personal luxury. We Americans are so entitled we've come to think of it as a necessity."

Bob's eyes widened. "Whoa. You're serious today, aren't you? I ask again… you okay?"

John smiled at his young friend, but the reaction on Bob's face told him he should have made a better effort.

"John, you've got to take care of yourself. People are depending on you."

"Tell me about it. So *many*. It's…"

"It's what? Tell me what's going on."

"Oh, nothing. Maybe growing pains, I don't know… maybe a small spiritual crisis."

Bob leaned forward. "Okay, now you need to tell me more. A spiritual crisis for a priest can be a serious problem."

"Tell me about it."

"How long has this been going on?"

"I don't know, really. It comes and goes. Maybe a few years."

"*Years?*" Bob's expression turned serious.

"Listen, Bob. Don't worry about it. You'll find that spiritual growth always involves ups and downs. Some desert experiences."

"Yes, I know, but *years?* You should talk to someone."

"I am."

"Good. Who?"

"You."

"Oh. Well, I meant a professional. Someone with training, and experience."

"Great idea, Bob. You know anyone who's specialties are angels, visitations, and visions?"

"You've been having…"

"No. Not me. That's the problem. This kid."

"A parishioner?"

"No, a young guy who wandered in off the street. At first, I thought he was looking for a handout. But that's not it. He's actually going through some kind of deep spiritual experience."

"That's great!"

"Well, yes. It is. He's a good kid, and he's had a rough life. So good for him."

"Is there a 'but' coming in this story?"

"I'm embarrassed to say it, but yes. I am happy for the guy, and I'm also… a little jealous. Envious. There. I've said it out loud. I'm struggling with the sin of envy." The fish and vegetable dish was colorful. A nice steak would have been good.

"That's healthy, John. If you understand it's something you need to work on, you'll be fine."

"No, you're not understanding me. I'm running into the sin of envy all over the place. When I see married couples, when I see people with normal jobs, when I hear of people enjoying their hobbies…"

Bob was quiet for a few moments. "Tell me more about the kid."

"I am *really* envious of this kid. He was baptized as an infant but never received the other sacraments. Hasn't been to Mass in years. And he's having these full-blown Moses-and-the-burning-bush experiences."

"Is he mentally ill?"

"See? There it is. I had that *exact* same reaction. Why do we do that?"

"Do what?"

"Assume that anyone who is having a profound spiritual experience must be crazy."

"Well, probably because we've spent our lives meeting people who claim to have those experiences, and in time, it turns out that most of them are."

"So, here's the irony," John said. "He's homeless, and I'm wishing I could have what he has."

"I think you're talking about something different."

"Am I?"

Bob's expression was that of a younger friend trying to figure out the older man. Probably wondering if *John* was a little crazy.

"Listen," John said. "This kid doesn't do drugs. He exhibits no symptoms of pathology. He only seems crazy when he talks about his spiritual experiences. And everything he's told me is in perfect harmony with the Bible.

Heck, he's even in harmony with the *catechism*. The strange thing is... he's never *read* the Bible *or* the catechism. He's lived on the street most of his life."

"Hmm. Well, if it is authentic, we should all sing praises, because this means God is moving in our midst."

"Exactly. And instead, I'm sitting there being eaten alive with envy."

"Mmm."

life to serving God. I spent almost ten years in higher education. I've done everything I know how to do. And yet... No visions. No angels, nothing. A daily grind, fourteen years of it, parades of people coming in to pull pieces off me and carry them away. There's almost nothing *left*. And God never sent *anyone* to help me. Not a single visitation."

"Until this kid."

"What?"

"He never sent anyone to you *until this kid...* who happened to wander in off the street? This kid who is teaching you about God."

"Well, I wouldn't say that."

"No? Sounds like it to me."

Bob could be a pain in the neck. He was prone to saying annoying, challenging things. And he would sit there and look at you, with no expression, like he was doing now.

"Look," Bob said, "I don't know what the story is with this kid. I haven't even met him. But I feel for him. I don't think I've ever shared this with you before, but when I was a kid, I spent a lot of time on the street. I was almost pulled into the gang scene."

"Really? I didn't know that. How did that happen?"

"I didn't think there was any other way for me. My mom, rest her soul, was working two jobs. Everyone I knew had a mom who was working two jobs, working the street corners or strung out on drugs."

"Oh. I'm sorry, Brother."

"I wasn't homeless, but we all had absentee dads and were left loose on the streets to make do for ourselves. The ones who did have men in their homes were worse off, because none of the men were biological and most of them were violent."

"Oh, my Lord. I never knew. How did you get out?"

"It's kind of a long story."

John shrugged. "It's a four-day retreat."

After a couple of seconds, Bob drew a breath. "I was sixteen years old, getting ready to be jumped in. Initiated. By that, I mean, the leaders of the gang had designed a test for me. This guy named Kujo, delivered the message. Kujo was younger than I was, but had been in the gang for several years, and had a special gift for violence. He told me I had been chosen to go into one of the rival territories and *kill* this low-level gangbanger who had been invading our territory."

"Lord have mercy."

"He did. Have mercy, I mean. Kujo had already given me the gun, and these older bangers, Kujo's bosses, were coming around to pick me up. I was practicing in front of a mirror, learning how to heft the weight of the gun and look cool doing it. Mom woke up and freaked out."

"Oh, I bet," John said. "What did she do?"

"She dragged me by the ear to our parish and plunked me down on a chair in front of our pastor. He was a tough old cuss, a sailor in an earlier life, I think. The two of them grilled me until I told them what I was doing with the gun."

"Oh. And *then* what?"

"I never went home again."

"Are you serious?"

Bob held up his right hand. "The absolute truth. Father hid me in the basement of the rectory until a couple of brothers came and picked me up. They snuck me out of the building under cover of darkness, took me to a monastery out in the country, and wham. Just like that, Father Bob had found his vocation."

"Dang."

"Yeah. Not your typical vocation story. Of course, it took me a while to find myself. I was so confused, I tried to run away several times, but they kept dragging me back."

"What did they do with you?"

"I've never worked so hard. Every morning, before it was light enough to pull weeds, they would make me read aloud to one of the brothers. They took rotations listening. They'd hand me off to the brother in charge of gardening, and we'd work in the chill at sunup through the heat of the day, to the chill at sundown. That went on for several months. At the end of each day, the abbot would have me sit for an hour, my muscles aching and fingers raw, while he told me God loved me and that my life had value. They all made an incredible investment of time and energy."

"Wow. That's amazing."

"I know. It is. A lot of mistakes have been made in the church, but in my case, they got it right. They literally saved me. I shudder to think what the rest of my life would have been like if I had been home that night when those bangers came to pick me up."

"No kidding," John said. "I'm getting chills just thinking about it."

··········

"Where are your parents?" Deuce asked.

Perry couldn't believe it. This was nuts. What was goin' on?

"You know. Mom is *dead*."

"I'm sorry to hear that. And where is your father?"

Emotions jolted up from a pit inside him. It was a mix of pissed off and freaked out. Here was his old man, right in front of him wearing a thousand-dollar coat, hair perfectly trimmed, not a whisker outta place in his beard, and two rows of perfect white teeth.

"Why're you *actin'* like this?" Perry asked.

"Look, son, I don't mean to pry. I'm trying to understand your situation so I can help you."

"My *situation?* No way you can *ever* understand my situation. That's impossible."

"I'm willing to try."

"Yeah? How 'bout you help *me* understand some things?"

"Okay. What is bothering you?"

"What's *bothering* me? Oh, *man*. Well, for starters, where'd you get those teeth?"

"Excuse me?"

See? Strange garbage like that. His old man never said stuff like excuse me.

"Did you pay a bunch of money for them teeth, or someone give them to you, or did they just magically appear, or what?"

"Uh. Well, yes, sure. I had work done. But... why would you ask that?"

"Why would I *ask*? You gonna act like you don't know what's going on?" The old man either had forgot everything or was actin' like it never happened.

"Son, I can't help you unless you can tell me what it is you need."

"See, that's what I'm talking about," Perry said. "You call me 'son,' but you act like you don't know me." The old man looked super confused, maybe a little scared

"*Do* I know you?"

Perry didn't know what to say. Weird as everything had been, maybe the old man really *didn't* remember nothin'. This was terrible. Maybe this is how it works. You die thinking you're going to heaven. Then you find out heaven ain't what you thought it would be. At first things don't seem too bad. Just a little strange. Then, you start to realize you *ain't* in heaven, and they send you off on a goose chase, lookin' for some path. While you lookin, every minute gets worse, and weirder than the one that came before it. What if that keeps happening for eternity? How bad could things get then? It was a terrifying thought. He didn't know if that was how it worked or not. He did know one thing for sure: he didn't wanna see whatever was gonna come next.

October 15

Perry woke up, but he didn't open his eyes. He could hear the morning sounds of the alley, smell the dumpster rot, and feel something uncomfortable under his back. Cold asphalt, pebbles, glass, some kinda slop like that. *I hate this alley.* Seemed like he'd been here forever.

He could tell he was laying close to the dumpster. He opened his eyes slowly, allowing his eyelashes to filter the light, take the shock of the morning sun gradually. *The blue sky, tall brick walls stained black with soot and mildew, and the orange...huh? What the hell is this?* He sat up. *The dumpster is orange? Aww, crud. What kind of messed-up day is this gonna be?* Things kept gettin' weirder and weirder. A big rat ran out from under the dumpster and bit him hard on the finger.

"What the hell!"

It was gone again, under the dumpster. Perry sat there, sucking the blood off his finger, defenseless against whatever was coming at him now. He didn't know what it would be, but he knew it would be strange, his life one big mind pretzel. The door across the alley burst open. A young girl rushed out, started unlocking a bicycle chained to the riser pipe. She had a big bag in her hand. Jumped on the bike and saw Perry looking at her. She froze for a second, looked him over, and took off on the bike like lightning.

Perry laid back down. Well, it was starting. He allowed his eyes to wander and found the sign over the door. *Ming-go Wing-go.* Two words, one over the other, and under them, the bottom part of a bicycle, showing part of a front wheel, the pedals, and tennis shoes with wings on 'em. *Huh. Pretty clever. Old man Ming gettin' creative. Ming-go Wing-go. Guess I better get up and go myself. Where? Who the hell knows? Why? Not a clue. But I can't lay here in this alley all day. Besides, that dumpster is rank.*

He dragged hisself up, stiff, knocked a couple pieces a trash off his legs. The dumpster was covered with black grime thick enough to hide a lot of the bright orange paint. A dingy white sticker with black letters said *Purity Containers. Cleanliness is next to godliness.*

"Slop." Perry spit on the grime. *Not everyone is a marketing genius, I guess. They oughta get some help from old man Ming.* He walked toward the end of the alley. Didn't feel like doing the boxer dance this morning. Junk was gettin' old. Wake up somewhere different every day, one bad surprise after another, a new kind of trash storm waiting around every corner. After his usual morning walk, he peeped around the corner of Summer Street toward the newsstand. Old Geppetto sittin' there on a stool, trash blowing down the sidewalk right in front of him, and him starin' like he didn't even see it. Broom leaned against the stand, the old man slumped, motionless.

Oh, man. That's not good. What happened? He started to move, and a person stepped out to block his path. Old skeleton face.

"The pain you are suffering was crafted by your own hand!" he shouted.

Perry tried to sidestep right, but the dude stayed in his face. "Be obedient to your parents in the Lord. That is what uprightness demands!" Perry stepped left. Dude stayed with him.

"Repent, you filthy sinner!" He had breath like a wild dog. "God himself bears witness! You have lived a life of rebellion, and have reaped the reward of pain, suffering, and death!"

Perry broke around him like a football running back, moving out into Summer street, then cutting back to move down the street to the right. A glance over his shoulder told him the dude was gone, so he eased up onto the curb, cautious. The sign over the store said Gillespie *News and Brews.* Geppetto didn't even look up when he approached. Perry hesitated a second, before saying

"Good morning."

Geppetto looked up, and Perry drew back a little. The old man's face was skinny, wrinkled, skin sagging below his sockets, barely covering his bones. His eyes were sunk way back in his head. They looked Perry up and down, criticizing him, judgin'.

"What the hell you want?"

Perry didn't know what to say. "Geppetto, it's me. *Perry.*"

"Who the hell is Geppetto? My name Giovanni. I don't know you. Get outta here before you scare away my customers."

"Mr. Gillespie, please. Don't you remember me?"

"You little tramp, I said get the hell out of here. You *stink*." He stood and picked up his old broom. Hard, boney fists wrapped around it, pointing it at him, threatening. "Don't make me hurt you, you little piece of garbage. You got to count of three to get outta here. Three."

Perry stepped back, feeling dizzy, disoriented.

"Two."

Perry walked backward till he was sure he could outrun the old man if he needed to, turned, and walked away. Under his breath, he said,

"Have a nice day, Geppetto."

Perry never was more alone in his whole life. He hated it here. His life at the green dumpster was bad, the blue one was worse, but this place with orange dumpsters was horrible. Everything here was cold, unfriendly. For the first time, he understood how important old Giovanni was in his life. Take away that one friendly face, and everything turned dark and dangerous. He didn't know what to do. He kept walkin', lookin' for somethin' familiar, somethin' that made sense. He had no idea where to go.

·····•·•····

A little while later, Dorchester was empty, hardly any cars, Perry bein' cool, hands in vest pockets, rolling a pebble back and forth with his toe. *Once they find yer hiding place, they'll steal yer stuff, put you right back where you started.* The street was quiet. Nobody around. This was the moment. He turned down Von Hilern, hurried to the end and ducked into the woods. Over by the tracks, he pulled apart the leaves and branches of his spot and stepped forward. A branch stabbed him in the eye.

"Booger noodles!" Teeth gritted, he squinted one-eyed at the place where the opening was s'posed to be, his other eye burning like fire. "The hell?" He pulled the branches apart with one hand, this time more carefully. Behind them was another row of branches and more behind that. In fact, this bunch of brush hadn't never been cut at all. Perry opened his eye with his fingers. He let the tears build up to wash it out. It was feeling a little better. He touched around it. Wasn't no blood on his fingers. Only regular tears from waterin', which was usual for gettin' poked in the eye. He put his hand over it to keep the sun out, stood there starin' at the brush. *Cuss it. Now the headquarters is gone. Things couldn't get no more screwed up if they tried.*

Perry walked back up, turned right on Dorchester. Ahead, he seen a woman pushing a shopping cart. Maybe it was his cart. He started walking faster, gaining on her. He caught up and grabbed her by the arm. She spun, and his heart stopped.

"Sister Mary Frances?" he gasped.

She was terrified. "Who sent you?" Like she'd seen a ghost.

"Sister Mary Frances, it's me. Perry."

"I ain't no sister, and you know it. What are you trying to pull?"

It was definitely her. She was real tired and dirty, and she didn't smell no better than Perry did. But it was her.

"You didn't join the convent?"

"Hell no," she said. "You know how much I woulda had to give up? No husband? No kids? It was too much to ask."

"You have a husband and kids?"

"Shut up!" she shrieked. "I don't know who sent you, but you can go back to hell. Get away from me!" She pushed her cart off the curb and started jaywalking across the street. It made Perry sick. He shuddered, standing in the shadow. What? Wasn't normally no shadow here. Above him, a billboard, way up there on glass stilts. But it wasn't like a board. It was like a giant movie screen.

A video started. Over the top of a grand piano, seein' the back of a dude in a tux. Beyond that, rows and rows of cheering people, stacked up in layers, a huge place. Dude was waving, holding both hands up, and then bowed to the audience. Big letters faded in: *Highly acclaimed by fans and critics alike*. The camera zoomed in to the back of the dude, flew past the long dark hair on his shoulders and out over the audience, then up, up, past the rows of faces, people dressed fancy, eyes all wide and gushy. More big words: *Newly released from Crown Records*. The back of the dude's head filled the whole screen. He turned and …

"Slop!"

Perry couldn't believe it. He was seeing his *own face* up there on the big screen. Dude had dark shades, perfect teeth, long flowing hair, but other than that, it was him. Words faded in, and a picture of a shining gold record disc: *Available in stores and online, Amadeus Live.* The screen went black.

After about a second, a different movie started. A big "T" with blue lightning dancing around it. *Tesla Electronics. Leading the way in power for over 130 years.* But Perry was still thinkin' about the last movie. "Amadeus Live. You kiddin' me? Dude's got my *exact* face." It was happening again, and it made Perry wanna puke. He'd never been so terrified.

••••••••••

Perry wandered aimlessly, left on West Fourth into Southie, walking for what seemed like hours. Two kids came out of a doorway in an old building carryin' bags over their shoulders. They were excited, happy. They looked at Perry as they walked past but didn't say nothin'. He stopped at the doorway and looked up at the sign. *K.O.'s Gym.* The words written over the top of two boxing gloves painted like they was hangin' from a nail. Perry paused for a long moment. What danger might be hiding inside that door? What nasty surprises? But the kids seemed happy. First happy thing he seen today. He had always been interested in boxing. In electronics store windows, he'd watch two boxers ducking, weaving, a dozen screens moving in unison. But he'd never seen inside a real gym before. Wonder what that would be like.

A guy grabbed his arm, and Perry yanked it away and stepped back.

"Lost and wandering sinner," dude said. "I have what you need."

Perry's heart nearly stopped. It was the skeleton creature again.

"Man, get off me." Dude was scarier every time he saw him.

"I have the answer you're looking for." Eyes were wild, bones jabbing out above hollow cheeks.

"Yeah? What's that?" How'd he even know Perry was lookin'?

"*The* answer. Jesus is *real*, man. Ask Him to be your personal Savior. Do it now!"

"Man, I don't want nothin' to do with your kind aJesus. Stay away from me!" The skeleton dude freaked out, jerkin' on his arm again.

"You're gonna burn in hell for eternity! Jesus is real!"

Perry yanked free, balled up a fist, and pointed with his left. "I ain't gonna tell you again, man. Get *off* me." Dude stepped back, huffin' and puffin'.

"Devil's comin' for ya, hear me, man? The devil's comin!" Perry took a step toward him, he spun and ran.

Those words. They made Perry sick, hollow inside. The door in front of him was waiting. *Hell, the day can't get no worse.* He pushed on the door and went in. There was a small space, and another door with the name of the gym. Under it, *Train hard or go home.* A loud rattling sound was comin' from the other side of the door. Shouting, heavy thuds. He took a deep breath and poked his head in. Steam that smelled like sweat. The rattling was a little speed bag, a young guy flailing it smooth and relaxed, the bag about to fly apart. The thuds were from a row of young dudes pounding heavy bags that was swinging and bouncing, trying to get outta the way. These guys was *serious.* Nobody looked at him. The shouting was from a big heavy guy with a towel around his neck, standing outside the ropes of a real boxing ring.

"Keep your left up! How many times you gotta hear that?"

Pow. Kid got socked in the eye, reeling backward toward the ropes.

"You must like that, why you keep dropping that left. You gonna let that old man pick away at you like that? Fight, Angelo!"

Pow. Another shot, this one to the ribs. The kid was trying to cover up but not fightin'. Perry moved closer to see the action. The guy pounding Angelo stopped, raised his glove to the heavy-set coach. He got up close to the face of the kid on the ropes.

"Angelo, you have talent. but you're work ethic is *terrible*. You need to be in here trainin' instead of hanging out on street corners. In here, you got a shot at bein' something. Out there, you're just another banger headed for a body bag."

The kid lay with his back on the ropes and stared at the canvas.

"What am I gonna do with you?" The older boxer shaking his head. The kid didn't say nothin.

"Listen, Angelo, you got to make a choice. If you want me to train you, you gotta show me something. I want you in here training five nights a week and on Saturdays, you do three-a-days, breakfast, lunch, dinner. Hear me?"

Angelo was silent.

"Angelo? Are you hearing me? I need a commitment from you. Are you in or are you out?"

Nothing.

The old fighter walked away. The big coach started unlacing his gloves for him, not saying nothin'. Angelo was still slumped against the ropes, boring holes in the canvas.

"I guess we're done," the old fighter said. "You don't want to be part of the program, clean out your locker. I need the space for other fighters who are serious." The older fighter shook his head slowly, reached up, took off his head gear, and turned around. Perry's breath caught.

"Father *John*?" It escaped before he could stop it. Nobody heard him. It looked *exactly* like Father John, 'cept his nose was smashed flat. And he maybe had a couple old cuts around his eyes, but other than that, a dead ringer for the priest over at St. Leo's. The big coach pulled the ropes apart with a hand and a foot. Before the old fighter slipped between the ropes, Angelo spoke up.

"K. O.?"

It stopped the older guy.

"Yeah?"

"I don't wanna clean out my locker. Don't make me, 'kay?"

The older fighter turned back to him. "This club is for serious fighters. Ones that can take a beating and keep coming back. I got no room here for guys wanting to take the easy way out."

"C'mon, K.O. Ease up, man. You kick me out, I got nowhere else to *go*." Angelo had tears in his eyes. Dude was in a tough spot. Couldn't stay, couldn't go nowhere else. Perry knew *that* feeling.

"Listen, Angelo. This is no game. This is real life. And in this world, you're gonna take a beating. You can take it in here, or you can take it out there. That's the only two choices you've got. There is no middle ground. You gotta decide, and nobody can do that for you. What's it gonna be?"

"I wanna stay." His voice was muffled, soft.

"I didn't hear you, Angelo," K.O. raising his voice, now. "I said what is it going to *be*?"

Angelo looked up with tears in his eyes, angry, defiant, but also beggin'. "I wanna *stay*, okay? How many times I gotta say it?"

K.O. crossed the ring in three shuffle steps, was in his face again. "You gotta say it every day!" Shoulders forward, leaning in. "Every day you gotta say, 'I'm here. I'm in. I'm ready to *fight.*'"

Angelo's face turned sideways, his neck straining back. K.O. stopped, took a breath, and let off a little.

"Listen, Angelo. I don't need to hear it with words. Words are cheap. I need to see it in your actions."

"*Okay*."

"I mean it. Five nights a week, full workout. No slouchin'. Coach tells me you're coastin', you're out. Saturday, you do three-a-days."

"Man..."

"Don't *man* me. *Every* Saturday. Breakfast, lunch, dinner."

Angelo started noddin', frownin'.

"And Angelo?"

"Yeah?"

"Every Sunday, I wanna see you bring your mom to Mass."

Angelo looked up, started to protest, thought better of it.

"And one more thing, if I hear you've been jumped in, you will *never* be allowed back inside this gym. I don't train gangbangers. Got it?"

"Yes, Father."

Booger noodles. It is him. It's Father Bianchi. Hard-nose version of him, but... dang. The priest held up a fist wrapped in cloth, and Angelo bumped it with his glove. Father John slapped him on the headgear, friendly like, and turned and walked back over to the coach. He slipped out the ring and bounced down the stairs. Perry stepped in front of him.

"Father John?"

"Yes?"

"Could I talk to you for a second?"

"Sure. Do I know you?"

"Name's Perry. 'Member me?"

Father K.O. looked him over a second. Not judging, just checkin' ta see if he knew 'im. "I'm sorry. My brains aren't what they used to be. Too many head shots. Is there something I can do for you?"

"I had a few questions."

"Okay. Can you give me a couple minutes? I need to get a shower and I'll be right out." Father John disappeared into the locker room, left Perry standing there.

....

Nothing else to do, Perry wandered around, checking things out. *All these dudes in here, the middle of the morning? Must be serious fighters.* Four speed bags rattling. Five, no *six* heavy bags bein' pounded. Jump ropes whirring, dudes crankin' out pull-ups with lean, tight biceps. Guys on the floor pumpin' crunches like they been there all day and ain't leaving anytime soon. *Serious gym. Man. K.O. got it going on.*

On the long wall above all the heavy bags, there was two rows of photographs in frames. Fighters threatening the camera. Names and dates under the pictures, like they was somebody important. In the middle of the wall, above all the rest, was a big picture, a young, lean, tough fighter, eyes like steel. Underneath, it said *John "K.O." Bianchi. Welterweight Champion of the World.*

"Holy *jeez—*"

"Watch out, now," a voice behind him said. "No cursing allowed in the gym."

He turned to find Father John behind him, clean now, wearin' the black shirt, white notch at the collar, totally looking like a priest. Face being busted up changed it some, but still, a priest, legit as sh… well, anyway.

"I need to get some protein in me," he said. "Join me for a shake? I'm buyin'."

"Thanks, Father. Sure." Minutes later, at the far end of the gym, seated at a little table, sipping a good-tastin' protein drink, Perry said, "Man, Father, you was really the champ of the whole *world*?"

Father John smiled and shrugged. "That was a long time ago."

"Yeh? What was that like?"

"Like getting punched in the face a lot." He smiled.

"Ha. Yeh, I bet that's true. Pretty crazy, K.O."

"It was. Those were good times. I enjoyed the challenge."

"How'd that happen? Becoming champ, I mean."

Father John held his gaze. "I thought we were going to talk about you."

"Yeh, but… you don't mind, I'd like to know. I never met a real champ before."

He shrugged again. "Well… it just kind of happened. My Papa Bianchi was a brawler when he was a young man. Back then, they fought bare fists, back alleys, knock the tar out of each other, and guys would gather around and place bets."

"Whoa."

"He was tough. Musta been mean when he was younger. But when I knew him, he was strong, kind, and patient. From the time I was knee-high, he taught me the basics of being a fighter."

"And you wanted to do that for a living? 'Steada bein' a priest?"

"Well, to be honest, I felt the calling to be a priest when I was a young boy. When I was in high school, the call was strong, but I was also having a lot of success in boxing, and I wanted to see how far I could go. Looking back on it, I realize that I never was whole until I put on this collar and embraced my true vocation."

"Wow. Crazy."

He nodded. "I remember one night, Mama came up to my room, tears in her eyes, and begged me to stop boxing. She wanted me to go into seminary right after high school. I did think about it. In the end, I didn't want to run out on Papa. He was my coach and I loved working with him. So, I went on with the fight game, and I'm glad I did."

"S'pose so, since you became the champ."

"That's not it. I went to a local college, which meant Papa and I got to work together for four more years. We were winning. People were starting to talk like we might have a shot at the title. We were working hard, having a great time." The look in Father John's eyes made it like being there with him. He got serious, staring at the table.

"One night, I was fighting this tough kid. Lightspeed Lewellen. He was the one person standing between us and a real shot at a title bout. If I couldn't beat Lightspeed, the only ways left to go were sideways or down."

"Whoa," Perry said.

"Man, Lightspeed was something else. He was all over me. He had these crisp, hard shots that came outta nowhere. I couldn't lay a glove on him, no matter what I did. It was like fighting a ghost." Father John looked back up at him.

"Yeh?" said Perry.

"Papa was always real cool in the corner, nothing bothered him. But that night, I could tell he was worried. It was a five-round professional bout. By the end of the fourth, I was getting pretty beat up." He pointed to a scar over his right eye. "This thing was bleeding pretty good. Papa couldn't get it to quit, and I was afraid they were gonna stop the fight. Early in the fifth, Lightspeed made one small mistake."

"Yeh?"

"He got overconfident, started show-boatin'. He thought he had me. I was pinned in the corner, and between my gloves I saw him look out at the crowd and smile. Maybe a tenth of a second. I caught him with a left hook, cranked it hard, rocked him, and drilled him with a right cross to the tip of his chin."

"Ooh." Perry winced.

Father John chuckled. "He went down like he was made of Jell-O."

"Aw, that's a *awesome*, story, K.O. Bet your papa was proud of that."

"He was. He jumped in the ring, scooped me up, was carrying me around. The crowd was going nuts. My hands were in the air. I could smell the blood, the sweat, the leather. Camera strobes all around me. It was like something out of a movie."

"That's awesome."

"They made the announcement, held my hand up, all that. I hugged Lightspeed, both of us bloody and soaking wet, and I went to the corner. Papa was grinning. He put his foot on the second rope, started to open a place for me to crawl through, and he looked at me real funny. It was like 'huh.' He fell face forward, down the steps, hit so hard I thought he'd split his skull." Father John stopped, blinked, and took a big sip of his protein drink.

Perry didn't say nothin'.

Father John swallowed. "Heart attack. Here one minute, gone the next. It was the strangest thing."

"Man, K.O., I'm sorry."

"Ah, that's life. It was tough at the time. I didn't know how I could go forward. But I *had* to. All I ever wanted was to make him proud. A well-known coach picked me up, and as they say, the rest is history."

"Man. I never heard a story like that."

Father John shrugged. "This life is all about relationships, Perry. Remember that. I'm sure thankful for the time I had with my papa."

"That's a crazy story."

"I suppose it is," Father John said, "but to me, it's normal because that was the path I walked. The strange thing is, even after becoming champion of the world, I still did not feel fulfilled. I could tell that was not my final destination. But I don't want to talk about me anymore. Everyone has their own path, Perry. Let's talk about you."

"Aw. Not much to tell, really."

"I bet your story is interesting. I'd like to hear it."

No way Perry wanted to tell K.O. *his* stinkin' story. "Man, Father, you was pretty rough on Angelo there."

"You think so?"

"Well, yeah, I mean… *pretty* rough."

"Perry, this is a rough neighborhood. I think you know that. Everybody here is in a long, drawn-out fight, am I correct?"

Perry nodded. *Man, was he ever.*

"So, in here, I train guys to have the skills to stay alive. People think boxing is a sport. And I guess it is. But in here? This is about *survival*."

Perry nodded. K.O. was makin' sense.

"I'm trying to save these guys' lives. They have only two choices. Heavy bag or body bag. Can you understand where I'm comin' from?"

"Yeh. I know more 'bout that than I *ever* wanted ta know."

Father John held his gaze. "Listen. This life is hard, and there are a lot of ways a guy can get taken out. The only hope any of us has is to learn self-discipline, hard work, and sacrifice. Understand?"

"Sometimes *that's* not even enough." Perry said.

Father John nodded. "That's true."

It got quiet for a minute.

"Perry… My life as a priest, the work I do with these young men, trying to help them find their way, means more to me than any belt or title ever could."

"That's awesome, K.O."

"So? Do you think you'd like to start comin' in here to train?"

It thrilled him. *Wouldn't that be something? That would be awesome. But it wasn't gonna happen.* "Naw, Father. I don't think I'm gonna be around here long enough. I'm just… passin' through."

"Passing through, huh?" He looked right into Perry with those steel eyes.

"I think so. Don't expect to be here too long."

"Do you know where you're going?"

"Naw, not really. Wish I did."

"Why not stay here? Settle in somewhere?"

"I'd like to, K.O., but it ain't up to me."

Father John looked at him closely for a couple minutes.

"Okay. But remember, Perry, no matter where you go, God goes *with* you."

"Thanks, K.O. I want that to be true."

"You can count on it, Perry." He extended his hand. "I will pray for you. And Perry, when you feel you don't have anywhere to turn?"

"Yeh?" Father John squeezed his hand, firm.

"Turn to God."

…••••••••••

Perry was shuffling, trying to figure it out. Everything they say about what happens after is total bull. Not one bit is right. They say you'll see a bright light and a doorway, but you don't. Well, unless you count the moon. There is a cloud, but not like they show in paintings and stuff. He used to go to the arcade before they found out he didn't have no home and started running him off. They had the new flashy games and a couple of old-school pinball games, like from back when his old man was a kid.

Dad said there weren't no arcades in the little town where he grew up. You went to like a laundry mat or bowling alley, and they'd maybe have one game, sometimes two. Every kid in town would line up to take turns pulling that plunger with a spring on it and beating the hell outta the machine, trying to make the ball go where they wanted it to go. That was what it was *really* like after you was dead. Like pinball. Only not like being the player, like being the *ball.*

Someone you can't see pulls the plunger, and you go shooting through space, knocking into all kinds of stuff you never see comin, and hitting unexpected turns and junk. Right when you think you gonna make it into the good place, one of those flappers comes outa nowhere and slaps the snot outa you, and off you go again. Like wakin' up and seein the dumpster has changed colors, or meeting Geppetto the grouch, or seeing Sister Mary Frances livin' on the street, or a billboard with yer *own damn face* on it, or maybe you're a professor, but that ain't you either, 'cause you're still wearing stinky rags and feeling like the scum in the bottom of the dumpster. Afterlife, snot. The afterlife *sucks.*

Somethin' big and shiny flashed, and he turned to see a black car about a mile long sliding by like some kinda slow-moving rocket. Like a sleek black rocket, so cool it don't *hafta* fly fast. Man, the back seat of the taxi with Geppetto was *nice.* What would it be like inside a car like *that*? Like what heaven might be. Guess he'd never know about either one now.

Halfway up the block, the rocket glided to a stop in front of a store. Sign said *Outta Sight Music*, a big pair of black-framed glasses, vinyl records for lenses. Some girls come running outta the store, screamin' and laughin', makin' fools outta themselves. The car sat there quiet, waiting. More girls come out, and more, and then more. Girls running from everywhere, like the buildings were spittin' 'em out. All of 'em swarming the car, tryin' ta see in, like ants on a popsicle stick. It was the craziest thing Perry ever seen. Some kinda madness, them girls all gone crazy at the same time. The driver side door opened, and a dude the size of a building got out, pushing gently, tryin to move the girls enough that he could stand up. Another giant got out of the passenger side. Same thing, barely able to get outta the car 'cause of the girls.

One of the girls, sounding like she is crying, screams "Amadeus!" *Huh?* That got Perry's attention. *Was this the dude? All this craziness over his own evil twin?* A couple seconds later, they was *all* screamin' it, pushin' each other, saying junk like, "I love you, Amadeus," and "Kiss *me,* Amadeus!" Perry froze in his tracks. This was more crazy than the professor. Crazier than anything he'd ever *seen.* The two big men moved over to the back door, about a mile from the front door, and started moving the girls away.

"Girls, girls. Give the man some room."

"Ladies, you gotta let him *breathe.* He'll get to all of you, you give him a minute."

Perry realized that this was his chance to see the guy face-to-face. He took off running, as the big men opened the door. Dude with long black hair, black shades, long black coat, the collar popped, steps out like he owns the whole planet. Girls started fainting and screaming. *Seriously? You gotta be kidding me.* He wanted to say, "Hey, I'm over here, ladies," but it wouldn't do no good, so he kept running. Amadeus was standing at the far side of the sea of women, smiling, waving, touching some of their hands.

Perry got close enough to see him good. *Whoa. It was him. It looked exactly like the professor, only if the professor was cool.* He had to talk to him. He had to find out what it was like to be him. He heard himself shout, "Amadeus! Over here!" His voice sounded different, surrounded by all those girl voices, and both the dude and his goons looked over. Perry started clawing his way through the women to get close, tell him what's up, and see if he could help him.

One of the goons turned to him, his back to Amadeus. He looked like a NFL lineman, squared off. *Man, what kinda threat am I to you?*

"Hey, man. I gotta talk to Amadeus!" he said.

The goon frowned. "Beat it, man. You serious?"

"No, you don't get it. I *gotta* talk to him."

"Yeah, man. All these nice ladies swarming around, I'm sure he's gonna take time for you."

"Come *on*, man."

Now the guy put his big meaty hands on him. "I ain't gonna ask you nicely no more. Get the hell outta here. You're messing up the man's *entrance.*" He shoved Perry so hard, he went over backward, back skiddin' on pavement, his feet up in the air, almost standing him on his head.

Perry looked up, a handful of girls pointing at him, giggling. As usual, he was rotten garbage layin' in the street. They turned their backs on him and started pushing, pulling, trying to get closer to Amadeus. The goon was pushing his way through the sea of ladies, back to the black rocket. A hot young woman got out of the car, holding a plate of glass in one hand and clicking her fingernails on it with the other.

She glanced at Perry, gave him a strange look for a second, turned to the giant, still standin' by the rocket. "We need to wrap this up in precisely forty-five minutes. Then we're back in the car, headed for the hotel. He's got to have some rest before dinner."

"Yes, Miz Traci," the giant said.

The other giant was barring the door, saying "Ladies, ladies, Amadeus is going to be ready for you in just a minute. Please line up single file. When you get in line, I'll open the door." The hot young woman went to the door and said,

"I'll take it from here." As she went into the store, the other giant went back to the car, and fist bumped his partner. They checked their watches, lowered their huge frames into the black rocket, and closed the doors. The rocket started shakin' from loud music inside.

Perry sat there, a lump starting on the back of his head and one in his throat. He had a skinned elbow, but the embarrassment hurt worse. "The afterlife *sucks*." He pulled himself up off the pavement, took one last look at the rocket, and turned to walk away.

Ain't no fire anyplace, but this is hell, that's for sure. Hell is seein' all the stuff you coulda did but didn't.

··········

Haruki's hand was on the tablecloth, finger tapping along with the three musicians playing light jazz. Stand-up bass, guitar, and saxophone under red and blue lights. A nice sound, a soft look. It was interesting how they could express their emotions, using hands, fingers and breath to manipulate inanimate objects.

Haruki looked around at the rich feel of the environment. Each table under a dim light, a soothing ambiance. He sipped a martini so dry it made his gums contract and breathed deep as the vapor opened his nostrils. Wealthy and powerful people sought out experiences that provided them with the finest sensations for the five senses. The only attraction for Haruki was the effect it had on those he was trying to manipulate. This place had everything he needed. Sights, sounds, complex aromas, tactile pleasures, and the finest treats for the gustatory sense.

The room was at about sixty percent of seating capacity. It was a popular place where elite professionals came to wind down. Later, it would be packed. His friend entered and held up a hand of greeting. Joseph was a man at the top of his profession. A cosmetic surgeon, he could transform an ordinary-looking person into a creature of beauty. Haruki liked that. A guy applying his talents, going around fixing the creator's screw-ups. He stood and they shook hands.

"Hey, Joseph. Great to see you again. How have things been for you?"

"Fantastic." Joseph smiled. He was dressed casually, open shirt collar, slacks, and comfortable shoes.

"Business is going well?"

He chuckled. "It would be impolite to say in public how well it is going."

"I'm happy to hear that."

"Haruki, I want to thank you again for setting me up the way you have."

"Well, I'm glad you are happy." They sat down at the table. "I've come to ask you a favor."

"Sure. Anything."

Haruki slid a manila envelope across the table. Joseph opened it and started looking through the glossy eight-by-ten photos.

"These look like surveillance photos."

"They were shot with a long lens. I don't want to get her hopes up until I know what is possible."

"Ah, I see." Joseph put on his glasses and started inspecting the photos carefully. Haruki enjoyed watching how his expert eyes took in every detail, a sculptor inspecting a slab of marble. Joseph went from photo to photo, sometimes holding them side by side, flipping back and forth. Haruki could tell he was making calculations, constructing a plan. Finally, Joseph slid them back into the envelope.

"What is it you would like to have done?"

"Everything possible. A super model if you can make it happen."

"Oh. That would take a lot, you understand. I couldn't do it pro bono."

"I'm not concerned about cost. I want to know what is possible."

"Well, her bone structure isn't bad. Her posture is decent. With training, it could be great. The ratio between her shoulders and her hips is about right once we get rid of some of the padding. That's relatively simple."

"So, an hourglass figure?"

"If you strip down the waist enough."

"Is bikini-model quality possible?" Haruki asked.

"Her breasts? They could use some work. What result are you looking for?"

"I don't want her to look like she is about to tip over, but I want her to be voluptuous."

Joseph nodded a few times. "Well, for that to happen, she's going to need significant augmentation of the breasts and the buns. From straight on, either front or back, she would look good, but her profile will need help. She's too flat in both the front and the back for a bikini model."

"Really? She looks a little chunky to me. Did you see that in the photos?"

"Of course," Joseph said. "But most of that is fatty tissue. Getting rid of the over-sized fat globules is not difficult. We will need to remove some excess skin after that process. The augmentation will be about providing the proper shapes and curves."

"I see." That was good news.

"She'll experience a lot of pain. You need to know that. And healing will be slow."

"That's fine. I think she can take it. What about her face?"

"She was probably relatively attractive in her younger days. Gravity has started getting the best of her, like it does everyone. But again, she has good bone structure. With some tightening and stretching, a few minute alterations, she can be beautiful. Temporarily."

"When you say 'temporarily,' what do you mean?" Haruki asked.

"I mean it's a matter of time until her new look will start to respond to gravity again. Unfortunately, I cannot stop the aging process. All I can do is forestall it."

"I understand. And what time frame are you talking about?"

"I'm as good as anyone out there. She'll look like dynamite on heels when I get done with her. But it is important that you know, you're going to spend a ton of money, and she's going to go through a hell of a lot of pain, for a temporary result."

"But how temporary?"

"Three to five years is reasonable if she takes care of herself. Maybe six. Tucks and touch-ups can keep it going for a while, but there are limits. There are doctors out there who will continue to stretch and pull until they've turned their patients into mutants. I won't do that. There comes a point when you're no longer acting in the patient's best interest."

"I understand," Haruki said again. "I won't be looking for follow-up treatments. Three years will be fine. She can probably complete several assignments for me in that time. By the end of three years, she'll probably be off the payroll anyway."

....

Next, Perry was in the cloud, and he was good for a change, enjoying hisself. The fluffy cloud was makin' him relax. Nothing was botherin' him. He was just kinda bein' there. It was a nice break.

"I heard what you were thinking." Perry's neck scrunched down into his shoulders from the sound of Henry's strong, soft voice.

"What? You heard what I was *thinkin'*?"

"When you were comparing your life to pinball."

"Oh. Sorry."

A long silence followed.

"It's just that things don't seem to be goin' right. And I'm tired."

"I know you are," Henry's voice said. "But you must persevere. Things are not always as they seem."

Perry didn't feel good no more. More like a little kid put in a corner.

"You suffer from a lack of understanding." Henry appeared out of the cloud.

"Man, you ain't kiddin'."

"It is true. You do not understand the old pinball game."

We talkin' about pinball now?

"The table is tilted"—Henry using his hands to illustrate— "so that the end of the board closest to the player is lower than the end of the board away from him."

Perry couldn't believe they was talkin' about pinball.

"All of the good things—the prizes, the awards, the bells, whistles, flashing lights—are up at the higher end of the board, difficult to get to."

Huh. Never really thought about that before.

"The easiest thing for the ball to do," Henry went on, "is to roll straight down and fall into the hole at the bottom of the board."

Perry listened. Henry was waiting. He did that a lot.

"The hole at the bottom of the board—this is the bad place. This is the place where you go if you lose."

Aww, slop. That's right. That is how it works. If the ball drops, yer turn is over.

"The flappers that come out of nowhere and slap you off into a new direction are designed to keep you from going into the bad place."

Oh, man. I never woulda seen that in a million.

"Those flappers, those rude slaps, are put there to help you get to the higher part of the board so you can have a chance of landing in the good place. If you land in the good place, you're rewarded with a lot of points and prizes, exciting sights and sounds, and also a *brand-new* game."

It was obvious now. Stupid. The cloud moved in, thick and fluffy, blocking Henry from his view.

"I'm sorry, for complaining," Perry said. "I never seen it like that before."

Perry waited. Henry didn't respond. After a moment, Perry said

"Henry? You still here?"

Silence.

Henry's a good dude, but scary. He can hear yer thoughts, and you don't never know when he's listening. Whoa. Maybe he's always listenin'. Just sometimes he don't feel like sayin' nothin'.

Perry sat still, tried not to think anything. Lasted about a minute.

October 17

The long black rocket was idling in park by the curb across from Gillespie's News and Brews. The sleek nose was facing toward Perry, who was a half block down, at the edge of the shopping plaza. If Perry looked straight ahead, he could see down the length of Lincoln Street, where it dead ended into Essex Street, or if he peeped around the corner to his left, he could see the front end of the limo. He was leaning against a corner of dark polished stone, trying to keep out of sight best he could, but the street was empty this morning. Amadeus was over by the news stand, talking to some tall suit. Perry was hopin' this might be a chance to talk to the great Amadeus. *But that suit. Don't never know what will happen when you come up on a suit.*

They was actin' like they was old buddies, slapping each other on the arm, laughin', cutting up. Geppetto sittin' there glaring at 'em like they was messin' up his day. *I guess Geppetto the grouch don't like nobody.* The two men crossed Summer, and stood by the rocket a couple minutes. The big suit leaned down, hugged Amadeus and walked away, toward the entrance to the big banking center there. Amadeus slipped into the rocket, and like magic, it glided up the street, right past Perry, slow and easy. He squinted his eyes, trying to see through the dark tinting on the windows, but he couldn't see Amadeus at all. *Rot. This guy is impossible to get close to.*

··········

Next thing, Perry was sittin' in the cloud by his dumpster again, lookin' at old Henry—green work shirt, ripped up suit pants, sitting with one leg crossed over the other, so Perry could see his dark knee. There was threads hangin' from the hem bein' stomped through. He was rocking the stained sneaker with the duct tape toe. He had his hands laced together, sleeves rolled up, ripped pocket flapped over, in a total relax. *How was a guy s'posed to keep up with all this?*

"What kind of hell is this?" Perry asked. "And what did I do to deserve to be *sent* here?"

With the mist drifting between them, old Henry asked, "Do you really think you are in hell, Perry?"

"It's *gotta* be hell."

Henry got real serious. "In your life, you have known times of darkness. You have known pain. But you know nothing of the torment of hell. All the pain, sorrow, and disappointment you have ever known does not equal a single moment in hell. There are situations *much* worse than this."

"*Seriously?* That's messed up."

Henry chuckled.

"It ain't *funny*, man."

"You think you have been cursed," Henry said. "But what if this is actually a gift?"

Perry couldn't believe it. "This? What kinda twisted person would give a gift like this? This is hell. It's gotta be."

Henry's face changed again, way more serious.

"Be respectful, little brother. You should choose your words with more care."

"Sorry." The cloud was rolling over his feet. "I just don't understand. Where is the gift in all this?"

"The gift you have been granted is rare. The perspective of possibilities."

"The what?" Perry shook his head. "I don't understand. What do you mean?"

"Most people can only see the one reality they are in at a particular moment," Henry said. "You have been granted the ability to see not only what is and what has been, but also what *could* be. A wider vision. The perspective… of possibilities."

"Well, I never asked for any of it."

"Sometimes the giver of a gift knows what you need, even more than you do."

"I need this? Like I need my head bashed in. Oh, yeh. Already got that. *Thanks*."

Henry was silent, looking at him.

"I'm sorry. I know you didn't do that to me."

"Perry," Henry said, "There is a darkness coming unlike anything you have ever known. You will know the terror of hell, truly. Do not disdain the gifts you have been given. Prepare yourself in prayer so that you may have the courage to survive the trial to come."

The mist swirled and old Henry was gone. Perry's heart was a big ice cube. Henry never said nothing like that to him before.

"Henry? Come back! Please! I won't talk like that no more."

The brightness of the cloud began to fade, like when the color goes out of a sunset, and everything turned to gray. Alone in the darkening mist, quaking with fear, Perry pleaded.

"Please… I don't want no more perspective of possibilities."

October 18

Father John liked visiting the hospital. He stepped out the back door of the church office, car keys in hand, along with a little prayer book and a small box containing oils for anointing the sick. It was difficult to see people suffer, but it was a rich field for faith sharing, and an opportunity to administer a sacrament that almost always brought a profound spiritual experience for the one anointed and also the priest.

"Hey, K.O.?" it made him jump.

Perry standing in the shadows of his carport. That was an invasion of privacy.

"Perry? What are you doing?"

"You got a second? I need to ask you somethin'."

"I'm on my way to visit sick people who need help. It would be better if you would go into the office and ask to set an appointment."

"Oh. Yeh, I get it. Gotta have an appointment. I know yer important. That's cool."

"It isn't because I'm important. I'm no more important than you or anyone else. It's just that I'm tasked with helping a lot of people, so my time is very —"

"I know yer time's *valuable*, man. That's okay. I'll catch ya later." The young man turned, shoulders slumped, and started shuffling away.

"Perry, wait."

He turned and looked over his shoulder. Something was really bothering him.

"I've got a couple minutes. Tell me what this is about."

Perry looked down at the ground, hands in his pockets. He reached out and touched a pebble with the toe of his old boot.

"I got some stuff I gotta figure out. No big deal."

"Come on, then. Let's sit down for a couple minutes and talk about it."

"No, man. Yer busy. I get it."

"Perry, please. Talk to me for a minute."

"This ain't somethin's gonna get *fixed* in a minute."

"Well, maybe we can start on it now, finish it later?"

Perry shrugged.

"Perry, what do you need? How can I help?"

"I need some advice."

"Okay, I'll help if I can. Tell me something about it." John started walking across the grass-covered grounds toward a bench under shade trees. Perry trailed behind, slowing the pace.

"Ask me a question, Perry."

"Well, K.O., what would you do if you had screwed up your life somehow?"

John considered that as he sat down. "Well… we all make mistakes. It's part of being human."

"Yeh, but I mean, what if you found out you coulda did something really big and important, but you blew it. What do you do then?" He dropped down onto the other end of the bench.

"Uhm… Perry, don't be too hard on yourself. We each have a different path to walk. Not everybody is sup*posed* to do something big or important. Sometimes it's enough to be yourself and do the best you can each day."

"No, but I mean what if you knew for *sure* that you coulda, but you didn't. What then?" Perry was very agitated. Angry, maybe. This wasn't the same light-hearted kid with the sharp wit and comedic timing.

"Perry, everyone looks back on their life and wonders what they could have done differently. I understand that you're in a tough spot, but you're not alone in asking those questions. The key is to start where you are today and move forward as best you can."

"Yer sayin' that 'cause I'm homeless. You think I'm a screw-up, so yer tryin' to make me feel better."

"Perry, I didn't say that."

"Didn't have to. You think I don't know that look? I seen it my whole life. But I never seen it from *you* before."

"I'm sorry. I wasn't meaning to be judgmental."

"I'm askin' something important, K.O. Somethin' about how *life* works. Yer right, I ain't the only one's made bone-headed choices."

"Perry, calm down. I'm trying to help. Please don't be angry with me."

"See, you talkin' to me like I'm a screw-up right there. And yer right, I am. You see me? Sittin' here in these filthy rags? What if I told you I coulda been a big-shot professor? Or maybe a famous musician? What would you say?"

"Perry, God loves you just as you are."

"Man, I ain't *talkin'* about that. I'm talking about what I *coulda* been. Can't you understand?"

"We all have to make do with what we're given," John said.

"Stop doin' that, man. You talkin' down to me. What if it was *you?* What if you found out you coulda been the Welterweight Champion of the *World*?"

John blinked. He looked away. It was strange, this kid jabbing his finger on John's secret boyhood dream. Perry couldn't know that the young John Bianchi had fantasized about that very thing.

"Perry, wishing something is possible doesn't mean the thing is actually possible."

"Yeh, but what if it *was*? What if that night, when yer mama came ta yer room, beggin' you ta be a priest, you'd a said 'No, Mama, I wanna keep workin' with Papa, 'cause I don't know how long I *got* with him.'"

A jagged icicle stabbed into John. A fracture of the sternum. Did he hear that correctly?

"How do you know..."

"Sorry. Probly shoudna' said nothin. It kinda slipped out."

"But... how do you *know?*"

"Yeh, how would I?" Perry said, challenging him.

"I can't answer that question. That's... wait. Who told you about my Papa?"

"Your Papa Bianchi the bare-knuckles boxer? The one taught you all you know about the fight game? How'd I know about *that?*"

It was like getting hit with a taser. His whole body was rigid. He could only blink.

"How did you?"

"You think you know more'n me. And I'm sure you do," Perry said. "But there's stuff I know that I don't think *nobody* knows, 'cause they ain't never walked *my* path neither."

Nothing. John had no tools to... what? Not possible.

"You ain't the only Father John Bianchi, I can tell you that."

"Wait… What?"

"The you that you are, ain't the only you there is. And I ain't the only one a me. And when you can understand that, maybe you can help me." He stood up abruptly.

"Perry, please. What is this?"

"Ha! Like I know. I know this… I can't make no appointment, 'cause I don't never know where I'm gonna be. Or when. So, I gotta come see you when I can, and not no other time. I gotta go. If I'm around, I'll come see ya on Saturday." Perry walked away.

Father John looked at the keys in his hand. He didn't really *feel* like going to the hospital now. He needed to go lie down.

A chilled breeze carried the scent of impending rain. He looked back up, scanning the church campus. Perry was… gone.

October 19

"I love it," Haruki said, smiling.

High above the city, he was gazing out of his glass-walled penthouse toward the North End of Boston, observing an unusual amount of congestion and bustle three miles away, near the old Naval Yard.

"You have an interest in maritime history?"

"No, my interest is not that broad. I am more specifically interested in ships of war."

"Oh, really? I don't guess I knew that."

The commotion was caused by a parade. Pete wondered why he had called him up here on a Saturday for a one-on-one meeting. Haruki seemed to be in a jubilant mood. Maybe he was going to prep Pete for a big assignment or something.

"See all that commotion down there? They are parading marching bands, color guards, decorative floats, all celebrating the launch of a warship that occurred over 220 years ago. Don't you find that interesting?"

"I do. I attended that parade one year. It was fascinating. There were people from all walks of life, a lot of veterans. There were young men and women in their twenties, home from recent wars, to great-grandfathers who served in World War Two. The veterans were given seats of honor at the ceremony after the parade."

"Oh, yes, they love to honor veterans, and they should."

"So, it isn't just ships of war. You also have a fondness for veterans?"

"No, not for Veterans. For *War.* Man's oldest tradition, going all the way back to Cain and Able."

"I've never really understood war," Pete said. "It seems like a huge waste of time and resources."

Haruki turned, a look of surprise on his face. "War is the purest form of human self-expression. It transcends all boundaries and brings the entirety of the human species face to face with their true nature."

"Which is?"

"*Animal* nature."

Pete didn't feel inclined to comment, but it bugged him. Sometimes Haruki could sound like a cold, heartless reptile. He was speaking in a calm voice, but his eyes showed a sizzling intensity.

"Those veterans down there lining the streets? They are being honored today, but not for the right reason."

"They are being honored for their *service* and their *sacrifice.*"

"Exactly. But they should be honored for their *insight.* That is what sets them apart. They know things about the human species that most people don't know."

Pete didn't want to hear about it, but it was clear Haruki wanted to enlighten him, so he asked, "What do they know?"

"Pete, if you want to be a person of influence, you must have a clear understanding of who and what humans are. Most people hold ridiculous ideas. They think humans are enlightened, intelligent, superior to all the other species. Some even hold that humans are god-like. But these veterans know the truth. They know humans are nothing more than vicious, soulless animals. That understanding is what they should be honored for.

••••••••••••

Virginia was sobbing without control, crying so hard she couldn't even find her car keys in her purse.

"Virginia, what happened? What did Father John do to you?"

"Dear, we're only trying to help. Tell us."

Virginia could scarcely breathe. She felt like helpless prey, surrounded by a pack of wild animals.

"You'll feel better if you talk about it. Get it off your chest."

She finally had her keys, pushed the button on the fob, and reached for the door handle. Gabby pressed her hand firmly against the door, preventing her from opening it.

"Virginia, this is not just about you. You have an obligation to the parish. Tell us, so that we can get to the bottom of this."

"I...I can't. Please. Let me go."

"We can't let you go dear, not until you tell us what happened. It is important. For the good of the parish."

It was a tug of war, Gabby pressing against the door with all her weight, determined not to let Virginia escape their grasp.

"Yes, for the good of the parish, Virginia. Tell us." The two other women closing in from behind her, snipping and yelping at her heels. She shoved Gabby in a rude way she would have never thought she was capable of, the older woman stumbling sideways, changing her focus from the holding the door to preventing a fall. Virginia seized the opportunity, slipped in quickly, and locked all the doors. She started the car and put it in reverse. The three women were slapping their palms on her windows, chiding, demanding. She felt like she was caught in some twisted zombie movie, the women completely out of their minds. She started forward slowly, allowing them time to move out of the way, but she was determined to get out of there. The day had started with hope and anticipation, and had devolved into disappointment, embarrassment, and crushing heart break.

October 20

During the nine a.m. Sunday Mass, from the altar, Father John saw Perry standing near the side exit at the rear of the sanctuary. He didn't know whether to be annoyed or terrified. He was leaning toward terrified. He couldn't help it. There was something spooky about this situation.

Father John was distracted during the introductory rites. He was about to participate in the single greatest miracle in all of Christendom, the consecration of the Eucharist, and he was having a hard time focusing, seeing Perry in his peripheral vision. *What did he mean when he said "You ain't the only Fr. John there is?" And how did he know all about Papa Bianchi?* On top of that, John knew that Gabby and her friends probably had vicious rumors slithering out there among the congregation about him and Virginia. There was literally nothing he could do about it.

After he concluded the Mass, John headed to his usual spot near the main exit. He grabbed an usher by the arm on his way there. "Joe?"

"Yes, Father?"

"Could you please go look outside and see if you can find a young homeless man hanging around? If you do, please tell him I would like to speak with him. His name is Perry."

"Sure, Father. I'll go look for him now."

Greeting the parishioners on their way out the door, John did his best to listen to each person, but this thing was making him crazy.

"Hey, K.O."

He turned and there was Perry, looking at him, sheepish. "Hey, Perry."

"Man said you wanted to talk to me?"

"Yes. Thank you for coming in. Can you hang around a few minutes, until I get out of these vestments?"

"Sure. Sorry 'bout last time. I didn't handle that too good."

"Don't worry about it. We're friends. I'll be out in a minute. Okay?"

Perry nodded.

As he hurriedly removed the heavy liturgical vestments and hung them in the wardrobe, John had no idea what he was going to say to Perry. He had no plan, only a need to understand the bizarre things that were happening. He rolled up the sleeves on his black shirt, said a quiet prayer, and reached for the door handle.

Perry was in the sanctuary staring up at a sculpted scene, burly roman guards swinging heavy hammers, nailing Jesus to the cross. Perry's face displayed a mixture of feelings. It was clear he was being pulled in. The eleventh station was an evocative piece of sacred art.

"Perry, thank you for waiting."

"No problem, K.O." He looked at John, then back up at the eleventh station. "You got some pretty interestin' stuff in here, you know that?"

"I agree. Beautiful and challenging art. How about if we have a seat in the reconciliation room? Would you like a bottle of water?"

"Sure."

Perplexing questions were common in the life of a priest. But in this case, the scenario was so strange, he was afraid even his good friend Father Bob would think he was cracking up, if he heard about it. He didn't need the bishop getting any bad reports about him. "Here you go, Perry." He handed him a cold bottle of water.

"Thanks, K.O. What's up?"

"Oh, nothing. I wanted to spend a few minutes with you. I'm pleased that you made it to Mass again today."

"I think you might be about the only one."

"I'm sorry to hear that. I apologize if our members made you feel unwelcome."

Perry shrugged. John hated it. "Here is the problem we have. The people inside the church are the same people that are outside the church. We're all far from perfect. I'm glad you hung in there and stayed for the whole Mass."

"Yeh, I figgered why not. It's a pretty interesting thing to watch. There was one old, old woman who smiled at me on her way out and patted my hand."

"That's nice," John said. "I invite you to do more than watch, Perry. I invite you to participate."

Perry scowled. "Participate how?"

"By saying the prayers, pondering the readings. I want you to feel you are a part of something, not an outside observer."

"Cool, Father. Thanks."

"I also wanted to follow up on our last conversation."

"Sorry."

"It's ok, Perry. I have a sense that unusual things are happening in your life. Would you want to talk about that?"

"Man," Perry said. "I don't even know where to *start*."

"I understand. When that happens to me, it usually brings up all kinds of questions."

"Yeh. Stuff's been happenin' to me I don't think never happened to *nobody*. I got a bunch a questions. I know you ain't got time for all that."

The things Perry said often sounded nuts. And yet the whole situation *felt* supernatural. John didn't actually want to dig into it. He would rather it would go away. In Church history, no matter what the year, if something out of the ordinary was happening to a person, be they priest or peasant, they were usually doubted, ridiculed, and sometimes even persecuted. Many of those people ended up being canonized as saints later. But that happened long after all their contemporaries were dead and gone. The last thing John needed was to get tangled up in something like that.

"Hey, Father John!" Perry snapping his fingers at him.

"Sorry. My mind wandered for a second. What was your question?"

"I said, what are you supposed to do when you're *dead?*"

John tried not to show any emotion. "Can you ask me that question in a different way, so that I can understand more clearly what you mean?"

"You know, when you die. What're you supposed to do then?"

"What're you supposed to *do*?"

"Yeah, like... what's the point? What's the game? What're ya supposed to do with yer time? How do you know if you're winning?"

"Winning? After you're dead?"

"C'mon, Father. You know what I'm talking about. Like pinball."

"Um... Not sure that I—"

"So, you're dead, right? Then what?"

"Are you asking what happens to you after you die?"

"No, I'm figurin' that out. What I mean is, what is the *point*?"

It was a strange mix of frustration and fear. The privacy of the reconciliation room was feeling creepy again.

"Father, you don't look too good. You're turning white and pasty… like the old man looks just before he starts throwin' up."

John laughed — tried to — it would have been better if Perry hadn't mentioned that.

"I am a little confused Perry. I'm not sure what you're wanting me to say…"

"Church teaches stuff about what happens after you're dead, right?"

"Rrrright…"

"So, what is it?"

There was a chill, John had the urge to get up and adjust the thermostat. As though talking to a child, Perry said,

"Like when Lazarus was dead but also wasn't dead, you know? Like that. Whadaya s'posed to *do*?"

"Nobody really knows what happens after you die, Perry."

"See, that ain't true neither. Plenty of people know. It's just that the experienced ones ain't talkin'. Except for that dude that calls hisself Henry, which he ain't, and he talks in riddles, so it ain't helpful, you know?"

"Perry… have you ever — um, let's see — spent any time in a hospital?"

"What're you talkin' about? I ain't got money for no hospital. I been hurt plenty, and I been sick too, but there's never been no money for a hospital. Dad and I always took care of ourselves. When we was alive, I mean."

"When you were…" John choked when he tried to say it.

"Yeah, I know, Father. It ain't normal. Not like they say it will be, with the bright light and all that. In some ways things are about the same, 'cept I keep waking up in strange cities, and like I said, that dude I told you about who comes out of a white cloud and talks to me about sh—stuff, and now there's more'n one a me and we keep popping up all over the place. I can't figure it out."

"There's more than one of…" It was like sticking your bare hand into a tub of crushed ice and water, only if someone had taken a funnel and poured it down the inside of your spine.

John couldn't talk. He couldn't move. He couldn't speak. He had a piercing headache. He was nauseated, wanted to run out of there. Instead, he sat and trembled. *Lord, please… help me… I have no understanding of these things. Guide me. Tell me what I'm supposed to do.*

"Look, Father, ain't no big deal," Perry said. "Don't be upset. I didn't mean to rattle you. I'll figure it out, else the guy in the cloud will tell me what to do next."

Just like that, the door to the reconciliation room was standing open and Father John was alone. He was confused. His senses were failing him. *He walked out, right? Got up and walked out the door while I was distracted, trying to process all the things he said... right? He walked out like a normal person, didn't he?* The ice water was pouring through the funnel at ten gallons a second.

··········

A few blocks away, the young waiter was checking his phone for new messages. It was a typical mid-morning shift — most of the breakfast people gone, the lunch crowd not due for another hour. The place was dead except for one table with three old ladies, an ugliest hat contest or something. Their plates were empty, and they were camped out there, all leaning forward with their heads together, chattering like they had the scoop of the century. His phone was no help. Even the social media feeds were boring. His thumb swiped screen after screen, navigating through a complete waste of a Sunday.

One of the old ladies held up her empty water glass, gave him a stink-eye look. He put his phone away, picked up a water pitcher. As he approached the table, he suppressed a yawn.

"But, Gabby, what did Virginia *say?*" the woman with the red hat asked.

"She said she couldn't bring herself to talk about it," Yellow Hat said. "She said it was too *shameful.*"

The waiter paused, holding the pitcher.

"Oh dear." Red Hat shook her head and held up her glass.

He started pouring.

"Sisters," Blue Hat said. "I hate to be the one to bring it up, but..."

"But what?" Yellow Hat asked.

"Well... somebody is going to have to tell the bishop."

··········

Later that afternoon, Perry peeped carefully around the back corner of the church building, lookin' at the side door. Nobody was around. Not even any cars goin' by. He hustled to the door, the one that couldn't latch 'cause he had stuffed the hole full of a crumpled-up church bulletin. He opened the door and slipped in quick, carryin' an empty water bottle in his hand. Tiptoeing over to the baptismal font, a creepiness bothered him. Like someone was watchin' him.

He looked up and there was Jesus, head drooping, sad look on His face. Staring down at him from the cross. He dunked the bottle and was chilled by the cool holy water. It made a loud glugging noise, causing his heart to thump almost as loud. He was sure he was gonna get caught. He wanted to fill the whole bottle, but he stopped about halfway. A clean getaway with half a bottle is better than getting busted with a full one. He slipped back out the same door.

Around the back of the church building, by the air conditioners, he took the lid off the bottle and placed his finger over the top. He started shaking it, to sprinkle holy water onto his head, his arms, his chest. Didn't seem like nobody could be allowed into hell if they was covered in holy water. Careful to not be louder than the air conditioner machines, he said,

"God, I don't need no money. Just keep me outta the bad place. And if it ain't too late… I hope this holy water can help me find my way into the good place. Amen."

He put the lid back on the bottle, dug around in his pocket, fished out a black felt marker, and wrote in big letters *HW.* He put the bottle into the corner of the cart and couldn't help but smile. He had got away with it.

October 21

The afternoon sun was warm, for October. The grass was cool, and the tree was throwing a little bit of shade in patches. Perry laid back, put his hands under the back of his head, and closed his eyes. All the stuff Father John had said was crazy. *Was there really a divisible mark? If there was, how come the new Henry said he was gonna end up in hell? It didn't seem like that part about bein' a king could be legit. But still, the mark might be, and if it was, that oughta be enough to keep him outta the bad place, shouldn't it? For a dead dude who ain't in heaven, those are pretty important questions. After being slapped around his whole life, it would be great if he could end up making it into heaven somehow.*

He had a sting of worry, thinking about Dad. The old man was nowhere to be found. Since he'd met the other Dad, the rich one with nice teeth, Perry was suspectin' his old man might really be dead. But if he was, that meant he was in heaven, havin' all those nice things. *But… how did Dad drink himself into heaven if Perry had worked and suffered his whole life and didn't make the cut? Oh, well. Who cares? If Dad made it in, good for him. One less thing to worry about.* That would be a big load off Perry's shoulders. He was tired. It was like he was falling. He let it happen. Strange sensation, the sounds of The Common falling away, getting more and more distant, down, down, through time and space into silence and darkness.

"D.M., I'm telling you it was probably the strangest conversation I've ever been part of."

D.M. was turned half around in the booth, trying to get the attention of the waitress. "I would think you'd be jumping for joy."

"Why would I be?" Deuce asked.

"Well, to me,"— he turned back toward Deuce — "it sounds like this solves your whole paternity problem."

"The kid said flat out that I'm his old man."

"That's not what I heard. He said you're the worst old man ever."

"Right. How would you interpret that?"

"He also said *his* old man is *dead*."

Deuce blinked. "I completely missed that. I guess I was so shocked by what he said before, I didn't even hear the second half."

The waitress arrived with two cups of coffee and a piece of chocolate pie.

"I wanted apple," D.M. said.

"Sorry, we ran out. Try the chocolate." She put the ticket face down on the table and walked off.

D.M. stared at the pie. "I don't *like* chocolate. I like *apple*."

"D.M.?" Deuce held his hands palm up.

"Right. So, what we've got is a very confused kid. Not a player in a conspiracy, not a surrogate for a powerful enemy. Just a disturbed street kid, which is what you originally thought."

"Oh, thank God." Deuce drew a deep breath. He started to exhale, but it got stuck. "But... wait."

"Yeah?"

"Who almost killed Mac? And why does this kid *look* exactly like Peregrine?"

··········

"I don't know why everybody's freakin'," Perry said. "It's like they won't even *talk* to me. Even Father John. Trippin', man. I went to the confession room, a sign's on the door, 'No reconciliation today due to emergency. Apologies.'"

"Perry, try to be calm," Henry said.

"I'm bein' calm." Perry swiped his hand angrily at the mist of the cloud. "I want to get this figgered out and nobody's helpin' me."

Henry raised a white eyebrow.

"Okay, you're helpin' me. I get that. But, man, can't you just connect the dots? Why I gotta struggle like this? Why I gotta be bouncing around like a lotto ball, wondering if I'm ever gonna get to roll down the chute?"

The white cloud usually made him wanna relax. Today, it was irritating. Perry swiped his hand in front of his face again, like trying to wipe steam off a window, but there wasn't no window. It stirred the steam up, made it worse, all swirling around, making Henry come and go.

"Henry, please don't leave me. Not today. I need you, man. I need you like I never needed nothin'. I'm all alone here, and I can't make all this stuff work out."

"I will never leave you, Perry." His voice was warm, strong sounding. It made Perry feel a little bit better.

"Thank you. Thank you so *much*, man. Without you, I got nothin'. I can't count on *nobody*."

"You can count on me."

"See, I want to believe that, but I don't *understand* you. I ain't never known nobody *like* you. You come and you go anytime you want, and I got no say in it. That makes me nervous."

"I am *always* with you, Perry. Do not be afraid. Everything is working together. You will see."

Again, his voice, or maybe his words, soothing, like warm water on yer skin, or a hot meal going into yer belly.

"Henry, why won't nobody talk to me anymore?"

"Why do you think?"

"I don't know. Father John and me used to talk together real good, like buds, you know? Now, he acts all nervous and uncomfortable around me. Last time I went there, he didn't show at all. Just left that sign."

"What changed, Perry?"

"I can't figure that out. It was like I said something that freaked him out."

"What did you say?"

"I can't remember. It's so hard to remember things now."

"Try."

Perry squinted down into the cloud, trying to see the image, remember the scene with Father John. "Well, I was talking about trying to get where I am trying to get to."

"And where is that?"

"I'm trying to get to the *good* place, remember? *You* tol' me about it."

"Yes, I remember. But what did you tell Father John that bothered him?"

"I can't remember."

"You told him you were dead."

"Yeh. So?"

Henry's brown eyes fixed on Perry's. Patient, waiting for him to catch up.

Perry shrugged.

"Perry, think back over your whole life. Did anyone ever tell you they were dead?"

"Well... no, I guess not."

"It is not something that people say."

"Oh. Yeah, but what if it's true?"

....

Mary was checking herself out in one of the mirrored columns, and she obviously wasn't thrilled. Rushing toward forty, she was grappling with the realization that age was catching up with her. She had obviously been feeling down lately. She turned and looked over her shoulder, turned sideways, pulled herself up to perfect posture, and checked her profile. Her shoulders drooped, and she went and sat down at her desk.

Haruki had been watching from the comfortable couch in his Chicago branch office. He stood, went to his desk, and touched the intercom button.

"Yes?" Her voice came through the speaker.

"Could you come to my office, please?" Looking at him through several clear Lexan walls, she nodded and reached for her tablet.

He met her at the door and welcomed her.

"How can I help you, Haruki?"

"Well, actually, Mary, I'm hoping I can help you."

Her blue eyes studied him, waiting.

"Please sit down."

She sat in an overstuffed chair, back straight, her tablet on her knees.

"Relax, Mary." He settled into the couch. "This is a personal conversation."

"Okay." She didn't relax much.

"I noticed when you stopped wearing your engagement ring. I'm sorry."

She looked down but didn't tear up or tremble. She was strong.

"I recognize that you're going through a difficult transition, and I would like to help you through it, if I can."

She looked up at him, defiant. "Thank you. I'll be fine. It might take me a little time."

"Good for you," he said. "Major life challenges define us. They can either send us downward into self-pity and self-harm or propel us upward to higher levels of living and self-realization."

"Thank you, Haruki. I appreciate that insight. I'll keep it in mind."

He nodded and gave her his most caring and engaging look. "Mary, I bet you were always the smartest girl in your class, weren't you?"

She shrugged like it was no big deal. "I suppose I was. Myself and one or two others."

"I thought so. I hope you realize that I hired you for your mind. I consider you to be a bright, intelligent woman with a piercing logic and a flair for problem solving. It is important that you understand that."

"Thank you."

"Having said that… did you ever wonder what it would be like to be the *other* type of girl? The one who had the perfect breasts and flat tummy, the perky little bum that the guys couldn't keep their eyes from?"

Her face clouded, disturbed. It was the reaction he expected.

"I want to show you something." Haruki opened a file and brought out a glossy eight-by-ten photograph of a young woman, conservatively dressed, a little chunky, thick glasses, and a crooked grin. He handed the photo to Mary. She scanned the photo, then looked at Haruki with a furrowed brow. He handed her another photo, this one a young woman in a bikini, long legs striding on a beach, hair blowing in the wind. She had the body of a voluptuous movie star, and a gorgeous face to match. She looked at that photo a little longer. Her eyes went from point to point in the photo, assessing all the dominant physical traits. She frowned and pushed both photos toward him. He didn't offer to take them.

"Those two photos are of the same young woman, exactly six months apart."

"What?" She went back to looking at the bikini photo, then the plain photo, then the bikini again. "You're joking."

"No. I borrowed these photos from a friend of mine. They are before and after shots of one of his patients. He does remarkable work, don't you agree?"

She looked at the bikini photo again, an expression of disbelief on her face. "I would say so." She looked back up at him. "Why are you showing me this?"

"Mary, your dock worker left you for another woman, didn't he?"

Her face flushed. "Well, it's a private matter, but... yes."

"And how did that make you feel?"

"How do you *think* it made me feel?" There was a fire in her eyes.

Haruki enjoyed that. "I think it must have hurt very badly."

"Yes."

"It must have been terrible to have him leave you, a woman of such powerful intellect, for a bimbo, simply because she has large breasts."

"And because she's a whore," Mary added. Haruki chose to let that one go by.

"So, how are you going to respond to this? Are you going to let yourself be eaten up with self-loathing, or are you going to fight, to defend yourself?"

She showed a mix of frustration and hurt. "How *can* I fight back? He doesn't want me anymore. He has made that clear."

"If you *could* fight back, if you could make him want you so bad that he couldn't stand it, would you?"

She looked at him with suspicion. She was no fool, and knew he was leading up to something.

"I might. It depends."

"Mary, you're going through an important test. You need to give yourself time to adjust to it, to find your proper footing. I want you to take a little time off and care for yourself."

Her eyes widened. "Are you laying me off?"

"No, nothing of the kind. I want to help you. I want to give you a great gift."

Her expression turned suspicious.

"Before I tell you what it is, I want you to realize that this is a once-in-a-lifetime opportunity. Consider your answer carefully. I won't make this offer twice."

"O-kay?" she said.

"I have booked a round-trip plane ticket for you, and eight weeks at an exclusive spa."

"Eight *weeks* at a spa?"

"It isn't just any spa. It is my friend's spa." He nodded toward the photographs.

A look of surprise crossed her face, a quick little smile, but she caught it and returned to her professional demeanor.

"You have my attention. Please tell me the details of exactly what you are proposing." Haruki smiled. Nobody talked to him like that. Mary had real courage.

"He calls it the Complete Self-Confidence Makeover. The same makeover the girl in those photos received. I am offering to treat you."

She looked at the bikini photo again, this time longer, and with a kind of hunger in her eyes. "I don't understand. Why would you do that? It must cost a fortune."

"Not a fortune, but a substantial amount," he said. "I have more than one reason for offering this. First, I want to help you get through this difficult time. I want to help you show that idiot dock worker exactly what he let slip through his fingers."

Her smile tried to come through again, but she suppressed it. She shook her head and offered the photos back to him. "It's too much."

"Nonsense. You are valuable to me because of your mind. With this makeover, your value to this organization would skyrocket. There would not be a woman on the planet who could outshine you. From my perspective, that's a good business investment. There's your second reason. Complete transparency. It isn't complicated."

She sat blinking, looking at the bikini, then back up at him.

"It is not a one-sided agreement. You will have to sign a three-year commitment to remain with the company, in return for the services rendered."

"I… I don't know what to say."

"Simply say yes. The plane leaves at eight a.m. tomorrow morning. But that's only half of the opportunity."

"Really?" she said.

"As I said, with my friend's help, you will enter an elite group of women who play at a different level. You could go down to the docks, surprise your ex-fiancé, and show him what he missed."

She smiled, no reservations this time. "I have to admit, that would be fun."

"Or..." He paused for effect. *"You could choose the nuclear* option." He handed her another photo, this one of a man so handsome, it was shocking. He was impeccably dressed, and a super model held onto his elbow.

She looked it over, and a different kind of hunger came into her eyes. “Who is this?” she asked, trying to be nonchalant. He handed her a copy of *Millionaire* magazine, the same photo on the front cover. The perfect teeth, the smiling eyes, the ruddy jaw line, and the gorgeous woman on his arm. “He is your next assignment, if you choose to accept it.”

“What?” She scrutinized the photo from top to bottom.

“I need to place someone in his organization. I think I can get you hired as his personal assistant. From there, you can be my eyes and ears inside his operation and have some fun. Enjoy whatever perks come along with the position. High pay, world travel, yachts, Leer jets.”

“Wait. I want you to be clear about what you’re asking of me. Do you want me to *sleep* with him?”

Haruki shrugged. “Only if you want to. That’s up to you. I bet it would burn your ex alive if you were on the magazine covers with this man while he was in line buying his six pack.”

“You’re going to get me a job with him… and have me *seduce* him?” Now she looked a little miffed.

“Mary, I apologize in advance, but I must ask you a personal question.”

“Okay.” Her head was erect, her jaw set.

“Are you a virgin?”

Her eyes dropped immediately and came back up to him, defiant. “You know I’m not.”

“So, you wouldn’t be doing anything you haven’t done before.”

“I’m not a whore.” Her eyes blazed. “I have *never* been easy. I’ve just had some… unfortunate relationship experiences.”

“Like the dock worker.”

“We were engaged to be married! I’m not ashamed of what I have done. Not one bit.”

“There.” Haruki pointed at her face. ”*That* is the spirit. That is *exactly* how you should feel. Never repent. Never apologize. Never regret. You only did what men and women have been doing since Adam and Eve hooked up under the apple tree. Never say you’re sorry to anyone. *Never.*”

She nodded, a troubled look on her face. “But Haruki… this seems different. This is going under the knife to get a perfect body, to ensnare a man for business purposes. It doesn’t seem right.”

He gave her his warmest, most empathetic smile. “I understand. We each must choose our own path. I would never for a moment want to pressure you to do anything you were uncomfortable with. I was only trying to help."

"I don't mean to sound ungrateful," she said quickly. She looked at the magazine cover and shuffled back to put the bikini photo on top of the three images.

"Forget I mentioned it." Haruki stood.

She remained seated, looking at the photo of the bikini. "He can really do this for someone like me?"

"You've seen the before and after. Those are untouched photos. He has a singular talent."

She sat quietly. He remained standing, signaling that the meeting was drawing to a close.

"Can I have time to think about it?"

"Unfortunately, I've got to make a move on this. I have inside information that the girl with him in the photo is going to be leaving his organization. She is being head hunted by a Fortune 100 company, to fill a vice-president position."

Mary's jaw dropped. The message wasn't lost on her. She was a sharp lady.

"Listen, Mary. I feel a little embarrassed here. I don't want you to think I was disrespecting you. Please forgive me. Let's forget this conversation ever happened. It was clumsy of me." He extended his hand and helped her up out of the chair. He started to move toward the door, but she clamped onto his hand and planted her feet. When he turned to look at her, her face was taut. "Are you okay?" he asked.

She looked him in the eye. "I'm better than okay. I'm going to do it."

October 22

Perry could see a group of young men hanging out in the cold. At the far end of the alley, the sky was turning colors as the sun dropped. The steam of their breath was rising in the evening air, into a halo of light that was becoming visible from a fixture over the exit door.

He couldn't hear what they was sayin', but he could tell they was kinda cutting up, laughing. One guy sipping off a small bottle of alcohol, a couple others sharing a smoke. He was pretty sure that wasn't no cigarette.

But it was the fourth guy that Perry was interested in. He looked like Amadeus. *But how could it be? How could Amadeus be here? This wasn't making no sense.* The dude that looked like Amadeus was quieter than the other three. He took a small sip off the bottle, then handed it right back. Didn't seem to be taking part in the clowning. Perry wasn't sure it was him, and it shouldn't be, but it did look like him.

One of the guys smoking looked up, saw Perry, and jerked his hand down. He pointed toward Perry, and all the others turned his way. Perry stepped back farther into the shadows. They all kept looking at him. After a minute, the one looked like Amadeus started walking toward him. Perry had been waiting for a chance to meet the famous piano player, but now that Amadeus was walking right toward him, all he wanted to do was cut and run. Too late. It was Amadeus for sure, and he was walking right up to him.

"Excuse me," Amadeus said, real polite.

"What?" Perry stuck to the shadows, started sliding along the wall, still thinking about getting out a there.

"I want to talk to you. Hold up a second. My friends think you're a cop. Are you?"

"I look like a cop?"

"No, not unless you're a narcotics cop."

"Man, I ain't no cop."

"Come down and meet my friends. Tell them that."

"I don't need to meet yer friends. Why would I want to do that?"

"I'm only being sociable."

"Well, my social calendar's all full up. I don't wanna meet yer friends."

"Well, what *do* you want?" Amadeus asked.

"Who says I want *anything*?"

"This is the third time I've seen you hanging around. That was you across the street from the magazine stand, and outside the music store, right?"

"Yeah. You sent yer goons to rough me up."

"No, you have it wrong. That wasn't my idea."

"You hired 'em, didn't you?"

"My agent did. But they weren't supposed to rough anybody up. I complained to their employer about the way they treated you. Is there something you want from me?"

Perry took a half step forward. "Yeah, how 'bout give me yer *life*?"

"What?"

Amadeus' face drained white. He stood very still. Stupid dude thought he was being threatened.

"Listen, I'm not looking for any trouble," he said.

Perry snorted. "I know the feelin'. But what you lookin' for and what finds you ain't always the same."

"Do you want an autograph or something?"

"You kiddin' me? How 'bout I give *you* a autograph."

"I don't understand."

"That makes two of us."

The dude stood there, looking around. His expensive clothes and his super-cool look, but he couldn't come up with nothing to say. Perry shook his head and started walking away.

"Fergit it. You can't help me. You're more messed up than I am."

"Where are you going? What's the matter?"

Perry stopped and turned to look at him. "What's the matter? You kiddin'? You're the *orange* dumpster, and now I see you here, at the *blue* dumpster. I'm tryin' to figure out what's going on."

··········

To say he was handsome didn't really communicate it. He was the most interesting man she had ever met. "You've got to understand," Haruki said, "Love is the key to everything, Mary."

Against the backdrop of a beautiful sunset, seeing him here beside her in his Lamborghini was surreal. His profile, what she was enjoying now, was like an ancient samurai statue come to life. He was tall, perfect posture, perfect teeth, luscious hair. She imagined her face on the bikini photo. *Will I look like that?* The idea excited her, and she pushed back against the doubt. *Why not? Why can't I have it? The technology exists, and his friend obviously has the training and talent.*

He smiled at her. He had not only the looks but also a magnetism that made it hard to keep her train of thought.

"Are you listening to me?" he asked in a playful tone. "You look like you're miles away."

"I'm sorry. I guess I'm a little out of sorts. This trip... it's a big step, you know?"

"Of course, I know. But you're going to be fine. You will be in the *best* of hands. A few weeks from now, you will be living a life that you've never dreamed of. I can't wait to see the new you emerge."

"I'm a little worried about who that new me might be."

"It isn't like that, I promise," he said. "What I should have said is that I can't wait to see the *real* you emerge. That astounding woman has been in there all this time, but nobody could see her. Except me. I've *always* been able to see her."

She looked into his shining eyes. Sincerity. Maybe something more?

"That astounding woman is getting ready to step out into the light of day," he said.

The way he talked about it made it sound nice. Not as frightening. She couldn't help wondering what it would be like. She drifted back to high school, to a chemistry class, where she was lab partners with the quarterback of the football team. Being near him made it hard for her to breathe. He was so gorgeous, so powerful, and he was nice to her. In fact, he had picked her for a lab partner. Probably only because she was smart. But still.

That had been her first experience of falling for a handsome guy. There had only been one brief exchange, finals week, during an after school study session, a couple moments where she was hoisted up onto a lab table. She was sure she was in love. Afterward, he acted like nothing had happened. He went on dating the lead cheerleader, and they never once spoke of it. It crushed her feelings, and it took her a long time to trust anyone again. But that first experience was so physically intense that even now, the smell of rancid chemicals excited her. Haruki made her feel like that, only multiplied a thousand times. Simply being beside him here in this car sent sensations through her body that were… well, embarrassing.

"Mary, you've recently had an experience of how powerful love can be. Love seeps down into every fiber of the human body and penetrates the deepest parts of the mind. After your makeover, while you're waiting for your new body to emerge, I've arranged for a personal trainer for you. Not a physical trainer. I think you will enjoy this. You're going to learn new and powerful ways to utilize psychology. How to harness the power of suggestion, and how to read people so well that some will think you're clairvoyant. You must learn how to control the power of love."

She listened, feeling waves of passion coming off him. Admiring how he could easily navigate traffic and, at the same time, give her the impression that she had his undivided attention. After the makeover, would she and he ever be able to… well, he said it himself. She was going to be in an elite group of women. Those were probably the type of women a man like him had relations with. Super-star females endowed with gifts so abundant that they could improve the lives of *twenty* women if the gifts were spread around evenly. Maybe there was a chance that she could get to know Haruki… better.

"Your dock worker understands the power of love," he said. "He drives it like a steamroller. You've had firsthand experience at what that feels like. I want *you* to learn how to drive it like this fine automobile. To be able to transport someone, to provide a luxurious experience, while at the same time remaining completely in control of every aspect of the situation. It is an enormous amount of power. Few could handle it. You have the mind to be able to manage that power and wield it to purpose. I predict you will fall in love with the power of love. You're going to be amazing."

"Haruki, thank you. I can't tell you how much I appreciate you giving me this opportunity. No, this honor. I am honored that you selected me."

He smiled broadly at her, and she melted. If she had that gorgeous body now, in this moment, she would show him her appreciation, and maybe even win his heart.

"Mary, I'm counting on the fact that you have recently learned what love is really about. You know from experience that the fairy tales are not true. The nice girl does not end up marrying the prince. Love is powerful, but love is not sweet *or* innocent. If you want to have a genuinely happy life, and all the perks and privileges this world has to offer..."

He was pausing to be sure she didn't miss the important part, but he needn't have. Mary was hanging on his words. Even so, when he said it, she was caught off guard.

"Mary, you've got to learn how to *weaponize* love."

....

The evening was cold, but the city's night life was starting to fire up. Perry was playing it casual. At the bottom of the concrete stairs, a giant dude was half standing, half sitting on a wooden stool. His tree trunk legs was stuffed into dress slacks, and he had on a heavy jacket and a purple felt gangster hat. His huge fist had some money sticking out of it. He was tryin' to blow smoke rings with his frosty breath. Dude looked up at Perry, kind of a frown. It was time to make his move. He headed down the stairs. Before he even got to the bottom, the giant's heavy voice said,

"Whadya want, little man?"

"I need to see a friend of mine. He's playing here."

"That right?"

"Yeh. That's right." Seein' Amadeus and his buds in the alley out behind the joint made him really curious. He had to get in and hear the dude play.

"Got ten bucks?" the giant asked, like he thought he already knew the answer.

"Yeh." Perry reached into his pocket and pulled out a crumpled ten.

The giant looked surprised. He shook his head. "We got a dress code."

"Lucky for me, I'm *dressed*," Perry said. What a jerk this guy was.

"That ain't gonna cut it."

"C'mon, man. Don't bust my chops. I gotta get inside."

"Never gonna happen. Not unless you think you can go through *me*."

Perry looked at him. He was big but prob'ly slow. Perry might surprise him, slip past, but then what? Guy would come in and drag him back out.

"Little Bruh, you need ta *bounce.*" He meant it. Perry still had the lump on his head from the last giant who shoved him down on the sidewalk. He turned and walked up the stairs. The giant grunted, carefully easing himself back down onto the stool. Yeh. He would be slow.

Perry was stuck now. He needed to get in, but he couldn't think of no way to deal with that giant. Ever' once in a while he'd peek down the stairs and the giant would look up and glare at him. No way he was getting in. Maybe he would wait around anyway, get another shot at talkin' to the great Amadeus as he left the club. Next time he would get down to it, not play word games in no dark alley. He had to do *some*thing.

As he started to walk away, his new old man and the professor came into view, heading for the stairwell. He waited in the shadows till they started down the stairs, then went and peeked down behind 'em. They walked down like they owned the place, went up to the giant, handed him a twenty, and slipped past like he wasn't even there.

OCTOBER 23

"Good morning, team members." Haruki was addressing another virtual meeting of the section heads. "How is everyone doing? Are you all getting geared up for the big Thanksgiving trip?" Several of them started to talk at once, then they all stopped to allow the others to speak first. Haruki loved it.

"I'm glad everyone is excited. Lisa is making the final logistical arrangements, so I expect everything will be wonderful. Now I need to steer us into the main topic of today's meeting. Mary is not here today. Sue is taking notes for the Chicago branch, and I regret to say that Mary will not be able to join us in the islands either. She is away on special assignment. I don't want you to think she was cheated. I can't reveal the secret yet, but later, when you find out about the assignment she is on, you will understand why she was happy to forego the trip." He sensed a little squirm from Lisa and smiled. *If that bothered her, just wait.*

In the small windows on the bottom of the screen the section heads were nodding approval. He had their attention. "Today I have great news. I am pleased to announce that each of you section leads are being promoted from regional initiative managers to national initiative managers."

The small windows at the bottom of the big screen showed smiles from the execs. The secretaries were neutral.

"That also means a major promotion for each of you secretaries as well. I'm going to reward you for your past loyalty by moving you up along with the section leads you have been serving." Now the secretaries were all beaming.

"Today I'm announcing a major shift in our corporate mission. In the past, we've said 'think nationally, act regionally.' As of today, our new motto will be 'think globally, act nationally.'" The people on the monitors were nodding, still smiling.

"Along with this transition, we're going to modify our corporate marketing to de-emphasize our for-profit activities and highlight our philanthropic initiatives. I will want input from each of you concerning which of your subordinates should be promoted to operate our profitable business activities, because you will be spending the lion's share of your time pressing philanthropic projects."

Pete raised his hand. "Haruki, can you give us a sketch of how our day-to-day activities will change?"

"Sure. Each day you will conduct one meeting with your subordinates and give them guidance on the for-profit activities they are charged with. Beyond that, you're going to be spending your time in personal meetings or phone calls with people of influence, promoting our philanthropic interests."

"That sounds great," Shawn said.

"This is going to require you to interface with national-level CEOs, as well as the movers and shakers in Washington. You will need to play at a much higher level to pull that off. So, at the same time I'm giving you these additional responsibilities, I am *doubling* your current salaries."

Audible gasps. Good. He was going to need momentum to sell what was coming next. "The people you see on national talk shows, the nightly news, the covers of magazines, are going to become your new best friends. You will not be *visiting* the elite personalities in the world, you are going to be living side by side with them, moving among them as *one* of them." Now everyone was fully on board. He could read their faces. They couldn't wait to hear more.

"Excuse me, Haruki," Steve said. "This all sounds fantastic. But I'm curious, why now?"

"A valid question. First, we are ready. Through the hard work and expertise of all of you, we've grown this company into an international powerhouse. Second, the time has come for us to give back, to pay it forward, and the metrics demand that we take immediate action."

He could see that everyone was with him.

"May I ask what metrics you are referring to?" Steve asked.

"I'm going to throw out a few numbers that will demonstrate what I mean. It's not important that you capture every detail. The facts will be provided to you later, and you will commit them to memory. For now, I only want you to see the big picture, okay?"

Everyone nodded.

"Here goes."

The secretaries all picked up their tablets.

"Earth has no more than twenty-four million, six hundred-forty-three thousand square miles of habitable land. Another way to express it, is fifteen point seventy-seven billion acres. Got it?" They were looking a little confused but nodding.

"My point is that the habitable land on our planet is finite. With that in mind, consider this. In the nineteenth century, the global population of Earth was estimated at 1.5 billion people. In other words, there were approximately 10.5 acres of available land for every person on the planet." All the people in the meeting were impressed by that.

"By the end of the twentieth century, the global population grew to 6.5 billion, reducing the available land to 2.4 acres per person." Faces clouded somewhat as they processed that tid bit.

"By the end of the twenty-first century, it is predicted that the global population will balloon to over 13 *billion* people, reducing the habitable land to a mere 1.2 acres per person." He paused for effect, giving them his expression of concern. They all stared at him, silent.

"These numbers are grim," Haruki went on. "But they understate the challenge. Rising tides, caused by global warming, could submerge land now occupied by over a billion humans within thirty years." Furrowed brows. He gave them time to process the information.

"Have any of you got a suggestion for how to solve this impending crisis?"

Nobody spoke.

"The problem will not be easily solved. This becomes clear when you realize that during the twentieth and twenty-first centuries, there have been two world wars, several major regional wars, many attempts at genocide in different parts of the world, countless localized plagues, and severe natural disasters that wiped out wide swaths of human civilization. All of that has not been enough to turn the tide of the human population explosion." They looked confused.

"I understand that you all are accustomed to dealing with local and regional issues. But today, I want to begin to show you how the local efforts you've been working on fit into a much larger context. I need you to step back and think on an epic scale, in terms of both geography and timeline." Haruki clicked a button, and his face dropped down so that there were five small windows, with the main part of the screen displaying a shot of Earth from outer space. A tranquil, blue-green orb floating against a black backdrop. "That much human expansion does not happen without cost. It is estimated by experts that as many as two thousand species are going extinct each year, at our current level of crowding."

As he was talking, the screen began displaying a series of images, slowly at first. Fossils of extinct creatures starting with crustaceans, fish, then dinosaurs, then early mammals, then larger mammals, moving more rapidly through time until it showed species extinct in recent decades, the Tasmanian tiger, the Dodo bird, and continuing to increase tempo, until it was a series of flashes, images of the most endangered species alive now. As the display increased in speed, he said, "Think about that. Five species go extinct *every single day.* As population density skyrockets, it is inevitable that the extinction rate will escalate." The display sequence was speeding through images of rhinos, giraffes, elephants, antelope, deer, lions, tigers, gorillas, monkeys, zebras, horses, bunnies, birds, cats, and dogs, stopping on a picture of a modern-day suburban family. The meeting attendees were now all frowning from under crinkled brows. Haruki clicked, and the family slowly faded away to a gray background.

When his face returned to the main display, he was showing his most grave expression. "Let me give you one example. Honeybees are in real trouble. Pesticides, and loss of habitat, have resulted in massive honeybee die-offs all around the world. This is sad because honeybees are awesome little creatures. But it moves from emotionally distressing to scientifically alarming when you realize that fully one-third of our global food production is dependent on honeybee pollination." A few of the people were taking notes, others were looking off like they were picturing the scenario he was presenting.

"Let's extrapolate the population numbers out to the twenty-second century. If the predicted rate of increase holds and remains constant into the end of the next century, we will be a planet of 24 billion people. That means there will be as little as a quarter of an acre of land per person. Sounds crowded, doesn't it?" They were all nodding.

"Now, take away a third of the food after the bees are gone." They looked more troubled.

"It is worse than it sounds, because the land that is habitable for humans is also the land that is suitable for food production." He paused to gauge their reaction. Not enough horror. "On that quarter-acre of land, you not only have to live, you must also grow all the food you need to live. That will be nearly impossible if you live in a tiny house in a temperate zone and eat a plant-based diet. If you try to raise a cow or a pig, you and your entire family will die of starvation."

The group was completely silent. He had their attention.

"Imagine what it would be like to wake to the screams of your children, bellies swollen, racked with disease, from lack of nutrition." An image appeared of a starving child dying in barren dirt. All the good feelings were gone. "And the neighbors on all sides of you are going to be in exactly the same situation. Every adult human you encounter is going to be out hunting for a way to feed their starving children."

He allowed them time to sit in silence, stare at that image and think. "Imagine that this is your child. I want you to connect with this problem at a personal level. I know it is difficult, but it is the only way to truly understand the problem."

It was a lot to absorb, and he needed them to move with him toward his conclusion. "Friends," he said, using his most compassionate face. "I know this information is troubling. I wish it were not true. But the facts cannot be denied. We are heading toward a global cataclysm. We are looking at the real possibility of global extinction within fifty to one hundred years."

More silence.

Finally, Steve raised his hand. "Haruki?"

"Yes, Steve."

"What are we to *do?*"

Haruki nodded, put on his somber look. "That is the question that faces all of humanity, Steve. Unfortunately, nearly all humans are asleep at the wheel, hurtling headlong into oblivion, giving these issues no serious thought."

"But Haruki," Pete said, "what are... *we*... going to do?"

Haruki pointed at the monitor, a proud look on his face. "*That* is the right way to ask the question. Personal accountability. Take-charge leadership. That is what I need from each of you."

They stared at him gravely, nodding.

"We need to discuss an important science term."

More silence.

"The term," he said, "is natural selection."

All the section heads glanced back and forth between the screen and their secretaries.

"There is no way to put this tenderly, so I'm simply going to be honest. Planet Earth is a beautiful piece of creation. A work of art, really. It could have existed into perpetuity, had it not been for the fact that the natural ecosystem was thrown out of balance."

"Are you talking about global warming?" Shawn asked.

"No, global warming is only a recent *symptom* of a larger and older problem. Until we face the truth and deal with the root problem head on, all the pathetic attempts to bring things back into balance will fail."

"Haruki, I'm sorry," Pete said. "I'm having trouble following you. What is the root problem?"

"The ecosystem was thrown off by the introduction of an invasive species."

They all were deeply troubled.

"I know this is hard to hear. I need you to turn off your emotions. Look at this from a science perspective. The unvarnished truth is humans have wrecked the ecosystem of the planet."

"*We* are the invasive species?" Steve asked.

Haruki nodded. "In time, you'll see that I'm right."

"Well, what in the hell are we going to do about *that*?" Pete asked.

"The problem with an invasive species is not that the species is harmful in and of itself. What makes invasive species dangerous is that they multiply too rapidly, dominate other more vulnerable species, use up too many of the food resources. That upsets the entire system."

"What are you saying?" Steve asked. "To save the planet, we have to wipe out *humans*?"

"No, not wipe out, Steve. Control. We need to control the rate of growth. This is basic science. If any species becomes wildly overpopulated, that species becomes unhealthy, vulnerable to disease, starvation, and eventual extinction. At the same time, all the surrounding species are threatened."

There was a loud silence. It was a lot for them to process. He waited.

"Are we talking about birth control?" Pete asked.

"Controlling the number of children born is a logical first step. China has taken a stab at it, but they've been clumsy. They limit all families to one child. For natural selection to work properly, we need to allow the most talented and gifted members of society to reproduce freely. Right now, the portions of the population who contribute the *least* to solving society's problems, produce three to five times as many offspring as the intelligent, contributing members. We need to reverse that, turning the pyramid on its head."

"How?" Shawn asked. "What are you proposing?"

•••••••••••

When Perry woke laying in the soft white cloud next his dumpster, the old man was lookin' at him with warm, friendly eyes.

"Hi, Perry."

"Hey, Henry." He sat up, stretched, rubbed his eyes.

"Perry, why do you and Giovanni like to play around with the Pinocchio story so much?"

He shrugged. "I don't know. It's from when I was a kid. Mom used to read it to me."

"Do you remember the story?"

Perry yawned. The cloud was all around him, wispy, white, drifting, and swirling. Henry's smiling face was there, inside the bright mist. "I don't know, man, been a long time. *Kind of* only, prob'ly."

"What do you remember about the story?"

Perry crinkled up his forehead. "Pinocchio was tryin' to be a real boy, right?"

"Yes. And what else?"

"Geppetto, the old man, really wanted a boy, but he didn't have one, so he made one… outta wood."

"Yes, that's it, Perry. Geppetto loved Pinocchio like he was a real boy, but he knew he wasn't one."

"And Geppetto wanted him to be a real boy too, right? They both wanted the same thing?"

"Good. You do remember the story."

"Yeah, I guess so. But Pinocchio screwed it up somehow, didn't he?"

"Yes. Do you remember how?"

Perry frowned. He didn't like quizzes. "Cause he wasn't a good boy. He ruined everything."

There was a long silence. Perry couldn't see Henry now, but he could feel him watching. He could see the cloud, and in the cloud, images of himself doing bad things. Stealing papers from a vending machine and sellin' 'em. Swiping a bottle from a wino who was passed out so he could give it to his old man. Stealing food off a plate at a sidewalk café when nobody was watchin'. Borrowin' stuff from construction sites. Bouncin' a can off the skeleton preacher's head. Stealing holy water from the church.

"I guess I really *am* like Pinocchio, huh, Henry?"

The silence continued. It went on so long, it got louder and louder. Perry sat there in it, feeling lousy.

Finally, Henry spoke again, very slowly, in a warm, soft voice.

"Perry."

"Yeah?"

"Who was Geppetto?"

"This a trick question?" The old dude was tricky. Had to watch him. Henry didn't say nothin', so Perry figgered he was gonna havta talk next.

"Geppetto was Pinocchio's old man, right? His Father?"

"Was he?" See. More tricky questions.

"Yes. He was Pinocchio's father, and he wanted him to become a real boy."

"So, Pinocchio was not a real boy."

"Right."

"Then how Could Geppetto be his father?"

"Because Geppetto *made* him."

"He made him out of wood," Henry said.

Perry was sure he had this part right. "Yes. He wanted a boy so bad, he made him outta wood."

Now Henry was giving him that look again. Like waiting for him to figure it out, so...

"Oh. He wasn't *really* his father."

Henry smiled at him, nodded. "Geppetto was Pinocchio's *creator*."

"Oh, wow. I never seen that before."

Henry didn't say nothin', just kinda sat there smiling, his dark skin a sharp contrast with his white teeth and the cloud, letting Perry think about it. After a minute, he got a little more serious.

"I have heard the questions you've been asking Father John."

Perry's turn to be silent. *How's he do that? How's he know that?*

"Perry, are you sorry for all the bad things you've done in your life?"

The cloud at his feet wasn't deep enough. He needed a place to hide.

"Yeh. I really am. I'm a terrible boy and a lousy son."

"Perry?"

"Yeh?"

"Little brother, I don't want to hear you talk about yourself like that anymore, okay? Never again."

Perry didn't understand but didn't know what to say.

"When you talk bad about yourself, you are talking bad about one of God's special people, you understand?"

"I... Naw, I don't think so." The suit in the park was shouting down at his dad, who was rolling on the ground drunk.

"Do you remember this moment, Perry?"

"Yes."

"How did you feel in that moment?"

"How'd I *feel*?" Perry had ta think about that one. "It was kinda mixed up. I was pissed at the old man for being such a screw-up... and I was pissed at the suit for saying bad things about my dad."

"I see. And in that moment — be perfectly honest — did you love your dad?"

Perry's head dropped, and he had a pang in his chest. "Yeh. Yeh, I did."

"You ran to him, helped him up, and helped him get home to the dumpster, didn't you?"

"Yeh."

There was a pause. Old Henry letting it sink in.

"Perry, in the moments when you did bad things, it was as if God the Father, who is your Creator, was sitting on a grassy hill watching you. He saw what you did, saw when it hurt you, saw how you suffered when there were consequences."

"I'm sorry."

"And in every one of those moments, God never stopped loving you. When you fell, when others hurt you, He loved you all the more."

Perry wiped his eyes on his sleeve. He needed a Kleenex. Or a rag or something. The steam of the cloud was making his nose runny.

"Geppetto wanted a son so badly that he created one," old Henry continued. "And of all the things he had ever created, Geppetto loved Pinocchio most of all."

Perry needed to sit and think about that. That changed the story. Made it seem… just diff'rent.

"While Pinocchio was a wonderful little puppet, Geppetto didn't want a puppet who would only move if he pulled his strings. He wished for him to become more. He wanted him to become more like *himself*."

Some more stuff to think about right there. But old Henry was talkin' again already.

"In order for that to happen, Pinocchio had to be free to participate in the process."

"How do you mean? That's one of them things you say that ain't like normal people talk. *Participate in the process*?"

Henry chuckled. His eyes looked real nice and kind. Like he was having a good time.

"Pinocchio had to *choose* to become real. It was hard for Pinocchio because he had limited experience. But in the end, Geppetto's love for him, and his love for Geppetto, saved Pinocchio, and brought both of their fondest wishes into reality."

Perry was trying to understand all that Henry had said. It was a lot.

"Perry, sometimes in a simple little story, great truths can be reflected."

"Man, you ain't *kiddin'*."

"What Father John told you was true. There really *is* a mark on your soul."

Perry kept his head down. His throat lumped up. If he was a little kid, he woulda been cryin'.

"Strive always to find deeper truths, Perry."

See? That was one of them things Henry would say sometimes made you feel like you oughta stop and write it down. Normal people don't say stuff like that. Another voice, bigger than a movie theater, all around him, said

"Choose the way of faithfulness, Perry. Set your heart upon my laws."

Perry was hunched over, eyes wide, hands moving up to cover his ears. He looked up at Henry, at his big smile.

"Who was that?" Perry whispered.

"That was the voice of El Elyon. The most-high God."

Perry didn't know what to say. He just looked at Henry with his mouth open.

"Your Creator," Henry said, still smiling, "wishes far better things for you. But you must *choose* these things for yourself. You must *decide* what you will become."

Man, he really needed a Kleenex. Didn't seem right to wipe it on his sleeve. Not in *this* place. Perry looked down at the cloud, tryin' to figure it out. When he looked back up, he was alone. Nobody wasn't there no more.

··········

In the waiting room of the spa, soft meditation music played, and pleasant aromas of nature wafted through the space. Mary was in a luxurious lounge chair, waiting for her orientation. She had her tablet on her knees, and she was engrossed. The screen revealed a fascinating story. The man on the cover of *Millionaire* magazine was everything Haruki had made him out to be. He was a self-made millionaire, starting with one hundred dollars' worth of stocks he bought while working at a grocery store in high school. Even back then he was an attractive kid. Fast forward a few years, and there were photos of him on the covers of business magazines and investor journals. Currently considered one of the top ten stock investors alive. There were photos of traveling on private jets, touring the Mediterranean on his 140-foot yacht, splitting his time between mansions in Switzerland, London, Canada, the U.S.—and an actual castle in Scotland. Wow.

Surprisingly, he was not divorced. He was a widower, madly in love with his college sweetheart until she died from cancer. Ahhh, and they had a little boy. The family photos in the magazine were heart-rending. The little boy standing beside his father at the funeral, face contorted in pain. But the little boy had recovered well. Now a handsome young man, he was a world-renowned concert pianist known to his fans simply as Amadeus. Wait, she had heard about this kid.

She opened another research tab and typed his name. Here it was. Photos of him performing in the world's elite classical venues. He had a reputation as a genius eccentric. The recent tabloid photos were racy, with cute young women on both arms, wild dancing at a rave club, police arrests, mug shots, and drug charges. Something about a scandal in Australia, a post-performance party that had gotten out of control. He was a wild kid. Typical for a young celebrity. Wow, his first album went gold, his second was racing up the charts. She made a note to get a copy of his music and become familiar with it. This assignment was becoming more and more interesting.

She went back to the millionaire magazine tab and looked more closely at the smiling photo. Was there anything about this stock investor that wasn't larger than life? It was a little icky poring over the intimate details. But wait… he granted the interview, and probably provided the photos, so he *wanted* people to know his story. Besides, if he were going to be her new assignment, this was only the beginning of the due diligence she would need to conduct. She could scarcely believe the adventure she was about to embark upon.

....

Haruki was getting frustrated. This was always going to be a tough sell, but he didn't expect the meeting to drag on like this. He was used to people falling into line.

"People, please calm down. An emotional response is not going to make these problems go away."

"Well, what kind of a response do you think *is* appropriate?" Steve asked.

"A science-based response. Mary is not here to report, but I wish she were. The report would be impressive. The Life Choice League has exceeded all expectations, preventing unwanted births. Since its beginning in 1973, over sixty million unwanted births have been prevented in the U.S. alone, without a single law being broken."

"Sixty *million?*" Steve echoed.

"Yes, and the vast majority of those are minority births, or the offspring of poor, under-producing people. The program is accomplishing precisely the effect it was designed for. The Life Choice League has been phenomenally successful, but it leaves so much undone."

"It leaves so much *undone*?" Pete said.

"Don't get me wrong," Haruki said. "It has been a big help. I believe the day will come when people laud the name Margarita Singer. She will be praised as a person who made extraordinary strides toward reducing population by founding the Life Choice League. But as you've seen by the numbers, it simply is not enough. War, disease, famine, and natural disasters are not enough, so volunteer abortions alone are certainly never going to be enough."

"Are you advocating *mandated* abortions?" Sue from the Chicago branch asked.

"I prefer to think of it as government regulated, Sue. It will require legislation. We want everything to be done above-board. It is too early to tell how the program will eventually take shape. It could be tied to annual income or to education level. Some people advocate a race qualifier, but that is never going to clear the political correctness barrier, so there is no sense even looking at it."

"But… isn't that the same thing?" she asked. "Tying it to income and education? Isn't that going to automatically select for minority races?"

"Excuse me, Sue," Haruki said. "You're getting ahead of yourself. In the first place, as I said, there's no telling what type of legislation will eventually be passed. Second, even though Mary is absent today, this is still a section lead meeting. Secretaries are here to assist with organization and information capture. Let's please limit the questions to section leads only."

"Yes, sir. I apologize."

He put on his generous expression. "It is a moot point, really, because getting rid of the minority races will not shrink the population numbers enough."

"What?" Steve gasped.

"Steve, please focus on the bigger picture."

"You want to get rid of minorities altogether?"

"Steve. Please withhold judgement until you've heard the logic behind the effort."

"So… who makes the decisions about who lives and who dies?" Pete asked.

"It's obvious. Those decisions must be made by people who have the vision, the emotional detachment, the moral courage, and the leadership skills to make hard choices for the greater good."

The faces in the small windows were stunned. He needed to sell harder.

"Let's back up a minute. This is not just about abortion. That is only one tool available to us. Try to look at this analytically. People tend to absorb a disproportionate percentage of their lifetime resources during the last few years they live, when they are least productive," he explained. "We need to adjust that."

More silence, and no direct eye contact.

"Listen, friends," Haruki said. "None of *you* have anything to worry about. I hope the Thanksgiving trip and your promotions demonstrate that I won't let anything bad happen to you or those you care about. I'm asking you all to move up to a higher level of service."

"How is this a higher level of service?" Pete asked.

"A higher level of self-*sacrifice*. I am asking you to carry the burden of making extremely difficult decisions, to preserve the planet and ultimately the human race."

They were less than thrilled.

"You'll be involved in something of historical significance."

"Yes, but what side of history are we going to be on?" Steve asked.

"History is a funny thing. What is false today will be true tomorrow. In the future, names like Stalin, Hitler, and Mao will be lauded as visionary people who did the *most* to save the planet. These people were completely misunderstood and unappreciated in their own time. And reigning supreme above all of them, orders of magnitude above them in accomplishment, will be Margarita Singer and the Life Choice League."

"Worse than Stalin, Hitler, and Mao?" Pete said.

"Not worse than, *Better.* Technically, Mao and Hitler are slightly ahead, with Mao being credited with reducing the population by seventy million. If we were going to be fair, we would have to acknowledge the fact that many of those deaths were a result of flawed management policy, not concerted effort. But even without that, Hitler has a firm hold on the lead. Hitler is credited with reducing the population by seventy to seventy-five million. Those deaths were a direct result of actions intentionally taken. Should his supporters be able to count his own people who were killed? I think so, but it is an on-going debate. Anyway you look at it, Hitler is still in first place. Mao is a close second, but Stalin, with his conglomerate population reduction of perhaps nine million people, isn't even in the same league." They were all staring at him.

"The important thing to remember, is that we are seeking a *lasting* solution to the population problem. In the cases of Hitler, Stalin, and Mao, their numbers were impressive, but they are fixed. Their effect died with them. They were all one-shot, flash in the pan blips on the timeline. They were clumsy, bombastic in their efforts."

Still nothing but blank stares. "Singer, on the other hand, engineered a poetic, evergreen, self-renewing system which continues to serve us today. She is long gone, and her legacy is still expanding, stronger than ever.

She has sixty million exterminated lives to her credit in the U.S. alone. She will soon eclipse Hitler and Mao. Her influence on the world stage is harder to quantify but she has certainly outdone each of them when you take that into account. In time, she will eclipse all of their efforts combined. But the most beautiful thing? Singer did her work elegantly, without firing a single shot. She set up a system where people volunteer their participation."

In the monitors, their mouths all hung open. Why were they not getting this?

"If you can bring yourselves to look at the bigger picture, you will see that what we do, we do out of love."

"Love for what?" asked Pete.

"For the planet, of course. For the sustainability of the human race."

"Haruki," Steve said. "You know I'm a naturalist. My hobbies are hiking, nature photography, and rock climbing. I spend my vacations white-water rafting, and I volunteer time each month picking up litter along stream beds. I donate to conservationist causes. I recycle. I eat a plant-based diet. My roof's covered with solar panels, for God's sake."

"That's all commendable."

"My point," Steve went on, "is that I love nature as much as *anyone*. I vote for pro-environment initiatives. But I'm sorry, I cannot in good conscience be a part of this."

"Settle down, Steve."

"How can we talk about saving the planet," he ranted, "while making plans to *kill* millions—no, *billions*—of human beings? No, thanks. Someone else can have the promotion intended for me."

"Don't be hasty, Steve. This is an important decision. Take some time —"

"I don't *need* time to think about it. I don't want any *part* of this."

"I am *telling* you to *take* time." Haruki caught himself barely in time to recover his civil tone. "I will hear your concerns tomorrow in a private meeting, Steve."

A heavy silence fell over the meeting. Steve had completely thrown off the momentum and timing. Haruki took a calming breath.

"There is a difference between running with the pack and being a true leader. Anybody can recycle, reuse their shopping bags, even use paper drinking straws, which don't actually work. But that is not what the planet *needs*. What the planet *needs* are people who have the commitment, the leadership traits to make *hard* choices. People committed enough to do the *untenable*, to rescue the planet from the *unthinkable*."

There was not a single nodding head. It was irksome. Haruki was expecting more support after all the generosity he had shown them. The meeting was drifting in the wrong direction. Time to roll out the incentives.

"Again," Haruki said, "I know what I'm asking is hard. It requires each of you to put aside your personal feelings and rise to the highest levels of leadership."

"Excuse me, but I'm not talking about *feelings*," Steve said.

"Steve, that will be quite enough. I already told you that I would discuss your concerns with you tomorrow, in a more appropriate setting." Steve was intentionally trying to sabotage his efforts. How dare he? "Keep in mind, the elite people we have been talking about already spend time every day grappling with these kinds of decisions. That is what leaders *do.* Your job will be to help them arrive at the *right* decision."

"But, Haruki," Pete said, "isn't there some *other* way we can save the planet? A way that is more *compassionate*?"

"This *is* compassionate. We will reduce the population of the world in sterile, professional conditions. The work will be performed by doctors, statisticians, and white-collar executives. It is impossible to tell what other methods may come out of our laboratories. It could be that something will develop to hasten the pace, and allow us to avoid a lot of legal wrangling. But this must be done. Would you rather have the world's children perish with bloated bellies in the dirt of a dying planet? Or would you rather wait until resource shortages lead to the collapse of civilization, and have attrition come through killing in the streets?"

Haruki took another deep calming breath. "I think you're looking at this all wrong. Everyone has a role to play in saving the planet. The Bible says, 'Amen, amen, I say to you, unless a grain of wheat falls to the ground and dies, it remains only a grain of wheat; but if it dies, it produces much fruit. Whoever hates his life in this world will preserve it.'"

They all looked bewildered. It was exactly the distraction he needed.

"Your doubled salaries will help you make the transition to moving among the world's elite. But there are other things to consider. To gain access to these people, you will need memberships at the exclusive country clubs and cigar rooms where they hang out. That is being taken care of as we speak."

Shawn's and Pete's ears perked a little. Steve was stoic.

"You will also need to have a completely different wardrobe, not only for yourselves but for your wives and children. There will be open accounts set up in the company name at the most exclusive clothiers. Your wife can't be seen wearing the same outfit she had on last month." The thing about the wives and children moved the needle a little. "The best way to connect with these high-level influencers is on a personal level. The company will be covering the expense of having all your children enrolled in the elite daycares and grade schools where the senators' kids or grandkids attend."

Shawn and Pete both liked that.

"You will be traveling a lot, both nationally and internationally. All travel will be either first class or private charter. All air miles, as well as any travel perks, will accrue to your personal accounts, and, of course, when schedules allow, you may bring your families with you. Admittedly, this is a difficult job in certain ways. I want to be sure your work carries great benefits for your families."

Hints of smiles were starting to return. The family thing was a strong motivator. But Steve's face was still made of stone.

"And since you'll be in Washington a lot, I'm arranging for each of you to have a leased residence in the city, in the exclusive neighborhoods where the elected officials live, so you can meet and become friends with these important people in a *natural* way—while you park your car, shop for groceries, or walk your dog."

Shawn and Pete seemed to be thinking about what that might be like.

"Playgrounds are great places to start business alliances," Haruki continued. "Let your children become best friends with the children of senators and congressmen, especially those who are chairs of important committees. You may live in D.C. full time, or only when the elected officials are in town, your choice. Your families will be enriched by enjoying the museums, art galleries, and national monuments. Your wives will have private lunches in five-star restaurants with the most powerful women in the world, while you save the planet by smoking cigars and swinging golf clubs."

Much of the resistance from Shawn, Pete, and Sue was evaporating.

"On a more... *sensitive* topic, you need to be able to treat these high-level influencers to the kind of favors that will get their attention. So, you'll have funding that is virtually unlimited, for sport fishing, exotic resort stays, the best golf courses in the world, and quid pro quo arrangements. We are going to do whatever it takes to get these initiatives passed. Oh, and of course you will each need a luxury car in Washington so you can fit in at the country club parking lot. I don't want you to have the hassle of renting transportation."

There was a marked change in the mood of the meeting. He could see the wheels turning in all heads, except Steve's. "Please understand," Haruki went on, "You will be white-collar influencers, offering guidance and incentives to people already in position to make things happen. The work you do will benefit all of mankind. It is only fair that you be compensated proportionately."

In the monitor, Sue's face was showing a more favorable expression, and his intuition told him to roll the dice.

"Mary has been running lead on the Life Choice League, and she has done a fine job. But her new assignment is going to keep her fully occupied, so we are going to have to promote someone to fill her responsibilities." Sue was staring at him.

"Sue, I've been thinking you might be ready for a promotion. How would you feel about stepping forward to take on Mary's responsibilities?"

"Me?" she asked.

"It would mean a four-fold increase in salary, a secretary of your own, a company car, the housing, travel, and entertainment allowances that you've seen Mary enjoy. I think you can handle the responsibility. What do you say?"

"Um... Haruki, thank you so much. I don't know *what* to say."

"You would become a leading champion of women's rights. The job is yours if you want it. If not, I'll promote one of your coworkers to the position. I'll give you twenty-four hours to think it over."

"Yes, sir."

"But be certain you can accept these responsibilities without reservation, Sue. I will need you to be all in. Your focus needs to be on the good that is being accomplished, not the cost."

"I'll let you know tomorrow."

"Fine."

She smiled. "Thank you for the opportunity."

••••••••••

At Gillespie Periodicals, Giovanni was sweeping the sidewalk when Perry's dad came shuffling along, staring at the ground, mumbling under his breath. He stopped to look into a green dumpster.

"Hey!" Giovanni waved his arms. He had to shout a second time before the old man looked up. "Come here, my friend!" He gestured with his arm for him to come over.

The old man looked around, as if to make certain he was the one being called, then shuffled across the empty street. Giovanni put down his broom and dusted his hands off on his pants.

"My friend, may I buy you a cup of coffee?"

The old man nodded, peering at him with bleary eyes. Giovanni placed his hand on his shoulder.

"We get in out of this cold, yes?"

Perry's dad hesitated, shrugged and followed him inside. Giovanni seated him at one of the little reading tables, patted him on the shoulder as he walked by, and busied himself with pouring two cups of coffee. He could feel Perry's dad looking at him, but he kept moving, casual, like it was no big deal. Like they did this all the time.

He reached into a bottom drawer and pulled out a pint bottle of bourbon, tucked that under his arm, and carried the two coffees to the table. "How 'bout I warm it up a bit?" He pulled out the pint. The man's eyes lit up and he nodded. Giovanni poured a generous shot of bourbon into each of their cups, screwed on the cap, and set the bottle aside. He raised his cup. "Salute!" Perry's dad nodded again, gave a shaky salute, and took a sip of the hot liquid.

Giovanni sipped also. *Where to begin?* He had known this was a conversation he could not avoid, and yet he did not feel prepared. "You have no been around for a while" he began, trying to act as casual as possible. The old man shrugged, looked to the side, and returned his eyes to the tabletop. He took a longer drink.

"You been doing okay?"

He shrugged. "S'pose so."

"Is good to hear. I'm glad." Giovanni wanted to give the man a few minutes, and a few sips of the liquor, let the booze take the edge off his pain before he had to tell him the news.

"I have a bundle of newspapers for you. You pick them up when we done here, okay? I been saving them for you."

The old man glanced up at him and away. "Mm." He was looking past Giovanni, out the window, focused on nothing. Drifting. Lost in there, somewhere. Giovanni needed him to pay attention, and it was hard for the man. He needed to gently work him up to it so it wouldn't be as much of a shock.

"I think the world of your boy."

Perry's dad's eyes were bleary, a little suspicious, but he nodded.

"I think you raised a fine young man. One of the finest young men I've known."

Perry's dad stopped mid-swig, a light coming on, an angry realization flashing across his eyes.

"Why didn' Perry pick up da bundle?" Scowling over the top of the coffee cup.

Giovanni had to be careful. Find the right balance of warming beverage without over doing it. The old man was a mean drunk.

"You seen those punks, the Hyenas, that little gang, no?"

Perry's dad looked at him with a dull stare. His eyes were yellow, cloudy, his whole face traced with tiny blue blood vessels.

"Those punks been giving me a hard time."

The old man was still staring, his eyes a little less bleary, the booze starting to kick in maybe.

"See, they came at me the other day, right out there at the newsstand. They try to rob my money, but Giovanni is no going down without a fight. When I resist, they all jump me at once." Perry's dad was intent now. Finally getting with it. The booze was working. Giovanni got up, went across the room, grabbed the coffee pot, came back, and refilled the cups. Perry's dad looked from him to the bourbon bottle.

"Help yourself."

The old man reached for it, almost knocked it off the table, grabbed it again like it was a live hand grenade. He tried to pour, but his hands were shaking so badly he missed the rim of the cup, poured some out on the table.

"Thit!" the old man shouted, looking up at Giovanni with an expression that showed the depth of a great tragedy.

"Is okay," Giovanni said. "I have more. We okay." He took the bottle, poured it into each of their cups, and screwed the lid back on. He sat quietly while Perry's dad took a deep swig, almost chugging the hot coffee. Giovanni waited. He was coming to the hard part and did not want to continue. It would hurt Perry's dad on his best day, and he never had best days anymore. The booze was the only help Giovanni could offer. It was not going to be enough.

"Dey attack jue?" The old man looking at him with a dull expression.

"Yes, they did. And they gonna kill me, too. Five of them, understand? They kicking me, hitting me, really putting it on me. I got a couple of them pretty good with my broom stick."

"Good," he grunted.

"But it was not enough. I was on the ground and they had me."

Perry's dad was looking at him again, interested to hear what came next.

"Someone came from the side and plowed into them. He was punching, kicking, like that. Those thugs were no able to concentrate on me anymore, see? He saved my life."

"Who did?"

"Friend," Giovanni said, "Your Perry did that. Perry came from nowhere and save me."

"Where *ith* Perry?"

"I knew they'd be very sore at Perry, so I took him in a cab, ten miles, across the river, and hid him in a hotel."

The old man's eyes narrowed, his face turning into a scowl.

"He was banged up. He paid a price for what he did, but it was not nothing he could not get over."

"Good." Perry's dad went back to sucking down the coffee. He drained the cup, wiped his filthy sleeve across his mouth and beard.

Giovanni wondered if it was safe to give him another cup or if it would be too much too quick. He hesitated. The man was still hurting from a cold night outside, so he decided to chance it. He poured another cup for him but not for himself.

"Friend, that is not the end of the story. There is more."

The old man looked up at him again.

"Perry was safe in hotel room. He was starting to heal up. He's a good boy, you know? He don't care too much for himself, only about others."

"Where'th my boy?"

"I had to come back to work, so I left him in the room, but he was worried about... well... he did not want to stay in the room I had for him. He took off, went back to the alley."

"Where'th my boy?"

"I gonna take you to see him. Stay calm."

"Where'th Perry?" This time it sounded more like he was pleading, about to start sobbing.

Giovanni sighed. "Friend, I do not want to tell you this, but those Hyenas caught him in the alley, jumped him while he was sleeping."

"Aww, thit!" He stood up, knocking over his chair, a bony fist pounding down on the table. The bourbon bottle fell over, Giovanni caught it before it hit the floor.

"Calm down." Giovanni held up the bottle and his open palm.

Perry's dad was wringing his hands, bleary eyes darting from side to side. He doubled up his fist, looked around, couldn't find anything to punch. "Awww!" His poisoned brain was unable to come up with words to say how he was feeling. Giovanni put the coffee pot away, started to put the bottle away, but thought better of it and slipped it into his coat pocket.

"Friend, I gonna help you through this. I owe Perry my life. I will do anything for you, okay?"

"I want thoo talk thoo my boy!" Perry's Dad insisted. He was shaking his head, unable to speak. Tears began to dribble down his wrinkled face.

"Brace yourself, friend," said Giovanni. "This is no going to be easy. You are not going to be able to talk to Perry, but I can take you to see him."

The old man's eyes opened wide, his face blanched, as if seeing a terrible specter.

"No, no, no!" He spun, crashing into the door, stumbling out into the street.

"Wait!" Giovanni cried. The old man was half running, half falling, bouncing off walls as he went.

....

Pete pulled into his garage and put the car in park. The minivan in the next stall was nothing fancy and, to be honest, getting up in miles. Peggy, his sweet wife, never complained. His big fancy job with Haruki was supposed to make them rich, solve all their problems, but somehow, six years later, all the money had slipped through his fingers. The casino. Guilt stabbed him. The money he'd lost at the tables could have easily bought her a new minivan. Heck, even a luxury SUV. Maybe paid off the house. He shook his head.

Haruki took him to his first casino, to celebrate his new position in the company. The flashing lights, the tuxedoes, the women in scant clothing were intoxicating. With his usual flamboyant generosity, Haruki bought all the drinks, even slid a full rack of chips in front of him, so he could have fun, and relax. Pete won almost seven hundred dollars that night and left there feeling like he was worth a million. That good feeling had faded long ago. Pete felt lousy almost all the time.

The whole experience of working at H&H had been a long string of painful disappointments, always one step away from the big prize. Close enough to success he could smell it, but it always slipped out of his grasp. He had to wonder if this new position wasn't going to be more of the same. He had never been comfortable with the things he had to do for Haruki, but this time the assignments were so sweeping, so dark. He wasn't sure he could get on board, even with all the perks. Steve was right. *Why didn't I have the courage to stand up and object like Steve did?*

This was going to require a serious talk with Peggy. It might be time to break away from H&H and start fresh. In a week he could get his resume together. He *should*. There had to be something out there that would allow him to make a decent living and also sleep at night. A light came on. Peggy was in the doorway, up on the little landing, looking out at him. He shut off the engine and smiled at her through the windshield. He pushed the button, and the motor on the big overhead door started humming.

"I thought I heard you pull in," she said.

"Hi, babe." He got out of the car and moved toward the steps.

"Usually, I hear the music thumping when you are a half block away."

He smiled again, tried a chuckle, but it was weak. He gave her a little kiss and held the door as she went back into the house.

"Everything alright?" she asked.

"What? Oh, yeah. Of course. How was *your* day?"

"Fine. Anything interesting happen at the staff meeting?"

He turned his back to her, hung the car keys on a hook, slipped his shoes off.

"We're going to have decisions to make."

She gasped. "Oh, Pete, please don't tell me you're losing your job, or getting a demotion or something. We're barely making it as it is."

"Why would you think that?" He turned to look at her, the fear in her face, the tears welling. "Baby, settle down." He moved closer and caressed her shoulders.

"I'm sorry," she said. "I know you work so hard. But… I feel like I can't take much more disappointment. I can't. I'm just… *tired*."

"Baby, we've got each other. Together we can do *anything*, right?"

She started sobbing. It ripped at his heart. All of this was his fault. He was the one who blew all the money. He needed to be the one who took the hit, not her. Mr. Gillespie had said it. Give the best of everything to your family.

"We're not losing our job," he said. "We're getting a promotion."

"Really?"

"Yes, really."

"You're not teasing me?" She wiped her palms against her eyes.

"Would I joke about something like this?"

"Pete, please tell me this is real. We've struggled so long."

"Babe, it's huge. Double the salary, all kinds of crazy perks you won't even believe."

She leaned into him and hugged him tightly. Happy tears now.

"Your man is always going to take care of you," Pete said. "You're going to have all new clothes, a new car, all kinds of stuff we've only dreamed about."

"Seriously?"

"Seriously. You're going to live like a queen. I'm finally going to be able to give you the kind of life you deserve."

"Oh, Pete!" She buried her face in his chest. "I knew you'd make it. I *always* believed in you. I can't wait to call my parents."

"Yeah. It'll be great. Everything is going to be… just… great." A huge hollow place opened inside of him.

··········

The two huge doors swung open all by themselves. They were made of some kind of dark, reddish wood, and looked real heavy. *Where is this?* Perry wondered. The way they opened, it was like he was supposed to go into the room, but he really didn't want to. It was a big, dark place.

He stepped in, careful, squinting, tryin' to see. The way things had been going, and after Henry had said he was for sure gonna go to hell, he didn't want nothing to do with dark places. The room was bigger than any room he'd been in. In front of him, a ways inside the door, he could make out a long wood table, longer than any table he'd ever seen. Even after his eyes adjusted, most of the room, even the other end of the table was lost in darkness. Spooky place. He was all alone.

Wait. In the shadows at the far end of the room, way over there, past the other end of the table, something moved. Perry froze. Did he imagine it? Out of the dark Kujo's face appeared. Behind him, a bunch of Hyenas stepped forward. They had ball bats, slapping them against the palms of their hands. The slaps echoed all through the darkness of the big room. Perry could see Kujo's snarl comin' at him. Perry's stomach was getting ready to vomit.

He turned, and tried to run, but he crashed into a giant wall of white. Then the wall divided and slipped past him. It *wasn't* a giant wall. It was two *actual giants*. As they came in the room, they lit up the room with a ton of light. Like they *were* the light. Like the light was *inside* them, busting out, and it lit up the whole room. Two huge white flames, only a lot brighter than any fire could ever be. Even though they were made of white hot fire, you could see the shape of the giants clear as day. They looked solid, but you could see right through 'em, the light flashing out of them like it would if it was comin' out of some kind of liquid crystal. They moved smooth, graceful, as nimble as any flame could be.

Perry could see the Hyenas plain now. Their faces had changed. Kujo looked real scared. His mouth hung open, eyes wide, starin' at the giants.

One of the giants turned and looked at Perry. It was the most terrifying thing Perry *ever* seen. Terrifying and beautiful. The face was calm, not excited at all. A glass face, the hot white flame rolling and moving inside, not like anything he'd ever seen. The giant held one hand down low in front of Perry, like telling him to stay back.

Perry was good with that, no problem.

The two giants were about the same size, but one was built real heavy, like the strength of a bull, the other was slim, with stringy muscles like a young boxer would have. They wore something like a short robe with a belt, the robe down to the middle of their thighs, and that was made of glass too. Below that, their legs were shaped like solid muscle, but made of flames inside of moving glass. They had on tall sandals with leather straps that crisscrossed the low part of their leg, and you could see through all of it, white flame, and flowing crystal. On their backs they wore a kind of cape, and each of 'em held a long spear made of metal. The spears looked powerful. White hot flames was sizzling through the shafts, like if they was filled with lightning, the tips of the spears, larger than Perry's hand were crackling and popping, little strings of lightning escaping and dancing about in the air.

The two giants looked at each other like “let’s do this.” They began to move forward in a slow walk. The capes on their backs exploded into giant wings. *Real* wings, with shining see-through feathers, powerful, like a giant white eagle made of fire and crystal would have. They held the wings out wide and shook ’em. Not big sweeps like an eagle does, but fast, and invisible, like a giant hummingbird.

One time Perry seen two big military helicopters swoop the harbor, low and fast. You didn’t just *hear* the sound, you *felt* it. Like two Chinese drummers pounding on your chest and your back. That’s how loud these wings was. He put his hands over his ears. The light in the room was way brighter now, *too* bright. So bright he almost couldn’t see the giants anymore. Perry was squinting, but it didn’t help.

A minute ago, it was Perry who was terrified. Now it was Kujo. His face was drained, his mouth hanging open, his eyes wide. He put his hands over his ears, backing away, stepping into the Hyenas behind him. All of ‘em dropped their bats, covering their ears, tryin’ to hide behind Kujo. The giants kept moving closer to the Hyenas, slow walkin’, beating their wings.

Perry couldn’t see the giants’ faces, but he could see how terrible the giants were, in the faces of the Hyenas. The Hyenas kept backing away and backing away. When the giants got to the end of the table, they swung the spears down, made a loud slap, catching the shaft of the spears with their other hand. The tips of the glowing hot spears cracked together in a big X at the end of the table, and lighting exploded out of them, and thunder clapped so loud it shook the floor.

The Hyenas was all curled up, the bright light pinning them against a stone wall. They were hugging each other, the younger ones crying. Kujo was about to die of fright. The wings stopped, and they held them out wide, perfectly still. The giants froze like crystal statues, but the flames were still moving inside. Perry had been hunching his shoulders hard. He relaxed now. Let his hands drop, to listen. The only sound was the sniveling of the Hyenas. The big room was bright with the light from the giants, and the Hyenas looked tiny and weak, shakin’ over there.

Perry smelled something familiar. Roasted *ham*? He turned to see a young girl coming in the door behind him. She was pretty, with flowing blonde hair, wearing a long white gown of shiny material that almost touched the floor. In her hair she had flowers, and she smiled at him real nice. She was carrying a platter, holding a huge roasted ham. It smelled so good it made his mouth water. She carried the ham over and placed it on the table. It had juices dripping out of it. He almost couldn't stand seeing it. She nodded toward the chair in front of him, held out her dainty hand inviting him to sit.

Really?

She nodded, smiling, like she knew some big surprise. He sat down and couldn't even see the Hyenas no more; the ham was so big. When you been livin' on little canned hot dogs and soda crackers, it's hard to stare at a big ham like that, and not grab it. But Perry wasn't sure whose it was, and he didn't want to get in no trouble. Not in *this* crazy place. Next, another young woman came in, carrying a platter with a giant roasted *turkey*. He could smell the turkey, *and* the ham. He could see the juices shining on the browned turkey breast, but he still couldn't believe it was real. She sat that platter on the table in front of him too, and another young woman carried in a big platter filled with grapes and every kind of sliced fruit he'd ever seen and placed it on the table behind the turkey and the ham. There was so much fruit, he could see it *over* the turkey. Another girl came in with a huge bowl of fresh cut salad. Every kind of vegetable he ever heard of, and some he didn't even know about. It was a *big* salad like he'd only seen before in dumpsters, but this one was brand new.

Next, a long parade started. More and more people, all dressed the same, all smiling at Perry as they went past, filling the table with more and more food. So much food Perry couldn't believe it. More food than he'd ever seen in his whole life. The platters stretched all the way over to where the giants was at the end of the long, long table. It was more food than a whole *grocery* store. Every kinda dish he ever heard of, even watchin' through windows at the cookin' shows, and a bunch he didn't recognize. It all smelled delicious and looked…

All he could do was stare.

A big rumbling movie theater voice, everywhere and nowhere like you was inside of the voice, said,

"I have set a table before you in the sight of your enemies."

Perry's neck scrunched down inside his shoulders. It was El Elyon's voice. Wasn't nobody had a voice like that. He'd know that voice *anywhere*. After a second, Perry saw that the high, high ceiling was lighted by the angels. It was a bunch of arches that met in the middle, way up there. He looked across the long table heaped with delicious food, hungry, but he was afraid to eat any of it.

He raised up in his chair enough to peek over the food at the Hyenas, and his heart stopped. Huddled against the wall was a bunch of the little demons from his Mama dream. He blinked. No, now it was the Hyenas again. *What?* Perry rubbed his eyes and looked again. Kujo was tiny, shrunk down to the size of a little demon, lookin' all around like he couldn't believe what was happening.

"Goodness and mercy..."

Perry's head ducked down again from the sound of it.

"...shall follow you all the days of your life."

Perry didn't know what to do. He sat real still.

The big voice made him jump. "Perry?"

"Yes?" he said timidly.

"It is my will that you should dwell in my house forever."

Perry's eyes filled with tears, and when he blinked, they ran down his face. He didn't care. He wasn't embarrassed. He didn't even care if Kujo saw him cry. He was happier than he'd ever been in his whole life. the banquet looked amazing.

"Sir," he said, "this is too much. I could never eat all this food in a hundred years."

The big voice was smiling on him. Another door opened on the side of the room, and in walked the most beautiful woman in the world.

"Mama!"

She was young and healthy, and she hurried over to him and hugged him, kissed him on his cheek. Next came Dad. He was young too, and clean. His hair was cut real neat, and his face was shaved. With big strides he came over and hugged Perry's shoulders, holding onto him, squeezing. The smell of his aftershave was the same as when Perry was little. Dad looked so, so happy. He kissed Perry on the top of his head, and it was more than Perry could stand.

"It's good to see you here, sport." Here Dad was, safe and healthy, like Perry had given up on ever happening. He grabbed Dad's arms and held on, crying like a little baby. Mama was huggin' both of them, and she was crying too.

Another parade started. Lots of doors opened, all the walls on both sides of the room, and people started streaming in. Geppetto, Father John, Mr. and Mrs. Ming, and a bunch of people he'd seen around on the street, and in the park, and down by the burn barrels, and some that he'd only seen in church, in paintings, and statues, and stain glass windows, and a bunch a people that he hadn't never seen at all. They came swarming in, pulling up chairs, joining the table, passing around food, talking, laughing, smiling.

There was every kind of person there. Men and women walking side by side with their arms around each other, staring into each other's eyes like they were the only ones in the world. Two young girls, like sisters, almost identical, whispering and laughing together. A mama walking, smiling down at a little girl who was holding her hand. A daddy with a young boy on his shoulders, the young boy hugging his cheeks, his chin rested on his daddy's head. A woman come holding a baby, smiling big, tears pouring down her cheeks, and the baby's chubby little fists grabbed her hair and pulled her down close. The woman laughed, and sobbed, and put her face against the baby's cheek.

But there *wasn't* every kind of person. There wasn't no old people. There wasn't nobody in wheelchairs. Nobody was walking with canes or walkers. Not even any crutches. The people were all healthy, happy, and they all gathered into a huge crowd around the giant table. Then they all started *singing.*

It was amazing. Like a great Christmas choir on the steps of a courthouse, but a thousand times bigger. A thousand times better. They was all looking up, so Perry did too, and the roof was gone. Musta been a thousand angels up there floating and singing, moving in a circle, holding their hands up, and above them another circle, and another, and another, level after level of angels holding their hands up, a warm light pouring down through the circles into the big room. All the people around the table raised their hands.

Perry's lungs was gonna bust. It was like something inside him had to get out. He opened his mouth, and a powerful singing voice started pouring out of him. He never sung like that before. He never sung so loud or so long. It was like he couldn't sing enough. Not enough to say how happy he was. How thankful he was. And his arms was straining, couldn't reach high enough. As he was singing, tears was pouring outta his eyes. He kept singing and couldn't do nothing but cry and cry.

El Elyon's voice spoke softly to him, close to his ear. "You are invited to attend this banquet Perry, but you must not appear in your rags. You must acquire suitable attire."

"I will," Perry said. "How?"

"Your clothes must be washed clean in the blood of the Lamb."

How can I get my filthy clothes washed? And in blood? he thought. *There must be a way, or El Elyon wouldn't be sayin' that, right?* Through his blurry tears, the cloud started swirling thick around him again, the whole banquet getting covered up, the cloud starting to soak up the sound.

"No!" Perry cried. "Come back!"

Everything beautiful was being torn from him. Again. Having that beautiful scene ripped away was like his muscles being ripped off his bones. Like the inside of his lungs being pulled out. It was the last straw. The last pain on the last day of a long, agonizing life. His whole body started to jerk and cramp and shake and twist. He couldn't control it. It was like clinging to the dumpster, vomiting the nasty green fluid, but worse. It was worse than the beat down in the alley. It was the worst pain ever. After what seemed like forever, it all stopped, and he lay still. Now he understood what it was to finally be dead. Things went blurry and faded into darkness.

October 24

"Steve, what's wrong? Are you sick? You're white as a sheet." He was in his home office, sitting back in his chair, staring into space when his wife came in. He snapped out of his thoughts, focused on her pretty face.

"No, I'm fine."

"Well babe, we've got dinner reservations in an hour. Are you going to be ready?"

"Becky, I hate to say it, but I think we've got a problem."

"Okay?" She gulped, and it ticked him off. That damn Haruki. When an employee agrees to join a team, devotes years of his life to help build something, there is an implied trust. The rug was being yanked out from under his whole life, from Becky's life, because of that psycho's lies and deceit.

"I'm sorry, honey. We'll be okay, but I've discovered a big problem with H&H. Something is not right."

"Okay?" She said again. She sat down in a chair, put her dainty little hands in her lap, and waited for the bomb to hit. He would have given anything to be able to avoid having to tell her this. And on their tenth wedding anniversary. For just once, it would be nice to have a special family occasion without H&H screwing it up. But this was too big to put off. He had to tell her.

"Before I tell you the details, I want to assure you that I will do anything, give everything to protect you and take care of the kids. I don't want you to worry about that, okay?"

"Okay."

"Haruki offered me a big promotion, double the salary, free memberships at exclusive clubs, extravagant clothing allowances, free cars, free international travel, a bigger package than I've ever heard of anywhere."

"Okay? That's good, right?"

"All I have to do is sell my soul to the devil."

"Oh."

"Something is not right about this. I tried to protest in the Section Lead meeting, but he cut me off and wouldn't let me speak. So, I decided I would take a few days off, travel to the other branches on my own and speak one on one with the other branch managers, try to talk them out of accepting these ridiculous incentive packages."

"Wait. Everyone was offered a package?"

"Yes. The very same package. Me, Shawn, Pete, and Mary. And our secretaries all move up with us."

"That does sound… irregular."

"Wait. Do you have your cell phone on you?"

"Of course. I have it right here."

"Let me see it."

She handed it to him, and he opened the case, and removed the battery. "Take that out and leave it in the other room, then come back."

"Okay? Steve, this sounds…"

"Just trust me, babe."

"Okay." She was gone a second, then came back in and sat down again. "What was all that about, Steve?"

"I don't trust Haruki. He might have listening devices in our phones."

"Honey, that sounds crazy."

"It does, right? Anyway, I decided I had to talk to my co-workers face to face without Haruki. That's when everything got weird."

"Weird how?"

"I booked the plane tickets. LA to Corpus Christi, Corpus to Chicago, Chicago to Boston. No problem."

"Okay? And?"

"And then I started trying to book ground transportation."

"Steve. These pauses are driving me nuts. Just tell me, okay? If you were trying to build suspense, you've done it."

"Sorry. Its just that I'm still trying to get my head around this myself. I started trying to set up ground transportation, from the airport to the branch office, in Corpus, and guess what?"

"Steve. Stop it. Just lay it out."

"Okay. Sorry. I couldn't book ground transportation from the airport to the Corpus Christi branch, because the Corpus Christi branch doesn't exist."

"What?"

"It doesn't exist. The address we use when we ship packages? Its bogus. There is no H&H branch. There is no building."

"What? Did you try calling Shawn directly?"

"I don't have a number for him. Haruki insists that we only communicate via video conferencing, over the company's proprietary system. Communicating through outside, unsecured channels is a firing offense."

Becky's face was turning pale. She looked frightened, which Steve hated. "Don't get upset, Becky. I'll figure this out."

"Try Chicago."

"I already did. And Boston. They're phantom offices. The only H&H branch office I can find anywhere in the world, is this one in L.A."

"Are you kidding me?"

"Do you think I'm kidding?"

"What are we going to do?"

"We are going to get dressed, go out and have a nice dinner, celebrate our ten years of marital bliss, and tomorrow, I'm going to call Haruki and tell him I'm out. And I might call a couple of Journalists I went to college with. This maniac thinks he can mess with my family like this, he's got another thing coming."

....

Perry woke up. Now where was he? Not in the cloud, not in any of the worlds he'd seen, somewhere else. Pitch darkness. He couldn't tell if he was sitting, laying down, maybe floating. No way to know. The squeal of an old-time radio tuner screeched out of the darkness. An orchestra faded in, then out, through some static, to some idiots making stupid jokes. Then to more static, to a male talk show host's voice.

"Sandy, if I've said it once on this show, I've said it a thousand times. The homeless problem in this city is out of control. I know the bleeding hearts want us to think of these people as victims, but the truth is, most of them are homeless by choice."

"Stan… that may be true, but in the story we're following tonight, a young man did fall victim to brutal violence."

"I know that, and I don't wish anyone harm. But I'm going to go out on a limb here, and predict that when the smoke clears, the evidence will prove that the violence was perpetrated by another homeless person, or by gang members. Two parts of the same problem. What does the evidence say so far?"

"Stan, all we've been able to determine, is that he was bludgeoned by a blunt object. A baseball bat was found abandoned at the scene, and it appears to be the murder weapon. DNA samples are being processed to confirm."

"So, early findings are consistent with my prediction," Stan said. "Have they identified the victim?"

"Yes, but they're not releasing the name because they are searching for the next of kin."

"Do we know anything at all about the victim?"

"Not much, other than he lived in a makeshift shelter beside a dumpster. Police say he engaged in petty crime, scavenging, and stealing. He stole food from restaurants and supplies from construction sites."

"So, it is just as I was saying. He was unremarkable in life, and in death, he disappears into a landscape of statistics that are becoming increasingly disturbing. This is the end of another wasted life like so many blighting our inner city."

"Still, it is sad to see this happen to such a young person."

"It is, sad, Sandy. And these tragic stories are becoming all too familiar. It is hard to fathom why any young person would choose to squander their life in that way."

"I agree, Stan. Officials who work with the homeless say they tried repeatedly to give him a fresh start, but he was too stubborn to accept help."

"Sandy, you've proven my point. His could have been a story of overcoming odds. Instead, his life ends as a tragic example of wasted human potential."

"I guess the core lesson in this is that we should not waste the opportunities we are given."

"Exactly. And in brighter news, next we'll interview the fireman who rescued a baby owl today, and we have this week's winning kitten story."

Silence.

Perry wanted to vomit. He wanted to cry. He screamed, but it was like the sound didn't go anywhere. It stayed close around him. He screamed again. He began to sob and curse. "Why would you let me hear that?"

No response came. Only darkness and silence.

Dark draped upon dark, growing darker still. He felt a pressure closing against him. The floor collapsed, and he was falling, rolling, tumbling over, and over. hands flailing, finding nothing, It was the worst feeling ever. A stab of panic. *This is it. I'm finally falling into the bad place.*

A rumbling male voice, deep and sinister like that of a great beast growling through a mouthful of spit, said,

"I told you God would let you down, Perry."

The downward motion was increasing. Perry was for sure gonna be sick.

The voice changed into a gravelly laugh. "You pathetic little boy. All your life, believing there was something more for you, like you might have a purpose. Look around you. What purpose is there to this? Live by a dumpster, be treated like garbage, even eat garbage, then be murdered and nobody comes to your rescue?" Now the laugh was loud.

Perry was falling fast, his stomach up in his throat. His fists were clenched, his teeth gritted. He couldn't even scream.

"You are a failure. You always *were* a failure." The voice was chasing him down, down, down, right on top of him. "Your mother was stolen from you by the very God you thought would save you. Your father is a complete loser. And you had the hubris to think you could save him. You? Pathetic little you?" The laughter roared. "He is dead, Perry. You failed. Your dad is rotting, and you promised you would protect him. You are a liar. And where are you now?"

Perry wanted to scream, but he was too terrified. The speed of the falling was still increasing, a whistle in his ears, wind racing up past him. The smell of rot was worse, stronger, taking his breath away.

"Where is your body, Perry? The mutilated body, the head the Hyenas crushed. Where are the broken bones? The bloody carcass? Do you even know?"

Perry didn't know. Didn't want to. "Shuddup!" he shouted.

The laughter came louder now, and was joined by a chorus of other laughter, howling with delight.

"Your body is being eaten by worms, Perry, and nobody cares. You are hardly even gone, and already your pathetic waste of a life has been forgotten. All you have left is your spirit, and your spirit is as pitiful as your putrid body."

Perry started crying. He couldn't help it. It hurt so bad. He was so scared. Nobody was comin', for sure.

"Is that fair, Perry? Is it fair that you have been abandoned?" The voice was louder than the wind rushing up past him. The voice was moving in circles around him, close, moist, wet, putrid. It smelled like rotten meat. "Of course, its not fair. Don't you see that all the talk about God, about mercy, about that ridiculous indelible mark, was all lies?"

"Nooo!"

"Doesn't that make you want to lash out?" He was streaking downward through the darkness, stomach in his throat.

"Shuddup!"

Again, the laughter roared, even more voices joining in.

"Haven't you had enough, Perry? Aren't you sick to death of the games, the riddles, the lies?"

"Yes! Stoppit!" He was ripping through space now, down, down, down, faster, faster. The skin on his cheeks was flapping below his eyes.

Right by his ear, the malevolent voice said "I can make it stop, Perry. But as long as you cling to those stupid lies you've been told, I can't help you." The voice got bigger and scarier. It was shaking Perry's ribs, it was so loud.

"Swear loyalty to me, you little insect. Give me complete control of your mind, and I can free you from all of those lies."

"I don't wanna go to the bad place," Perry pleaded.

"The *bad* place?" The laughter exploded. Sounded like thousands laughing. "This from a cockroach who spent his life crawling in and out of dumpsters? You've seen what your God will provide for you. I give you my word: if you serve me, I will provide something much grander."

"I... I don't..."

"Perry, *stop sniveling*!" The voice was terrifying.

Perry was nauseated, his hair sticking straight up, gritting his teeth against the sickening motion. His eyelids were flapping, so he squinted them tight. He was sure he was gonna crash down somewhere terrible any second now. His fear was so bad, he was shaking all over. He was falling so fast, but when he opened his eyes again, he could see something... as though he was looking out through a swift waterfall of black water, something like a different world, a city street, a sidewalk, traffic going by, and the back of a familiar man.

"Geppetto!" he shouted. The old man didn't seem to be able to hear him. "Geppetto! Help me!" he cried. He reached forward, and his hand passed through the waterfall, and passed through Geppetto's shoulder. The old man turned, jumped back in terror, banging his head on a metal light pole.

"Geppetto, please! Help me! Go Get Father John!"

A strong wind ripped past his face, and the waterfall disappeared. Again, there was nothing but darkness, and the sickening sensation of falling faster and faster.

"You stupid little boy," the malevolent voice sneered. "You think that old man can help you? You think your priest can reach you here? No, Perry. You are mine. Mine and mine alone. There is no one here to save you but me, and you're running out of time."

"Nooooo!" cried Perry, gritting his teeth, clinching his eyes shut.

"I can save you, Perry. But you have to let go of those foolish lies people have been telling you. Do it now!"

"Leave me alone!" Perry shouted, the wind rushing up under his chin.

"Say it, Perry. Curse your false god, and I will save you."

"Noooo!" He shouted. "*God, save me*!"

A different voice, huge and strong, hit like an earthquake.

"Enough!"

All motion stopped. It was jarring. A bright spotlight pinned Perry to an ordinary gray floor. Wings were flapping, and it sounded like a bunch of rat's toenails clawing to get away, then there was silence.

Perry flopped over on the floor, panting, exhausted.

Nobody said nothin'.

OCTOBER 25

"Team," Haruki began, "I have called this emergency meeting because our H&H family is facing a moment of tragedy. I ask you all to brace yourselves. I have the sad duty of delivering awful news."

Shawn gulped. He didn't need any bad news right now. He had been tossing and turning all night, haunted by images of war, genocide, starving children, and legions of baby ghosts rushing in on him. It had been a *terrible* night. Now what?

"It breaks my heart to tell you that we've lost Steve."

"Steve quit?" Pete asked.

"No, Pete. Please. Let me say this. Steve is… he's *gone.*"

Shawn's blood turned to ice.

"Yesterday evening, Steve was out to dinner with his wife. When he left the restaurant to get the car, he was attacked." Haruki stopped, gulped, reached for a glass of water, wiped his eyes with a thumb and index finger. "A man in black clothing pulled a gun on Steve, demanded his wallet, which Steve gave him, then he demanded Steve's Rolex, and witnesses say that Steve tried to fight with him over it. It is unclear whether the gun went off accidentally or if the man intentionally pulled the trigger, but Steve was shot in the chest. He died before the ambulance arrived."

Everyone in the meeting was stunned. Shawn had a lump in his throat, and the hair on the back of his neck was standing on end. Goose bumps covered his skin. All he could think of was Steve saying, "I don't want any part of this."

"Did they catch the assailant?" Pete asked.

"As luck would have it," Haruki went on, "one of the witnesses was a private investigator with a license to carry a concealed weapon. He was trying to get into position to intervene when the assailant's gun went off. He pulled his weapon and shot the assailant before he had a chance to flee. The assailant was lying dead beside Steve when the police arrived. It was a terrible, terrible mess." Haruki's voice cracked.

Nobody said anything for a few seconds.

"Has the attacker been identified?" Shawn asked.

"He was just a drug addict, a young man wanting to steal money, probably to score a fix."

Shawn had a thousand questions but didn't feel like asking for answers to any of them. Not from Haruki.

"What breaks my heart..." Haruki stopped and visibly gulped. "I keep wondering what is going to happen to Steve's pretty young wife and child now that Steve isn't here to provide for them." Haruki stopped, shook his head, and his face twisted into a painful grimace. For a split second, he looked up at the monitor, to see how everyone was reacting.

The look in those eyes, sent a shudder that rattled Shawn from head to toe.

October 28

"Haruki, I'll hand this off to one of my guys and let 'em teach that snooty little professor a lesson."

"Which guys are you talking about?"

"Well, I've got Kneecap and Slice. I could get one of them. Or both, you wanna do it right."

"No, Guy. That will not suffice. The boy's father is much tougher than he looks. We don't want to scare the boy. We want to crush the father. We want to take all the fight out of him in one heavy blow. Thuggery will only make him angry."

"Okay."

"This is a sensitive operation and must be handled with a high level of finesse." He handed Guy a piece of paper. "Call that number. When the line opens, don't wait for anyone to speak. Say 'forty-two, forty-two, forty-two,' then give the target's name, home address, and place of work. That is all. Hang up."

"This ain't got no name on it."

"You don't need a name, Guy. Did you hear me? I just gave you the instructions. You must follow them to the letter, exactly as I said. Understand?"

"Sure, Mr. H., I understand. But I don't see why it would hurt for me to have a name."

Haruki sighed. "Guy, this gentleman is one of the best in the business. He does high-profile work. The most valuable asset he has, is his anonymity. Understand?"

"Sure, Boss. Everybody likes anonymity. I don't think I should give my name either, would that be okay?"

"Guy. Listen to me. Don't give your name. It would cause a problem if you did. We need complete anonymity throughout the entire chain of communication."

....

Melanie, the parish secretary at St. Leo's, was working on the list of people who had signed up to volunteer for the committee which would plan the parish's spring picnic. It was a good list, for this early. A strong list of workers, but it was lacking one or two good leaders, who could organize the others.

A call came in, and she picked it up on the second ring.

"Good morning, thank you for calling St. Leo's, Melanie speaking."

"Good morning, Melanie. This is Sarah, in the bishop's office. How are you?"

"Oh hi, Sarah. I'm fine. How can I help you?"

"Melanie, the bishop would like to have a one-on-one with Fr. Bianchi. Can you look at his schedule please?"

"Sure, I have it right here. What are we looking for, maybe a half-hour slot for a phone call?"

"Uhm. No, actually, the bishop would like him to clear his whole schedule tomorrow morning."

"Oh, okay Let's see..."

"And he wants him to come here, to the bishop's office."

"Oh. I see."

November 2

Perry seemed disturbed today. He was dark, and brooding.

"Perry," Father John said, "I would like to revisit our conversation about Lazarus."

"It's okay, Father. Henry already told me we was talking about the wrong dude."

"What?"

"Henry says there's a different Lazarus."

Perry was slouched, face clouded over.

"*Anyway*, I want to explain something more about Lazarus being raised from the dead. You see, there's nothing more terrifying for us humans than the specter of death."

"Man, that's right. Death ain't no joke."

"No, it isn't. So, I want to tell you another story."

Perry sighed. "Okay."

"God's chosen people were wandering in the desert, and they became very tired and frustrated."

Perry nodded. "I know what that feels like."

"They began to do terrible things, which made God angry with them."

"Oh." Perry looked down. That bothered him.

"He sent snakes into their midst, and the snakes were biting them, and people were dying."

"Serious?" His face full of fear. "God must have been really mad, huh?"

"If you read the whole story, you will see that God had good reason. But God is merciful, and when His people begged Him for help, He heard them."

"Yeah? What'd He do?"

"He told Moses to make a statue of a serpent wrapped around a staff."

"Huh. You mean that big walking stick Moses carried in the movie?"

John laughed. "Yes, Perry. It was that staff. You've seen that old movie?" Perry frowned. No sense of humor today.

"Yeh. Mostly that's what I've seen, *old* movies. I seen that one a long time ago. What'd Moses do next?"

"Next, God told Moses to raise the staff up before the people, and if the people would look upon that statue, God would heal them, and they wouldn't die."

"That's some crazy stuff right there, Father John."

"It is. It's such a powerful story, that even today the image of a snake wrapped around a staff is the image used by medical doctors."

"Oh. I seen that. Like on the side of a ambulance, right?"

"Exactly," Father John said.

"That's a cool story." Perry brightened a little.

"It is, and it's an *ancient* story. That story is a gift to us from God that allows us to know that we can trust Him, and that He always wants to show us mercy, even when we make bad mistakes."

"That's cool. But I never knew that was from the movie."

John smiled. "That ancient story about the snake on the staff is what we call a foreshadowing. It is a hint about things to come."

Perry scowled.

"Remember, we agreed that the most terrifying thing of all is death, right?"

"You know it." Perry visibly shivered.

"So, when Jesus came to Earth, he came to bring us the greatest gift of all."

"Yeah? What was it?"

"He came to give us freedom from the fear of death. That is why he brought Lazarus out of the grave."

"Yeah, but Lazarus *died* again."

"True," John said. "But only in our human way of looking at things."

"You got a *different* way to look at things?"

"We know that God looks at things very differently than we do."

"Oh. I s'pose so. That makes sense."

"And after three days in the tomb, Jesus raised Himself, and conquered death forever."

"Nah, that part ain't right. Death is alive and well, I can tell you that."

"People do die. You're right," John agreed. "But think about this, Perry. If we never left this life, we would never get to go on to another."

"And you think the next life is better."

"This life is the only life we know, but Jesus tells us that this life is only a small part of the whole story. He tells us there are mansions waiting for us."

"So how do we get to see the *rest* of it? How do we get to the good place? It ain't as easy as it sounds, finding that path."

"It isn't easy. In fact, if we had to do it on our own, it would be impossible. God is perfect, and pure, and holy. So much so that nothing tainted by sin, or anything bad, can ever come into His presence."

Perry's face fell.

"And yet," John went on, "God loves each of us and wants us to come be with Him."

Perry looked down at the floor, sad. "I don't see how that's ever gonna happen. I don't think *nobody* is *all* the way good."

"Exactly. But like with the snakes in the desert, God made a way. Jesus came into *our* world, to take all *our* sins—all the bad—of all the people who *ever* lived, on *Himself*."

Perry looked suspicious. "That's a lot a bad things."

"Yes. And it's hard to think about that because Jesus is so *good*. Jesus is the only man who was ever perfect. He is God Himself, come to us in the form of a simple man."

Perry's brow furrowed.

"God *became* a man. He came to live the life of a man so He could die for all of *our* sins. When Jesus went to the cross, Perry, He had done nothing to deserve punishment. He was good and pure. He was holy. He only suffered, because he wanted to save us. He suffered and died for our sake."

Perry was looking up at the crucifix.

"When the soldiers raised Jesus up on the cross—nails in his hands, thorns piercing his brow—it was the fulfillment of the foreshadowing that happened when Moses raised the snake on the staff. And three days later, when Jesus rose from the dead, death was conquered forever."

"Huh?"

"The image of the snake on the staff was a sign of hope for the people in the desert. The image of Christ on the cross has become the sign of hope for all of mankind."

"Whut?"

"Perry, when we see that image, we can know with certainty that God has paid the price of our failings, and that death has been conquered once and for all. We each have an invitation to come and join Him in a new life and the new kingdom that is far beyond this one that we know."

"So how come everything's gotta be so hard?" Perry asked. Tears were forming in his eyes. "Why can't we all go be in that new place right *now*?"

"Only God understands why there must be suffering in this world," John explained. "This life does have a purpose, but we will never fully understand it until our life is over and we enter into that new kingdom."

Perry was staring at the floor again. No, past it, deeply troubled by something only he could see.

"But there is something very important about this story that you must remember."

Perry looked up. "What's that?"

"You must remember that only the people who chose to look upon the image of the snake on the staff were saved. And only those who choose to look to Jesus on the cross will be safe from true death and be able to enter the kingdom. It is not something to be taken lightly."

Perry looked up, astonished. A flash in his eyes, irritation.

"Father John, why'd you wait so long to *tell* me this?"

John held his gaze. "What do you mean?"

"You tellin' me all this time all I needed was to get one a them little crosses, and ever' time I do somethin' bad, I look at it, and I can get to the good place? I could a *been* there by now. Why didn't you *tell* me?"

Sometimes Perry said the strangest things. "No, it isn't that simple. It isn't a good luck charm."

"No?" Perry's expression challenged him. "You just said anyone who looked at the snake or the cross could quit bein' dead and get to the good place."

John shook his head.

"Yes, you *did* say that. You *just now* did."

"Slow down, Perry. I did say that, but I think you misunderstand what I mean. It isn't magic. That's not how it works."

"Man, why you gotta be like that? You're bein' just like Henry, talking in riddles, and sh – awh. I don't *come* here fer that. If you ain't gonna help me, I ain't got time ta be comin' here for riddles." Perry stood up, scowling, and turned to leave.

John got up. "Wait."

"No." Perry faced him. "I been comin' here, askin' you fer help all along, and you say you know how to find the path, but you don't tell me, and now you gonna start talking in *riddles?*"

John blinked at the angry young man in the doorway. *What just happened?*

This street boy, alone in the world, probably needed God more than anyone John knew. Despite all efforts, John was making things worse. What if the boy gave up on the Church, and turned to drugs or to the gangs? He could be lost for the rest of his life. Maybe for eternity. *Please, Father,* he prayed. *Give me the right words.*

"Please come back and sit down, Perry."

"You gonna tell me what you know?"

"Yes. I will."

"An' no riddles?"

"No riddles, I promise."

Perry hesitated a moment, skulked back in, hesitated, and slumped down.

"K.O., I ain't *got* eternity. I'm runnin' outta time. If there's a secret, you gotta give it up, man."

"I'm sorry. I wasn't trying to talk in riddles."

"Well, you gonna tell me the secret of findin' the path or not?"

John held up his hands. "Calm down. I'm going to tell you. Calm yourself so you'll be ready to hear, okay?"

Perry took a deep, stuttering breath, let it out. "Okay. I'm ready. I'm listenin'."

"The secret to finding the path is not a riddle, Perry. It is a *mystery.*"

Perry looked at him with suspicion.

"Here it is, the deepest truth of all truths. It is important that you hear me, that you believe me, and that you try to understand the mystery."

"Okay."

"Perry… Jesus *is* the path."

Perry's brow crinkled into a scowl, and he looked up at the crucifix. He looked back at John.

"Jesus said it plainly, but many, many people miss it because it is too simple."

"What'd he say?" Perry asked.

This boy had been lied to and mistreated so much in his life; John was afraid he might not be able to accept the gift.

"Jesus said '*I* am the way, and the *truth*, and the *life*. No one comes to the Father except through *me*.'"

Perry's eyes filled with tears. He gritted his teeth, put his head down.

"Father John, I been tryin' so *hard*. I been *tryin'* to get to the Father, but I can't do it. It ain't *workin'*."

"Perry, remember the indelible mark. God the Father *wants* you to join Him in the new kingdom. It is not *your* idea, it is *His*."

"So what I gotta *do?*" His frustration was palpable.

"You don't have to do anything. You said it yourself, nobody can earn this. You have worked hard your whole life, but you can't work hard enough to deserve this — ever — because nobody is all the way good. Remember saying that?"

Perry nodded; his face still tilted down at the floor. He reached across quick, grabbed a Kleenex from the box on the table, held it to his face.

"There is a place in God's kingdom reserved especially for you," John said. "All of Christ's suffering, people beating Him, spitting on Him, looking down on Him, was all for you. Christ took those nails in His hands and died on the cross to erase *your* sins."

Perry's eyes were swimming in tears. John's own heart was being pulled from his chest.

"I ain't worth it." Perry said. He choked back a sob.

"And yet, there He is." John pointed to the crucifix.

Perry stared at the figure of Christ crucified, blinking, tears dribbling down his cheeks. A look of horror came across his face. Then profound sadness. "I ain't worth it," he said to the crucifix.

Perry slid out of the chair, collapsed into a lump on the floor—his face down, forehead to the rug. "I ain't worth it." His fists clenched. "I ain't *worth* it," he gasped, pounding the rug. "I ain't *worth* it!" He covered his face with both of his dark-stained hands, sobbing, his entire frame quaking. "I ain't worth it." Now it was a desperate plea.

John slid out of his own chair and knelt, praying with all his heart. Praying with his soul, in gratitude for the miracle of this fine young man, this poor, lonely little sheep who was so strong and so tough, but so good and loving on the inside.

John couldn't find words to express his feelings. His heart, his mind, his spirit, his entire self was streaming toward heaven in an ecstasy of gratitude, humility, and release.

After long moments, Perry's sobbing stopped, and the room became quiet. The presence of the Holy Spirit was as powerful as John had ever known it. The love of God filled the room. A pervasive stillness settled. A miracle. God present right here, right now.

John placed his hand on Perry's back. In a kind voice, he said, "Perry, God the Father of Mercies, through the death and the resurrection of his Son, Jesus, has reconciled the world to himself and sent the Holy Spirit among us for the forgiveness of sins, through the ministry of the Church. May God give you pardon and *peace.* I absolve you from your sins in the name of the Father, and of the Son, and of the Holy Spirit."

Perry had undergone a change and would never be the same. Maybe John Bianchi would never be the same either.

....

"Perry, wake up," a woman's soft voice said.

He did wake up, but he didn't open his eyes. Was this a dream? This morning was different from all the other mornings that had happened before. Nothing hurt. He could tell there was a warm, soft glow around him, and he could smell the slightest hint of something nice.

What is that? He'd smelled it before. At St. Leo's there was a garden, with a statue of a beautiful lady and a bench, and surrounding that statue was thorny bushes. In the spring, Perry liked to sometimes lay on that bench in the morning, when nobody was around, and close his eyes. When the cool morning breeze moved just right, he could barely catch the soft, almost invisible smell of the roses. That's what he was smelling now.

Perry smiled. That bench was one of his favorite places on the whole Earth. From the time he was little, he liked to lay there and pretend the statue of the beautiful lady was his mother, standing over him, kind of reaching down to him a little, protecting him. It was a strong feeling. It made him warm inside, and also kinda sad, because he missed Mama so much and for so long. But the beautiful lady was always there. He could feel his eyelashes getting wet, just thinking about it.

Yeh, that's where I am. The bench at St. Leo's. He could feel one of his arms hanging off the bench and his legs kind of half bent over the end. But it didn't quite feel right. The bench was usually cold and hard, but right now he was in a soft place. His head was hanging back, like over a soft pillow, his face to the sky, and he could feel warm light shining down on him. *This definitely isn't the bench.*

He started letting his eyes open a little so he could see past his eyelashes. Tears were making everything blurry. The light around him was bright and warm, and there was blue and white. *Prob'ly clouds and sky.* Someone else was there. A face. Lookin' down at him. It wasn't a face made of concrete. He opened his eyes all the way.

The beautiful lady, her face close to his. Not the statue, the *actual lady*, with a blue cloth draped over her head, her face soft and pretty. Tears were filling her eyes just like his, but hers were lit up with love.

Perry was surprised to find he was laying across the beautiful lady's lap, and she was holding him with one arm around his shoulders, like if he was a little boy. Even more surprising, his filthy rags were gone, replaced with a robe of smooth, shiny material, white like the people at the banquet had wore. She stroked his hair, and he started crying for real.

Nothing that came before mattered now. There used to be something else, but he couldn't remember what it was. He never had any minute that was this nice. He didn't know there could *be* this kinda minute.

The beautiful lady touched his face with her fingers and laid her hand against his cheek. That started something like a flood. Happy feelings pouring into him. The love of Sister Mary Frances, and Mama, and Geppetto, and Dad before he got sick. The joy of the great banquet, and the thrill of hearing the voice of El Elyon say his name, all mixed together and coming to him at the touch of the beautiful lady.

It was a strange feeling, like somehow, he all of a sudden understood who he was and *why* he was. It all made sense now, everything that had happened, and it was all exactly like it was supposed to be. Like something real heavy had been fastened to his back and it was time to let it go.

For the first time, Perry didn't feel tired. He was a kind of happy he hadn't ever known before. For the first time ever, he didn't *want* nothing. Like he already *had* everything. And somehow it all came to him at the touch of the beautiful lady.

She started getting real blurry. They were both crying, the sweetest minute he'd known. The fog rolled in, and Perry was the only one there, laying in the soft cloud, but he wasn't sad. He didn't think he was able to be sad now. And he didn't think he'd ever be alone or sad again.

••••••••••••

"Perry." Henry's voice, warm and strong, came out of the cloud. "You are moving to the next level now, little brother."

I wonder what that means. Perry listened. Silence. He barely breathed. He didn't want to mess up this nice feeling.

"You have learned much and have proven that your heart is as pure and good as I knew it was. Now you will go where you have not been and become something new, something you never thought was possible."

More silence.

Stillness.

Peace.

Relief washed over him. Sounded like he was finally gonna go to the good place. All the good things from his life were coming back now, piling up, covering him — the love of his friend Geppetto, his deep feelings for Dad, the love he'd always held for Mom, Father John, the beautiful lady, Henry in his green work shirt and old suit pants. Every smile, every fluffy cloud, every sunbeam, every rainbow after every rain, bunnies, and fawn deer, and little songbirds, and butterflies all in one. Powerful.

Like a wave in the harbor, not washing over him but sweeping him along, like being *inside* the wave, knowing its power, being part of it. Water was running from his eyes, down his cheeks, and he let it flow, washing, cleaning, making him pure, carrying away the grime of the city. He felt new and fresh and whole and ... loved. He felt loved. Like his mother loved him. Like his dad nuzzling his neck while carrying him to bed. Like Sister Mary Frances with her hand on his shoulder.

It was too much. Too much good, too much happiness. Too much beauty. Too much... perfectness. He didn't deserve to be here. He could *never* deserve this. He would try, wherever this new place was, to deserve this minute. He would try hard, knowing he never could. There wasn't nothing nobody could do to deserve this. He put his face in both his hands, burrowed down into the cloud.

He tried to speak but could only find a whisper, a soft whisper, like the wispy cloud around him, inside of him. "Thank you… Thank you…"

With his face in his hands, his eyes closed, for the first time in his life, Perry could see clear. For the first time, he understood. Everything — all his pain, all his loss, all his long suffering — was for one thing, to bring him to this minute right here. To bring him to where he could finally let the old Perry go, once and for all. He understood now that the old Perry *had* to die and never wake up, so that this new thing, whatever it was gonna be, could become.

The cloud began to turn now. As though he were back on the merry-go-round, moving slowly. Lying under a warm summer sun, eyes closed, lashes wet, face washed clean by rivers of holy water. The merry-go-round began to tilt slowly, held secure by the cloud, turning but also rolling and tumbling. It was a strange feeling, but he wasn't afraid. Everything was going to be… not fine, amazing.

He was finally gonna get to see what he'd always been lookin' for.

··········

Thank you for taking the time to read this first book in the series. Perry will appear again in the second book, Three To One, along with the other major characters, and some new ones you haven't met. Amazon will not always notify you of new release dates. Please sign up for the T.S. Epperson mailing list, to be among the first to hear about new releases at: https://BookHip.com/MKAXXMZ

Other Titles by T.S. Epperson

Thank you for reading book one, *Once To die.*

In this modern era, reviews make the world go around. If you have the charity within you, please go online and post a few encouraging words. That will help other readers find this story, and empower the author to publish more works. Thank you again.

You are invited to read the other books in "The Other Side of Dead" Series:

Unto Ash
The Other Side of Dead, a Short Prequel
Available as a free download at: www.BookHip.com/MKAXXMZ
Once To Die
The Other Side of Dead, book 1
Three To One
The Other Side of Dead, book 2
Coming spring of 2023
Without End
The Other Side of Dead, book 3
Coming Summer of 2023
Judgement Day
The Other Side of Dead book 4
Coming Fall of 2023

For other titles and collaborations by T.S. Epperson, go to Multivalent-press.com/T.S.Epperson

About the Author

T.S. Epperson is one of the pen names for Tom Epperson, who lives in South Carolina. Due to his background in Workforce Education and Development, Tom is fascinated with colorful and complex characters. Twelve years spent working on staff at a Catholic parish of 1,500 families, changed his understanding of the rhythm of life.

Everyone is on a unique journey. Tom was born the seventh of twelve siblings. He was an altar boy beginning at age seven, and a bar band musician beginning at age eight. His childhood was a happy rhythm of walking to daily Masses in the morning, and participating in music rehearsals in the evening. On Friday and Saturday nights he would close down the bars with his older brothers' band and then serve or attend Mass again Sunday morning.

His life has been and still is, a constant effort to balance the worldly with the spiritual, as his writing reflects. Tom is a hopeless optimist and a romantic realist. He is the proud father of two adult sons, the finest of the finest, and lives with his wife, who is his companion in a sweeping time travel adventure. So far, they have traveled nearly four and a half decades. Together, they strive to live more in the present than in the past, and his favorite thing is to stand in salt water and teach his Grandchildren how to lure exotic creatures from the sea.

Acknowledgments

The influence others have contributed to the creation of this novel series is almost inexpressible. The list of names is beyond what I can address here. So many people formed this story over many years, and I am profoundly thankful to them all.

I must make effort to thank those who have sacrificed the most, and born the weight of the long process which has brought us to this moment. To my advance readers, editors, writing coaches, marketing advisors, thank you. The story would be inferior if not for your contributions.

I also thank and am thankful for the many friends and mentors who shaped the spiritual elements of the story over the years. My Parents were the most influential among them.

Most importantly, I want to express my deep gratitude to my broad and diverse family, but especially my loving wife, who patiently encouraged me and stood patiently beside me while I chipped away in search of this story. To my daughter-in-law, and my grandchildren who encourage and inspire me, and to my sons, who are my partners in creativity, and are more talented and gifted than I am. What a joy it has been to travel together following the breadcrumbs of our respective muses.

For all of these people and so many others, for the difficult times and setbacks which have allowed me to see the complexity of the human experience, for the moments of consolation and redemption that kept me going, for life, the universe, and all that is, I thank God, the only true author. What a beautiful story you are unfolding through the ages.

Thank you.